MEN IN UNIFORM

CA

_P_RINCE

MEN IN UNIFORM:
COLLECTION

January 2017

January 2017

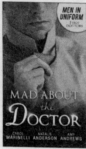

January 2017

February 2017

MEN IN UNIFORM:
CAPTIVATED
by the
PRINCE

SUSAN STEPHENS   **LYNN RAYE HARRIS**   **ANN MAJOR**

MILLS & BOON

First Published in Great Britain 2017
By Mills & Boon, an imprint of HarperCollins*Publishers*
1 London Bridge Street, London, SE1 9GF

MEN IN UNIFORM: CAPTIVATED BY THE PRINCE © 2017
Harlequin Books S.A.

The Italian Prince's Proposal © 2003 Susan Stephens
Prince Voronov's Virgin © 2011 Lynn Raye Harris
The Amalfi Bride © 2007 Ann Major

ISBN: 978-0-263-92776-4

09-0117

Our policy is to use papers that are natural, renewable and recyclable products and made from wood grown in sustainable forests.
The logging and manufacturing processes conform to the legal environmental regulations of the country of origin.

Printed and bound in Spain
by CPI , Barcelona

THE ITALIAN PRINCE'S PROPOSAL

SUSAN STEPHENS

For Steve, my hero.

Susan Stephens was a professional singer before meeting her husband on the Mediterranean island of Malta. In true Modern Romance style they met on Monday, became engaged on Friday and married three months later. Susan enjoys entertaining, travel and going to the theatre. To relax she reads, cooks and plays the piano, and when she's had enough of relaxing she throws herself off mountains on skis or gallops through the countryside singing loudly.

CHAPTER ONE

CROWN PRINCE ALESSANDRO BUSSONI OF FERARA narrowed amber eyes in lazy speculation as he continued to stare at the brightly lit stage. 'She'd do.'

'I beg your pardon, sir?'

There was no emotion in the question. The man sitting next to the Prince on the top table at the lavish Midsummer ball wore the carefully controlled expression of a career diplomat, and had a voice to match. Thin and lugubrious, with sun-starved features, it would have been impossible for Marco Romagnoli to provide a sharper contrast to his employer, and Crown Prince Alessandro's blistering good looks were supported by one of the brightest minds in Europe, as well as all the presence and easy charm that was his by right of birth.

'I said she'd do,' the Prince repeated impatiently, turning a compelling gaze on his aide-de-camp. 'You've paraded every woman of marriageable age before me, Marco, and failed to tempt me once. I like the look of this girl—'

And it was a lot more than just her stunning appearance, Alessandro acknowledged silently as his glance went back to the stage. The girl possessed an incredible energy not dissimilar to his own—an energy that seemed to leap out from the gaudily dressed performance area and thump him straight in the chest.

All he had to offer her was a cold-blooded business deal, but... His sensuous mouth curved in a thoughtful smile. In this instance mixing business with pleasure might not be such a bad thing.

'Are you serious, Your Royal Highness?' Marco

5

Romagnoli murmured, taking care not to alert their fellow diners.

'Would I joke about so serious a matter as my future wife? Alessandro demanded in a fierce whisper. 'She looks like fun.'

'Fun, sir?' Marco Romagnoli leaned forward to follow his employer's eyeline. 'You are talking about the singer with the band?'

'You find something wrong with that?' the Prince demanded, swivelling round to level a challenging gaze on his aide's face.

'No, sir,' Marco returned in a monotone, knowing the Prince would brook no prejudice based on flimsy face-value evidence. 'But if I may ask an impertinent question…?'

'Ask away,' Alessandro encouraged, his firm mouth showing the first hint of amusement as he guessed the way Marco's mind was working.

'She'd do for what, exactly, sir…? Only she's rather—'

'Luscious? Bold? Striking? In your face? What?' the Prince prompted adjusting his long legs as if the enforced inactivity was starting to irk him.

'All of those,' Marco suggested uncomfortably, his glance flashing back to the stage, where Emily Weston was well into her third number and clearly had the affluent, well-oiled crowd eating out of her hand. 'I can see that a young lady like that holds a certain attraction for—' Marco Romagnoli eased his fingers under a starched white collar that seemed to be on the point of choking him.

'Go on. Don't stop now,' Prince Alessandro encouraged, reining in his amusement.

Taking a few moments to rethink his approach, the usually unflappable courtier replied carefully, 'Well, sir, I can see she's a beauty, and undoubtedly perfect for certain activities. But you surely can't be thinking—'

'You mean I should bed her, not wed her?' Alessandro suggested dryly, as he looked back to where Emily had the microphone clutched between both hands for a slow number, looking as if she was about to devour it.

'I couldn't have put it better myself, sir. In my opinion such an ill-judged match would only create more problems than it would solve.'

'I disagree,' the Crown Prince of Ferara countered, 'and nothing you can say will persuade me that the girls you have paraded before me would fill the role any better—or vacate it without causing problems.'

He paused, and took another long look at the stage. 'As it is not my intention to break any hearts, Marco, this is the perfect solution. I want a straightforward business deal and a short-term bride—'

'Short-term, sir?'

Alessandro turned to answer the disquiet so clearly painted across the other man's face.

'I know,' he said, leaning closer to ensure they were not overheard. 'You're thinking of all the other implications such an arrangement would entail—I would expect nothing less of you, my old friend.'

The Prince's companion grew ever more troubled. Even if he could have shed the role of cautious professional advisor, Marco Romagnoli had known Alessandro from the day of his birth, and was considered an honorary member of the royal family.

'I wouldn't wish to see anyone take advantage of you, sir,' he said now, with concern.

'I shall take good care to ensure that none of the parties involved in my plan is taken advantage of,' Alessandro assured him. 'Thanks to our country's archaic legislation I can think of no other way to solve the problem of succession. If my father is to have his wish and retire I must marry immediately. It's obvious to me that this young woman has spirit. When I put my proposition to her I think she will have an instant grasp of the advantages that such a match can bring to both of us.'

'Yes, sir,' Marco agreed reluctantly, flinching visibly as Emily launched into a raunchy upbeat number.

'I have seen enough, Marco,' the Prince said, reclaiming his aide's attention. 'And I like what I see. Please advise the young lady that Alessandro Bussoni wishes to talk with her after the performance tonight. No titles,' he warned. 'And if she asks, just say I have a proposition to put to her. And don't forget to ask her name,' he added as, without another word, Marco Romagnoli rose to his feet.

After the show, Emily Weston, the singer with the band, was having a tense debate over the phone with her twin sister Miranda.

'Well, how *do* you deal with them?' she demanded, shouldering the receiver to scoop up another huge blob of cleansing cream from her twin's industrial-sized pot.

'Who do you mean?' Miranda snuffled between ear-splitting sneezes.

'Stage Door Johnnies—'

Miranda's summer cold symptoms dissolved into laughter. 'Stage Door Whosies?'

'Don't pretend you don't know what I'm talking about,' Emily insisted, flashing another concerned glance towards the dressing room door.

'I didn't think there was such a thing as Stage Door Johnnies nowadays,' Miranda said doubtfully.

'Well, I can assure you there is,' Emily insisted. 'What else would you call uninvited gentleman callers who won't take no for an answer?'

'Depends on who's doing the calling, I suppose,' Miranda conceded, blasting out another sneeze. 'Why don't you just take a look at him first, before you decide?'

'No way! That's never been part of our agreement.'

'But if he looks like Herman Munster you can send him packing...and if he's a babe, pass him on to me. He'd never know the difference. If Mum and Dad can't tell us apart, what chance does this man stand? What have you got to lose?'

'Look, I'll have to go,' Emily said as another rap, far more insistent than the last, bounced off the walls around her head. 'I told his messenger I couldn't see anyone I didn't know immediately after a show—pleading artistic temperament. He still hasn't taken the hint.'

'He sent someone round first?' Miranda cut in, her voice taut with excitement. 'He sounds interesting. He might be a VIP.'

'I doubt it,' Emily said as she peered into the mirror to peel off her false eyelashes. 'Though when I said I wouldn't see him I thought his representative muttered something about Prince being disappointed—'

'Emily, you dope,' Miranda exclaimed through another bout of sneezing. 'Prince Records is the recording company my band's been hoping to sign with. And you've just turned away their scout.'

'Can't I get one of the boys to see him?' Emily suggested hopefully. After all, there were five male members in Miranda's band.

'Are you kidding?' Miranda exclaimed. 'First of all they'll be in the pub by now...and secondly, do you seriously think I'd trust them to discuss business without my being there?'

Remembering the dreamy idealism of Miranda's fellow musicians, Emily could only respond in the negative. 'It might have helped if you had warned me this might happen,' she protested reasonably. 'Have to go,' she finished in a rush, wiping her hands on the towel across her lap as another flurry of raps hit the door. 'Whoever this is, he's not about to give up.'

Cutting the connection, Emily grabbed a handful of tissues as she shot up from her seat in front of the brilliantly lit mirror. Then, scooting behind a conveniently placed screen, she called out, 'Come in.'

This was the craziest thing she had ever done, Emily thought nervously as she swiped off the last of her make-up and stuffed the used tissues into the pocket of her robe. She tensed as the door swung open.

'Hello? Miss Weston? Miss Weston, are you there?'

She had heard male voices likened to anything from gravel to bitter chocolate, but this one slammed straight into her senses. Italian, she guessed, and with just the hint of a sexy mid-Atlantic drawl. She pictured him scanning the cluttered space, hunting for her hiding place, and felt her whole being responding to some imperative and extremely erotic wake-up call.

'Make yourself comfortable,' she sang out, relieved she was hidden away. 'I'm getting changed.'

'Thank you, Miss Weston,' the voice replied evenly. 'Please don't hurry on my account.'

Just the authority in the man's voice made the hairs stand on the back of her neck. And there was a stillness about it that made her think of a jungle cat, lithe, impossibly strong—and deadly.

It was in her nature to confront threats, not hide from them. So why was she skulking behind a screen? Emily asked herself impatiently. Could it be that the force of this man's personality had taken possession of what, in Miranda's absence, was her territory?

'Can I help you?' she said, struggling to see through a tiny crack in the woodwork.

'I certainly hope so.'

There was supreme confidence and not a little amuse-ment in the response, as well as the type of worldliness that had Emily mentally rocking back on her heels. It was al-most as if the man had caught her out doing something wrong—as if she had no right to be looking at him.

Drawing a few steadying breaths, she tried again. But all she could see through the crack in the screen was the broad sweep of shoulders clad in a black dinner jacket and a cream silk evening scarf slung casually around the neck of an impressively tall individual. A man whose luxuriant, dark wavy hair was immaculately groomed and glossy…the type of hair that made you want to run your fingers through it and then move on to caress— She pulled herself up short, closing her eyes to gather her senses…senses that were reacting in an extraordinary manner to nothing more than a man's voice, Emily reminded herself. She spent her working life objective and detached…yet now, when it really mattered—when Miranda's recording contract was at stake—she was allowing herself to be sideswiped off-beam by a few simple words. 'I'm sorry, Mr…er—'

'Bussoni,' he supplied evenly.

'Mr Bussoni,' Emily said, her assurance growing behind the protection of the screen. 'I'm afraid I didn't give the gentleman who works for you a very warm welcome—'

'Really? He said nothing of it to me.'

She was beginning to get a very clear picture of the man now. The image of a hunter sprang to mind…someone who was waiting and listening, using all his senses to evaluate his quarry. 'I understand you'd like to discuss the possibility of signing the band?' she said carefully.

There was another long pause, during which Emily formed the impression that the man was scanning all her neatly arranged possessions, gathering evidence about her and soaking up information—drawing conclusions. And from his position in front of the mirror he could do all of that—and still keep a watch on her hiding place.

Taking over last minute from Miranda meant she had been forced to come straight from work. There had been no time to find out about the event, let alone who might be in the audience. She had certainly not anticipated the need to be on her guard—to hide everything away. 'You are from Prince Records?' she prompted in a businesslike tone, hoping to bounce the man into some sort of admission.

'Do you think you could possibly come out here and discuss this in person?'

It was a reasonable enough suggestion. But Miranda was never seen without full war paint, and after liberal applications of cold cream Emily's own face had returned to its customary naked state. If she hoped to impersonate her twin an appearance right now was out of the question.

'I know this must sound rude, after you've taken the trouble to come backstage, but I'm rather tired this evening. Do you think we could talk tomorrow?' she said, knowing Miranda should have recovered and taken her rightful place by then.

'Tomorrow afternoon, at three?'

Emily's hearing was acutely tuned to his every move. He was already turning to go, she realised. Suddenly she couldn't even remember what she had on the following day, let alone specifically at three o'clock in the afternoon. The only thing she was capable of registering—apart from an over-active heartbeat—was that the recording contract for Miranda's band was vital.

'OK. That's fine,' she heard herself agreeing. 'But not here.'

'Anywhere you say.'

Possibilities flooded Emily's mind. She dismissed each one in turn…until the very last. 'Could you come out to North London?' Her mother and father had insisted that if Miranda's cold had not improved by tomorrow she should be brought home to recuperate. Emily knew she could rely on her parents to fill in any awkward gaps…smooth over the cracks when she changed places with her twin.

'I don't see why not.'

'That's if you're still interested?'

Interested? Alessandro thought, curbing his smile just in case Miss Weston decided to suddenly burst out from her hiding place. If he had been fascinated before, now he was positively gripped.

He ran one supple, sun-bronzed finger down the slim leather-bound diary he so longed to open, and traced the length of the expensive fountain pen lying next to it before toying with a pair of cufflinks bearing some sort of crest.

The handbag on the seat had quality written all over it, rather than some flashy logo. And the smart black suit teamed with a crisp white double-cuffed shirt hanging on a gown rail was Armani, if he wasn't mistaken.

His gaze swept the threadbare carpet that might once have been red to where a pair of slinky high-heeled court shoes stood next to a dark blue felt sack, ornamented with a thick tassel. Alongside that, a pull-along airline case—

'Mr Bussoni?'

His gaze switched back to the screen.

'Mr Bussoni, are you still interested?'

There was just a hint of anxiety in the voice now, Alessandro noted with satisfaction. This contract obviously meant a great deal to her. He cast a look at the discarded stage costume... Something jarred. No, he realised. Everything jarred.

'Only on one condition,' he said, adopting a stern tone as he assumed the mantle of time-starved recording executive.

'And that is?' Emily said cagily.

'That you come to supper with me after our meeting.' Alessandro was surprised when a curl of excitement wrapped around his chest as he waited for her answer. 'You may have questions for me, and there's sure to be a lot we have to discuss,' he said truthfully, satisfied that he had kept every trace of irony out of his voice.

Emily let the silence hang for a while. Miranda would definitely have to be better by then, she thought crossing her fingers reflexively. 'That's fine,' she confirmed evenly. 'I'll let the rest of the band members know—'

'No,' the voice flashed back assertively. 'It only needs one person to take in what I have to say...and I have chosen you, Miss Weston. Now, are you still interested in progressing with this matter, or not?'

'Of course I'm interested,' Emily confirmed, suddenly eager to be free of a presence that was becoming more disconcerting by the minute.

'That's settled, then. I'll write my number down for you. Perhaps you'll be good enough to get in touch first thing...leave the address for our meeting with my secretary?'

'Of course.' She felt rather than heard him prepare to leave.

'Until tomorrow, Miss Weston.'

'Until tomorrow, Mr Bussoni.'

Emily held her breath and tried to soak up information as the door opened, then shut again silently. The man might have three humps and a tail, for all she could tell, but her body insisted on behaving as if some lusty Roman gladiator had just strolled out of the room after booking her for sex the next day.

After he'd left it took her a good few minutes to recover her equilibrium. And when she moved out from behind the screen everything seemed shabbier than she remembered it, and emptier somehow, as if some indefinable force had left the room, leaving it all the poorer for the loss.

By early afternoon the next day, Emily had cancelled all her appointments for the rest of the week and was ready to take her sister back to their parents' house.

Drawing up outside the front door on the short gravel drive, she switched off the engine and tried for the umpteenth time to coax her twin into facing reality.

'This man is different to anyone I've ever encountered before. It would be a real mistake to underestimate him, Miranda.'

'He made quite an impression on you, didn't he?' Miranda replied, slanting a glance at her twin.

'I didn't even see him properly,' Emily replied defensively. 'And don't change the subject. It's you we're talking about, not me.'

After assuming a low-profile role in an orchestra for a number of years, Miranda had attracted the attention of a leading Japanese violin teacher. In order to fund the lessons Emily's twin had started a band—a band that in the beginning had taken up only the occasional weekend; a band that was now taking up more and more of her time...

'I only need this recording contract for a year or so,' she said now, as if trying to convince herself that the scheme would work. 'Just long enough for me to launch my career as a solo violinist.'

Emily frowned. She wanted to help, but only when she was confident Miranda understood what she was letting herself in for. 'Are you sure Prince Records understands that? They would have grounds to sue if you let them down.'

'They won't have any trouble finding someone to replace me; the boys are great—'

'I'm still not happy,' Emily admitted frankly. 'I just can't see what you'll gain going down this route.'

'Money?' Miranda said hopefully.

Emily shook her head as she reasoned it through aloud. 'You're not going to be able to honour a recording contract drawn up by a man like Mr Bussoni and put in the practice hours necessary to study the violin with a top-flight teacher like Professor Iwamoto.'

'It won't be for long,' Miranda insisted stubbornly, unfolding her long limbs to have a noisy stretch. 'I'll cope.'

Before Emily had a chance to argue Miranda was out of the smart black coupé and heading up the path.

'Don't be silly,' Emily said, catching up with her sister at the front door. 'The more successful the band, the less likely it is that this crazy idea of yours will work. I know the money would be great, but—' The expression on her twin's face made Emily stop to give her a hug. 'I know you're still pining over that violin we saw in Heidelberg.'

'That was just a stupid dream—'

'Well, I don't know much about violins,' Emily admitted, 'but I do know what a sweet sound you produced on that lovely old instrument.'

'Something like that would cost a king's ransom anyway,' Miranda sighed despondently. 'And it's sure to have been sold by now.'

Emily made a vague sound to register sympathy while she was busy calculating how much money she could raise if she sold her central London apartment to the landlord who already owned most of the smart riverside block, and then rented it back from him. Miranda need never know. It was a desperate solution, but anything was preferable to seeing her sister's opportunity lost. 'If I can help you, I will,' she promised.

With a gust of frustration, Miranda hit the doorbell. 'You do enough for everyone already. You won't even let me pay rent—'

'If I didn't have you around, who else would keep the fridge stocked up with eye masks?' Emily demanded wryly.

Their banter was interrupted when the door swung open.

'Girls—'

Then another idea popped into Emily's head. 'I've got some investments—'

'No!' Miranda said, shaking her head vehemently. 'Absolutely not.'

'You're not arguing,' their mother said wearily, giving them both a reproving look.

'Heated discussion, Mum,' Emily said as she shut the door behind them. 'Where's Dad?'

'In his study, of course.'

Of course. Emily stole a moment to inhale deeply, taking in the aroma of a freshly baked cake coming from the kitchen, along with the gurgle of boiling water ready for tea.

'You look tired,' her mother said softly, touching her arm. 'And as for you, Miranda—' Her voice sharpened as if her maternal engines had revved to a new pitch. 'What you need is a good dose of my linctus, and a hot cup of tea—'

'Did I hear the magic words?'

'Dad!' the girls cried in unison.

After giving them both a bear hug, Mr Weston linked arms with his daughters and followed their mother into the kitchen.

'It will be easy for you, Emily,' her mother asserted confidently, after Miranda had outlined her plan to secure the recording contract. 'You're not emotionally involved like Miranda. And you'll run rings around this record company man when it comes to securing the best terms for Miranda.'

Emily was surprised by her reaction to this vote of confidence. It was unnerving to discover that her mother's assessment of the situation could be so far off the mark. Intuition told her that running rings around Alessandro Bussoni was out of the question. But her main worry was the strange way her heart behaved just at the thought of him joining them in the tiny house. The man behind the voice would fill every inch of it with presence alone, never mind the unsettling possibility that she might brush up against him—

'Are you sure you're all right with this, Emily...? Emily?'

Finally the concern in her father's voice penetrated Emily's dream-state, and her eyes cleared as she hurried to reassure him. 'Of course, Dad. Leave it to me,' she insisted brightly, 'I can handle Signor Bussoni—'

'Italian!' her mother exclaimed, showing double the interest as she unconsciously checked out her neat halo of curls. 'How exciting. And when did you say he was arriving?'

'Right now, by the looks of it,' Emily's father said as he peered through the window.

CHAPTER TWO

'OH, NO!' Miranda gasped, looking to her sister for guidance.

'Stay upstairs until he's gone,' Emily suggested briskly. 'I'll come and get you when the coast's clear. Mum. Dad. Act normal.'

'Yes, dear,' her mother said breathlessly, exchanging an excited glance with her father.

Don't look so worried,' Emily called after Miranda. 'I promise not to turn anything down without your approval.'

Exchanging quick smiles, the girls were just on the point of parting at the foot of the stairs when they stopped, looked at each other, and then swooped to the hall window.

Standing well back from the glass, Emily ran a finger cautiously down the edge of the net curtain.

'Oh, boy,' she murmured, watching the tall, darkly clad figure unfold his impressive frame from the heavily shaded interior of a sleek black car.

'You said Herman Munster,' Miranda breathed accusingly.

'I said he might have been Herman Munster for all I could see of him,' Emily corrected tensely.

'Looks like you were both wrong in this instance,' their father commented dryly.

Alessandro felt a frisson of anticipation as he double-checked the address his private secretary had passed on to him that morning.

He wasn't used to waiting, and eighteen hours was far too long in this case.

But then he wasn't used to speaking to someone hiding

behind a screen either, or accepting anyone's terms but his own—which was how he now found himself getting out of a rented Mercedes outside a perfectly ordinary semi-detached house in North London.

He smiled a little in amused acceptance. He couldn't recall a single instance of being turned down by a woman, let alone agreeing to a time of her choosing for an audience as begrudging as this one. His sharp gaze took in the small rectangular lawn, freshly mowed, and then moved on to the splash of vivid colour provided by a pot of petunias to one side of the narrow front door. For someone who moved between palaces, embassies or the presidential suite in some luxury hotel when he was really slumming it, this chance to sample suburbia was a novelty... No. A welcome change, he decided as he swiped off his dark glasses.

Behind a snowy drift of net, the Weston family watched Alessandro Bussoni's progress towards the house in awe-struck silence.

'He's absolutely gorgeous,' Miranda murmured. Their distracted mother barely managed a weak gasp of, 'Oh, my!'

'Go, before he sees you,' Emily suggested urgently, having already turned her back on the window.

'But your make-up,' Miranda said, hopping from foot to foot, torn between going and staying.

Emily's hand shot automatically to her face. 'What about it?'

'You're not wearing any,' Miranda exclaimed with concern.

'Can't be helped. He'll still think I'm you. Why shouldn't he? Anyway, you're not wearing any make-up,' Emily pointed out.

'Only because I'm sick.'

'Well, there's no time for me to do anything about it now,' Emily said firmly. 'I'll be fine. Don't worry about me.'

'Sure?' Miranda asked hopefully.

'Sure,' Emily said briskly, hoping no one had noticed that her hand was shaking as it hovered over the doorknob.

'I'm going to change,' Miranda shouted, on her way up the stairs. 'Then I'm taking over from you.'

'No!' But even as Emily's gaze raked the empty landing to call her sister back she knew it was too late. Sucking in a deep, steadying breath, she seized the doorknob tightly and began to turn...

'You go and wait in the lounge, pet.'

'Dad—'

'Go and compose yourself,' Mr Weston urged gently, refusing to let go of her arm until Emily allowed him to steer her away from the door. 'You look like you could do with a few minutes. I'll keep him busy until you're ready.'

'You're an angel,' Emily whispered, reaching up on tip-toe to give her father an affectionate peck on the cheek. But a moment alone was all it took her to realise that she couldn't go ahead with the charade after all, and she rushed upstairs to find her sister.

The twins waited motionless, hardly daring to breathe as they stood just inside the door to Miranda's bedroom. It felt as if the conversation downstairs had been going on for ever while their father satisfied himself as to their visitor's identity and then invited him into the house, but at his signal they started down the stairs.

Emily was dressed in her customary relaxing-at-home-uniform of blue jeans and a simple grey marl tee shirt. Her well-buffed toenails, devoid of nail varnish, were shown off in a pair of flat brown leather sandals, while her long black hair was held up loosely on top of her head with a tortoiseshell clip.

In complete contrast, Miranda had somehow found enough time to coat the area around her large green eyes with copious amounts of silver glitter, add blusher to her cheeks and staggeringly high platform shoes to her seemingly endless legs.

Surely there could be no mistake, Emily thought, giving her twin the final once-over before they reached the sitting room door. Signor Bussoni would immediately presume it was Miranda he had seen on stage. 'Relax,' she whispered, taking hold of her twin's wrist. 'It'll be all right.'

'Then why are you shaking?' Miranda remarked perceptively.

'Girls? What's keeping you? You've got a visitor.'

'We're coming now, Dad,' Emily called back, hoping she sounded more confident than she felt. She had no idea what she was up against, and had nothing to go on but that disconcerting voice. For all she knew it might be Herman Munster hiding behind that impressive physique and those super-sleek clothes.

'Come on, love. What's the hold-up?' Popping his head round the door, her father drew her into the room. 'Your mother will have tea ready in about fifteen minutes,' he said. 'You two know each other,' he added, with an expectant smile.

Emily felt as if her powers of reason had vanished. Her mind's eye wasn't simply unreliable, it was positively defective, she decided, gazing up into a man's face that was almost agonising in its perfection. Thick ebony-black hair, cut slightly longer than was customary in England, was swept back and still tousled from the wind. Conscious he would think her rude, she forced her gaze away, only to discover lips that were almost indecently well formed and the most expressive dark gold gaze she had ever encountered.

Restating his name with a slight bow, Alessandro viewed the two sisters standing one behind the other. 'Miss Weston,' he murmured.

Lurching forward in response to Emily's none too subtle prompting, Miranda extended her hand politely. 'Delighted to see you, Signor Bussoni,' she said, letting out an audible sigh when Alessandro raised her hand to his lips.

'And I you,' he said in a voice as warm as the sunlight that had tinted his skin to bronze. 'But, forgive me, it is the other Miss Weston I have come to see.'

'The other Miss Weston?' Miranda squeaked, looking helplessly behind her to where Emily was standing rigid, wishing the ground would swallow her up.

'Indeed,' Alessandro said in a voice laced with humour. 'You did invite me, Miss Weston,' he said, looking straight at Emily.

Shock rendered both sisters speechless, and for a moment no one moved or spoke. If their own parents couldn't tell them apart, how could Signor Bussoni? Emily wondered tensely. She breathed a sigh of relief as her mother breezed into the room.

'Ah, Signor Bussoni, what a pleasure it is to have you in our midst.'

'The pleasure is all mine, I assure you,' Alessandro said, inclining his head towards the older woman in an elegant show of respect.

'I see you've met my girls.' Looking from Emily to Miranda, she clearly couldn't contain herself another moment. 'Have you heard Miranda play yet?' she said expectantly. 'The violin,' she prompted, when Alessandro stared at her blankly. 'Her interpretation of the Brahms ''Violin Concerto'' is second to none, you know. She won a competition with that piece.'

Emily's face flared hot as she realised that her mother was completely oblivious to the tension building around her.

'The violin?' Alessandro's face betrayed nothing but polite enquiry, but beneath the surface his mind was working overtime. Had he been hoist by his own petard? His plan had seemed audacious enough, but this family appeared intent on embroiling him in something even more ambitious. He glanced again at the girl her mother had called Miranda. Her provocative clothing and extravagantly made up face marked her out as a showgirl...but apparently she was a classical violinist. And then his gaze switched to the fresh-faced beauty he had come to see...the angel with the faintly flushed cheeks and the incredible jade-green eyes who masqueraded as a showgirl by night... To say the contrast intrigued him was putting it mildly. But what the hell was he getting himself into? Taking another look at Emily, he found he could not look away. He would have carried right on staring, too, had it not been for her sister's protestation providing him with a distraction.

'Oh, Mother, really,' Miranda said now, looking at Emily to back her up. 'Signor Bussoni doesn't want to hear about all that—Emily, say something.'

Emily, Alessandro mused, running the name over and over in his mind and loving its undulating form, its perfect proportions, its old English charm... Emily, Emily— Her mother fractured his musings with terrier-like determination.

'Emily won't stop me telling Signor Ferara all about your wonderful talent, Miranda. If no one speaks of it, how will you ever play that violin you so loved in Heidelberg?'

'Mother, please,' Emily cut in gently. 'I imagine Signor Bussoni's time is very precious. He's come here to talk about recording contracts for Miranda's band. I'm sure there will be other occasions when he can hear her play the violin.'

'Oh...' Mrs Weston hesitated, looking from one to the other in frustration.

'That would give me the greatest pleasure,' Alessandro agreed. 'But it was you I heard singing last night,' he stated confidently, turning to Emily, his bold gaze drenching her in the sort of heat she had only read about in novels.

'Emily took over for me because I caught a cold and lost

my voice,' Miranda confessed self-consciously. 'As a rule, no one can tell us apart.'

'I see,' Alessandro said, nodding thoughtfully as he studied Emily's face. He would have known her anywhere...even if there had been five more identical sisters lined up for his perusal.

Emily tried hard to meet his stare, but he disturbed her equilibrium in a profound and unsettling way.

'Singing is just a hobby for me,' she started to explain. 'You would have signed up the band right away if Miranda had been onstage—'

'Possibly,' Alessandro murmured, confining himself to that single word while his eyes spoke volumes about his doubt. He couldn't have cared less if Emily had a voice like a corncrake...and beauty was in the millimetre, he realised, as he filled his eyes, his mind and his soul with the face and form of a woman he desired like no other. Emily Weston was everything he wanted...everything he needed to set his plan in motion. No, much more than that, he realised, and only managed to drag his gaze away from her when the telephone shrilled and everyone but he made a beeline for the door.

'Let me,' Emily's father insisted calmly, easing his way through the scrum.

'Won't you sit down, Signor Bussoni?' Mrs Weston said awkwardly. 'Miranda, go and fetch the tea tray.'

'Do you mind if I—?' Swaying a little, Miranda stopped mid-sentence and passed a hand over her forehead.

'You've still got a fever. You really should go to bed,' Emily observed, taking hold of her twin's arm. 'You'll never get better if you don't rest. I'll see her upstairs,' she said, turning to her mother. 'If you'll excuse me for a moment, Signor Ferara?' she added to Alessandro. 'I'll come down and serve the tea,' she promised, ushering her sister out of the door. 'Just as soon as I see Miranda settled.'

'That won't be necessary.'

Alessandro's voice stopped Emily dead in her tracks.

'You're not going—' she said quickly...far too quickly, she realised immediately, noting the spark of interest in his eyes. Her heart thundered as he shot her an amused, quizzical look. 'Well, we haven't discussed the contract yet,' she said, attempting to make light of her eagerness for him to stay.

'Emily,' Miranda murmured weakly, 'I really think I should...'

'Of course,' Emily said, welcoming the distraction as she looped an arm around her sister's waist. 'Let's get you to bed.'

'Can I help?' Alessandro offered.

'That won't be necessary,' Emily said, urging her sister forward.

'Emily's right, Signor Bussoni,' Miranda murmured faintly. 'I'll feel better after a short rest. My sister has my full confidence. I am quite content for you to put your proposition to her.'

Alessandro answered with a brief dip of his head. 'I feel equally confident that your sister will find my proposal irresistible, Miss Weston.'

'I'm very grateful to you, Signor Bussoni,' Miranda replied as she stood for a moment, framed by the door, her carefully made-up face illuminated by an oblique shaft of late-afternoon sunlight.

Beautiful, Alessandro thought dispassionately, and if you stripped away the paint and glitter almost a carbon copy of her sister. But there was no attraction there. None at all. Not for him, at least.

'You will sort it out for me, won't you, Emily?' Miranda said anxiously as they left the room together.

'When have I ever let you down?' Emily teased gently as they started up the stairs.

'Never,' Miranda said softly, turning to give her sister a kiss.

Emily came back into the room to find Alessandro comfortably ensconced on the chintz-covered sofa, with her mother beside him chatting animatedly. But the moment she arrived his focus switched abruptly.

'Do you handle all your sister's business affairs?'

Emily prided herself on her ability to recognise exceptional adversaries on sight. And she was facing one right now, she warned herself. 'Not all,' she said carefully. She saw his eyes warm with amusement and knew he had her measure, too.

'Just contracts?' he pressed.

Emily's heart gave a wild little flutter, like a bird trapped in an enclosed space.

'We're not here to talk about me, Signor Bussoni—'

'Alessandro, please,' he said, embellishing the instruction with a small shrug intended to disarm, Emily guessed, as she watched her mother's eyes round in approval at what she clearly imagined was an enchanting display of Latin charm. But her mother had missed the shrewd calculation going on behind that stunning dark gold gaze, Emily thought, feeling her own body respond to the unmistakable masculine challenge.

'I'm sure you're very busy, Signor Bussoni,' she said, struggling to sound matter-of-fact with a heart that insisted on performing cartwheels in her chest. 'And it's the contract for Miranda's band you've come to discuss after all.'

'Correct,' he agreed.

His voice streamed over Emily's senses like melted fudge. How could a voice affect you like that? she wondered. Surely the cosy little room with its neatly papered walls had never housed such a dangerous sound as Alessandro Bussoni's deep, sexy drawl.

'It seems you and I have rather a lot to discuss, Miss Weston,' he said, reclaiming her attention. 'Far more, I must confess, than I had at first envisaged. I'll send my car for you at eight this evening.'

As he stood the room shrank around him.

'But surely you will stay for tea, Signor Bussoni—?'

'No—' Emily almost shouted at her mother. 'I'm sorry,' she said, instantly contrite. 'But Signor Bussoni must have other appointments—' was that a note of desperation creeping into her voice? She made a conscious effort to lower the pitch before adding, 'It's enough that he's making time to discuss Miranda's future tonight, Mother.'

He inclined his head to show his appreciation of her consideration.

'Until this evening, Miss Weston.'

'Signor Bussoni,' Emily returned with matching formality.

'Alessandro,' he prompted softly.

Emily felt her gaze drawn to dark, knowing eyes that seemed to reach behind her own and uncover the very core of her being. She felt deliciously ravished by them and immediately on guard, all in one and the same confusing moment.

A thrill ran through her as he lifted her hand and raised it to his lips. The contact was brief, but it was enough for her logical brain to be set adrift and her veins to run with sweet sensation. Then her father returned from his telephone call and she was able to take refuge behind the bustle of departure, easing into the background as Alessandro strode back down the path to his car.

Was he psychic? Emily wondered, as the unmistakable figure emerged from the grand entrance and came down the hotel steps at the precise moment the limousine she was arriving in swept to a halt outside.

Nothing would have surprised her about Alessandro Bussoni, Emily realised as he beat both the doorman and the chauffeur he had sent to collect her to the car door. As it swung open her mouth dried, and her body felt as if it was contracting in on itself in a last-ditch attempt to conceal anything remotely capricious in her appearance, though she had taken the precaution of wearing an understated navy blue suit with a demure knee-length skirt.

'Welcome, Miss Weston,' he said, reaching into the limousine to help her out.

Or to stop her escaping? Emily thought in a moment of sheer panic when his fingers closed over her hand.

'Please. Call me Emily,' she managed pleasantly enough, while her thought processes stalled.

Precaution, my foot! She should have worn a full protective body suit...with ski gloves, she reasoned maniacally, as a flash of heat shot up her arm. What was she thinking? The first rule of business was to keep everything cordial but formal. And here she was, unbending already as if she was on a date! Gathering herself quickly, she removed her hand from his clasp at the first opportunity.

'I must apologise for not coming to pick you up in person, Miss Weston,' Alessandro said, standing back to allow her to precede him through the swing doors.

Emily made some small dismissive sound in reply, and was glad of the distraction provided by a doorman in a top hat who insisted on ushering her into the hotel. But she was so busy trying to keep a respectable distance from her host she almost missed his next statement.

'I wanted to come myself, but there were some matters of State I was forced to attend to: matters that demanded my immediate attention—'

'Matters of State?' Emily repeated curiously. But it was hard to concentrate on what he was saying when they were attracting so much interest.

When the first flashbulb flared she glanced round, imagining some celebrity was in view. But then she realised that the cameras were pointing their way, and a small posse of photographers seemed to be following them across the lobby.

She smiled uncertainly as she tried to keep up with

Alessandro's brisk strides. 'It must be a quiet night for them,' she suggested wryly.

'What? Oh, the photographers,' he said, seeming to notice their presence for the first time. 'I'm sorry. You get so used to them you hardly know they're around.'

Having seen a pack of photographers waiting around on the night of the charity event, snapping away at anything and everything, even the spectacularly ornate heels on one woman's shoes, Emily took it for granted that hotels of this calibre attracted the attention of the world's media as a matter of course.

'I suppose they have to do something while they're waiting for the main event to arrive.'

'Main event?' Alessandro quizzed as he broke step to look at her.

'You know…personalities, showbiz people, that sort of thing.'

He pressed his lips together and he gave her an ironic smile, his dark eyes sparkling with amusement. 'I guess you're right. I'd never thought of that. It must get pretty boring for them…all the hanging around.'

But it wasn't just the photographers, Emily thought. She couldn't help noticing all the other people staring as Alessandro ushered her across the vast, brilliantly lit reception area.

Hardly surprising, she decided, shooting a covert glance at her companion. He was off the scale in the gorgeous male stakes. His dark suit was so uncomplicated, so beautifully cut, it could only have come from one of the very best tailors…yet somehow the precision tailoring only served to point up his rampant masculinity. His crisp, cotton shirt, in a shade of ice blue, was a perfect foil for his bronzed skin, and somehow managed to make eyes that were already incredible all the brighter, all the keener—

She looked away, knowing she would have to pull herself together if the evening was to fulfil its purpose as a business rather than a social occasion. 'Matters of State?' she repeated firmly, determined not to let him off the hook.

She was rewarded with a low, sexy laugh that revealed nothing except for the fact that she was fooling herself if she imagined that she would be able to overlook the power of his charm for one single moment.

At a small, private lift, tucked away out of sight from the main lobby, she watched as he keyed in a series of numbers. Heavy doors slid silently open and then sealed them inside a plush, mirrored interior. There was even a small upholstered seat in the corner should you require it, Emily noted with interest, and apart from the emergency intercom a telephone for those urgent calls between floors. The only users of this exclusive space would be pretty exclusive themselves, she deduced with a thoughtful stare at her companion.

'You didn't answer my question yet,' she prompted.

'I've taken the liberty of ordering a light supper to be delivered to us later.'

He might have said it pleasantly enough, but the effect was offset by a flinty stare that suggested that he alone would direct the course of their conversation.

Alessandro knew he was in for a rocky ride the moment he saw the defensive shields go up in Emily's eyes. And no wonder she thought him harsh. He was struggling to reclaim control of a situation that was slipping away from him as fast and as comprehensively as sand through a sieve. Logically, all he had to do was bring her to the point where she would sign the contract drawn up by his lawyers, but she had turned everything on its head, this woman he felt such a crazy compulsion to woo.

'Rather than go out to eat I thought it better that we devote ourselves entirely to the matter in hand,' he said, hoping to placate her. The last thing he wanted was to explain what this was about in a lift!

'You said something about matters of State earlier,' Emily pressed doggedly, 'and, if you remember, I asked—'

Words had always been the most effective weapon in her armoury, but where Alessandro Bussoni Ferara was concerned they seemed utterly ineffectual. Emily was starting to seethe with exasperation.

'So, what's this?'

In the split second between her lunge to grab his wrist and Alessandro's reaction to it Emily knew she had made her biggest mistake. What on earth was she doing, assaulting a strange man in a lift, snatching hold of him, grabbing on tight to the gold signet ring on his little finger? And why was he allowing her to hang on to him, even though he was twice her size and could have moved away from her in an instant? Worse still, the flesh beneath her sensitive fingertips felt warm and smooth and supple— She blinked, and recovered herself fast, removing her hand self-consciously from his fist where it had somehow become entangled.

'It's my family crest,' he volunteered evenly. 'Does that satisfy your curiosity?'

No! Not nearly! 'Your crest?' she said curiously.

His whip-fast retaliation left Emily with no time to hide the cufflinks on her own white tailored shirtsleeves.

'Shall we start with your explanation for these?' he countered smoothly, bringing her wrist up.

The sheer power in his grip was impossible to resist. But Emily found she didn't want to, and incredibly, was softening. 'That's my—'

'Yes?' he pressed remorselessly.

'My cufflinks are engraved with the crest of my Inn of Court,' she admitted, averting her face.

'Ah,' he murmured, as if pleased to hear his suspicions confirmed. 'Barrister?'

Emily nodded tensely. 'And you?'

Now it all made sense, Alessandro realised—the tasselled sack to hold her robes and wig, the pull-along airline case to transport her briefs, along with all the other papers she would have to carry around...the severe cut of the restrained outfit she wore to court beneath her gown hanging up in her dressing room at the hotel while she sang that night, the only nod to feminine sexuality displayed in the power heels of her plain black court shoes—

'This is our floor,' he said as the lift slowed.

Another evasion! Controlling herself with difficulty, Emily hunted for something...anything...to derail her mounting irritation—unfortunately, the first thing she hit upon was how well the light, floral perfume she had chosen to wear mingled with Alessandro's much warmer scent of sandalwood and spice, and that didn't help at all! As the lift doors opened she sprang to attention, noticing that he stood well back to let her pass. Now she registered disappointment. Disappointment that he didn't yank her straight back inside the intimate lift space, close the doors and make it stop somewhere between floors...for a very long time indeed.

'Emily? Did you hear me?'

Refocusing fast, she saw that he had already opened the arched mahogany double doors to his suite and was beckoning her inside.

'I'm sorry—'

'I said,' he repeated, 'would you care for a glass of champagne?'

'Oh, no, thank you. Orange juice will be fine until we conclude our business.'

'And then champagne?'

'I didn't say that, Signor Bussoni—'

'Alessandro.'

'Alessandro,' Emily conceded. 'And when our business is concluded I will be leaving.'

'Whatever you like,' he agreed evenly. 'I've no wish to tangle with lawyers in my free time.'

The throwaway line ran a second bolt of disappointment through her. She would have to be under anaesthetic not to register the fact that Alessandro Bussoni was a hugely desirable male. It was time to tighten the bolts on her chastity belt, Emily told herself firmly, if she had a hope in hell of being ready for what promised to be a tough round of business negotiations.

And she would deal with the lazy appraisal he was giving her now how, exactly?

She only realised how tense she had become when Alessandro turned away to pour them both a glass of freshly squeezed orange juice and each of her muscles unclenched in turn. Keep it cool, Emily warned herself silently. Cool and impersonal. It's only business after all...

CHAPTER THREE

LEAVING her handbag on the pale, grey-veined surface of a marble-topped console table, Emily dragged in a deep, steadying breath as she took in her surroundings.

The hotel room was decorated in English country house style, but at its most extreme, its most sumptuous: a symphony of silks, cashmere, damask and print. And Alessandro's accommodation wasn't just larger than the usual suite, it was positively palatial. In fact, Emily guessed the whole of her parents' house would fit comfortably into the elegant drawing room where they were now holding their conversation—a room that at a rough estimate she judged to be around forty feet in length.

'Not very cosy, is it?'

His voice startled her, even though it was pitched at little more than a murmur.

'Sorry?' she said, turning around.

'This room,' Alessandro said, holding her gaze as he carried the juice over to her.

'It's very—'

'Yes?' he said, noticing how studiously she avoided touching his hand as he passed her the crystal glass.

'Well...' Emily chose her words carefully. She didn't want to cause offence—maybe he loved this style. 'It tries very hard—'

'—to condense all the flavours of your country into a single room in order to impress the well-heeled tourist?' he supplied, looking at her with amusement over the top of his glass.

'Well, yes,' Emily said, discovering that a smile had edged on to her own lips. 'How did you guess? That's my opinion exactly.' Nerves were making her facial muscles capricious, unpredictable...and somehow she found herself smiling up at him again.

'Let's hold our meeting somewhere more...snug,' Alessandro suggested. 'Don't look so alarmed,' he said, shooting her a wolfish grin that failed entirely if it was meant to reassure her. Thrusting a thumb through the belt-loop of his black trousers, he slouched comfortably on one hip to put his glass down on the table. 'My bedroom can hardly be described as snug—it's almost as large as this room. Fortunately there are two bedrooms, and I've had the smaller of the two turned into an office for the duration of my stay.'

'I see,' Emily said, watching him extract some documents from the folder on the table and wondering why all she could register was how tanned, and very capable his hands were—

'Daydreaming again, Emily?'

'I beg your pardon?'

'And I beg you to pay attention when I ask you if you would care to join me in my office—so that our meeting can begin.'

His tone was amused—tolerant. And her expression must have been blank and dreamy, Emily realised, hurriedly adopting an alert look.

'Shall I lead the way?'

Retrieving her handbag, Emily hurried after him, but as he opened the door to the next room, and stopped beside it to let her pass, she juddered to a halt. The remaining space inside the doorframe was small...too small.

The difference in size between them seemed huge, suddenly, though it was his aura of confident masculinity that was his most alluring feature, Emily thought as she skirted past him. 'Very impressive,' she managed huskily, pretending interest in all the high-tech gizmos assembled for his use in the skilfully converted bedroom.

'Why don't you sit over there?' he suggested, pointing towards a leather button-backed seat to one side of a huge mahogany desk.

Perching primly on the edge, Emily watched in fascination as Alessandro sat or rather sprawled on his own chair with all the innate elegance of a lean and hungry tiger.

'Would you care to open the discussion?' he invited.

Folding her hands neatly in her lap, Emily attempted to sweep her mind clear of anything but the facts. 'Well, as you know, I'm here to secure the best possible deal for my sister's band—'

'For your sister, primarily?'

'Well, yes, of course, but—'

'Miranda needs the money a recording contract will bring her in order to buy a rather special violin and to complete her training, is that correct?'

'That's putting it rather crudely.'

'How else would you put it, Emily? What I want to know is, what's in it for me?'

'Surely that was self-evident when you saw the band perform. They're excellent—'

'Without you?' he cut in abruptly. 'How do I know what they'll be like? What if I said I'd sign the band if you remained as lead singer?'

'I'm afraid my obligations at work would not permit—'

'Ah, yes,' he cut in smoothly. 'I'll come to that later. But for now let's consider your proposal regarding the recording contract for your sister. How does she intend to fulfil both her commitment to the record company and to her tutor at the music conservatoire?'

'I'm here to ensure that whatever contract she signs allows her to do both—for the first year at least.'

'And then she will drop the band?' Alessandro suggested shrewdly.

'She will fulfil all her contractual obligations,' Emily stated firmly. 'I can assure you of that.'

'As well as put in the necessary practice hours to become a top-class international soloist? Somehow I doubt it,' he said, embroidering the comment with a slanting, sceptical look.

'You clearly have no experience of what it's like to strive to achieve something so far out of reach,' Emily said, overruling her cautious professional persona in defence of her sister, 'that most people would give up before they had even started.'

'Perhaps you're right—'

'Many artistes are forced to take other jobs to pay their way through college,' she continued passionately, barely registering Alessandro's silent nod of agreement.

'Not just musicians or artistes—'

But Emily was too far down the road either to notice his comment or to hold back. 'You're making assumptions that have no grounds in fact,' she flung at him accusingly.

'And you're not even listening to me,' Alessandro replied evenly, 'so how do you know what I think?'

'You've already decided she can't handle both commitments,' Emily said, realising she hadn't felt this unsteady since delivering her first seminar as a rookie law student. 'Right now, Miranda's not feeling well. But as soon as she's feeling better I know she'll do everything she says she will.'

'You say—'

'Yes, I say,' Emily said heatedly. 'I know my sister better than you...better than anyone—' She broke off, suddenly aware that all the professional expertise in the world was of no use to her while her emotions were engaged to this extent.

'I'm sure you're right,' Alessandro agreed quietly, showing no sign of following her down the same turbulent path. 'But why on earth choose a band as a way of making money? Why not find it some other way?'

Emily made an impatient gesture as she shook her head

at him. 'Because she's a musician, Alessandro. That's what she does.'

'A cabaret singer?'

'What's wrong with that?'

As he shrugged, Emily guessed every stereotypical piece of nonsense that had ever been conceived around nightclub singers was swirling through his brain.

'Miranda makes an honest living,' she said defensively. 'Would you rather she gave it up…gave up all her ambitions…just to satisfy the prejudice of misguided individuals?'

Alessandro confined himself to a lengthy stare of good-humoured tolerance, and then held up his hands when a knock came at the door just as Emily was getting into her stride. 'Excuse me, Emily. I won't be a moment.'

As Alessandro left her Emily felt a warning prickle start behind her eyes. No one had ever made her lose her temper like this before…not once. She hadn't ever come close. Plunging her hand into her handbag, she dug around for some tissues, then rammed them away out of sight again when he came back.

'Come on, Emily,' he said, staying by the door. 'Supper's arrived.'

'I think I'd better go.' She resorted to hiding her face in a hastily contrived search for the door keys in her handbag.

'After supper,' Alessandro insisted as he held out his hand to her.

Was she meant to take it? Emily wondered as she stared up at him in surprise.

'Come,' he repeated patiently.

It was tempting. Maybe supper would give her a chance to relax, regroup, gather what remained of her scattered wits. She was here for Miranda, wasn't she? And the job she had come to do wasn't nearly finished. Eating was harmless…civilised. Lots of deals were cut over power breakfasts and business lunches; she'd done it herself on numerous occasions.

Romantic suppers?

Muffling the tiny voice of reason in her head, Emily convinced herself that the meal was nothing more than a brief interlude, a welcome break that would give her the chance to get her professional head screwed on ready for the discussions to come. But when she walked back into the first room she saw that a great deal more than a light snack awaited her.

'When you said supper, I imagined...' Her voice tailed off as she surveyed the incredible feast that had been laid out for them along the whole length of a highly polished mahogany table.

'Aren't you hungry?' Alessandro demanded, cruising along the table, grazing as he went. 'I know I am.'

She tried not to notice the way he seemed to be making love with his mouth to a chocolate-tipped strawberry.

'You can eat what you want when you want,' he said, sucking off the last scrap of chocolate with relish. 'And we can keep on talking while you do,' he added, his curving half-smile reaching right through her armour-plated reserve to stroke each erotic zone in turn. 'Would you like me to make a few suggestions?'

Withdrawing the plundered stalk from between his strong white teeth, he deposited it neatly on a side-plate.

Emily forced her mouth shut, but kept right on staring at him.

'Food?' Alessandro offered with an innocent shrug as he cocked his head to one side to look at her.

'That's fine, I can manage,' Emily said, almost snatching one of the white porcelain plates from his hands.

'Shrimp, *signorina*?'

'Don't you ever take no for an answer?'

The look he gave her sent a flame of awareness licking through every inch of her body.

'Relax, Emily. I deliver what I promise—just a light snack, in this instance.'

'I'm perfectly relaxed, thank you,' Emily retorted, concentrating on making her selection from the platters of delicious-looking salads...a selection she was making with unaccustomed clumsiness, thanks to the route her thoughts were taking.

Was it her fault that those beautifully sculpted lips provided a rather different example of a tasty snack...or that stubble-darkened jaw? Not to mention the expanse of hard chest she supposed must reside beneath his superior-quality jacket and shirt—and, talking of superior quality, what about the muscle-banded stomach concealed beneath that slim black leather belt? Distractedly, she spilled half a bowl of coleslaw on top of the mountain of food she seemed to have absent-mindedly collected on her plate.

'I don't think the pudding will fit,' Alessandro pointed out, removing a serving spoon holding a heaped portion of sherry trifle from her hand.

'Of c-course not,' Emily stammered, while the erotic mind games kept right on playing—ignoring her most strenuous efforts to put all thoughts of whipped cream and tanned torsos out of bounds.

When later she found herself drawn towards a tower of honey-coloured choux balls drizzled with chocolate, he asked, 'Do you like chocolate, Emily?'

'I love it. Why?' she said suspiciously.

Alessandro shrugged as he piled some profiteroles onto a plate, adding some extra chocolate sauce and pouring cream for her. 'We have a chocolate festival in Ferara every year; free chocolate is handed out all over the city. We even have a chocolate museum—you should make time to see it.' As he handed her the plate his amused golden gaze scanned her face. 'What do you say?'

'Thank you.' Was she accepting an invitation to consume a plate of delectable pudding, or something rather more?

'Imagine this, Emily—a thousand kilos of delicious chocolate sculpted into a work of art before your very eyes; artists coming from all over Europe to compete for a prize for the best design—'

He turned to pour them both a steaming cup of strong dark coffee from an elegant silver pot.

'Clean sheets are placed underneath each block so that the onlookers can help themselves to slivers as they watch—' He stopped, and stared straight into her eyes, his expressive mouth tugging up in a grin. 'Well?'

Emily's pulse-rate doubled. 'No cream, no sugar,' she blurted, certain he intended to provoke her—a chocolate festival, for goodness' sake!'

Murmuring her thanks as he pressed the coffee cup into her hand, she glanced up, only to encounter a dangerous gaze alive with laughter. She was right to be wary, she realised, looking away fast.

But thankfully this was his final sally, and he allowed her to finish her meal in peace. When they returned to his luxurious bedroom-turned-office, he kept the lights soothing and low as he slipped a CD into the music centre.

Emily smiled. Brahms, she realised, surprised he had remembered her mother mentioning Miranda's competition piece.

He poured champagne and brought two crystal flutes across before settling himself down on the opposite sofa.

'Better?' he murmured, watching her drink. 'Do you mind if I take my jacket off?' he added, loosening a couple more buttons at the neck of his shirt.

'Not at all,' Emily said, forgetting her pledge to keep champagne celebrations until later as she watched him ease up from the chair to slip off a jacket lined with crimson silk. Freeing a pair of heavy gold cufflinks from his shirt, he dropped them onto the table and rolled up his sleeves to reveal powerful forearms shaded with dark hair. There couldn't have been a more striking contrast to the type of pasty-faced executive she was accustomed to dealing with.

'So, Emily,' he challenged, eyes glinting as he caught her staring at him. 'Do you still think I'm one of those misguided individuals you referred to?'

For his opinion of cabaret singers, yes; where everything else was concerned—

'I take it from your expression that you do.'

His smile had vanished.

'Let's get one thing straight between us before we go any further. I don't give a damn what people do, as long as they're not hurting anyone else in the process. But I do care about motives—what makes people tick. What makes you tick, Emily?'

Racing to put her brain back in gear, the best she could manage was a few mangled sounds.

'Barrister by day,' he went on smoothly, 'moonlighting as a cabaret singer by night. There's no harm in that, if you can cope with the workload. And it's even more to your credit that you were moonlighting to help your sister out of a fix. What is not to your credit, however, is the fact that you intended to deceive me. Why was that, Emily?'

'I admit things got out of hand—'

The lame remark was rewarded by a cynical stare.

'You really thought you could pull this off?' he demanded incredulously. 'What kind of a fool did you take me for?'

Emily's face burned scarlet as she struggled with an apology. 'I didn't know you—I'm really sorry. I didn't think—'

Alessandro held up his hands, silencing her. 'As it happens, you're not the only one who hasn't been entirely straightforward.'

'Meaning?'

'Let's consider this plan of yours first.'

'My plan?' It was clear he was on a mission to tease out

her motives whilst taking care not to reveal any of his own, Emily realised.

'Amongst your misconceptions is the notion that your sister's crazy scheme is actually going to work.'

'Will you help her or not?'

'Without my co-operation your sister will never play the instrument she has set her heart upon.'

'What do you mean?' Emily said anxiously, finding it impossible to sit down a moment longer.

Stretching his arms out across the back of the sofa, Alessandro tipped his head to look at her. 'Why don't you sit down again, Emily?' he suggested calmly. 'You do want to help your sister, don't you? You do want her to be able to play that violin she saw in the instrument maker's shop near the castle in Heidelberg?'

Emily could feel the blood draining out of her face as she stared at him. 'How do you know about that?' she said in a whisper.

'I make it my business to know everything relevant to a case before I enter into any negotiation,' he said steadily. 'I never leave anything to chance.'

Emily's professional pride might have suffered a direct hit, but the only thing that mattered was Miranda's future... But what was Alessandro Bussoni really after? Why had he gone to so much trouble? And how did he come to have such a hold over a German violin maker?

'The violin in Heidelberg—' she began, but her voice faltered as she remembered Miranda playing the beautiful old instrument. 'What did you mean when you said that my sister might never get to play it?'

'Without my co-operation,' Alessandro reminded her, his expression masked in shade.

'I don't understand.'

'Sit down again, Emily. Please.'

'I think you owe me an explanation first.'

'The particular instrument you refer to is a museum piece

almost beyond price. It was being displayed by one of to-day's most celebrated instrument makers—'

'*Was* being displayed?' Emily asked. 'Why are you talking about it in the past tense?'

'Because it's no longer there,' he said evenly.

'You mean it's gone back to the museum?' Relief and regret merged in the question.

'Not exactly.'

'What, then?' Her look demanded he answer her fully this time.

But Alessandro still said nothing, and just stared at some point over her left shoulder.

Slowly Emily turned around, her eyes widening when she saw what he was looking at. A beautifully upholstered taupe suede viewing seat was angled to face a large entertainment system. Nestled in the corner of the unusual triangular-shaped seat rested a violin, propped up between two cream silk cushions. 'Should it be out of its case?' she mumbled foolishly, sinking down on the sofa again.

'I imagine that's the only way it's ever going to be played,' Alessandro said, levelling a long, steady gaze at her.

Emily's heart was thundering so fast she could hardly breathe. She had to turn round to take another look, just to make sure she wasn't dreaming—to prove to herself that she really was in the same room as the violin Miranda had played in Heidelberg.

'But you told me it was a museum piece—beyond price,' she said, not caring that her battered emotions were now plainly on show. 'I don't understand.'

'Everything has its price Emily,' Alessandro said with a small shrug as he regarded her coolly.

He was waiting. For what? For her to say something? But how could she when her brain had stalled with shock and her whole body was quivering from some force beyond her control? To make matters worse, Emily couldn't rid herself of the idea that she too was a prize exhibit—and with a rather large price tag dangling over her nose.

'You bought it?' she managed finally.

'I bought it,' Alessandro confirmed.

'But why on earth—?'

'As a bargaining counter.'

'A bargaining counter?' Emily spluttered incredulously. 'What are you talking about?'

'Will you allow me to explain?'

Emily clenched and unclenched her hands. She didn't like the look on his face one bit. 'I think you better had,' she agreed stiffly, feeling as if she was clinging to Miranda's dream by just her fingertips now.

'It would be far better for your sister if she had enough money to continue her studies without the distraction of working with the band.'

'Well, of course,' Emily agreed. 'But—'

Alessandro's imperious gesture cut her off. 'Let me finish, please. It would be better still if she could have the use of that violin behind you—'

'Is this before or after she wins the Lottery?' Emily demanded, rattled by his composure.

'What if I told you that I am prepared to give the violin to your sister…on permanent loan?'

A thundering silence took hold of the space between them—until Alessandro's voice sliced through it like a blade. 'Well, Emily, what do you say?'

'What would she have to do for that?' Emily demanded suspiciously.

'Your sister? Nothing at all.' Alessandro's mouth firmed as he waited for Emily's thought processes to crest the shock he had just given her and get back up to speed.

Emily's eyes clouded with apprehension as her brain cells jostled back into some semblance of order. 'What would *I* have to do?'

A smile slowly curled around Alessandro's lips, then

died again. She was so bright…so vulnerable. It was as if he had spied some rare flower, moments too late to prevent his foot crushing the life out of it.

Standing up, he crossed the room. He needed time to think…but there was none. Opening a door, he reached inside the small cloakroom where he had been keeping the flowers. He had ordered the extravagant bouquet to seal their bargain. As he grabbed hold of them he realised that his hand was shaking. He paused a beat to consider what he should do. He could ram them in the wastebin, where they belonged, or he could keep on with the charade…

Turning to face Emily, he held out the huge exotic floral arrangement. There was real hope in his eyes, and a sudden tenderness to his hard mouth.

'I'm sorry, Emily, I meant to give these to you earlier.' She looked so wary, and Alessandro knew he was the cause. What had started out as a straightforward business transaction had developed into something so much more. If Emily Weston accepted his proposal he would be the luckiest man in Ferara… No—the world, he thought, trying to second-guess her reaction.

'For what?' Emily said, glad to have the opportunity to bury her face deep out of sight amongst the vivid blooms as he handed them to her. 'I've never seen such a fabulous display,' she admitted, forced to pull her face out again when they began to tickle her nose.

'For agreeing to become my wife,' Alessandro said softly.

For a full ten seconds neither of them seemed to breathe, and then Emily whispered tensely, 'Are you mad?'

Alessandro's rational self gave a wry smile, and told him she might be right. But thirty generations of accumulated pride in Ferara insisted that no woman in her right mind would refuse the opportunity to become princess of that land.

'Not as far as I am aware,' he said coolly.

'I think you must be.'

'I said I had a proposition for you. I made no secret of it.'

'Yes, a recording contract...for my sister—from Prince Records,' Emily said, thrusting the bouquet away from her as if she felt that by accepting it she was in some way endorsing Alessandro's plunge into the realms of fantasy.

'I have no connection whatever with any company called Prince Records,' he said, brushing some imagined lint from the lapel of his jacket.

'What?'

'You assumed I was a recording executive,' he elaborated. 'I allowed you to go on believing that...while it suited me.'

'I see,' Emily said, finding it difficult to breathe. 'And now?'

'The deception is no longer necessary,' Alessandro admitted. 'Because I have something you want and you have something I want. It's time to cut a deal.'

Emily felt as if her veins had been infused with ice. She might be twenty-eight and unmarried, but when her prince came along she wanted more than a business deal to seal their union...she wanted love, passion, tenderness and a lifetime's commitment—not a charter of convenience to close a cold and cynical deal. 'So, who the hell are you?' she demanded furiously.

'Crown Prince Alessandro Bussoni di Ferara,' he said. 'I know it's rather a mouthful—Emily?'

Snapping her mouth shut again, Emily whacked the bouquet into his arms. 'Take your damn flowers back! My sister might be in a vulnerable position right now, but let me assure you, Alessandro, I'm not.'

'Your sister put herself in this position—'

'How dare you judge her?' Emily flared, springing to her feet to glare up at him. 'You don't have the remotest idea how hard she works!'

Alessandro felt as if he had been struck by a thunderbolt, and it had nothing to do with the fact that no one—absolutely no one—had ever addressed him in this furious manner in all his life before.

Just seeing Emily now, her eyes blazing and her hair flung back, her face alive with passion, intelligence and a truckload of determination, he felt a desperate urge to direct that passion into something that would give them both a lot more pleasure than arguing about her sister.

Was he falling in love? Could it be possible? Or was he already in love? Alessandro forced a lid on the well of joy that threatened to erupt and call him a liar for wearing such a set and stony expression in response to her outburst, when all he wanted to do was to drag her into his arms and kiss the breath out of her body. Had the thunderbolt struck the first moment he saw her, commanding that gaudily decorated stage…putting the harsh spotlights to shame with her luminous beauty—a beauty that had refused to stay hidden even under what had seemed to him at the time to be half a bucket of greasepaint?

'If you'll excuse me, I'll go and call my car for you,' he said steadily, revealing nothing of his thoughts. 'I can see you're upset right now. We will discuss this tomorrow, when you are feeling calmer—'

'Don't waste your time!' Emily snapped defensively.

'With your permission,' Alessandro said, swooping to retrieve the discarded bouquet from the floor by her feet, 'I'll have these couriered to your mother.'

'Do what the hell you want with them!'

But as she calmed down in the limousine taking her safely home through the damply glittering streets, Emily was forced to accept that without financial assistance Miranda would never achieve her full potential. A grant might be found to cover her lessons with the Japanese violin professor, but no one was going to stump up the funds necessary to buy her a violin of real quality.

But how could marriage to a stranger provide the answer? She gave her head an angry shake, then began to frown as she turned Alessandro's preposterous suggestion over in her mind. With the right controls in place it might be possible...it would certainly secure Miranda's future.

The ball was in Alessandro's court. If he was serious he wouldn't be put off by her first refusal; he would be back in touch with a firm proposition very soon... *Very soon.* How long was that? Emily wondered, feeling a thrill of anticipation race through her.

CHAPTER FOUR

EMILY'S family sat in a closely knit group on the sofa in front of her, their faces frozen with disbelief.

'And so we'll all board Alessandro's private jet and fly out to Ferara for the wedding,' Emily finished calmly.

Her mother recovered first. Glancing at the vivid floral display that took up most of the front window, she turned back again to Emily, her face tense with suppressed excitement. 'Are you quite sure about this?'

'Quite sure, Mother.'

'No,' Miranda said decisively. 'I can't let you do this for me.'

But as Miranda cradled the precious violin in her arms it appeared to Emily as if the wonderful old instrument had finally come home.

'Believe me, you can,' she said firmly, turning next to her father. 'Dad? Don't you have anything you'd like to say?'

Her father made a sound of exasperation as he wiped a blunt-fingered hand across his forehead. 'I've never understood this romance business. I just knew your mother was right for me and asked her to marry me. She accepted and that was it.'

'You can't mean you approve of this, Dad?' Miranda burst out, distracted from her minute inspection of the violin. 'Just because it worked for you and Mum doesn't mean it's right for Emily. She doesn't even know this Alessandro Bussoni—'

'Well, I only got to know your father in the first year,' their mother pointed out. 'And Alessandro's a prince.'

As Miranda groaned and rolled her eyes heavenwards, her father made his excuses.

'I have work to finish if we're all going off on this jaunt next week.'

'A jaunt?' Miranda exclaimed, watching him hurry out of the room. 'Doesn't Dad know how serious this is?'

'Alessandro has given me a cast-iron contract,' Emily said calmly. 'I've read it through carefully and even had it double-checked in Chambers.'

'And you're sure that Miranda's fees will be paid in full?'

Miranda flashed a look of dismay at her mother. 'Mother, really!'

Emily put a restraining hand on her sister's arm. 'Fees, as well as a grant, Mother, plus an indefinite loan of the violin.'

'And the only way Alessandro's elderly father can abdicate is if Alessandro marries you?'

'That's right, Mother. You see, we need each other.'

In spite of her bold assurances, Emily wondered if she really was quite sane. She could recall every nuance of Alessandro's telephone call—the call that had come through almost the moment she'd walked into her apartment after their meeting. He had signed off the deal with a generosity beyond anything she could have anticipated. At least, those were the tactics he had employed to make her change her mind, she amended silently. Tactics. She rolled the cold little word around her mind, wishing there could have been more—wishing she could have detected even the slightest tinge of warmth or enthusiasm in Alessandro's voice when he'd upped his offer to ensure her agreement. But it had been just a list of commitments he was prepared to make in exchange for her hand in marriage. He might have been reading from a list—perhaps he had been, Emily thought, trying to concentrate on what her sister was saying.

'And all you have to do is marry some stranger,' Miranda exclaimed contemptuously.

'Don't be like that,' Emily said softly.

Miranda made a sound of disgust. 'Well, I think you've all gone completely mad.'

Emily might have agreed, even smiled to hear the word she had so recently flung at Alessandro echoed by her sister, but noticing how Miranda held the violin a little closer while she spoke only firmed her resolve. 'This marriage lasts just long enough to allow Alessandro's father to abdicate in his favour and Miranda to complete her studies with Professor Iwamoto. That's it. Then it's over. So don't any of you start building castles in the air—'

'Castles,' her mother breathed, clapping her hands together as she gazed blissfully forward into the future. 'Who'd have thought it?'

'I'll make it work. I have to,' Emily said, when she was alone in her bedroom with Miranda later that day. 'I've got nothing to lose—'

'You've got everything to lose!' Miranda argued passionately. 'You might fall in love with Alessandro, and then what?'

'I'm twenty-eight and have managed to avoid any serious romantic entanglements so far.'

'Only because you're a workaholic and no one remotely like Alessandro has ever crossed your path before,' Miranda exclaimed impatiently. 'What are you going to do if you fall in love with him? He's one gorgeous-looking man—'

'Which makes it all the easier to keep the relationship on a professional level,' Emily cut in, seizing on the potential for disappointment. 'He's bound to be spoiled, selfish, inconsiderate and self-obsessed. Just the type of man I have always found so easy to resist.'

'And what if you get pregnant?' Miranda persisted.

'Absolutely no chance of that.'

'Now you do have to be kidding. You'll never be able to resist him. And Alessandro looks like one fertile guy—'

'It's never going to happen without sex.'

'What?' Miranda stared blankly at her.

'I've had it written into the contract,' Emily said, congratulating herself on her foresight. 'It seemed like a sensible precaution. And it saves any embarrassment for either party.'

'"It saves any embarrassment for either party",' Miranda mimicked, trying not to laugh. 'Get real! You'll never know what you're missing.'

'Exactly,' Emily confirmed. 'And I intend to go back to work when all this is over, so I don't need any distractions.'

'Alessandro isn't a distraction; he's a lifetime's obsession,' Miranda pointed out dreamily.

'Maybe,' Emily conceded. 'But he'll want out of this contract as much as I will do. Don't go making Mother's mistake and reading more into it than there is. This is a straightforward business deal that suits both of us. It's a merger, not a marriage.'

'Then I'm sorry for you,' Miranda said softly. 'For Alessandro, too. And it makes me feel so guilty—'

'Don't,' Emily said fiercely, clutching her sister's arm. 'Don't use that word. You have to support me, Miranda. It's too late to back out now. I've already arranged to take a career break. Just think—I'll be able to pay off my mortgage with Alessandro's divorce settlement, so you're helping me to achieve my dream, too.'

'In that case, I guess we're in this together,' Miranda said, pulling a resigned face.

'Just like always,' Emily admitted, forcing a bright note into her voice as she tried not to care that her marriage to Alessandro was doomed before it even began.

'Like for ever,' Miranda agreed, on the same note as her

twin. But her face was full of concern as she looked beyond Emily's determined front and saw the truth hovering behind her sister's eyes.

It was a beautiful summer's evening of the type rarely seen in England. The milky blue sky was deepening steadily to indigo, and it was still warm enough to sit out on the hotel balcony in comfort. The uniqueness of the weather was perfectly in accord with the mood of the occasion, Emily mused as she watched Alessandro come back to her with two slender crystal flutes of champagne. The business of signing the contract was over, and now it was time to celebrate a most unusual deal.

A little shiver ran through her as she took the glass. Marriage to a man like Alessandro would have been an intoxicating prospect whatever his condition in life... If there had only been the smallest flicker of romance—but there was none.

'To us,' he murmured, breaking into her thoughts with the most inappropriate toast she could imagine.

'To our mutual satisfaction,' Emily amended, only to find herself qualifying that pledge when she saw the look on his face. 'With the outcome of our agreement,' she clarified.

'Ah, yes, our agreement,' Alessandro repeated with a faint smile. 'It may not have been spelled out to you exactly, but you will be entitled to keep the title of Principessa if you so wish... Emily?'

'That's really not important—'

'Not important?'

She could see she had offended him. 'Look, I'm sorry. I—'

His dismissive gesture cut her off. Turning his back, he stared out across the rapidly darkening cityscape. 'Once we are married the title is yours for life, whether or not you choose to use it.'

'I will have done nothing to earn that right,' Emily protested edgily.

'Don't be so sure,' Alessandro countered, spearing her with a glance. 'There are bound to be difficulties before you settle into the role.'

'Please don't worry about me, Alessandro. I'm quite capable of looking after myself.'

Emily was convinced that she was right, but she hadn't reckoned with the speed with which Alessandro would put the plan into operation. By the end of the week even travel arrangements had been finalised. Emily and her family would fly to Ferara in Alessandro's private jet while he remained in London to conclude his business dealings there.

As the day of departure drew closer, the speed of change in Emily's life began gathering pace at a rate she couldn't control. It felt as if the carefully crafted existence she had built for herself was being steadily unpicked, stitch by intricate stitch. The first warning sign was when a young couple arrived unannounced to take her measurements and speak in reverent terms of Brussels lace and Shantung silk, Swiss embroidery and pearls. At that point Emily realised that if she didn't put her foot down she would have little to say even about the style of her own wedding dress. As if to confirm her suspicions, just a couple of days later clothes began arriving at her apartment—without anything being ordered as far as she was aware—as well as boxes of shoes by the trunkload.

Feeling presumptuous, almost as if she was attempting to contact someone she hardly knew, she picked up the telephone to call Alessandro at his London office.

She was so surprised when his secretary put her straight through that for a few moments she could hardly think straight.

'I know it's a bit crude,' he admitted, covering for her

sudden shyness with his easy manner. 'But time has been condensed for us, Emily, and I wanted you to feel comfortable—'

'Comfortable?' Emily heard herself exclaim. 'With clothes labelled "Breakfast, lunch, dinner: al fresco; breakfast, lunch, dinner: formal"! And that's only two of the categories. There must be at least a dozen more—'

'You don't like them?' Alessandro said, sounding genuinely concerned.

'I'm sorry. I don't mean to sound ungrateful.'

'Should we meet and discuss it, do you think?'

'Yes.' She should have pretended to think about his offer for a moment or two, she realised.

'Shall I come for you now?' There was a note of amusement in his voice.

'That would be nice,' she managed huskily.

Alessandro took her to lunch at one of the city's most exclusive restaurants. Somewhere so discreet that even a prince and his beautiful young companion could pass a comfortable hour or two consuming delicious food in a private booth well away from prying eyes.

Laying down her napkin after the most light *millefeuille* of plump strawberries, bursting with juice, sweetened with icing sugar and whipped cream, Emily wondered how she was going to refuse Alessandro's fabulous gifts without offending him.

'Is something troubling you?' he pressed, signalling to the waiter that he was ready to sign the bill. 'You surely can't still be worrying about those clothes?'

'I don't know what to think about them,' Emily admitted frankly, hiding her confusion behind the guise of practicality. 'There are just so many outfits—it would take me the best part of a year just to try them all on.'

'So leave it for now,' he suggested casually. 'Grab a few things you like, and I'll have the rest delivered to the palace. You can take your time over them in Ferara. I just thought as we were in London it was too good an opportunity to miss.'

'You're very kind...too kind,' Emily said impulsively. Her heart was hammering painfully in her chest, while Alessandro's gaze warmed her face, demanding that she look at him.

'I just want you to be happy,' he murmured.

A muscle flexed in his jaw, as if he was struggling with the situation almost as much as she was. 'For the duration of the contract,' Emily said, as if trying to set things straight in both their minds.

Inclining his head towards her, Alessandro gave a brief nod of agreement. 'Talking of which—' Reaching inside the breast pocket of his lightweight jacket, he brought something out, then seemed to think better of it and put it back again.

'Are you ready to go?' he said, standing up. 'I thought we might take a stroll around the park before I take you back.'

As they left the restaurant Emily was aware that the same men who had followed them discreetly from her apartment were just a few footsteps behind them now.

'Don't worry,' Alessandro said, linking her arm through his, seeing her turn. 'They're the good guys.'

'Your bodyguards?'

'Yours, too, now that you are to be my wife,' he reminded her.

The thought that she was to be Alessandro's wife excited her, in spite of everything, but the thought that she would never go anywhere again without bodyguards was the flipside of the coin. She needed Alessandro to guide her through this confusing new world, Emily realised. There were so many things she had to ask him...

'Would you like to come back to my place for coffee?'

The few seconds before he replied felt like hours. So long, in fact, that Emily began to feel foolish—as if she had made some clumsy approach to a man she'd only just met.

'Better not,' he replied with a quick smile.

'Don't worry—I just thought—'

Alessandro could have kicked himself. Emily's invitation had been irresistible—almost. But if they went back to her apartment there could only be one outcome and, to his continued surprise, Emily Weston had awoken a whole gamut of masculine instincts within him—prime amongst which, at this moment, was his desire to protect her. To protect her, to woo her, and then make her his wife. And he had already accepted that the timing of that last part of his plan might not coincide exactly with their wedding day.

'There's still time for that walk in the park.'

They were sheltering from rain beneath a bandstand when he said, 'You'd better have this.'

'What is it?' Emily said curiously, watching as again he dipped his hand inside the breast pocket of his jacket. She frowned when she saw the ring he was holding out to her.

'It would cause quite a stir in Ferara if you weren't seen wearing this particular piece of jewellery,' Alessandro explained, as coolly as if it was a laptop that came with the job.

Of course there would be a ring…she should have known. And it was a very beautiful ring. But shouldn't an engagement ring be given with love…and with tenderness?

'Don't you like it?'

It really mattered to him, Emily realised, taking in the fact that the ring was obviously very old and must have been worn by Alessandro's ancestors for generations—possibly even by his late mother.

'If you prefer you could just wear it on public occasions.'

'I love it,' she said firmly. And I can see how much it means to you, her eyes told him. 'It's just with all these fabulous clothes, and now this…' The words dried up as he took hold of her hand. His expression was lighter, as if a great burden had been removed from his shoulders.

'Thank you,' he said softly. 'I was hoping you'd like it. It has been passed down through my family.'

'Tell me more,' Emily encouraged, forgetting everything else as she surrendered to Alessandro's voice, and his touch...but most of all to the sudden realisation that she wasn't the only one who needed reassurance.

'I know it isn't the usual huge and very valuable stone,' he began, 'and perhaps it isn't the type of thing you might have been expecting. But this ring has a provenance that no other piece of jewellery can boast.'

It might have been made for her, Emily realised as he settled it on her finger. Dainty ropes of rubies and pearls wound around the circumference with a ruby heart as the centrepiece of the design. 'Tell me about it,' she repeated.

'There was a Prince of Ferara named Rodrigo,' Alessandro began. 'He fell in love with a beautiful young girl called Caterina. Rodrigo had this ring made for her...'

As his voice stroked her senses Emily tried to remain detached and remind herself that Alessandro was only telling her a story. But it wasn't easy when her mind was awash with alternative images.

'On his way to ask for Caterina's hand in marriage, Rodrigo's horse shied, throwing him unconscious into the lake. Robbed of her one true love, Caterina decided to join a religious order.'

Emily tensed as Alessandro switched his attention abruptly to her face. 'What happened to her?' she asked quickly, full of the irrational fear that he could read her mind and know it was full of him rather than the characters he was telling her about.

'Caterina's horse shied on the way to the convent,' he said casually, the expression in his eyes concealed beneath a fringe of black lashes. 'When she recovered consciousness this ring was right there by her side.'

The ruby heart seemed to flare a response, making Emily gasp involuntarily.

'So, did she join the religious order?'

'She couldn't.'

'Couldn't?'

'That's right.'

'Why not?'

'I should take you home now, if you are to have an early night before your flight to Ferara tomorrow,' he said restlessly, as if he wished he had never started the story. 'I have another business meeting in about—' He frowned as he glanced at his wristwatch. 'About ten minutes ago.'

All the romance…all the tenderness…had vanished from his voice as if it had never been. Of course it had never been, Emily thought, angry for allowing herself to get carried away. Alessandro's fairy story was just part of the play-acting they were both forced to endure…and the ring was just another prop.

'I'll take good care of it,' she said, closing her fist around the jewel-encrusted band.

'I'm sure you will,' he murmured as he straightened up. 'Shall we go?'

It was an instruction, not a question, Emily realised. 'You don't have to see me home,' she said quickly. 'I've made you late enough already.'

'I'm taking you back,' he insisted in the same quiet determined tone that made it impossible to argue with him.

Alessandro left her at the door to her apartment, refusing yet another invitation to cross the threshold. *'Li vedro in Ferara, Emily,'* he said, waiting until she had closed the door.

'Yes. See you in Ferara, Alessandro,' Emily confirmed softly, turning away from him to face the empty room.

CHAPTER FIVE

IT SEEMED to Emily that everyone in Ferara had cause to celebrate apart from the main characters in the drama that was about to unfold.

From one of the windows in the turret of the huge suite she had been given for her few remaining days as a single woman she had a good view of the cobbled thoroughfare outside the palace walls. Bunting and banners in the distinctive Feraran colours of crimson, blue and gold hung in colourful swathes across the street, along with numerous posters of the soon to be married couple...Emily Weston and Prince Alessandro Bussoni Ferara. Es and As, intertwined.

For once Emily was forced to agree with her mother. It hardly seemed possible!

She had been awake since dawn, when all the unfamiliar sounds of a new day in Ferara had intruded upon her slumbers. Only then had she begun to drink in the unaccustomed luxury of her new surroundings—and with something closer to dread than exhilaration. The setting was everything she might have dreamed about—if she'd been a dreamer. One thing she had not anticipated was how it might feel to be set adrift in a palace that, however fabulous, was full of endless echoing corridors where everyone but she seemed to know exactly what was expected of them.

Ferara, at least, was far lovelier than she had ever dared to expect. On the drive from the airport the countryside that had unrolled before her had been picture-postcard perfect. A landscape of lilac hills shrouded in mist, some crowned with quaint medieval villages shielding fields cloaked in vines, and clusters of cypress trees standing on sentry duty against a flawless azure sky.

The Palace of Ferara was constructed around a sixth century Byzantine tower, and seemed from a distance to be balanced perilously on the very edge of a towering chalky-white cliff face. Rising out of the low cloud cover as they had approached by road, both palace and cliff had appeared to be suspended magically in the air. But as they'd drawn closer Emily had seen that the stone palace was both vast and set firm on towering foundations.

No wonder a Princess of Ferara needed so many clothes, she mused as she retraced in her mind those parts of the palace she had already been shown. The sheer number of rooms was overwhelming.

Tossing back the crisp, lavender-scented sheets, she swung her legs over the side of the bed and headed towards the glass-paned doors leading onto her balcony. Even in the early-morning sunshine the mellow stone already felt warm beneath her naked feet. Staring out across the city, she felt like an excited child, monitoring the progress of some promised treat... Except that she wasn't a child any longer, Emily reminded herself, pulling back. She would have to be totally insensitive not to realise that the people of Ferara had high hopes for this marriage, and all she had to offer them was a sham.

She dragged her thoughts from harsh reality and they turned inevitably to Alessandro, and how long his business would keep him from Ferara. The best she could expect was that he would turn up for their wedding. Then they would get on with their own lives—separately. She would stay on in Ferara, of course, and act out her part as promised. But what did Alessandro have planned? Would she see him at all?

Shaking her head, as if to rid herself of pointless speculation, she reached for the telephone and dialled an internal line. After several rings she remembered that Miranda and her parents would probably have already left for their promised tour of Ferara.

So, what did a 'soon to be' princess do in her spare time? Ring the office, she told herself, trying another number.

'Force of habit,' she explained to the uncharacteristically bewildered Clerk of Chambers who normally organised her working life with unfailing efficiency. 'Yes, OK, Billy. See you at the wedding then.'

She tried to hang on to the familiar voice in her mind, but when she replaced the receiver the room seemed to have grown larger and even emptier than before she placed the call.

Shower, dress, and draw up a plan, she decided, trying to ignore the stab of tears behind her eyes as she headed purposefully towards the lavish marble bathroom. She would have to pull herself together and find a meaningful role for herself if the next couple of years weren't going to be the longest of her life.

She felt better when she came out of the bathroom, hair partly dried and hanging wild about her shoulders, and with a fluffy white towel secured loosely round her hips. She had waltzed herself halfway across the ballroom-sized bedroom, humming her own version of Strauss, before she realised she was not alone. As her hands flew to tug up the towel and cover her breasts she realised there wasn't enough material to cover everything—

'Calm down. I'll turn my back,' Alessandro murmured reassuringly.

It wasn't easy to stay calm when your heart was spinning in your chest!

'Who let you in?' she said, backing up towards the door of her dressing room.

'I apologise for arriving unannounced.'

He could try a little harder to *sound* contrite, Emily thought, conscious that her nipples had turned into bullets. 'I thought you had business to conclude in London.'

So did I, Alessandro mused wryly. But thanks to you, Emily, I couldn't stay away. 'Can I help you with that?' he offered, moving towards her as she debated whether to simply brazen it out and turn to open the dressing room door, or try to manoeuvre the handle with her elbow whilst clinging on to the towel and preserving what little remained of her dignity.

'That won't be necessary,' she said, choosing the latter option.

'Oh, come now, Emily,' Alessandro murmured, moving closer. 'I have seen a woman's body before…'

That was all the encouragement she needed to try and bludgeon the handle into submission with an increasingly tender arm.

'It's not as if anything's going to happen,' he added sardonically, 'remember that "no sex" clause?'

'Yes, thank you, I do remember,' Emily said, conscious that every tiny hair on her body was standing to attention.

'See? I'm not even looking,' he insisted, leaning across her to open the door. 'Your modesty is utterly preserved, *signorina.*'

Launching herself into the dressing room, Emily slammed the door shut and leaned heavily against it as she struggled to catch her breath.

'Don't be long,' Alessandro warned from the other side. 'I've got something to show you…something I think you might like.'

Emily's gaze tacked frantically around the room as she tried to decide what to do next. Dropping the towel, she sprinted naked to examine her daunting collection of new clothes.

Everything was cloaked in protective covers and there were photographs of each outfit on labels attached to the hangers; labels that came complete with directions as to where matching accessories might be found. But her investigations were hampered by too much choice. And just what was the appropriate outfit for after you'd stepped out of the shower only to be discovered naked by possibly the most delicious male on the planet? A male, furthermore, with whom you could anticipate no hanky-panky whatsoever!

Modest enough to prove you weren't the least bit interested in him, she decided, and casual enough to put them both at their ease.

Decision made, Emily dived into the bottom of the wardrobe and tugged out her trusty jeans and tee shirt.

'I hope you slept well?'

'Very well, thank you,' she replied politely, giving Alessandro a wide berth on her way back across the room. 'I had no idea you had arrived home.' Reaching the massive fireplace, she intended to rest one trembling arm on the mantelpiece, but missed when she found she couldn't reach. Acting nonchalant, she leaned against the wall instead, and levelled a bogus confident stare on Alessandro's face.

'Come over here,' he said softly, indicating the cushion next to his own on the cream damask sofa.

As one corner of his mouth tugged up in a smile Emily's battered confidence took a further plunge into the depths, while her heart seemed capable of yet more crazy antics. 'Why?' she said suspiciously.

'Because there's something that I'd like you to see,' he said patiently.

Emily took care to measure each step, so as not to appear too keen.

'Sit down,' he invited, standing briefly until she was comfortably settled on the sofa.

Maintaining space between them, Emily folded her hands out of harm's way in her lap and waited.

Reaching down to the floor at his feet, Alessandro brought up an ancient brown leather casket and set it down on the table in front of her. Releasing the brass catches, he lifted the lid. 'For you,' he said, tipping it up so that she could easily see the contents.

Emily gasped, all play-acting forgotten as she peered into the midnight-blue interior, where a quantity of diamonds flashed fire as the early-morning sunlight danced across their facets.

Reaching into the casket, Alessandro brought out a diamond tiara, together with earrings and a matching bracelet and necklace. 'You will wear these with your wedding dress,' he said, laying them out on the table in front of her.

'Don't you think that's a bit much?'

'To my knowledge, no Princess of Ferara has complained before,' he said, sweeping up one ebony brow in an elegant show of surprise.

'Well, I had planned a more restrained look—'

'You'll do as you're told,' Alessandro cut in firmly. 'The people of Ferara expect—'

'The people of Ferara,' Emily countered, 'are receiving short shrift from us both. And I can't...I won't appear any more of a hypocrite than I already am. They deserve better—'

'You will honour this contract,' Alessandro returned sharply, 'and leave the people of Ferara to me. They are my concern—'

'Shortly to be mine,' Emily argued stubbornly. 'If only for the duration of our agreement. While this contract runs its course,' she continued, 'I intend to fulfil my duties to this county, and its people, in full. And I warn you, Alessandro, I will not be side-tracked from my intended course of action by you.'

'Then you will do as I ask and wear this jewellery,' he insisted, clearly exasperated. 'It's for one day only. That is all I ask.'

Emily mashed her lips together as she thought about it. The royal tiara to hold her veil in place and cement Alessandro's position as ruler of Ferara? She would agree to that. 'I would love to wear the tiara, but this ring is what your people care about,' she said, touching the ruby and pearl band. 'All the other jewellery is very impressive, but, just as you said, no jewel, however valuable, can boast the history of this one modest piece. Why overshadow it? I think your people would appreciate seeing simplicity in their Princess. I've no wish to flaunt your wealth.'

There was a long pause during which Emily couldn't fathom what was going on in Alessandro's mind. His face remained impassive, but behind his eyes myriad changes in the molten gold irises marked the course of his thoughts. Even sitting with his back to the sun, with his face half in shadow, the light in his eyes was remarkable, Emily mused, leaving tension behind as she slipped deeper into reverie.

'You're an exceptional woman, Signorina Weston—'

She started guiltily out of her daydream as Alessandro began putting the fabulous jewels back inside their velvet nest. She could hardly believe what he was saying...doing. She had won her first battle—and so easily— 'You agree?' she said, holding her breath.

'I agree,' Alessandro said, almost as if he surprised himself. 'Everything will be locked up for safekeeping. The tiara will be returned to you on the day of our wedding.'

'Thank you,' she said with relief, getting to her feet as Alessandro stood up to go. 'Will I see you again before then?' It was a question she longed to know the answer to...a question she knew she had no right to ask him.

'I imagined you would be too busy with your preparations,' Alessandro said, looking at her intently. 'I have meetings arranged right up to the morning of the ceremony...I thought I'd give you time to sort through all those clothes,' he added, clearly of the opinion that any woman should be thrilled by such a prospect.

But Emily wasn't impressed. As far as she was concerned, the over-abundance of outfits in her walk-in wardrobe represented nothing more than a selection of costumes for the short-running drama production in which she was about to appear.

'I'd like to do something worthwhile...learn something about Ferara,' she insisted. 'The clothes can wait.'

For a moment Alessandro seemed taken aback. 'Well, good,' he said. 'I'll find someone to have a chat with you—'

As her stomach clenched with disappointment, Emily's lips tightened. 'Don't bother,' she said tensely. 'I'll find someone myself.'

After eating breakfast alone in her suite, Emily knew it was time to make good her boast to find someone who would tell her a little about Ferara. Catching sight of an elderly gardener through one of her many windows, she hurried out of the room.

He was as gnarled as an oak tree and, right now, as bent as one of its branches as he leaned over the plants he was caring for. Emily remained discreetly half hidden as she stared at him, wondering if she had made the right choice.

She needn't have worried about disturbing him. He was oblivious to everything around him apart from the roses he was tending.

Emily smiled as she watched him. The old man's love for his plants was revealed in his every move. He had probably worked in the palace gardens most of his long life. Ferara was that sort of place. Who better to tell her everything she wanted to know? He might not speak too much English, but her Italian was...not too bad, she consoled herself. They should be able to have a conversation of sorts—and anything was preferable to returning to the silence that dominated her ornate, but ultimately sterile rooms.

'*Buon giorno!*' she began hopefully, walking towards the solitary figure. 'I hope I'm not disturbing you.'

'Not at all, *signorina*. I'm delighted to have the company.'

'You speak English,' she said, unable to keep the excitement from her voice.

'I do,' the elderly man replied, leaning heavily on the handle of his fork. 'What can I do for you, *signorina*?'

'Don't you feel the sun?' Emily said, shading her eyes with her hand. 'It's terribly hot out here.'

'Yes, I feel the sun,' he agreed. 'I love to feel the sun. I love to be outside...with my roses,' he elaborated, gesturing around him with one nobly hand whilst star-bright amber eyes continued to reflect on Emily's face. 'Do you like flowers?'

'I love them,' she replied.

'Roses?'

'Especially roses,' Emily sighed, as she traced a petal wistfully. 'They remind me of my parents' garden in England.'

'Do you feel homesick already?' he asked perceptively.

It was as if some bond formed between them in that moment. And as they smiled at each other Emily felt herself relax. 'I'm surprised they flourish here in this heat so late in the summer,' she said, reining back the emotion that suddenly threatened to spoil these first moments with a potential new friend and possible ally.

'My own system of filtered sunlight and judicious watering,' the old man told her proudly. 'Like me, these roses love the sun. And, like me, in this hot climate their exposure to it must be rationed. Otherwise we'd both shrivel up.'

He chuckled, and his eyes sparkled with laughter, but Emily could see the concern behind them, and regretted that she was the cause.

'What's this one called?' she asked, determined to set everything back on an even keel as she pointed to an orange-red, rosette-shaped bloom.

'A good choice,' he commented thoughtfully, stabbing his fork into the ground to come and join her. 'This rose is named after Shakespeare's contemporary, the great English playwright Christopher Marlowe. Here,' he invited, selecting a bloom to show her and holding it up loosely between his fingers, 'inhale deeply, *signorina*. You should be able to detect a scent of tea and lemon. Lemon tea,' he declared, chuckling again, pleased with his joke.

'Mmm. It is a distinctive scent,' Emily agreed after a moment. 'But what is the connection between Christopher Marlowe and roses?'

'You don't know?' he demanded.

It seemed as if she was going to have to learn something about her own culture before starting on his, Emily realised. 'I'm afraid I don't,' she said ruefully.

'Christopher Marlowe pressed a rose inside the pages of a book he gave to a friend after an argument...to express his regret over their disagreement.'

'And did his friend forgive him?'

'Who could resist?' the old gentleman retorted, his eyes widening as he surveyed the array of beautiful blooms nodding in the breeze in front of them.

Before Emily could stop him, he cut one for her.

'Here, *signorina*, take this. Press it between the pages of a book...and always remember that if a rose is shown love and care it will flourish and bloom, wherever it is planted.'

Taking the flower from his hand, Emily smiled. 'Do you work here every day?'

'I intend to,' he told her, eyes shining with anticipation. 'I intend to make this rose garden the most talked about in all of Ferara...all of Europe!'

They talked for some while, and then she left him to his work.

'I'm sure you will,' Emily agreed. 'It's so very beautiful already.'

'Would it bother you if I came here to talk to you again?'

'Bother me?' he exclaimed with surprise. 'On the contrary *signorina*. I should love it.'

'In that case,' Emily said happily, 'see you tomorrow.'

The old man bowed as she started to move away. 'Until tomorrow, *signorina*. I shall look forward to it.'

After her encounter with the elderly gardener Emily felt more confident that she had something to contribute to palace life. A plan was taking shape in her mind: a scheme to improve the living conditions of all Alessandro's employees—though she had to admit to a moment's concern when her private secretary said she knew of no one matching the old man's description in royal service.

Turning it over in her mind, Emily returned to her desk to catch up on some correspondence. On the top there was a large red journal she didn't recognise, and, opening it at the flyleaf, she saw it was from Alessandro. He had written simply, 'For Emily from Alessandro—a record of your thoughts'. And then, at the bottom of the page, he had added the date of their forthcoming marriage.

'Do you like it?'

She nearly jumped out of her skin. 'I love it,' she said bluntly, running the fingers of one hand appreciatively down the length of its spine.

'Your secretary showed me in,' he explained. 'I hope you don't mind?'

'Not at all.' The now familiar surge in her pulse-rate had reached new and unprecedented levels, Emily discovered as she continued to stare at Alessandro standing on the balcony outside her room. Surely there would come a point where she'd got used to seeing him? But how could anyone look that good in a pair of jeans and a simple dark linen shirt? She surmised he was off-duty, and wondered what he planned to do with his free time. 'Is this a gift for me?' she said, glancing down at the journal.

He answered with a grin and a shrug.

'Five years of entries?' she teased lightly. 'I presume you couldn't get any less?'

His silence allowed her to draw her own conclusions. 'Well, I've never had anything like it before.' she admitted frankly, 'so, thank you.'

'May I come in?' he said, leaning on the doorframe.

'Of course.' She wondered if her heart would ever steady again. 'I was only going to write some letters.'

'But I thought you wanted to have a look around Ferara?'

'I do.' She tried not to read anything into the remark, but her pulse rate rebelled again. 'I'm very keen to learn more. Actually, I've already made a friend of one of the gardeners.'

'Did he tell you much about our country?'

'He was a very interesting old gentleman, as it happens. And, Alessandro?'

'Yes?'

Emily waited, noticing how his eyes reflected his thoughts—there was a something in his expression now that suggested this might be a good time to air her idea. 'I know you've been very busy, and that small things aren't always apparent, but...'

'Get on with it,' he encouraged with a gesture.

'After talking to the gardener I got the impression that his apartment could do with some renovation—just some little touches that would make his life easier.'

'And you'd like to take charge of these?'

'Yes. I think it would be worthwhile.'

'I'm sure it would,' Alessandro agreed. 'And as far as learning more about Ferara is concerned—well, I've taken the afternoon off, so I could show you around, if you like.'

A shiver of excitement raced down Emily's spine as she let him wait for her answer.

'The chocolate festival,' he prompted, 'the one I told you about? It's usually held in February, but there's to be a special demonstration in celebration of our marriage.

Because of the heat at this time of year it's taking place inside the grand hall of one of the municipal buildings.'

So, his talk of a chocolate festival hadn't been a wind-up after all, she realised, feeling a rush of anticipation. 'I'd love to go.'

'That's settled, then,' he said. 'We'd better leave right away if we want to catch the best demonstrations.'

When they arrived, Emily was amazed to find the streets of Ferara had been recreated within the cool, vaulted interior of the ancient building, complete with chocolate stalls, chocolate sculptures in various stages of completion, and crowds milling about. There was a ripple of excitement when Alessandro was spotted with his bride-to-be, but after the initial surprise they were able to move around the vast marble-floored exhibition area quite freely. It was Emily's first real exposure to her new countrymen, and at first she held back a little self-consciously, but Alessandro grabbed her hand, drawing her forward, giving every indication of being proud of his choice of bride.

He was either a very good actor, Emily decided, or—a very good actor, she told herself firmly, knowing how easy it would be to let her imagination get the better of her where Alessandro was involved.

'Let me get you some chocolate,' he offered, weaving through the press of people, towing her behind him. He took her to stand beneath one of the towering pillars where an artist was already busy at work, then reached out and caught some of the glossy flakes as they showered down. He began feeding them to her, until Emily had to beg him to stop.

'Stop? Are you sure?'

'No,' Emily admitted, laughing because she was sure her face had to be smeared with chocolate.

To anyone unaware of their tangled relationship they would have passed for two people in love, laughing and enjoying the festival for what it was—an explosion of hap-

piness and goodwill to celebrate the marriage of a man who
was clearly much loved by his fellow Ferarans.

Freed from the tensions imposed by their arranged marriage, they actually enjoyed each other's company, Emily
realised, smiling ruefully as she accepted the clean handkerchief Alessandro produced from his pocket.

'Is there anything else you should have warned me
about?' she probed cheekily. 'Cream bun fights, perhaps?'
She gazed up at him as she tried to wipe some of the chocolate smears off her face, loving the feeling of closeness
that had sprung up between them.

'I think I can safely promise you one or two more interesting customs throughout your time here.'

Emily's smile faltered. Trying not to spoil the mood, she
shook herself out of the doldrums. 'Tell me about these
different traditions,' she pressed with another smile.

'If you haven't guessed already, our wedding's a great
excuse for giving some of the best a second airing. Everyone in Ferara loves a carnival. You'll definitely be seeing
my country at its best.'

'I'm looking forward to it,' she said. And she was, especially if Alessandro was to be her guide.

'You're still covered in chocolate,' he commented as she
made another attempt to clean her face.

'Well, if I am it's all your fault,' Emily countered with
a laugh that swiftly turned into an uncertain silence.

That remark was the closest she had ever come to flirting
with him. And in view of his comment that seemed to remind her of the time limit on her visit, flirting was out. Not
only that, but her teasing manner was attracting quite a bit
of interest. 'I must look a mess,' she said self-consciously.

'You look lovely,' Alessandro argued, removing the
handkerchief from her hand. Dampening one clean corner with his tongue, he very gently wiped her face for
her. 'There's—that's better,' he declared at last with satisfaction.

Emily fought the urge to stare into his eyes, suddenly terrified that what she might see there would not match her own feelings. 'I suppose we'd better be getting back.' She broke free and went to stand some distance away before he had the chance to put distance between them.

This was crazy, Emily realised. When all she wanted was to be with him here she was calling an end to the day almost before it had begun! How had she ever imagined she could throw herself in the path of a man like Alessandro and walk away unscathed? Suddenly she couldn't wait to get away. The smell of the chocolate, the heat of the crowd and the noise reverberating round the lofty building stabbed at her mind, and she was almost running as she burst out through the imposing double doors that led to the open air. Shielding her eyes against the unforgiving rays of the midday sun, for a moment she was completely disorientated. Starting down the broad sweep of stone steps, she nearly stumbled.

'Emily! Are you all right?'

The voice was unmistakable—deep, and concerned. Tears sprang to her eyes as he caught hold of her, and she hated herself for the weakness. Somehow she had to get back her pre-Alessandro control, Emily raged inwardly. But she needed his steadying arm to guide her down the steps…

'It's hot, and you've consumed vast quantities of chocolate,' Alessandro said soothingly. 'I think we should take a gentle stroll back to the palace. I'll organise a light lunch—'

'Oh, no. I couldn't eat anything,' Emily said truthfully, though her lack of appetite was a direct result of the ache in her heart; nothing at all to do with the sunshine or an over-abundance of chocolate.

'I think for once you're going to do as I say,' Alessandro said sternly as he led her carefully down the steps. 'You almost fell up there. Then what would I have done? I can't have a wedding without a bride.'

'I'm sure you'd find someone without too much trouble.'

'But they wouldn't be you, would they?' he said tolerantly.

'Does that matter?'

'Yes, it does. So you're just going to have to humour me. The sun is strong and you're not used to it. Here, lean on my arm. We'll take it slowly…walk in the shade. I don't suppose you've eaten properly.'

'I've had lots of chocolate,' she pointed out mutinously.

'An unrelieved diet of chocolate might get a little boring, even for you. A light salad, some iced water—'

She hoped he was right. Maybe the heat *was* getting to her…the heat, and feelings she was sure he didn't reciprocate. Alessandro was simply making the best out of a difficult situation, she thought, flashing a look up at him…while she was falling in love, she realised with a stab of concern.

Alessandro returned Emily's troubled glance with a smile and a reassuring squeeze. He had been right to take her out of the heat. He should have anticipated how many people would attend the event, but he had just wanted an excuse to be with her. The chocolate festival had been the perfect opportunity.

Falling in love had been the last thing on his agenda, he realised as they made their way slowly back to the palace. But here, under the centuries-old shade of the cypress trees, the warmth of the sun was like a balm that enveloped them both in its healing rays. If he could have done, he would have willed all the mistrust, all the uncertainty that had tainted their relationship to float away on the light breeze that sighed through the branches over their heads…

Emily was perfect, and the mood of his people was wholly supportive, he realised with pleasure as he courteously returned several greetings. She would make a wonderful first lady: a true equal to stand beside him and care for these people he loved so much. She could hardly wait to make a start on improving the lot of those around her...sharing her own happiness with others. He snatched a look at the woman who in one short week would be his bride. She was deep in thought, but not so preoccupied that she couldn't take account of every smile that came her way and return it with sincerity. He felt a rush of deep affection for her...something that transcended physical attraction and looped a band of love around his soul.

He had never once felt like this, Alessandro realised, relishing the simple trust she placed in him, linking her arm through his. The privilege of being allowed to care for her made him happier than he could ever have imagined. It fulfilled him...completed him. Falling in love with Emily was the most natural, the most inevitable step he had ever taken. But if he rushed things he knew he ran the risk of damaging their relationship, perhaps irrevocably. He would have to take things easy...take it slowly, give them both time to get to know each other.

It wasn't enough that the chemistry between them was almost frightening in its intensity and that every male instinct he possessed insisted he take her straight to his bed. He knew with utter certainty that if he wanted more, he had to wait—

'D'you know, Alessandro?'

She captured his attention so easily, he realised happily. 'Tell me,' he prompted softly.

'I love Ferara...I love your people... They're all so friendly, so genuine and so welcoming...' She hesitated.

'And?' he said gently, sensing there was something more she wanted to say.

'I really think this might work...between us,' she elaborated awkwardly, though there was no need, Alessandro thought with an inward smile as he drew her a little closer. He had already come to that same conclusion himself, some time ago.

CHAPTER SIX

FOR the next couple of days Emily hardly saw Alessandro, except in passing. But she knew he was swept up in protocol, and fine-tuning their wedding arrangements. Her own family was busy with last-minute preparations, too, so any spare time she had she spent talking to her new friend.

With only one night to go before the wedding, she finally found the courage to ask him more about where he lived. Now that she intended the welfare of the palace staff to be one of her main areas of interest while she was in Ferara, this looked like as good a time as any to make a start. 'Does it suit you?'

'Suit me?' he asked with a wry grimace.

'I'm sorry,' Emily said, realising he probably didn't have much choice. 'I suppose your accommodation comes with the job.'

His nod of agreement suggested she had hit the mark. Emily decided to press on. 'Are you comfortable there?'

'Not bad,' he agreed, after much thought. 'Though the kitchens are a long way from my apartment. By the time I get my food it's usually cold.'

'Don't you have your own kitchen?'

'My own kitchen?'

'A kitchenette?' she amended quickly. This new turn in her career was proving to be harder than she had expected. 'Somewhere to prepare yourself a bite to eat…a drink?'

'No. Nothing like that,' he told her, rubbing the back of his neck with his hand as he thought about it. 'Sounds like a good idea, though.'

'I'm sure I could arrange something for you.'

'Could you?'

'Would you let me try?'

'Only if you agree to give me cookery lessons as well,' he said, dismissing the idea with a wry grin and a flick of his hand.

'I'm not thinking of anything very elaborate,' Emily said encouragingly, 'just a small fridge, and perhaps a kettle and toaster to start with. If you had those, at least you'd be able to make yourself a quick snack whenever you felt peckish.'

'Good idea!' her new friend said enthusiastically. 'I'll leave it with you, then.'

'Excellent,' Emily said enthusiastically. 'I'll let you know what progress I've made when I see you tomorrow—'

'Tomorrow?'

Emily's hand flew to her mouth. 'My wedding day—' Her stomach churned with apprehension. How could time have passed so fast?

'So, where is your husband-to-be?'

'Prince Alessandro?'

'Yes, yes,' her elderly friend retorted impatiently. 'My son. Where is he? Why has he left you on your own?'

'Your—' Emily's mouth fell open as the full extent of her blunder overwhelmed her. 'You didn't say!'

'And would you have been so open with me if I had?' Alessandro's father demanded as he levelled a shrewd look on her face.

'Well…I…I don't know,' Emily admitted frankly. 'You must think me a terrible fool—'

'On the contrary,' he replied. 'I think you anything but a fool. My son, however—'

'Oh, no, please,' Emily said, shaking her head. 'You don't understand—'

'What don't I understand?' the old Prince demanded, straightening up so that even in his gardening clothes Emily could be under no misapprehension as to his status.

'I… Well… This is not the usual sort of wedding.'

'You love him?' he asked her directly.

'Well, I...' Emily paused, unsure of what to say.

'I said,' he repeated sternly, 'do you love my son?'

'Causing trouble again, Father?'

The deep, familiar voice went straight to Emily's heart. 'Alessandro!' she exclaimed breathlessly. Who said a prince could descend on you unannounced, wearing snug blue jeans and a close-fitting white top, looking as if he had just climbed out of bed? And his hair was still damp from the shower, she noticed on closer inspection.

'I see you've met my father,' he said, shooting her a wry grin.

He betrayed nothing of their developing friendship, but, remembering his concern for her after the chocolate festival, Emily felt a shiver of awareness shimmer over every part of her as he moved past her within touching distance. He had been more than tolerant. He had been... As she struggled to find the right word she watched him throw his arms around the older man and kiss him warmly on both cheeks several times before hugging him again. To be the object of such fathomless affection—to be capable of bestowing it—

She looked at Alessandro as if seeing him for the first time, and knew without question that she loved him.

'*Papa! Mi sei mancato!*'

His father's voice was equally fierce as he clutched his son to him. '*Anche tu, Alessandro.* I've missed you, too, *vagabondo*!'

Another hug and they were done, leaving Emily still gaping.

'You have neglected your bride so badly she has forgotten that tomorrow is her wedding day,' the old man accused, wiping his eyes on his sleeve. 'You are a bad boy, Alessandro—neglecting us both like this.'

'I never neglect you, Papa,' Alessandro argued, flashing

a glance at Emily as he tightened his arm around his father's shoulder. 'It's just that business sometimes—'

His father pressed his lips together in a show of disapproval. 'Business, business, business,' he proclaimed with a dismissive gesture. 'And your bride, Alessandro? What about your bride?'

Emily was forced to laugh as Alessandro executed a deep bow, flashing her a smile as he straightened up. 'I can only offer you my most humble apologies, Signorina Weston. Whatever punishment you decide to exact, I shall accept without question.'

Don't tempt me, Emily thought, feeling the effects of his statement reverberate around her senses.

'Once again,' Alessandro continued easily, tossing her an amused and comprehending look, 'I regret that unavoidable matters arose, demanding my immediate attention—'

'Your *bride* demands your immediate attention,' his father broke in sternly. 'Your wedding is tomorrow, in case you had also forgotten that, Alessandro.'

'I had not forgotten, Father,' Alessandro responded softly, glancing at Emily.

'It doesn't matter,' Emily insisted, shaking her head to hide her confusion. 'Alessandro is very busy, Your Royal Highness. And I have plenty to occupy me,' she managed vaguely. 'I'll leave you two together—'

'You will do no such thing,' the old Prince informed her imperiously. 'You will stay here with me and talk a while longer. After tomorrow Alessandro may begin the process of taking precedence over me. But today, as far as I am aware, I am still the undisputed ruler of Ferara, and I wish to talk with my future daughter-in-law. Alone,' he added pointedly. 'Make yourself busy somewhere else, Alessandro. Emily and I have much to discuss.'

'Father,' Alessandro said, executing a small formal bow. 'Your wish is my command.'

* * *

The wedding had more similarities to a big-budget film than any ceremony Emily had ever attended before. And, in true cinematic fashion, preparations for her starring role began just before dawn, when her private secretary called to inform her that the beauticians and hairdressers had started to arrive.

Breakfast was delivered on a tray with legs, presumably so that she could enjoy her last breakfast as a single woman safely tucked up in bed. But Emily was already out and about when the young maid knocked timidly on the door. Together they decanted the fruit juice and croissants onto a table overlooking the rose garden.

'You can take the rest away. I shan't eat it,' Emily insisted ruefully, scanning the cooked delicacies and plates of cold meats and cheeses, knowing she couldn't face them. 'Oh. Leave me an orange,' she said as an afterthought. She knew they had come from the palace orchard and were absolutely delicious.

'Yes, *signorina*,' the maid said with a courteous bob.

Just as Emily had thought, her simple breakfast proved to be the only oasis of calm in a day that was testing in the extreme. Pulled from pillar to post, she found herself constantly surrounded by strangers all charged with seeking perfection. The unfamiliar attention was daunting, and what made it worse was being treated suddenly as if she was on a higher stratum from everyone else. It made normal conversation impossible.

As her hair was dressed up, ready to hold the weight of the tiara, and the finest film of coral rouge was applied to her cheeks, Emily began to feel increasingly like an inanimate object. No one seemed able to meet her eyes. No one spoke unless she instigated the conversation. And no one seemed prepared to volunteer an opinion on anything, preferring to wait for her to state her own views as if they were the only ones worth listening to. The lack of verbal interplay was driving her crazy. And her nerves were building to crisis level as what had been a theoretical exercise became all too real.

Just when she thought she couldn't stand one more minute of it, her face broke into a smile.

'Dad! Mum! Miranda!' Breaking free of the posse of primpers, Emily fled across the room towards her family.

'But, *signorina*...your veil,' the designer called after her.

'Give me a moment, please,' Emily said, keeping her head firmly buried against her father's shoulder.

'Five minutes,' her father bartered, keeping her close as he encircled Miranda's shoulders with his other arm. 'Then you can have her back, I promise.'

There was such quiet determination in his voice that even the highly-strung designer was forced to concede defeat.

Her father sounded just like Alessandro, Emily thought fondly, raising her head to watch the couturier make an imperious signal and lead his group out of the room.

'There's still time to change your mind, Emily,' Miranda whispered, looking around anxiously at their mother, who nodded agreement.

'It's not too late,' her father agreed gruffly. 'I can have you out of here in a jiffy—'

'No, Dad,' Emily insisted firmly. 'There's too much at stake here—for everyone concerned. I'm going ahead with it.'

'Oh, the violin arrived! It is absolutely—' Miranda's hand flew to her mouth. 'How could I mention that?' she asked herself distractedly. 'When you're having to put up with all this?' She made a wild gesture to encompass the various stations dotted around the room set up by hairdressers, beauticians and designers.

'It's not so bad,' Emily teased. 'No, honestly,' she said sincerely, catching hold of Miranda's hand. 'Nothing would induce me to stay here if I didn't want to. It's not so bad living here at the palace with Alessandro.' She raised her eyebrows a fraction as she looked at her sister.

'You mean—' Miranda flashed a glance at their mother and father, who quickly pretended interest in the view outside the window.

'No, I don't mean what you're thinking,' Emily said softly. 'But he's great fun to be with when you get to know him. And he's so kind.'

'Is that all?' Miranda said, sounding disappointed.

'It was never meant to be anything more,' Emily pointed out, working at her smile. 'And you look beautiful,' she said, desperately trying to turn the direction of the conversation. 'And Dad, Mum, you look fantastic,' she added for good measure.

'You're absolutely sure about this?' her father said, looking at her again with concern.

'Yes,' Emily said, raising her eyes to his to prove that her composure really was restored. 'You can call everyone back in again now. I'm ready.'

The ancient cathedral in Ferara was on so vast a scale it might have been built for some lost race of giants. As Emily arrived beneath the towering stone archway that marked the entrance a murmur rose from the congregation like a collective sigh.

'This situation is about as real as a film,' her father murmured, echoing Emily's thoughts. 'The only difference is, I doubt any of us will be able to forget this once the show's over.'

'Courage, Dad,' Emily replied as she squeezed his arm. 'We'll get through this together.'

'I'm supposed to be supporting you, remember?' he growled out of the side of his mouth as the opening chord burst from the organ and an angelic choir soared into the first anthem.

Emily was about to move forward when one of the several attendants who had joined the procession from the palace attracted her attention.

'*Signorina, scusami l'interrruzione,*' he murmured, bowing low. 'This is an ancient custom in our country. The bride's flowers are traditionally a wedding gift from the groom's family.'

'How lovely,' Emily said, exchanging her bouquet with a smile.

'His Serene Highness is most keen that traditions should be upheld,' the attendant added, backing away from her in a deep bow.

As Emily's curled her fingers around the slender stems of the roses she knew they were more than a gift. The fragrant arrangement signified the approval of Alessandro's father, and that mattered to her more than any one of the fabulous wedding presents that had arrived at the palace.

She could not remember ever feeling so keenly aware...so alive. And as she steadied herself for the walk up the aisle she found she could identify each strand of scent—incense, the roses resting in her arms, and the heady mix of countless exclusive perfumes. And above all the dazzling sights and sounds and scents, even though she never looked directly at him once, she was aware of Alessandro, waiting in silence for her at the end of the vast sweep of aisle.

Moving forward, Emily felt the burden of her long train ease as the squad of young train-bearers, chosen from schools in Ferara at her own request, took up the weight. And after a few brief moments of adjustment, when she feared she might lose the priceless tiara as the veil was tugged this way and that, they managed to keep pace with her perfectly.

She walked tall and proud at her father's side between the massed ranks of European royalty, wearing the slim column of a gown she had insisted upon. Only the splendour of the diamond tiara denoted her rank—that, and the floating pearl-strewn veil that eddied around her like a creamy-white mist. The only real colour was in her cheeks and in the coral-tinted roses her old friend had provided—Christopher Marlowe roses from the palace gardens, with every thorn removed, simply arranged and tied with silk ribbons in the colours of her new country: crimson, blue and gold.

She was aware of her mother in deep blue velvet, and Miranda, ravishing in palest lemon, as well as some other bridesmaids whom she had met only briefly. And then, as the organ sounded a fanfare of celebration, Emily focussed on the long walk ahead of her—the walk to join Alessandro, who stood waiting for her at the foot of the steps to the high altar.

The aisle itself was a work of art, paved in marble and carved by long-dead artisans to such effect that the scenes portrayed appeared more like faded photographs scanned onto the cool surface rather than the painstaking work of supreme craftsmen.

In front of her a vast window of such intense blue it appeared to be backlit by a power even greater than the sun threw splashes of colour across the faces of the dignitaries, some of whom Emily recognised, but she only sensed rather than saw every head turn her way, because her own gaze had found Alessandro's.

Even though she knew he was entering into marriage with no thought of love or romance, his strength lent her courage, and, seeing a flicker of concern in the eyes of his father, when Emily dropped her curtsey in front of him she smiled reassuringly as he reached forward to bring her to her feet.

Then she was standing next to Alessandro, with every fibre of her being pulsing with awareness… Alessandro, who appeared a daunting figure even in such a setting, where the scale of the building challenged normal perception. She matched her breathing to his, steadying herself, willing herself free of expectation, knowing that if she harboured none she could never be hurt.

But as the ceremony reached its climax a heady sense of destiny overcame her. Too much incense, she told herself firmly. But, whatever happened, she would do her best for the people of Ferara during her tenure as their Princess.

'You may kiss your bride.'

Reality struck home like a real physical blow. Would he kiss her? Or would he humiliate her in front of everyone? Was this hard for him? Impossible?

Too churned up to interpret anything, let alone the expression in her husband's eyes, Emily tensed as she waited. She didn't know what to expect.

He smiled, as if he was trying to imbue her with some of his own confidence. Alessandro, always considerate...thanking her for keeping her part of the bargain, Emily reasoned, wishing against her better judgement that it could be more. She felt his firm lips touch her mouth, pressing against the soft yielding pillow of her lips as she sighed against him—then a chord from the organ broke the spell and he linked her arm firmly through his.

And they were walking down the aisle together, man and wife, smiling to the left, and then smiling to the right—but never once smiling at each other.

They had their first row on their wedding night.

Elevated to a magnificent suite of rooms adjoining Alessandro's own, Emily prepared for bed alone. Her head was ringing with the effort of maintaining a front for so long. But at least she could console herself with the knowledge that she had begun to fulfil the requirements of their contract.

Who was she trying to kid? Emily wondered angrily as she sat down in front of the gilt-embossed dressing table mirror. A ceremony couldn't plug the chasm in her heart, or blot out her certainty that everything she had planned—so carefully, so meticulously—was already falling apart around her ears because she had made the classic mistake of allowing feelings to get in the way.

The fact that Alessandro was a prince didn't matter at all—the fact that they had a business contract between them rather than a love affair mattered more to her than she could ever have imagined. It hurt like hell, she realised wistfully.

Plucking out the last of the pins holding her hair in place, she allowed it to spill over her shoulders and began to brush it with long, impassioned sweeps.

It was hard to believe she had been naïve enough to think she could simply pick up the pieces of her carefree single life and transfer them to Ferara with the rest of her luggage. Naïve? Her naïvety had been monumental, Emily thought, shaking her head angrily and then tossing the brush aside.

The wedding changed everything she realised, remembering the solemn vows she had made. Alessandro was her husband now, and she was his wife. And with those simple facts came hope, desire, expectation—and, most pressing of all, she thought, ramming her lips together as she tried not to cry, was the need to spend at least your wedding night with your husband.

Once they'd left the cathedral there had hardly been a chance for her to speak to him. And even when they had opened the reception by dancing together there had been constant interruptions. And she hadn't helped matters, Emily thought, remembering how stiffly she had held herself. There had been a moment when the toasts were made—Alessandro's hand had closed over her own as they'd sliced through a tier of the wedding cake and she had felt her whole body rebel and strain towards him. But she had clenched her fist over the handle until her knuckles had turned white and hurt...and apart from that—

She started at the knock on the door.

She had sent everyone away, taking the chance, once she had showered, to slip into a clean old top that had somehow found its way into the bottom of her suitcase. It didn't matter what she looked like. It could only be the maid with some hot milk, she reasoned, hurrying to the door.

'Alessandro!'

She felt foolish, standing there with bare feet, wearing nothing except an old faded top while her husband looked every bit as resplendent in a simple black silk robe as he had in full dress uniform, with medals and sash of office.

'I just came to see if you were all right...if you had everything you need,' he said, appearing not to register her choice of clothes as he scanned her sumptuous quarters as if running a mental inventory.

'I'm fine,' Emily replied. 'Just a little tired.'

'You looked beautiful today.' As he turned to look at her his gaze was steady and warm. 'Thank you, Emily.'

'It was nothing,' she lied, forcing a smile. But her glance strayed to his mouth as she remembered his kiss at the culmination of their marriage ceremony...chaste and dutiful maybe, but it still possessed the power to thrill her like no other kiss could ever hope to again. Recklessly she relived it now, briefly, self-indulgently, closing her eyes for just an instant as faint echoes of sensation shimmered through her frame.

'I think it all went well,' Alessandro said, breaking into her reverie.

'Yes,' she managed tightly. 'It all went very well. Miranda is in seventh heaven. The violin is everything—'

'Can we talk about us for a moment?'

His expression was hidden in shadow as he moved away from her towards one of the heavily draped windows, but Emily knew something had upset him. Perhaps he thought the violin too high a price to pay for a woman for whom he felt nothing.

'There's no reason why it should be awkward between us—' he began.

Awkward between them! What the hell was he talking about? Alessandro thought angrily, balling his hands into

fists while in his mind the image of some rare bloom over-
laid the fever. He swung around to look at her. Petals
bruised easily, too easily—

'Are you all right?' Emily said, reaching out a hand.
Then, remembering her position, she let it fall back again
by her side.

He was completely naked under the robe; she was sure
of it. Her speech had thickened as erotic possibilities
crowded her mind... No one need ever know. They could
be lovers and still end the contract as agreed. Just the possibility was a seduction in itself... The walls were twelve
feet thick in this part of the old palace, she remembered.
And their rooms were interconnecting. Most of the servants
were still celebrating at one of the many parties in the palace grounds—she could still hear periodic explosions from
the fireworks outside.

'I'm not aware of any awkwardness between us,' she
said, in an attempt to prolong the conversation, trying not
to stare too blatantly at the outline of his hard frame so
clear in silhouette as he stood with his back to the window.

She was standing close to him now...close enough to
detect the tang of the lemony soap he must have used in
the shower. Closing her eyes, she inhaled deeply, then murmured dreamily, 'Don't worry, Alessandro. I'm completely
at ease—'

She gasped in alarm as his fist hit the wall.

'"Don't worry, Alessandro"?' he mimicked softly, dangerously, and so close to her lips she could feel his warm
breath on her face. 'How can you ask me not to worry?
Am I the only one tense here? Don't lie to me, Emily,' he
warned, pulling back. 'You're about as at ease with all this
as I am.'

He took a couple of steps away, as if he couldn't bear
to be close to her any more than she could bear to be parted
from him.

'Please don't waste your breath on innocent protestations,' he said. 'I know you're lying to me. We're both in this over our heads, and you know it.'

'We knew what we were getting into—'

'Oh, did we?' He cut in sceptically. 'You're quite sure about that, are you, Emily? You're quite sure nothing's changed between us now that we're man and wife?'

He had taken the same mental journey she had, Emily realised with surprise. And each nuance in his voice betrayed the fact that he was every bit as disturbed by his thoughts as she was by her own.

'It's our wedding night—'

'So?' he demanded harshly.

'My no-sex clause—' She felt so foolish, so exposed. 'We could—'

'Forget it?' he suggested.

His gently mocking tone nudged her senses until she was unbearably aroused; the wet triangle of lace between her legs stretched taut in the struggle to contain her excitement.

'I don't think so, Emily,' he said harshly.

Every last remaining strand of common sense told her he was right, while her instinct, her desire, every hectic beat of her heart said she would stop at nothing to change his mind... But once the terms of their contract were satisfied he would need to move on, Emily reminded herself. Marry a woman of his own choosing—someone, as he had already intimated, who could shoulder the responsibilities of Ferara as an equal partner. There would be no place for her in Ferara then, so she would just have to find some way to rein in her hunger for that country's prince sooner rather than later.

Switching on the smile that had served her so well throughout the day, she agreed tonelessly that she did have everything she needed. But, just when she was complimenting herself on the cool way in which she'd handled the situation, Alessandro threw everything into confusion again.

'I suppose we could do as you suggest—keep the terms of our contract and yet have an affair,' he suggested bitterly.

There were a few moments of stunned silence, then Emily laughed nervously—as if to show she knew he couldn't possibly be serious.

'What do you think, Emily?'

'What do I think?'

What *did* she think? She wasn't incapable of any thought, Emily realised as she watched him caress the door handle. Her belly ached with need for him. She was utterly beguiled by his strength, by the subtlety in his hands and by the strong, flexing power in his fingers... She wanted to know how all that would feel, transferred from hard steel to soft flesh—

'Well?' he said harshly.

Could he be serious? Her body seemed to think so.

Even as he watched her eyes darkening, and saw the tip of her tongue dart out to moisten her lips, Alessandro knew it wasn't enough. Even if Emily agreed, a sexual relationship with his beautiful new wife would only leave him more frustrated than ever. And he wanted more. He wanted much more. He wanted her love. He knew he had to do something...say something...or he might tip them both headlong into a situation from which neither of them would ever recover. He lifted his hands in a gesture of surrender.

'Forgive me, Emily. I don't know what I'm saying. I'm very tired—'

Yes, he was tired, Alessandro acknowledged. He was tired of all the play-acting, tired of pretending he didn't feel the most urgent need to consummate their marriage and ease the physical torment he was certain now that she felt every bit as much as he did. He longed to make Emily his wife, and in more than name only. He wanted them to be bound together, body and soul, for the rest of their lives.

But the weariness dragging at his mind had another

cause, he accepted restlessly as he started to pace the room. What exhausted him the most was the secret he was forced to keep. The secret he bound so close because it was the one thing in the world that could take her away from him. And, in spite of the physical desire that raged through his body, he couldn't—he wouldn't—run the risk of losing her.

'We're both tired—and no wonder,' Emily observed gently, trying to hold her husband still from his angry pacing when she knew she had little more to soothe him with than her voice.

'I know,' Alessandro said, shaking his head as he stopped dead to look at her, as if for the first time. It was as if she understood everything...and nothing, he realised, passing a single finger down the side of her face. But it wasn't her fault...none of it was her fault.

Emily longed to grab hold of his hand then, and kiss it, and hold it against her cheek to warm him with her strength...her love... But the moment had passed, and now he was tense again. She could feel it in the air without looking at him.

'My behaviour just now was unforgivable,' Alessandro said, moving away from her. 'I'm sorry if I frightened you. The last thing I want is to make this any harder for you than it already is.' Reaching the door, he turned to face her again.

'Is there anything...anything at all, Emily...that I could provide for you here in Ferara to make you happy?'

'I am happy,' she protested quickly.

'Don't give me a glib answer because that's what you think I want to hear,' he warned. Leaning back against the door, he said softly, 'I mean it, Emily. Whatever you want—whatever it takes to make you happy—just name it.'

You, she thought, meeting his gaze steadily. That's all I want...you. First, last and always.

'You mentioned an idea for upgrading the palace apartments for staff—we could set up weekly meetings—'

'Yes,' she said quickly. Even a regular business meeting with him would be better than nothing at all. 'I think that's a wonderful idea.'

'I'm pleased you think so.'

Emily returned his smile. The first real smile she had seen on his face all day. But if he'd wanted her half as much as she wanted him they would have been setting up a very different sort of assignation, she reminded herself sadly.

One thing was sure: he wouldn't have been leaving her to spend their wedding night alone.

CHAPTER SEVEN

ALESSANDRO'S father sat up in bed to stare at his son in tolerant mystification.

'You come to my rooms at dawn to ask an old man like me what to do about the state of your marriage? Is this really my son Alessandro talking? I would hardly have believed it possible—before Emily came into your life,' he added, shaking his head. 'And had it not been for the nonsense you have told me about this—*contract*—' he spat out the word '—had it not been for that misplaced kindness to me, you would never have found yourself in this mess in the first place. How could you do such a thing, Alessandro? And how could you imagine such a travesty would work?'

I did it for you, Father...only for you, Alessandro thought, taking the rebuke in silence. And in spite of everything he couldn't find it in his heart to regret a thing...except that by trying to help his father it seemed that he had only succeeded in causing him more pain.

'Emily is like a tender bud—'

'I know, Father! I know!' Alessandro exclaimed impatiently, swiping the back of his neck with his hand as he sprang to his feet to pace the room like a tiger with a thorn in its pad. 'She is like no other woman I have ever met,' he went on, shaking his head in utter incomprehension. 'She shows no real interest in the priceless jewels she is entitled to wear, or the designer clothes I arranged to please her. She chooses instead to devote herself to the needs of our country, and to the small improvements she can make here at the palace. These...these are her passions.'

'Are you complaining, Alessandro?'

'No, Father! No. It's just that I am having to learn a

whole new way of dealing with a woman. I feel like a youth embarking on his first love affair—'

'Perhaps this *is* your first love affair,' the old Prince murmured sagely.

'So, help me, Father. Tell me what to do.' Alessandro stopped, and levelled a blazing stare on his father's face. 'You must help me. Before I lose her.'

'You know what to do,' his father told him calmly. 'You know in your heart what is right, Alessandro. And if you want to make *me* happy, you will forget all about this foolish contract. Make this marriage work, Alessandro, or spend the rest of your life wishing that you had. It's up to you.'

Alessandro stopped pacing and stared unseeing into the distance. 'Monte Volere,' he murmured to himself. 'I shall take her to Monte Volere.' Then he turned around. 'Monte Volere, Father!'

'September...harvest-time in Monte Volere,' his father commented thoughtfully. 'A very good place to recharge the batteries of the heart.'

Alessandro felt the tension leave him as he watched a smile of contentment curl around his father's mouth.

'I think you've redeemed yourself, Alessandro. It's an excellent idea,' the old Prince declared with satisfaction.

'How soon can you be ready to leave?'

'Leave?' Emily said, still reeling from being shaken out of her slumbers by an Alessandro she had never seen before—black jeans, black tight-fitting top, black leather jacket slung across the broad sweep of his shoulders, tousled hair and yesterday's beard throwing shadows across the harsh planes of his handsome face.

But they were man and wife now, and her husband seemed to need her. 'Is everything all right?' she asked, instantly alert. 'Is it your father? Has something happened?'

'Yes. No. And, no—not yet,' he said, warming to her concern. 'My father's fine; don't worry.'

Alessandro was all tension and energy, like a coiled spring about to unwind—fast, Emily realised. 'So...?' she began curiously.

'How long?' Alessandro repeated, not troubling to hide his impatience now.

'Er...not long,' Emily admitted. 'I'd have to shower and—' She broke off uncertainly. 'Do I need to pack anything? Bring anything with me?' she elaborated, drawing up the sheet when the intimacy of his stare brushed something savage in both of them.

'You can shower when we get there. Come as you are.'

'In my nightclothes?'

'Why not?'

'Because it might cause a scandal?' Emily ventured cautiously.

Alessandro's look suggested that throwing her over his shoulder and storming off might cause a far bigger one.

'You're probably right,' he conceded reluctantly. 'So be quick. Just sling on your jeans and let's go.'

Jumping out of bed, Emily tore into her dressing room and, reaching into the very back of the wardrobe, where she had managed to conceal them from the army of wardrobe mistresses who had taken control of her clothes, she pulled out her jeans.

But the position of Princess came with conditions attached. One of the most onerous was that her appearance should never give cause for gossip or alarm. Discounting the crumpled denims out of hand, she grabbed a smart pair of navy trousers and a short-sleeved white blouse. They would do, Emily decided, gathering up her hair and securing it with a band and a couple of clips.

'Ready?' Alessandro said, barely looking at her as he grabbed hold of her forearm and dragged her with him.

'Ready,' Emily said, trying to catch her breath as she settled back in the passenger seat of a flame-red Ferrari.

'Good,' Alessandro said, narrowing his eyes as he concentrated on the road, his foot flat to the floor.

With the palace disappearing into the distance behind them, Emily was relieved to find Alessandro's driving fast but a good deal smoother than his chauffeur's. He drove without speaking, and finally, when she was almost bursting with curiosity, he announced that they would be stopping for lunch at a small village in the hills.

The Prince of Ferara's arrival with his new wife at an unpretentious café in the main square caused disbelief, followed swiftly by purposeful activity. And that was thanks largely to Alessandro's manner, Emily realised as she watched him putting people at their ease. He had barely finished introducing her around—and giving a pretty good impersonation of being proud of his choice of wife—when several women emerged from the kitchen, bearing local delicacies which they placed on the freshly scrubbed outdoor tables.

'You will need your strength,' one of them informed Alessandro coyly, nodding encouragement as she held out one of the first large oval dishes of pasta for him to taste.

'My strength?' he queried, making a point of not looking at Emily, though she noticed the smile he was gracious enough to hide behind a huge red-chequered napkin.

'*Si*, Principe,' all the other women chorused gaily, much to Emily's embarrassment.

Then one of the men threaded his way through the women, flexing a battered cap in his hand. 'Today is the Palio del Timone, Principe,' he explained. 'Each year we have a tug o' war with the neighbouring village; you have arrived just in time—' He stopped, as if he felt he had gone too far.

'Go on,' Alessandro encouraged, putting down his fork to listen.

'If you took part...' The man hesitated again.

Alessandro got to his feet and clapped him on the shoulder. 'Of course I will take part.'

'Federico,' the man supplied, flashing up an expectant glance.

'Federico,' Alessandro said, shaking him by the hand, 'you have just recruited a new member to your team. I am honoured to serve with you.'

Rubbing his hands together with glee, Federico turned. 'Did you hear that? I believe this year we may just have the edge!'

As the excitement rose to fever-pitch, Emily remembered Alessandro had been in a rush when they left the palace. 'Are you sure there's time for this?' she murmured with concern as she joined him.

'Why not?' he demanded, looking at her in amusement. 'How much of a hurry are you in, Principessa?'

As she went after him Emily's face was bright red, provoking delighted smiles and knowing looks from those women close enough to observe the exchange.

If their marriage had been consummated, Emily reckoned, a little embarrassment would have been a small price to pay. But as it was it seemed particularly unjust—especially as the women were still nudging each other and winking at her.

The news that Alessandro was to take part in the competition had spread like wildfire, and it seemed as if the entire population of the village had managed to crowd themselves into the small paved area around the café. Silence fell as he crossed the square to greet the opposing team. It was obvious that his side was at a considerable disadvantage, as most were older than their rowdy young opponents from the neighbouring village.

'Do you think you can redress the balance?' Emily asked anxiously, as she watched him strip to the waist. His naked torso was all the answer she needed, and a murmur of approval rose around them as he handed her the black top.

'Take up the slack,' the man from the café ordered, pointing to the thick rope lying on the ground. 'Principessa,' he added, 'when you drop the flag, the men must put their weight and their strength behind that rope. The first team to haul the others across that white line wins the Palio.'

Emily tried to concentrate—but was there anything more delicious than seeing Alessandro put his weight and his strength behind that rope? she wondered, watching the flex of muscles on his sun-bronzed body. If there was, she could only imagine it would be Alessandro completely stripped of his clothes.

His glance flashed across at precisely that moment, filling Emily with a very different kind of excitement from the rest of the spectators. And as she dropped the flag he gave a slight smile that seemed to promise her a contest no less involving than the one he was embarking upon.

Emily watched the denim mould around his impressive thighs as he dug his heels into the ground, gravel spitting up either side of his feet as he heaved. Each muscle and sinew was clearly defined as he threw every bit of his strength behind the rope, working to drag the other side closer to the line.

It was all over very suddenly. A groan from the losing side and a triumphant shout from Alessandro's who, brandishing the rope, punched the air with their fists. Then there was a noisy round of back-slapping and congratulations, as well as good-natured banter before Alessandro came back to reclaim his top.

'I'll just take a shower, then I'll be right with you,' he promised, wheeling away to accompany Federico. 'Then we'll go,' he called back to her over his shoulder. 'Be ready.'

The villagers wanted Alessandro to share in their cele-

brations, and were disappointed when he told them he had
to leave. But, having exacted a promise from him to return
the following year, they accepted his decision and fell back.

'If we are to reach Monte Volere before bedtime, I must
go now,' he explained, provoking another round of nudges
and tempting Emily to disillusion everyone on the spot. Her
husband's hair might have been still wet from the shower,
and his top clinging damply to the water droplets around
his neck—giving the impression that he was in such a hurry
to get back to her he hadn't troubled to dry himself properly—but she knew he only wanted to get to his country
estate before dark.

Beyond the narrow streets and close-clustered village
houses the countryside opened into a vast, sprawling plain.
As the tawny volcanic soil paled to blonde they sped on
through the pale, freshly tilled earth on an arrow-straight
road, until another range of hills, even higher than those
they had left behind, loomed in front of them.

'Not long now,' Alessandro promised as he began to
negotiate a series of tortuous hairpin bends. 'I'm going to
stop when we get to the top,' he informed her. 'Then you'll
see one of the most spectacular vistas in all of Ferara.'

Emily formed a sound of appreciation in her throat. But
the last thing on her mind after the events in the village
was a sightseeing trip. And even if Alessandro's suggestion
of an affair between them had been his idea of a joke, she
had believed this trip to his country estate signalled his
intention to bring them closer—if only for the sake of appearances. Now she knew the visit was nothing more than
proof he intended to keep his word and show her around.
And, keen as she was to learn more about Ferara, she was
keener still to learn more about her husband.

'Save it,' she muttered ungraciously.

As Alessandro shot her a curious glance Emily regretted
the outburst. He was only doing what he thought was
right—what he thought she would enjoy.

'No. I insist,' he said firmly.

She had to admit he was right about the view. As she climbed out of the car Emily felt like an eagle staring down at the lake, tiny below them, shimmering in the heat haze like a panel of jewel-encrusted silk.

'It's absolutely stunning,' she murmured, fighting off the insane urge to move close enough to slip her arm through his.

'This region of Ferara has many similarities to the fiords of Norway,' Alessandro said. 'Don't stand too close to the edge,' he warned, coming to stand between Emily and the sheer drop only a metre or so in front of her feet.

Emily smiled, then felt unaccountably bleak when he started back to the car as if there was some other fabulous camera opportunity waiting just around the next bend for them.

'You will find there is a lot of variety in Ferara,' Alessandro remarked as he turned the car back onto what was now little more than a steep mountain track. 'I hope you will eventually come to love it as much as I do.'

And the point would be...? Emily thought his remark strange, bearing in mind the peculiar circumstances of their marriage. 'Mmm,' she managed non-committally.

But if the view he had shown her had been the eagle's perch, then his estate at Monte Volere was the eagle's eyrie, she discovered as Alessandro turned in beneath a narrow stone archway. Set on the highest point of a hill cloaked with vineyards, the pink and cream stone of the old manor house glowed rose-red where shadows were painted by the failing light.

'Why have you brought me here?' she said curiously.

Alessandro turned to stare at her, an amused expression tugging at his mouth. 'Rest and recreation—'

'No. Really,' Emily insisted.

'Really,' Alessandro replied steadily as he drew to a halt

in front of the old building. 'I thought you needed to get away from everything…everyone…for a few days.'

'To be alone?'

But Alessandro had already climbed out of the car.

'I'll show you to your room,' he called over his shoulder as she followed him up the steps. He opened an oak door and beckoned her inside.

My room? Emily thought, banishing the sense of disappointment. She stared across the stone-flagged hall as Alessandro sprinted up the stairs.

'Well?' he said, leaning over the carved wooden banister. 'Aren't you coming?'

The room he showed her into had been made cosy with throws, rugs and cushions in a variety of warm colours. One wall was almost completely devoted to a huge fireplace, carved from a single block of mellow honey-coloured sandstone. This housed a black wrought-iron grate and, because there was no need for a fire, an earthenware dish containing dried pot pourri to provide a splash of colour on the terracotta tiles. A wide-armed fan whirred lazily on the ceiling, stirring the scent of dried rose petals into the air. The thin coating of yellow ochre paint on the rough plaster walls had paled to lemon where the sunlight had faded it over many years, and exposed oak beams supported the high, sloping ceiling over the vast four-poster bed. Dressed with crisp white bedlinen, this offered a breathtaking view over the surrounding countryside—something Emily discovered when impulsively she flung herself down on it and bounced up and down.

'I'll be right across the landing if you need me,' Alessandro said, closing the door quietly behind him before she had a chance to say a word.

Suddenly Monte Volere didn't seem so appealing—she didn't even want to be there any more. Gusting a long, shaky sigh, Emily stared around the empty room. If this was Alessandro's idea of a honeymoon— She mashed her lips together, remembering he wasn't much good at wedding nights either. But she wouldn't let it get her down. No expectations, no disappointments, she reminded herself—and at least the bed looked comfy.

As Emily had anticipated, the high bed was extremely comfortable. The ceiling fan turned rhythmically over her head, soothing her while it kept everything airily pleasant. Over and above all this, she had taken a leisurely bath to ensure she got a good night's sleep—but, glancing at the clock, she saw it was three o' clock in the morning.

Safe to say success has *not* crowned my ventures, she thought, staring across at the closed door onto the landing. Irrationally, she felt an overwhelming urge to open it. Open it, and then what? Emily asked herself impatiently, giving her pillows an extra thump. And then leave the rest to fate, she decided, after another period of restless thrashing. Swinging her feet onto the cool tiled floor, she padded silently across the room. With care, she managed to lift the heavy wrought-iron latch without making a sound. Cautiously, she tested the door. The hinges were well oiled, and the movement was squeak-free. Opening it a little more, so that it looked like an invitation rather than an oversight, she hurried back to bed with her heart thundering in anticipation.

Above the sound of the fan she thought she could hear something…footsteps, maybe—measured, rhythmical—pacing, she decided. It had to be Alessandro, since he had already told her that the staff at Monte Volere came in on a daily basis, so she knew they were all alone in the house.

Arranging herself on the pillows, Emily fluffed out her long hair, moistened her lips, listened—and waited.

Across the landing Alessandro, after tossing and turning all night, found himself pacing the floor like a pent-up warrior on the eve of battle. Emerging from his angry introspection for a few moments, he noticed Emily's door open.

Feeling sure that he had closed it behind him earlier in the evening, he felt a rush of concern for her. Pulling on his jeans, he crossed his room to investigate.

Leaning against the wall just outside his bedroom, he paused, consciously stilled his breathing, and listened. They were still alone in the house; he was sure of it. The only noises he could detect were the typical muted creaks and groans of old timber as it cooled and relaxed after the heat of the day.

But, just to make absolutely certain Emily was safe, he crossed the landing, taking care to move silently, and stared into her room.

With her senses on full alert Emily detected the movement even though she heard nothing. Licking her lips one last time, she closed her eyes and concentrated on taking deep, calming breaths. Her limbs felt deliciously suspended and a seductive lethargy rolled over her...her nerve-endings grew increasingly sensitive as she lay still and contemplated Alessandro's imminent arrival.

Emily...his wife, Alessandro mused, incredulous that it was so as he gazed at her still figure. Could it be possible that she was even more beautiful asleep than awake? Then, remembering the strength of character that burned in her eyes, and the firm set of her mouth whenever she was angry with him, he smiled and shook his head in a quick gesture of denial. And she was lovelier still when she smiled, he remembered. And when she laughed...

His gaze lingered on her mouth. The temptation to cross the room, to match his length to hers and to tease open those full, sensuous lips...lips he was sure waited like the rest of her to be awakened—

He stopped himself. The open door was her protection, he realised. How could he surprise her when she was beginning at last to trust him? He could not take advantage of the open door. He would not frighten her by entering the room when she was asleep. Spinning around, he returned to his own room after making sure that his wife's bedroom door was closed securely behind him.

Breakfast was a tense affair. Cursing herself for behaving like a lovesick fool, Emily accepted that she had received no more than she deserved...which was precisely nothing.

Alessandro seemed cool and distant, though as polite as ever. Dismissing the cook who had come in to prepare the food for them, he insisted on waiting on her himself at breakfast.

'This really is far too much for me,' Emily protested, when he handed her a dish piled high with freshly peeled and sliced peaches, and a second plate covered in a selection of cold meats and cheeses.

'Eat,' he commanded impatiently, returning to the table where their breakfast buffet had been laid out only to return with some warm bread rolls. 'You'll need your strength today.'

'Need my strength?' Emily said suspiciously. 'For what?'

'We've got a busy day ahead of us.'

Watching him tear into his own roll, and stab at a plate of cheese with the energy of ten, Emily felt her spirits take a dive. Hiking, she guessed—at the very least. Mountaineering, probably—both of which filled her with dread. 'You mean a day of physical activities?'

'Mmm,' Alessandro confirmed gruffly, his eyes glittering with a dangerous light. Draining his coffee cup fast, he pushed it away. 'Grape-treading,' he rapped purposefully.

'Grape-treading?' Emily echoed, following him with her eyes as he strode to view the massed fields of vines through the open window. The occasion was sure to be fascinating to watch, she thought. Her glance embraced Alessandro's powerful forearms and the broad sweep of his chest. What part would he play in the proceedings? she wondered, hoping it would require him to strip to the waist again.

'What?' he demanded, thrusting his fingers into the back

pockets of his jeans as he turned around. 'What are you staring at?' he repeated, more insistently.

Emily tore her gaze away from the well-muscled thighs so tantalisingly defined in snug-fitting denim. 'Nothing,' she said dismissively, with a flip of her hand. 'I'd like that very much. For you to take me to the grape-treading, I mean.'

'Good.'

That voice again, she realised, turning her face away so that he couldn't see her reddening under his calculating and extremely disturbing gaze. 'I had no idea that such archaic practices survived,' she said, rustling up her most professional manner.

'Just about everything is mechanised these days.' Alessandro said, accommodating her approach. 'But for the highest quality wines only an experienced eye can judge the grapes. So we keep our vines low and pick by hand. It is hard work, and must be completed quickly before the heat of the sun raises acidity levels.'

She tensed as he prowled closer. 'I see...'

'Oh, do you?' he murmured sardonically, somewhere very close to her ear.

'But surely you can't tread all those grapes out there?' she said edgily, staring fixedly out of the window as she waited for her face to cool down.

'Of course not, ' Alessandro said, standing right beside her. 'The grape-treading is purely symbolic. It marks the start of the harvest.'

He refused to take the hint as she moved away, and suddenly was right in front of her again.

Glancing from side to side, Emily realised she was boxed into a corner between an old oak dresser and a bookcase. How on earth had that happened? she wondered, sagging with relief when he moved away.

'Different varieties of grape ripen at different times,' he continued evenly, as if their game of tag, at which he was clearly a master, had never taken place. 'And when they are all safely gathered in we celebrate, with a proper Festa del Villaggio. The custom of treading some of the grapes the old way after the first picking is said to placate the forces of nature.'

Emily began to relax. The history of the grape was surprisingly interesting...or perhaps it was more relief that, having distracted them both by explaining it, Alessandro was allowing the sexual tension between them to ease. She inclined her head to demonstrate her fascination with the subject, hoping her body would take the hint and calm down, too.

'It is also carried out to ensure good weather,' Alessandro went on, in the same soothing tone. Without any warning, he crossed the room, seized her arms, and held her close. 'So, Emily,' he demanded impatiently, 'will you come?'

'I'd love to.' After all, she persuaded herself as his hands relaxed, the chance to get to know her husband a little better, to see him interacting with the villagers, was an opportunity that might never come again.

'Great. You'll have to get changed first.'

'You mean it's today—right now?' She should have guessed! 'Why can't I go like this?'

'Well, if you want to look like you're heading for court—'

'Without a jacket—?' As she pulled a face his lips tugged up in a half-smile. 'You're teasing me.'

'Am I?' he murmured provocatively.

'OK, so now what? Point me in the direction of the nearest shops?' Emily demanded, confronting Alessandro, hands on hips when he started laughing. 'Please, Alessandro. Don't be difficult. I want to go with you. Just tell me where the shops are and I'll go and buy something suitable to wear.'

'OK. I'll take you.'

'Thank you,' Emily said graciously.

'We can walk there,' he said, when she stopped at the passenger door of the four-wheel drive he'd told her he used to get about the estate.

'Walk?' Emily couldn't imagine how she had missed a dress shop as they drove through.

'Certainly,' Alessandro said, striding away in the direction of the fields. 'It will only take ten minutes or so to reach Maria Felsina's cottage.

'Cottage?' Emily demanded, increasing to a trot to keep up.

'You'll see. Come on,' he urged, speeding up again. 'We haven't got all day. You don't want the grape-treading to start without us, do you?' he called over his shoulder.

A suspicion had taken root in Emily's mind. 'You mean we'll actually be taking part?'

Alessandro's loafers slapped rhythmically against the hard-baked earth. 'Of course,' he called back. 'Why else would we be going?'

'I don't know…I'm not—'

'Not what?' Alessandro demanded impatiently. He blazed a stare at her. 'Do you want to come with me?'

'Of course I do. But—'

Taking her arm in a firm grip, Alessandro marched on in silence.

As they stood in front of the modest dwelling, waiting for the door to open, Emily still felt bemused at the possibility of shopping for clothes inside such a tiny cottage.

'Don't look so worried,' Alessandro said as he turned to look down at her. 'Maria will find you something to wear.'

Emily made a conscious effort to relax. 'I'm fine,' she said.

All the signs of a much loved home surrounded them. There wasn't a single weed to be seen in the garden, and the colourful flowerbeds to either side of the newly swept path were crammed with blooms. The shuttered windows beside the front door were underscored with planters over-flowing with blossom, while heavily scented climbers jostled for space around the doorframe.

Closing her eyes, Emily tried to concentrate on the sounds of the bees buzzing and the birdsong; the mingled perfume of flowers, all so delightful and distinctive. Had she been alone, she might have succeeded. But Alessandro was standing very close, claiming every bit of her notice— and why was he making such a fuss about kitting her out for the grape-treading? Surely she would only need to roll up her trouser-legs and don some sort of overall—?

She came to full attention as the door swung open. A short, generously proportioned woman, as creased and as brown as a walnut, slapped her hands together when she saw Alessandro and cried out with pleasure, 'Alessandro! *Piccolino!*'

'My nanny,' Alessandro explained, swinging the old lady off the ground with an answering shout.

Emily watched as a frantic exchange of questions and answers ensued between them.

'Maria apologises for being at the end of the garden tending her geese,' Alessandro translated. 'Her favourite, Carlotta, is to take part in the annual goose race and must have extra care. True,' he assured Emily when he saw the look on her face. 'One day I'll take you to see the race. These birds are treated like favoured members of the family. And the winner...' He gave a low whistle of appreciation.

'Fed to the family?' Emily guessed wryly.

'Certainly not!' Alessandro said with a grin. 'There is a substantial cash prize at stake—to keep the winning goose in luxury for the rest of its life. It is up to the owner to ensure that this is the case. A matter of honour,' he explained, pinning a serious expression on his face. 'And now Maria invites us into her home.'

'*Si,*' Signora Felsina insisted, nodding her head enthusiastically as she beamed at Emily.

Stepping over the stone threshold, Emily looked around curiously. The tiny cottage windows allowed in little natural light, but several old-fashioned oil lamps had been lit so that everything was softly illuminated. She could smell something delicious cooking on the old black range, and noticed that the best use had been made of the narrow window ledges, which housed an array of pungent green herbs flourishing in terracotta pots.

Contentment was contagious, she discovered, hoping they could stay for a little while. Everything was ordered for comfort. Every object had been arranged to please the eye. And all of it gleamed with the unmistakable patina of regular attention. A bolt of desire pierced her heart as she glanced across at Alessandro—desire that went way beyond the physical to claw at her soul. Did he feel it, too? Did he long for a sanctuary like this to call his own? Could he feel the tug of a real home? The longing to create a similar haven was overwhelming her—

'Sit, Principessa, sit—'

The heavily accented voice of the older woman interrupted Emily's reveries.

'Here,' she insisted, tossing rugs and cushions aside. 'Sit here, Principessa.'

'Emily. Please…call me Emily.'

Something in Emily's voice must have troubled the older woman. Her hand lingered on Emily's arm as she turned to confront Alessandro.

'Alessandro,' she said, her voice mildly chastening. 'Your bride is not happy. What is wrong, Alessandro?'

Emily tensed at the bluntness of the remark, but Alessandro seemed not to have taken offence.

At his non-committal grunt Maria shook her head, and took herself off to pour out three fizzing glasses of homemade ginger beer from a vast stone flagon. 'You sit, too,' she said, turning around to face Alessandro. 'You take up too much space,' she complained fondly as she transferred the squat glasses onto a wooden tray.

'Here, let me,' he said, ignoring her instruction and removing the tray from her hands. 'Now, *you* go and sit down, *tata*.'

Emily watched as the old lady hurried to obey his instruction, noticing her beam of delight when Alessandro used what surely must have been his childhood name for her.

Settling herself down into a chair so plumped up with cushions her chubby sandal-clad feet barely touched the ground, Maria Felsina held her glass aloft as she made a smiling toast to Emily.

'Emily,' Alessandro echoed softly.

Draining her glass with relish, Maria leaped to her feet and declared, 'And now you must eat—'

'Oh, no—' Emily protested. She was still full from breakfast, but Alessandro's glance warned her to stay silent. 'Thank you,' she said, seeing she might cause offence by refusing one of the sugar-frosted buns. 'These look delicious.' And they were, she realised, as the moist, feather-light sponge slipped down her throat.

In spite of the warm late-summer weather, there was a low fire in the grate, and as she ate Emily longed to open some buttons at the neck of her tailored shirt. She went so far as to toy with the top one—but when Alessandro caught her glance for some reason, the innocent action suddenly struck her as irredeemably provocative. She looked away, but not before she saw one of his sweeping raven brows rise minutely in an expression that was both accusing and amused.

'My wife has come to you for clothes, *tata*,' he said, turning his attention back to his old nurse.

'Will they fit?' Emily murmured discreetly.

Alessandro must have translated this, Emily thought,

judging by their peals of laughter. Before she could feel embarrassed, Maria took her hand and stroked it gently, as if to atone for the outburst. Then, confirming Emily's reading of the situation, she turned a face full of mock reproach on Alessandro and wagged a blunt-nailed finger at him.

'Maria is the best dressmaker on the estate,' Alessandro explained. 'She'll soon sort you out with something to wear.'

'In time?' Emily said anxiously.

Her concern crossed the language barrier, and with a vigorous nod of her head Maria indicated that she should follow her into the next room. Taking her through a low door, Maria pointed to some bolts of cloth stacked in one corner of the room, and then at the old treadle sewing machine standing against the wall.

There was a makeshift gown-rail—just a piece of rope suspended between two hooks on a low joist—and crammed onto this were cotton skirts in a startling profusion of colour and pattern, together with white puff-sleeved tops, all with the same scooped necks and tie fronts.

'*Ecco*, Principessa!' Maria exclaimed. And then, after viewing her thoughtfully for few moments, Maria swooped on the rail and unhooked an armful of clothing.

'Oh, no! I couldn't possibly!' Emily protested, seeing the top was so low her belly button would get an airing, never mind anything else. When Maria pressed it into her hands she bundled it behind her back, hoping Alessandro, who had just appeared at the door, hadn't noticed.

His eyes sparkled dangerously in the dim light. 'Well? Go and try them on,' he urged softly.

'Will you—?'

'I'll come back when you're changed,' he said reassuringly.

Next, Maria held out a selection of skirts for her to choose from, and Emily surprised herself by selecting the gaudiest one.

Maria smiled, nodding approval of her choice, shaking out the fabric equivalent of a sunset.

The prospect of wearing something so showy...so decadent...was exciting. Pulling on the skirt, Emily began to do battle with the blouse, managing at last to adjust the front into something approaching respectability.

'No, no,' Maria protested, waggling her finger. 'Like this, Principessa,' she said, with a broad grin on her face.

Before Emily could stop her Maria had tugged the elasticated top below her shoulders until there was more cleavage on show than ever. But the older woman still wasn't satisfied, and, plucking at Emily's bra strap, she shook her head in disapproval.

With a rueful laugh Emily finally capitulated and, reaching behind her back, freed the catches on her bra. As the last restraint was removed even she had to admit the result was impressive.

Indicating there was one last thing to be changed, Maria darted down to reach beneath an old wooden chest. Pulling out a pair of simple brown leather sandals, scarcely more than a thong to stick between the toes on strips of toughened leather, she pushed them across the stone-flagged floor towards Emily.

'Grazie,' Emily said, flashing up a smile as she slipped them on. They were surprisingly comfortable, she found, wiggling her toes and relishing the freedom. As she straightened up, Maria reached for the pins that were already finding it a struggle to contain Emily's heavy mane of shiny black hair. They were cast aside, and with a final flourish Maria carefully drew her fingers through the resulting cascade, arranging it like a gleaming cloak around her protégée's shoulders.

Standing back, she beamed with satisfaction and, taking hold of Emily's arm, turned her around to view her reflection in the mirror.

Even the short time she had been in the hot climate had

warmed Emily's skin-tone to gold, and the brazen hussy staring back at her bore no resemblance whatever to the tight-laced professional she was accustomed to seeing. Instead, a full-breasted woman, with wild, untamed hair streaming across her shoulders, gazed back proudly. Toned legs, full lips, and dark up-tilted eyes suggested endless possibilities…endless fantasies…

As Maria gusted with approval Emily started to move towards the door. At the last moment she hesitated; dressing up, play-acting, was one thing, but her husband was all too real—and she didn't know him well enough to be able to predict how he would react when he saw his wife parading about like some fugitive from a bawdy etching. There was a distinct possibility she might unleash a whole lot more than she could cope with.

At the sound of a low, appreciative whistle she froze.

'That's quite an improvement.'

Leaning up against the doorframe, his arms loosely folded, Alessandro made no attempt to hide his interest in her newly adopted persona. 'You really look the part,' he murmured, giving Maria a wry nod of approval.

Raising her head defiantly, Emily stared him square in the eyes. What part was that? she wondered suspiciously.

'Leave the rest of your clothes here,' he said, straightening up. 'We'll pick them up later. Come on,' he pressed, 'everyone will be waiting for us.'

And, before she could refuse, he stretched out, caught hold of her, and swept her out of the door.

CHAPTER EIGHT

THEY were in a huge barn filled with the young men and women of the village. The contrast to the dappled light of the afternoon was apparent the moment Alessandro slid shut the huge wooden door behind them. Inside the barn Emily was conscious of a heady, sensuous quality to the heavy golden air that was lacking on the outside.

Ribbons of sunlight slanted across a sea of smiling faces, while the scent of young, clean bodies merged with the more pungent aroma of ripe fruit. There was an air of expectancy, and even sound seemed in thrall to the mellow mood, Emily discovered, when a murmur of welcome rose like a wave, subsided first to a whisper, and then to silence as Alessandro raised his hands.

She saw that here there was no protocol; her husband was greeted as warmly and as naturally as if he was just another man from the village, come to show off his new bride. His loud greeting was matched by the shouts of the other men present and then, turning to Emily, he urged her forward.

There was complete silence as everyone waited to see what she would do.

She felt her cheeks grow hot, and for a moment she held back. But the firm touch of Alessandro's hand on her arm gave her no choice and, stepping forward, she executed a smiling curtsey to the assembled crowd.

'Thank you,' Alessandro rasped, very close to her ear.

Emily turned and smiled back at him, the cheers resounding in her ears. She felt a warm rush of happiness to know that her action had pleased him.

She watched as he tugged his shirt over his head, and

then saw that she wasn't the only woman looking at him with naked appreciation.

And some of the village girls weren't afraid to move closer. Instinctively, Emily moved onto the offensive. Almost before she knew what she was doing she had placed herself between Alessandro and his admirers.

As he toed off his shoes he saw what she was doing, and threw her a half-smile that rippled through her body with startling consequences.

Was it a challenge? Emily wondered, conscious that the other women had backed off. Keeping her eyes locked on Alessandro's, she kicked off her own sandals.

Matching her stare for stare, he leaned forward and rolled up the legs of his jeans.

Holding his gaze, Emily tossed back her hair, then, emulating all the other women, she picked up the hem of her skirt and secured it into her underwear. She had never been consciously proud of her legs before, but now she was—especially when Alessandro's eyes broke their hold on her own to lavish a lingering and frankly appreciative gaze on them.

He was naked apart from his jeans, and his hard, muscled torso gleamed like a priceless bronze in the sultry haze, setting him apart from all the other men. It wasn't simply the power in his body, Emily realised as their eyes locked again, or even his extra height. It was that bone-melting menace in his dark, angled stare.

Prowling the floor around her, it seemed almost as if it was now Alessandro's turn to draw an invisible barrier between Emily and the rest of the men, so that even amidst the crowd she was undeniably and unmistakably his.

Emily's breath caught in her throat. Involuntarily, she touched her tongue to her lips, and one of the young women, misreading her expression, took it for uncertainty. Leaving her partner on the outskirts of the crowd, she alone dared to breach the invisible circle her Prince had drawn around his wife.

Taking Emily by the arm, she drew her across the sawdust-covered floor towards the huge open vat that stood at one end of the barn. Leading her up the steps, she brought her onto the high platform of seasoned oak.

'Come,' she said softly, in lightly accented English. 'You must be the first to climb in, Principessa.'

A low murmur of approval rose from the men, then died the instant Alessandro shifted his position and started moving towards her.

'I'll lift you in,' he murmured, just as she was about to climb over the side.

Convincing herself that the only reason she would allow him to do that was because there were so many people watching and she couldn't refuse, Emily proudly inclined her head. There was something about the very special atmosphere surrounding them that made her acutely aware of the power of her femininity. It was a force she could use, or not, as she chose...

But she had overlooked the fact that she had not felt Alessandro's arms around her since they had danced together at their wedding reception. And now, thanks to her own reckless choice of clothes and the sensuous ambience in which they found themselves, she was intensely aroused.

The touch of his hands around her waist was electrifying. She closed her eyes and told herself not to read anything into it. But Alessandro took delight in lowering her as slowly as he could, so that it seemed to Emily as if a lifetime of pleasure was encapsulated in the few seconds it took to sink down into the mountain of grapes. The silence around them had thickened and taken on a new significance, as if everyone in the barn was holding a collective breath. As she sank lower she could feel the swollen fruit bursting beneath her feet, until her legs were completely submerged to the very top of her thighs.

When Alessandro vaulted over the side to join her a great cheer went up, temporarily diminishing the sensuous mood. It seemed his presence in the vat was the sign for everyone else to climb in, and a mad scramble ensued as tiny spaces were claimed; couples were so closely entwined it was impossible to see where one handsome youth ended and his pretty young partner began.

In the melee, Emily was thrust up tight against Alessandro, her feet struggling for purchase on the warm, slippery juice and split skins. She was forced to cling onto him just in order to remain standing. Relaxing gradually, as he steadied her, she became aware of his heart thrumming rhythmically against her breasts and his naked chest like warm marble beneath her hands.

The air was intoxicating, and stimulating, filled with the perfume of grapes and juice and heightened emotion. There was so much noise, so much covert—and not so covert—activity between the couples, that Emily felt shielded by it, free to indulge in her wildest fantasies, to become someone else altogether, someone far more daring and provocative than she could ever hope to be...

Then, as if at some silent signal, the noise stilled as suddenly as it had begun. Out of the silence rose a moistly slow and regular beat. It was impossible to ignore and useless to resist, and, after missing only a couple of the moves, Emily found herself joining in with the rest and stamping her feet in a rhythmical pattern.

As the pace increased the atmosphere became charged with a new and primal energy, and, clinging on to Alessandro, Emily felt her senses respond urgently. She softened against him, each of her muscles yielding in turn, until finally she was moulded into him, moving to his rhythm, their rhythm, to the insistent, unavoidable rhythm that consumed them both.

As she abandoned herself time stood still and meant nothing. She no longer knew where she began and he ended. The only certainty was that she was safe in his arms, and it was to his eyes that her overheated glance flew for approval.

Soon her clothes were drenched and she was coated all over with the sweet, sticky juice. She noticed that some of their companions were already beginning to peel away, clambering out over the sides of the vat in untidy, exhausted groups. She noticed too how a haze of passion seemed to linger behind each departure, hovering in the air around her and in the lingering exchange of slanted glances as couples retired silently into the shadows, arms intertwined and bodies fused in tense expectation.

Quite suddenly she was alone with Alessandro.

Leaning against the side of the great vat, his arms outstretched and resting lightly on the rim, he studied her calmly. Emily felt as if even the air she breathed was saturated with sensuality. She was trembling as he moved towards her, remained quiescent when he swept her into his arms, and felt bereft, even for those few moments of separation, after he had lowered her down over the side of the vat...

Vaulting over to join her, Alessandro twined his fingers through hers and drew her quickly down the steps with him, across the floor of the barn towards another door she hadn't noticed before. From there he took her across a small cobbled yard, made shady by a roof of densely intertwined grapevines, and, unlatching another door, he brought her inside the facing building, and shot home a sturdy black bolt.

They were locked in together, closed off completely from the outside world. Streamers of sunlight strung from the roof trusses high over their heads brightened the honey gold air humming around them, and as Alessandro mounted some open wooden steps with Emily in his arms she registered hazily that he was carrying her up to the hayloft.

Alessandro brought her to a mezzanine level, where the

floor was hidden beneath a deep, soft carpet of sweet-smelling hay. Setting her down gently, he sat beside her and drew her onto his lap, stretching out his long legs as he eased back against the bales of hay.

Emily felt as if she might drown in his eyes, as if the depth of expression had been there all the time, waiting for her, if only she'd had the courage to see it. There were no divisions between them now, only the gasping, pleading murmurs escaping her lips that left Alessandro under no illusion as to how much she wanted him and how hard it was for her to wait.

Pausing only to snatch apart the grape-stained ties of her blouse, he dragged the fabric away and plunged his tongue between her breasts to lick the sticky juices off. Feasting on sweetness, his questing mouth found first one succulent extended nipple and then the next, while Emily, meshing her fingers through his hair, could only beg him not to stop.

'I have no intention of stopping, *cara mia*,' Alessandro husked, holding her firm beneath him. 'Not until every last drop of juice has been licked from your body.'

And as he moved back to his task Emily found her pleasure increased when she could watch her body responding to his touch. The sound of her own rapid breathing, coupled with the deeper, throaty sounds of contentment from Alessandro, added a piquancy to her enjoyment she could never have anticipated as he fulfilled his pledge with devastating thoroughness. And, in spite of her impatience, Alessandro continued to prepare her with the utmost care, as if he knew how inexperienced she was.

When at last his hands reached down to throw back her skirt, she thrust up her hips in desperate haste, willing to go to any lengths now to make it easier for him. But he broke away, swinging to his feet as he reached for the buckle on his belt. Then, dropping back to his knees by her side, he took her face between his warm hands and kissed her very slowly, so that she was in no doubt how deep his feelings ran.

'Don't be frightened,' he murmured, reaching to strip off the rest of his clothes.

Emily gave an involuntary gasp and looked away. Nothing could have prepared her for the sight of Alessandro naked, and aroused. 'No,' she gasped instinctively, pulling back.

'No?' he queried softly, reaching up inside her blouse. His slow, seductive strokes soothed her, and then he took each engorged nipple-tip between his fingers and tugged a little. Smiling down at her, he murmured, 'Are you quite sure about that, Emily?'

The only answer possible was a series of small gasps—gasps that became cries of delight as he replaced the touch of his hands with his mouth.

'Do you still want me to stop?' Alessandro taunted her softly, whispering the words against her neck, so that she shivered with pleasure and pressed against him all the more.

'No,' Emily moaned, wanting only his touch and his kisses, not his questions.

'Are you sure?'

She reassured him frantically with every persuasive phrase she could think of. He would be a wonderful lover, she was sure of it, and that certainty increased her desire for him until it filled her whole world.

'So, you're not scared of me now?' he pressed gently.

'Scared?' Emily scoffed faintly, turning her face away so that he could not see how brazen he had made her…how she longed to be full of him, stretched by him, pleasured endlessly only by him.

'There's nothing to be ashamed of if you are,' he pointed out softly. 'At one time it was quite usual for women to save themselves for their husbands—'

'Don't tease me,' she warned huskily.

'I'm not teasing you,' Alessandro assured her, kissing
the top of her head while his hands moved over her with
long, calming strokes.

'I'm not very experienced,' Emily admitted, wanting
more as she moved sinuously against him. 'And I'm
twenty-eight,' she breathed provocatively, as if the time had
come for him to remedy the situation.

'As old as that?' he growled, attending to her breasts.

Emily let out a soft cry as he began to suckle greedily
whilst rolling the other nipple between a firm thumb and
forefinger. He knew exactly how to tantalise her to the point
of reason and beyond, until her body, her mind, her whole
being craved only one thing.

'So what if you're not experienced?' Alessandro demanded, stopping to gaze at her. 'I think I know what you
need…'

'Alessandro—'

'"Alessandro,"' he mocked softly, positioning her beneath him. She felt his breath fan her neck, and sighed as
the shivers raced and competed with every other sensation
delighting her senses.

'What's wrong, Emily?' he demanded, easing her thighs
apart. 'Is it time to stop teasing you?'

'Alessandro,' Emily whispered putting her finger over
his lips, 'don't hurt me…'

'I would never hurt you—'

'I don't mean that…I mean don't do this unless—'

'Unless?' He drew her hand to his lips to drop kisses on
her soft palm. 'Tell me, Emily,' he insisted softly.

'I know this is just a marriage of convenience—'

He leaned back a little and stared at her thoughtfully. 'Is
that all it is for you, Emily?'

'What is it for you?' she persisted, still craving reassurance.

'Our marriage is anything we choose to make of it,'
Alessandro said, kissing each fingertip in turn. 'And in an-

swer to your question, I would never hurt you…not intentionally.'

A starburst of emotion clouded her thoughts as he kissed her lips. His hands were growing more demanding, so she couldn't marshal her thoughts except to know that Alessandro was so skilled a lover… And she was lost.

Tugging off her skirt, he tossed it away and then returned his attention to her nipples. He began teasing them again with light passes of his fingertips, watching with satisfaction as she moaned and writhed beneath him.

Holding him captive with her fingers meshed through his hair, Emily savoured the touch of his mouth and his tongue, the nip of his teeth on her own swollen lips as his hands moved over her body transporting her to a fierce, elemental place where thought was nothing more than the slave of sensation. And now when he held back she played him at his own game, rolling away, luring him on.

But Alessandro was too fast and caught her easily, bringing her back beneath him and holding her firm between powerful thighs that seemed banded with steel. And now all that lay between them was a tiny white lace thong.

He had brought her to a highly aroused state, and Emily knew that it pleased him to see her so eager for his possession. Coaxing her thighs apart, he encouraged her to lift them for him, his amber eyes glittering with satisfaction as he used one hand to secure her arms above her head and the other to trace with a tantalisingly light touch the damp contours of the swell between her legs. She felt as if her whole being was concentrated in that one small area, as if every sensation she had ever experienced was magnified and centred there. Long, shuddering sighs told him how good it was, that it was the most intense sensation she had ever experienced, while Alessandro's murmurs to her in his own foreign tongue encouraged and enticed her all the more as he trailed his fingertips across the pouting site of her arousal.

When he tugged the thong off and she lay naked beneath him, wanting him so badly, there was a part of Emily that still held back at the thought of what such a powerful man might do to her. But even now Alessandro could sense her fear, and his hands were skilful and persuasive, making her forget everything but her desire for him. And when he dipped his fingertips between her wet swollen lips, the last of her doubts was erased by an intensity of sensation she could never have imagined. Crying out shamelessly, she begged him to take her then, but he refused to be hurried, only tempted her with the tip of his erection, pulling back just before she had a chance to draw him inside her. And then, releasing her hands, he gave her absolute freedom to decide the pace.

But once he was inside her Alessandro reclaimed control, increasing the pressure to fill her completely, stretching her beyond anything she could ever have imagined, until pleasure blanked out every thought but her craving for fulfillment. Holding her firm, he murmured reassurances, repeating her name when her sobbing cries marked the onset of the powerful spasms he had set up with such care.

Could anything ravish his senses more than this? Alessandro wondered, as he savoured the sight of Emily bucking beneath him.

Only one thing, perhaps, he realised as he plundered the moist, hidden depths of her mouth to taste her sweetness—and that would be the sight of his beautiful wife holding their child at the moment of its birth.

'I don't know if I like them,' Emily protested as Alessandro held out a linen cloth sagging with the weight of warm green figs plucked straight from the tree.

He made a sound of encouragement as he gave his collection a little shake. 'But ripe figs don't travel well,' he insisted. 'I promise you, Emily, you have never tasted anything like this before.'

It was so hard to resist him... No, impossible, Emily realised as she gazed up into golden eyes whose beloved intensity had become so familiar to her over the past few days at Monte Volere. Did they only burn with fire like that when he looked at her? she wondered, smiling up at him as she picked out one of the plump ripe fruits and raised it to her lips. Even that innocent gesture seemed redolent with meaning now. She heard herself sigh, felt her body quiver with awareness...anticipation. She seemed to be in a permanent state of arousal...

After taking her to his bed in the homely old manor house Alessandro had introduced her to physical love in a way that made her want him all the time...every moment of every day, waking and even sleeping...so that she reached for him unknowing in the middle of the night, and then woke to find him making love to her again.

'Well?' he demanded softly as she sank her teeth into it.

Savouring the mouthful of intense, perfumed sweetness, Emily made a sound of contentment deep in her throat. 'It's the second best thing I ever put in my mouth,' she admitted, flashing him a glance.

Alessandro threw his head back and gave a short, virile laugh. 'Wait until you taste the wine from my vineyards,' he murmured provocatively. 'There are several contenders that should be considered before you make your mind up.'

'I won't change my mind,' Emily promised, slanting him a look as she linked her arm through his, relishing his strength and his body warmth through their light, summer-weight clothes.

'Ah, but my wine contains the essence of life,' Alessandro declared, laughing at her puzzled expression. 'You'll see what I mean when you drink it.'

He wasn't joking, Emily realised later, as she watched him select a bottle from the rack. She was even more sur-prised to see him moving about the well-equipped kitchen with a familiarity that suggested he was accustomed to fending for himself.

'Who taught you all this?' she demanded softly, linking her arms loosely around his waist as he whipped up an omelette. Leaning her face against his strong, muscular back, she inhaled his warm musky male scent... Being with him like this felt so wonderful...so right.

'Maria Felsina,' he said, reaching for the olive oil. 'Before she became a most sought-after dressmaker, specialising in traditional clothes, she lived with our family. She was the one who greeted me when I returned home from school for the holidays—from university, too. We spent more time together here at Monte Volere than at the palace. This is the one place where I can relax and be myself.'

'I can see that,' Emily agreed. 'Even at the grape-treading I noticed the way the people accepted you as one of them.'

'I am one of them,' Alessandro said simply. 'We all call Ferara home.'

'Did you see much of your parents when you were a child?'

'My parents were swept up in their duties at Court—'

'I hope you will find time for your own children—' Emily stopped, aghast, wondering how such words could shoot out of her mouth having made no connection first with her brain. She had no plans to have children, and was quite sure that Alessandro felt the same. Her cheeks were still on fire when he turned to look at her, and there was an expression on his face that seemed to confirm it would have been better to keep her opinions to herself. 'That is, when you have children eventually yourself—some time in the future,' she said, stumbling over the words.

The look of bewilderment, of sheer panic, on his wife's face pierced Alessandro's heart. 'Don't look at me like that, Emily,' he insisted, sweeping her into his arms. 'You've said nothing wrong.' Dipping his head, he stared deep into her eyes to assure her, 'I plan to have lots of children with the woman I love—and sooner rather than later.'

Alessandro forced back the urge to tell Emily about the final requirement before his father could retire. His desire had never been stronger, he realised as he pressed her to him. But now was not the time. Their love was little more than a tender shoot, and she was at her most vulnerable. He didn't know how she would react when he told her, and crucial business meetings were about to take him away. When he told her, he wanted the time to be right... He had to be there, to reassure her...

'Alessandro?' Pressing him away from her, Emily stood back. Did his silence mean some woman had been found for him...some woman who would bear his children...a fitting partner to rule Ferara alongside him?

'I wish I didn't have to go away,' he said tensely. 'But as you will discover, Emily, with great privilege comes great responsibility. You know I wouldn't think of leaving you unless there was absolutely no alternative.'

Did she? Emily wondered, staring up at him. But then he dragged her back into his arms, as if he couldn't bear to watch the doubts scudding across her face.

'Stop this, Emily!' he told her fiercely. 'When I am a father I will be with my children; I will take equal part in their upbringing and I will spend as much time with them as any father, possibly more.'

'I believe you—'

'That's better,' he said, tipping the creamy egg mix into the pan. 'I cannot bear to see you upset. You'll feel better when you eat.'

If only it was that easy, Emily thought as she poured out two glasses of wine while Alessandro slid a delicious looking golden omelette onto a plate and dressed it with salad for her.

'You must promise me that you will stop worrying,' he insisted, nodding towards the table. 'I don't want to come home to a waif who has pined away. Haven't I told you, *cara mia*? Everything's going to be all right. My wife will take an equal part in everything I do.' He stopped in the act of pouring his own egg mix into the pan. 'What's wrong, Emily?'

Fork suspended, Emily could only stare at him. The idea of some other, unknown woman sitting so close to Alessandro, living with him…bearing his children…was insupportable.

'I promise you,' Alessandro said steadily, bringing his own food across to the table, 'we will share everything, and that's a promise.'

'Good,' Emily said, swallowing a huge mouthful of food, effectively staunching her end of the conversation. She tried not to choke on it as she considered the possibility that negotiations between Ferara and Alessandro's bride-to-be might be going on right at this very moment—even as they ate.

When was she ever going to accept that as soon as their contract came to an end Alessandro would want a proper marriage?

No time soon, she realised as they chinked glasses. But it was too late for regrets. She couldn't turn the clock back, and the truth was she was in love with her husband— deeply, passionately and ultimately, though she wished desperately it could be otherwise, hopelessly.

CHAPTER NINE

IT SEEMED no time at all since they had driven beneath the stone archway that marked the entrance to the Monte Volere estates to share their magical time, and now they were back in the Feraran capital, faced with reality. Even though Alessandro had reassured her about their impending separation, Emily felt as if her worst fears were taking on a darker, clearer shape. Alessandro had assured her that their parting would be for a couple of weeks at most. So why did she feel so sure it would be longer...?

This morning he would leave. The time for his departure had come around before she'd even had time to complete her move into his apartment at the palace, let alone discuss the worries that were now occupying her mind every waking moment. The little she had managed to glean about his trip left her in no doubt that it would be arduous, maybe even dangerous, and the last thing she wanted was to burden him with personal concerns...

Dressed casually for what she knew would be a rushed farewell, she waited in her old apartment, surrounded by all the chaos associated with her move. Pottering about aimlessly, she tried to concentrate on practical matters, picking up one thing, and then another, and switching their positions haphazardly in between glancing at her wristwatch as she counted down the minutes to his departure and wondered how much time they would have left together. Alessandro was already overrunning his schedule, and at the palace his daily life ran to a remorseless timetable.

'Emily, I'm so sorry.'

She nearly jumped out of her skin when he breezed into

the room, but he came straight over to her and, seizing both of her hands in his, raised them to his lips.

'Forgive me, *cara sposa*—'

'Matters of State?' Emily teased softly, forcing a smile through the foretaste of loneliness that was already stealing into her mind. The last thing she wanted was to worry Alessandro in the last few moments they had together. She needed to know that he was oblivious to the undercurrents chipping away at her happiness, and felt a rush of relief when he grinned back at her.

'How I hate these distractions,' he murmured, tugging her towards him.

'What? Me?' Emily demanded fondly, staring into his eyes.

'Everything but you,' he growled softly. Pulling her over to the sofa, he insisted she sit down.

'You'll be late,' Emily reminded him, glancing at the delicate ormolu clock on her mantelpiece.

'So I'll be late for once. It's not something I make a habit of.' He paused and looked down at her, his dark golden gaze direct and full of warmth. 'But this is special.'

'What is?' Emily said curiously.

'You,' he said wryly, brushing a strand of hair away from her face. 'For you I would make the whole world stand in line and wait, because I love you. I love you more than life itself, Emily. Forgive me for leaving you, but know that, however much you miss me, I shall miss you more.'

Tentatively Emily traced the line of Alessandro's claret-coloured silk tie from the point where it secured the crisp white collar around her husband's strong, tanned neck, down his toned torso to the slim black leather belt on his midnight-blue suit.

'And I love you more than I ever thought it possible to love anyone,' she whispered. 'I have never trusted anyone so completely in my life—with my life—you are my life.'

Bringing her hands to his lips, Alessandro turned them

and kissed each palm in turn. 'For ever, Emily,' he murmured, looking deep into her eyes. 'And now...' The corners of his mouth were starting to tug up in a grin. 'I've got something for you.'

Shifting emotional gears in tandem, Emily threw him an amused look. 'A crown?' she teased, remembering the last occasion on which he had said something similar.

'Not a crown,' he said with a wry shrug. 'I could get one for you, but I thought you weren't so keen on that type of thing.'

She loved the way his eyes crinkled at the corners when he grinned at her like that. 'OK, so don't keep me in suspense.'

Reaching inside his jacket, Alessandro drew out a slim volume of poetry. 'Christopher Marlowe,' he murmured softly as he pressed it into her hands. 'Well, Emily, do you like it? Does it please you?'

'It pleases me very much,' Emily whispered as she traced the worn binding reverently with her fingertips. He couldn't have brought her anything she would have liked more, she realised. 'I love it,' she whispered. 'It's the most beautiful...the most special thing I've ever been given.'

'I was hoping you would say that,' he said, cupping her chin to draw her forward for a tender kiss on the lips. 'Because I want you to read a page every day while I am away, and then you will know how much I love you. And now—'

'You must leave?' Emily said, trying to be brave about it.

'Soon,' he agreed, putting his finger over her lips.

She pulled away. 'I'm sorry, Alessandro. I feel so—'

'How?' he demanded softly. 'Emily, speak to me.'

'Once the terms of our contract are satisfied—' She shook her head, unable to go on.

'You can't stop there,' he warned.

'Has a bride been found for you?' She spoke so softly she couldn't be sure at first that he had heard.

'A bride *has* been found,' Alessandro confirmed. 'But I found her myself, and she is sitting here in front of me now.'

'So, you really do love me?'

Alessandro's brows rose as he stared at her, and when he spoke again his voice had adopted the low, teasing tone she loved so much. 'You guessed,' he teased gently with a heavy sigh. 'I guess that means my secret's out.'

As he brought her into his arms Emily felt safe again, as if her fears had been of her own conjuring—and all for nothing.

'I love you,' she murmured against his lips. 'But I don't know how I am going to live without you.'

He put his finger over her lips and smiled into her eyes before replacing his finger with his lips. 'You don't have to live without me, *mio tesoro*,' he said at last. 'This will just be a very brief separation.'

'Promise?'

'I promise,' he vowed softly, wrapping her fingers around the book of poems as he got to his feet. But at the door he stopped, and dragged her to him. 'I'd take you with me, but—'

'I'll be fine. Go,' she whispered fiercely, 'before you change your mind.'

'I have already changed my mind,' Alessandro confessed, raking his fingers impatiently through his hair.

'But you're running late,' Emily murmured without much conviction as he dragged her back into his arms.

'One of the privileges of being a prince is that I set the agenda,' he husked against her ear. 'And I have just re-membered something very important...something that cannot wait...'

'Here?' Emily breathed, feeling her heart pound against his chest as he pressed her back against the door.

Miming that she should be quiet for a moment, Alessandro dug in his pocket for his mobile phone. 'File a

new flight plan,' he ordered briefly when the call was connected. 'I have been unavoidably delayed.'

In the short time since Alessandro had been away, Emily
had to admit that one of her greatest successes had been
his father's apartment. With his approval she had transformed it, relegating the angular, uncomfortable furniture
to the areas of the palace she thought might eventually be
opened to the public and replacing it with a selection of
well-padded armchairs, cosy throws and rugs. A small
kitchen had been created, and a supply of fresh fruit, cakes
and other delicacies were ordered to be delivered on a daily
basis.

'You've done too much for me already,' he protested one
day, while Emily was balanced on the top of a pair of
stepladders, fixing some dried autumnal arrangements to
the wall.

Turning quickly to reply, she paused and put a hand to
her forehead. She never usually felt dizzy…

'Why don't we call one of the servants to do that for
you?' he suggested.

Hearing the anxiety in his voice, Emily hurried to reassure him, realising he had been on his feet helping her for
most of the morning. 'I'm fine,' she said. 'Are you getting
tired?'

'No, it's you I'm thinking about,' he said. 'Why don't
you come down from there? You look pale.'

'Don't worry about…' As her voice faded Emily blinked
her eyes several times, fighting for equilibrium. She had
never fainted in her life before, or been sick, but all at once
it felt as if she was going to do both.

'I'm sorry, I think I'm going to be—' Hand over mouth,
she slid cartoon-style down the stepladder, and made a dash
for the bathroom.

She got there just in time. Turning on the cold tap, she
filled the basin and immersed her face in the icy water.

Then, pulling back, she looked at herself in the mirror. Wet-faced and ashen, she steadied herself against the wall. She was no fool, she knew all the signs: she was pregnant. The only problem now was how was she ever going to bear the wait until Alessandro returned.

'Are you all right in there?'

'Yes, I'm fine,' she called brightly. Hurriedly wiping her face on a towel and arranging her hair as best she could in just a few seconds, she swung open the door, making sure she had a reassuring smile on her face for Alessandro's father. 'Let's get back to those catkins and hazel twigs,' she said as she walked past him.

'No, no,' young lady,' he said, waggling his finger at her. 'You've done more than enough for one day in your condition—'

'My condition?'

He couldn't conceal the sparkle in his eyes as he looked at her. 'You know what I mean,' he insisted, ushering her to a chair. 'I'm only surprised my son hasn't thought to inform me.'

'Inform you? What should Alessandro have told you?'

The old Prince considered this in silence for a few moments, then his face crumpled with concern. 'You mean he doesn't know yet?'

'That I'm pregnant? Emily said with a shy smile. 'No, Alessandro doesn't know about our baby yet. I've only just found out myself. But I'll tell him the moment he returns—'

'He should have been the first.'

'These things happen,' Emily said with a shrug as she smiled back at him.

'He'll return soon—immediately,' Alessandro's father amended thoughtfully. 'I'll have a messenger dispatched to bring him back here at once.'

'Could you do that?' Emily said, hardly daring to believe that Alessandro might be back with her so soon.

'Of course. And as soon as Alessandro knows about the baby we can make the announcement.'

'Won't it be a little early to go public with the news of my pregnancy?' Emily said with concern.

'Excuse my eagerness, but as well as celebrating my first grandchild I shall be celebrating my freedom.'

'Your freedom? What do you mean?'

'I shall be free…free to concentrate on my roses,' he explained excitedly. Now that you are expecting the heir I can abdicate formally. Forgive me, Emily. I am so eager to renounce the throne and pass it on to Alessandro I can hardly think straight.'

'What did you mean about making the announcement of my pregnancy official…before you can abdicate?' Emily said carefully.

'Alessandro must have explained—'

'Of course,' she said quickly. 'But it's always good to hear it again. I have so much yet to learn about my new country.' She felt as if each separate word was being wrenched out of her, and each one of them caused her pain—pain that only increased when she saw the expression of suppressed excitement, of longing, and of a dream so close now he could almost touch it written clear across her father-in-law's face.

'Well, as you know,' he began, struggling to keep his excitement under control, 'the first condition was that my son should marry before I could contemplate abdication—'

'Contemplate…' Emily murmured.

'That's right. Marriage, of course, was the first step. And the announcement of your pregnancy…the birth of your child, Alessandro's heir…is what my country's archaic legislation requires before I can abdicate in his favour. I never mentioned it before…for reasons of delicacy,' he explained gently. 'I know you can't force these things—'

Oh, can't you? Emily thought, feeling as if her heart had

just splintered into a thousand little pieces. 'No,' she agreed huskily. 'That's true.'

'But now, with this wonderful news...wonderful for all of us,' he said expansively, opening his arms in an embrace-the-world gesture. 'Emily, come to me. Let me thank you for this gift of life.'

Like an automaton, Emily accepted the old Prince's arms around her shoulders and even managed to return his kiss. He had done nothing wrong, she reasoned. She couldn't blame Alessandro's father for his son's *oversight*...

Oversight, Emily thought incredulously, much later alone in her own room. She hadn't even moved fully into Alessandro's apartment at the palace and now she was pregnant with his child. Everything that seemed to have been built on firm foundations between them had been founded on a lie. There was only one thing left to do now— and it didn't involve staying a minute longer than she had to in Ferara.

Picking up the telephone, she called her sister's mobile.

'What do you mean, she's gone?'

His father looked at him in anguish. 'I said she should tell you—'

'Tell me what?' Alessandro demanded in a clipped voice devoid of emotion. 'I'm sorry, Father,' he said, shaking his head as if he had never been more disappointed with himself. 'None of this is your fault. If I hadn't been visiting such a volatile place I would have taken Emily with me and none of this would have happened.'

'I think it's more complicated than that,' the elderly Prince ventured cautiously.

'What do you mean?'

Clapping his son on the shoulder, the old man let his hand linger for a squeeze of paternal affection. 'I'm sorry, Alessandro. I can't tell you—'

'Can't tell me!' Alessandro exploded. 'What can't you tell me about my wife? Has she been unfaithful to me?'

'No!' the old Prince exclaimed with outrage. 'She has not.'

'Then what?' Alessandro demanded angrily. 'Why else would she leave me?'

'You left her...*here...alone*,' his father reminded him. 'A stranger in our country, young and vulnerable. She was lonely—'

'We had an arrangement,' Alessandro reminded him bitterly.

'An arrangement?' his father exclaimed incredulously. 'If that's all you think of your marriage, Alessandro, then perhaps Emily was right to go.'

'Right! She is my wife!' Alessandro thundered. 'And whether you like it or not, Father, we have an arrangement—'

'Bah! Don't talk to me of arrangements, Alessandro,' he warned. 'I'll have none of it. I will not have my happiness at Emily's expense...or yours,' he added, seeing the torment that was fast replacing the anger on his son's face.

Mashing his lips together in impotent fury, Alessandro turned his back and stalked to the window. 'Then where is she?' he growled in an undertone.

'Somewhere where she is appreciated, I imagine,' his father told him mildly.

'And where might that be?' Alessandro said, turning slowly on his heels to confront him again.

'I'll leave you to work that out. But don't take too long, Alessandro. Don't let her slip through your fingers.'

Grinding his jaws together, Alessandro sucked in a breath as he made his decision. 'If she really wants to go, Father, there is nothing I can do to stop her. But if there is even the slightest chance—'

'You're wasting precious time, Alessandro.'

Inclining his head in a curt show of silent agreement,

Alessandro paused only to give his father a brief, fierce embrace before setting off for his own rooms, where he would pack an overnight bag and ring the airport to file his flight plan for London.

'As it happens, Emily, I do have something for you. Something I think you'll like—the fallout from a nice juicy bankruptcy. Your clients are major creditors—after the usual banks and Inland Revenue et cetra. Respectable elderly couple, allegedly fleeced out of their life savings by some toff from the Shires.'

'Billy, you're a diamond,' Emily said gratefully, playing to her Chief Clerk, whose thick Cockney accent and market stall *joie de vivre* masked a mind of Brobdingagian scope and efficiency. She had been expecting to pick up the dregs on her return to Chambers—the cases no one else wanted. But this was right up her street. 'Do we have all the papers?'

'Do pigs have wings? But your clients are available for a conference this morning.'

'Good. Give me what we've got. Set up the meeting. Oh, and Billy?'

'Yes?'

'If any personal calls come through for me...I'm not available.'

'I understand,' Billy said non-committally, straightening his impeccable tailor-made waistcoat on his rapid passage out of the room.

Collecting up her things, Emily went to settle herself into the office Billy had allocated to her. She was back to being a 'door tenant' for the time being—a part-timer in Chambers—and would have to submit to being shuffled about wherever there was available space.

Across Europe the new generation of young royals all combined professional careers with the responsibilities of their rank, so there hadn't been a single comment when she'd returned to work. And by using her maiden name she was largely assured of anonymity. So far, at least, the paparazzi had failed to mark any change in the blissful state of the Crown Prince of Ferara's marriage.

It had been Miranda's suggestion that she return to work and take time to think things through. They stuck by each other through thick and thin, Emily mused, knowing she needed her sister's support like never before. She knew Miranda would never suggest she should try and forget there had ever been a man called Alessandro...but that wasn't going to stop her trying, Emily thought as she reached for the intercom button.

'Billy, can you bring those papers in right away, please?'

The meeting with her elderly clients went well. As Emily had anticipated, they were both dressed in their Sunday best, and trying their hardest to appear at ease, when in fact, after planning carefully all their lives to enjoy a well-earned retirement, they were now staring into the abyss. Fortunately they had kept a meticulous diary of events, and with that she could build a case.

Emily found nothing unusual in taking over a case at the last minute, but it did mean that crucial parts of the thick file had to be read and assimilated before the first court hearing that same afternoon. Fortunately she thrived on the pressure; cases like these were what had attracted her to law in the first place.

She broke concentration reluctantly when a knock came at the door, knowing it could only be one person.

'Sorry to disturb you, Emily,' said Billy. 'I thought you should know you've had one call.'

'From?'

'Your sister.'

'Oh?' Emily said with concern.

'She said not to worry you.'

But the way Billy had delivered the message suggested

she should look deeper into the matter without delay, Emily thought, automatically scanning her diary. 'Could you get hold of her for me, please, Billy?'

'Already on line one,' he announced briskly, on his way out of the door.

'Miranda?'

'Sorry to trouble you at work, Em. I know you left a message with Billy to say you were too busy to speak to anyone, but I thought you should know—'

'You don't have to apologise.'

'Alessandro's in town. He wants to see you. I didn't know what to say.'

Emily's heart must have stopped. She only knew she had never been more grateful for her sister's support at the other end of the line. 'Did you tell him?'

'Where you'll be? No. I'm waiting for you to give me the go-ahead on that. But, Emily?' Miranda added anxiously.

'Yes?'

'I really think you should see him. At least give him a chance to explain.'

'I don't know.'

'Please, Em. If you'd spoken to him, heard how worried he sounds, you wouldn't be so hard on him. He knows you're appearing in court today; he just doesn't know which one…'

The silence hung between them and deepened, until finally Emily said softly, 'I can't keep running away from him for ever, can I, Miranda?'

Dragging the documents she had been reading before the call back towards her, Emily read the name of the man she would be accusing in court that day—the man who had tricked and betrayed an elderly couple. Alessandro had betrayed and tricked *her*, she remembered bitterly—and into a marriage of convenience that included an innocent child. What sort of man did that?

Alessandro managed to slip into the visitors' gallery just as the court usher called out, 'All rise,' and the judge walked in and took her seat.

He missed the first few moments of procedure—case number, names, et cetra—and was barely aware that another man, seeing him arrive, had also moved into the gallery a couple of rows back, and was desperately trying to catch his attention. The only thing he saw, the only thing he cared about, was Emily, fully robed and bewigged, standing in front of the judge.

He drank her in like a life-restoring draught, feeling his resolve and his determination increase with every second that he gazed at her. Just being so close was like a healing process, and he hadn't even realised how heartsick he was until this moment. He was in such agony he had to clench his fists to stop himself calling out to her. Taking a deep breath, he battled to compose himself. He would win her back. He had to...

His heart sang with pride while his mind seethed with questions as reason and logic made a steady return. Staring at her, he found it impossible to equate the woman he'd thought he knew—the clear-faced, intelligent woman below him now in the well of the court—with someone who could give herself to a man as freely and as lovingly as Emily had and then simply disappear without a word. Had she fallen out of love with him? His guts churned as an ugly worm of suspicion burrowed into his mind.

He had been so sure that she loved him—but then how could she have left him so abruptly if that was so? And, feelings apart, she had broken the contract that meant so much to her—to her sister. His father was heartbroken by their split, yet Emily had said she loved him, too. What could have taken her from them without even the basic courtesy of a note...something...anything to explain her behaviour? It had to be something so momentous, he reasoned, that only a face-to-face meeting would allow it to be brought out into the open. Yet a face-to-face meeting was the very thing Emily seemed intent on avoiding—but she *would* meet with him, he was determined on that…

The efforts of the man sitting behind Alessandro to attract his attention failed until the judge called a mid-morning recess. The very last thing on Alessandro's mind was a reunion with someone from his old school. Let alone Archibald Freemantle, he realised, grinding his jaw as he fought to remain civil.

His whole mind was focused on one thing and one thing only, and that was making things right with his wife. Maybe his pride had taken a battering when she deserted him, but the overriding emotion he had felt then, as now, was one of loss. Loss so insupportable he had no strategy to cope with the devastating effect it was having on every aspect of his life. Without Emily he had no life, Alessandro thought bitterly, forcing his attention back to the irritating individual in front of him.

'Archibald,' he said coolly, extending his hand as courtesy demanded, then removing it as fast as good manners allowed. 'What brings you here?'

'This case, old boy,' Archibald exclaimed, with such a heart-felt sigh it threatened to mist up his gold-rimmed spectacles.

'Oh?' Alessandro said vaguely, trying to be discreet about his desire to spot Emily…if only for a moment…just a glance would do, he realised, cursing himself for being a lovesick fool.

'You must have realised it's m'brother,' Archibald said, huffing again. 'Freemantle Minor,' he clarified, reverting to the argot of school.

Alessandro tensed. It didn't seem quite the moment to comment, *Oh, that rat,* so he confined himself to a murmured, 'Ah, now I recognise him.' The man in the dock, he realised, and a flash of amusement briefly eased his torment. Toby Freemantle had started his career as a small-time crook, going through coat pockets at school—until he was asked to leave. It appeared he had pursued his calling into adult life.

'Would have got off,' Archibald said hotly, clearly determined to elicit Alessandro's support, 'had it not been for that bitch barrister the wrinklies hired. Apparently she's hot stuff—said to be one of the best legal minds around. For a woman,' he added scornfully.

Rage powered up through Alessandro's frame at this casual dismissal of Emily's abilities, but only a muscle flexing in his jaw threatened to betray his feelings.

'I'm sure the judge presiding would be delighted to hear you make such a remark,' he commented laconically. 'Oh, and by the way, Archibald...'

'Yes?'

'That woman is my wife.'

Making a hasty exit, Emily was keen to escape to Chambers, where she could forget her personal problems and immerse herself in the case ready for cross-examination the next day.

Head down, arms encircling her bundle of papers, secured with the traditional pink ties, she failed to see the tall, imposing figure waiting at the head of the broad sweep of marble steps... Until an arm reached in front of her to grab hold of the mahogany banister and block her way.

'Emily—can we talk?'

Her mind locked with shock, even though she had expected Alessandro to find her. Unable to cope with the thought of seeing him again, she had simply banished it from her mind.

Seeing the security guards on alert, and moving towards them fast, Emily nodded them away first before she spoke. 'Alessandro. I didn't expect to see you here.'

Why was she lying to him? She bit down on her lip. All

her cool, all her reserve, every bit of the calm logic that guided her in the courtroom had vanished.

It was useless reminding herself that this was the man who had lied to her, who had used her like a breeding mare to gain an heir for his country, when the need to feel his arms around her instead of having one of them obstruct her path in such a stiff and telling way was all she cared about.

She could hardly breathe. She couldn't bring herself to look at him. But then, she didn't need to, she realised wretchedly. She could feel him, sense him, scent his clean male warmth and imbibe his very essence without using her eyes.

If she didn't keep his betrayal, his lie of omission at the forefront of her mind, she might just go mad from wanting him.

'Emily, please…won't you even speak to me?'

She wouldn't survive if he hurt her again. 'This is a difficult case—'

'I can see that. I'm sorry to intrude on your work, but your phone is always switched through to your answering service.'

'I don't have much time—'

'As I said, I apologise for approaching you like this, but I could think of no other way.'

The whole situation was a catastrophic mess, Emily realised tensely. Leaving aside her own feelings, Miranda's first solo concert was coming up in the New Year—a concert where she would be playing the violin Alessandro had loaned to her.

'Emily—' Alessandro's voice had roughened, and was considerably louder. It brought her back to full attention. 'I have to talk to you,' he insisted. 'But not here; not like this, please.'

Emily's face flushed red as she stared up at him. She had never thought to hear so needy, so desperate a note in his voice.

'I know I've let you down—'

He had found out she knew about the baby clause; she could hear it in his voice...in what he didn't say. She had to hear his explanation. 'I feel as if I hardly know you any more,' she murmured, speaking her thoughts out loud.

'Well, I only know that I've hurt you, Emily. And that I can't let it end like this. I can't go on any more without your forgiveness.'

My forgiveness...my forgiveness, Emily thought wretchedly as her hand moved instinctively to cover her stomach. 'If you could give me the rest of the afternoon...'

'You have to eat,' he said instantly. 'Why don't we meet at my hotel for dinner? Eight o'clock? You won't want a late night.'

'Yes... Yes, please.'

'Shall I send a car for you?'

Her mind was in freefall. She needed time to think, to prepare, to plan how she was going to tell him about their baby. 'No, that's fine. I'd rather you didn't.'

Emily stood motionless, watching Alessandro take the steps down to the foyer. He moved with long, purposeful strides, his head held high, and the gaze of every woman, and not a few of the men, zoned in on his rapid departure.

Only when he had gone through the doors that led to the street did she begin very slowly to follow after him. He was still her husband...and in spite of everything she knew without doubt she still loved him.

She fought hard in court...wasn't her marriage worth fighting for, too?

The invisible men, as Emily had learned to call them, had obviously telephoned ahead, as the door to Alessandro's suite swung open before she could even knock.

As he stood back to let her pass the temptation to touch him, to look into his eyes, was almost irresistible. But she could feel remoteness coming off him in waves, pushing her away.

Shrugging off her winter coat and scarf, she put them on a chair first, and then, having first drawn a deep, steadying breath, she turned around. 'How are you, Alessandro?'

He looked amazing. Black trousers, black round-necked cashmere sweater framing his tan...

'How am I?' he said, dipping his head to give her a keen look. 'That's an interesting question, coming from you, Emily.'

Picking up her coat and scarf, he walked across the room and deposited them inside what must be a cloakroom.

'Apparently I'm some sort of monster,' he said with his back to her, 'since my wife walked out on me without a word of explanation.'

CHAPTER TEN

THE expression in her husband's eyes frightened Emily. It was as if all the angry frustration, all the bafflement possible had been captured and condensed in his gaze. And as for herself... She took a steadying breath and struggled to find the words she had so carefully rehearsed in the taxi from her apartment. But she was in too much pain to speak—pain so bad it felt as if her heart had been ripped out of her chest and stamped on.

It seemed like several lifetimes before she managed to say, 'I spoke to your father—'

'And?'

She had never heard him sounding so curt, so cold. And she wasn't doing much better. Her own voice was strangulated, false. She had to wait and take a few deep breaths before she could relax enough to start again. 'He told me—'

'Told you what?' Alessandro cut in harshly. Why was it that angry words hung in the air longer than any others? he wondered furiously. The very last thing he had intended to do was shout at Emily the moment she arrived, but his emotions were in turmoil. No one knew better than he that the rest of their lives depended on what happened between them in the next few hours. 'Go on,' he said, making a conscious effort to soften his tone.

Emily knew she had to set him straight about his father's role, if nothing else. 'It was something he thought I already knew...something he believed you would have told me,' she went on, trying to stay calm. 'He said he couldn't abdicate until you...until I had your child.'

Alessandro's face went blank and unreadable—like a stranger's, Emily realised with an inward shudder. She saw

149

the change come into his eyes first: a slow infusion of pain, then guilt, and finally something approaching fear.

'I thought I'd lose you,' he said, so softly she could hardly make out the words. 'I believed it was too much for you to accept all at once. You would never have agreed—'

'You're right about that,' Emily flared, her own voice shaking with emotion. 'I would never have agreed to barter the life of a child—even for the sake of my own sister's happiness.' She stopped. There was an iron band around her chest; she could hardly breathe. She wheeled away from him in bewilderment. 'I thought you loved me,' she cried accusingly.

In a couple of strides Alessandro had crossed the room and grabbed her chin, forcing her to look up at him.

'Don't you understand anything, Emily? I do love you. More than you will ever know. No! Look at me!' he insisted when she tried to turn her head away. 'I love you,' he repeated fiercely. 'I have loved you from the first moment I set eyes on you. I don't suppose you believe in love at first sight; neither did I, before I met you—' He shook his head and looked away, as if the emotion was too much for him to bear. 'I was frightened I might lose you if I told you the truth. I can see now that I was wrong. But if you won't accept my apology then I don't know what I can do…what I will do without you…'

'When would you have told me?' Emily demanded tensely when he'd let her go.

'If you had become pregnant there would have been no need to tell you,' he admitted with a short, humourless laugh.

'That's very blunt.'

'Yes,' he agreed bitterly.

'And if I hadn't become pregnant?' She needed to choose her words with more care, Emily realised distractedly, still agonising over her own startling news and wondering how she was going to break it to him. 'When...when would you have told me?'

'I'm not sure,' Alessandro admitted bluntly. 'I needed time...time to be sure you trusted me before I could identify the *right time*.'

'I see.'

'No, you don't,' he said, taking hold of her again. 'I was wrong. I can see that now. I should have told you right away. I need you to forgive me, Emily. I need you to accept my apology so that we can rebuild everything I have damaged, however long it takes... Emily?'

When she told him about their baby—what would he think of her then? Emily wondered numbly. He had been so honest, so frank and giving in his own apology, while she harboured the greatest secret of them all, jealously guarding it inside her like some precious gift she had not yet chosen to bestow. Instead of making it easier for her, Emily realised, Alessandro's openness had only made it all the more difficult.

'This isn't easy for you,' he said. 'I realise that. You need time to think. I'm going to take you home. No, I insist,' he said, holding up his hands. 'I'll keep in touch, and when you're ready—'

'No,' Emily said urgently—this wasn't supposed to happen. 'I don't want you to take me home.' This was the moment. She needed to tell him...whatever the consequences might be for herself.

She could see how pale he was beneath his tan, hear the enormous pressure he was forced to endure because of her reflected in his voice. She couldn't bear it. She couldn't bear to see him suffering and know that she was the cause.

'Don't apologise to me. We're both at fault,' she said, the words all coming out in a rush. 'We had no chance to get to know each other—'

'Listen to yourself,' he said. 'You're half-frantic with worry, and all because of me. There's no excuse for my behaviour,' he said harshly, cutting off any chance she might have had to say more. 'I'm going to get your coat—'

'No, Alessandro, wait—'

But he was already back, and helping her into it. 'I'm taking you home, Emily. I've upset you enough for one night. I won't hear any arguments.'

But her home was in Ferara, Emily thought as he ushered her out of the door. With Alessandro…

'I don't want to pressure you,' he said, releasing his hold on her arm at the door to her apartment. 'I've put you through enough. If you come back to me, Emily, it will be for ever, so I want you to be sure.'

'We never expected it to come to this.' Emily shivered suddenly as he kissed her on both cheeks, as if in that moment the shadow between them had made itself visible.

'We never expected to fall in love,' Alessandro countered softly, shooting her a wry half-smile as he turned to go.

Emily had thought she'd had sleepless nights before, but she'd been wrong. *This*…this was a sleepless night.

Finally she gave up on sleep altogether, and, clambering out of bed, crossed the wood-strip floor to the enclosed balcony that had been one of her main reasons for buying the riverside flat.

She could never have anticipated that her meeting with Alessandro would go so badly wrong…that she would be so lacking in force, in ability to put her point across. She was ashamed of the way she had caved in, Emily realised tensely. But the atmosphere had been so fraught, their reunion so fragile… If Miranda had been at home they would have talked things over. But Miranda had already embarked on a tour of the provinces that preceded her debut in the capital… And, though she had lost track of time, Emily knew it was the middle of the night—Miranda would be asleep.

Wrapping herself in a mohair throw, she curled up on one of the sofas and stared bleakly out at the river, stretching darkly into the distance like an oily rag. The main road was freshly salted with icy sleet and made her long all the more for the mellow colours and warmth and sunshine of Ferara.

Whatever time it was, her mind was still buzzing. She hadn't managed to sleep since Alessandro had left a little after twelve. Burrowing deeper into the soft throw, she squeezed her eyes tightly shut and wished harder than she had ever wished for anything in her life that things could be different... Wasn't cheating a man out of his child on a par with cheating a defenceless elderly couple out of their life savings?

The unmistakable sound of her laptop signalling incoming mail broke into that disturbing thought, and, peering at the clock, she saw that it still wasn't quite four-thirty in the morning.

Racking her brains for friends in the Antipodes, or even late-working New Yorkers, she padded across acres of wood-strip flooring into the open-plan space that constituted her living area. Leaning over her desk, she clicked the mouse and brought up the screen.

Tight schedule—now leaving first thing tomorrow— make your decision about returning to Ferara—let me know soonest—Alessandro.

Her heart gave a little flurry just to know that he was awake—and thinking of her. But, reading the e-mail again, she went cold. She couldn't leave London. There was still the court case to settle. And it wasn't going well; there were all sorts of outstanding issues.

Fingers flying, she typed a reply and sent it straight back.

*I can't make that sort of decision yet. I have a tight
schedule, too.*

She hovered anxiously over the machine, realising that
he couldn't read her mind and know all the difficulties she
was facing at work. Out of context the message would just
seem petulant.

His reply came through right away.

I understand you need more time.

Frowning a little, Emily pulled out her chair and sat
down in front of the computer.

*The case I'm involved in is proving more complex than
I had anticipated.*

This time she gave herself a little more space before
touching 'send', and checked what she had typed again for
possible misunderstandings. She hugged herself as she
waited for Alessandro's reply. It didn't take long.

When will your case be completed?
Difficult to say. Two weeks max, at a guess.
Before the holidays?
Hopefully before the holidays.
I'll send the jet.
No need.
But that's a yes?

She hesitated about ten heartbeats—a split second.

Yes.
I'll send the jet.

Emily sat staring at the screen until dawn sketched rosy fingers across a sullen, snow-laden sky, but there was no more mail that night from Alessandro.

Touching the screen by his name before she switched off, she wondered what lay ahead for them both with the holidays approaching fast. The possibility of seeing him again was the only present she had on her Christmas list.

Unforeseen delay in resolving case—no chance I can make it for Christmas.
Sorry.
Emily

Alessandro took out his frustration on his desk with a blow so hard he found himself nursing his fist, wondering if he had broken anything.

He had chosen e-mail specifically as a mode of communication to give them both a breather. A voice on a telephone could reveal so much...too much. E-mail was brief and to the point. And utterly without emotion—or should be...had always been...up to now.

Hating himself for putting his heart on the line, he stabbed back.

What's the problem?

Sitting in her office, surrounded by papers, Emily rested her forehead on the heel of her hand and stared at the screen. She felt sick from early pregnancy blues augmented by a very real concern for her clients. It was beginning to look as though she would win the case, but the chance of securing some money for the elderly couple was appearing increasingly unlikely.

The likelihood of reaching any type of satisfactory conclusion before the long drawn-out holiday season interrupted everything was negligible.

She touched the screen by Alessandro's question, as if it was possible to draw some comfort from him by doing that, then pulled her hand away. Having him at the other end of the line, waiting for her reply, was no compensation for having him with her. And knowing he was out there somewhere, but not knowing where, made her feel lonelier than ever. It made her feel weak and vulnerable—something she could have done without. Because that was no help to her elderly clients, whose future peace of mind lay in the scrambled mounds of documentation scattered across her desk. But the least she owed Alessandro was an explanation for staying in London over Christmas…

Freemantle has no money—no assets—no nothing. Can't leave my clients in the lurch—have to keep trying.

Try what? Emily thought, absentmindedly dispatching the message before she had quite finished it. If Toby Freemantle was stony broke—

Her eyes flashed to the screen as Alessandro's reply came up.

Trace his maternal grandmother's will. She left him all her art treasures. His brother boasted to me that whenever creditors came to call the paintings were stored in their mother's attic. Keep me informed. Alessandro.

Instantly alert, Emily straightened up, and tapped in. *Thank you—I will.*

And then, not because she thought it was prudent, or that he would even care, but because her heart took over, she lapsed into a personal style.

*I hope you have a good Christmas, Alessandro—say
sorry from me to your father. Emily.*

Making a sound close to a tiger in a rage, Alessandro
replied.

*Sure to—Father in South Africa, looking at rose gar-
dens—signing off, Alessandro.*

Alessandro had been right, Emily thought, waving off two
very happy elderly people, her hands clutching tight the
bottle of champagne they had insisted on buying for her.
She wouldn't drink it now, because she was almost four
months pregnant, but it signified their peace of mind, and
that was all that mattered. She would take it to the
Christmas gathering at her parents' house.

Thanks to Alessandro, the works of art she had tracked
down with the help of the fraud squad had raised millions
at auction, brightening the London scene on the run-up to
the big Christmas shut-down. There had been more than
enough money to satisfy all the creditors and even set Toby
Freemantle up for life—when he came out of jail.

As the elderly couple disappeared around the corner, arm
in arm, she knew her first e-mail had to be to Alessandro.
She had to thank him, let him know the outcome of the
sale.

Great news—do you ski?

Rocking back on her chair, Emily stared at the screen
again.

Almost as hesitantly as she might have said the words,
she tapped in, *Yes—why?* then clicked the mouse and
waited.

We have issues to resolve sooner rather than later. I plan to spend Christmas in a small village called Lech, in the Arlberg region of Austria. I'd like you to join me.

Emily's heart leapt at the invitation. But she had promised to attend her mother's famous Christmas lunch, she remembered, frowning.

'Of course you must go with Alessandro,' Miranda insisted, when Emily telephoned her twin to run the idea past her. 'You don't think Mother will try and make you stay in England if she thinks there's a chance of a *rapprochement* with Alessandro, do you?'

'No, but—'

'But what?'

'I haven't told him yet,' Emily said tensely, tracing her still flat stomach.

'Are you going to wait until he can see for himself?'

'I don't know. I—'

'Look, Emily,' Miranda said, beginning to sound impatient. 'I've got to go to rehearsal. You're the one who always knows what to do. You know what you have to do now. You're just allowing emotion to get in the way of clear thinking.'

Emily allowed herself a wry smile. 'Are you surprised?'

'That you've let things go this far? Yes. It's a fact that Alessandro wasn't entirely open with you. Get over it. Aren't you doing just the same to him now? If you want the truth, it looks like a bad case of double standards.'

'Please don't be angry with me. You know I've forgiven him. But he wouldn't give me a chance to explain—'

Miranda heaved a heavy sigh down the phone, cutting her off. 'I'm not angry with you, Emily. I'm just worried about you—and Alessandro. Please say you'll go.'

'I can't just turn up pregnant in Lech.'

'No, you can't,' Miranda agreed thoughtfully. 'So maybe I'll—'

'No! Don't you dare say a word to him,' Emily warned. 'This is something I have to handle by myself.'

'Promise?'

'Have I ever let you down?'

'This would be one hell of a time to make it a first,' Miranda said bluntly.

Emily could feel her sister's concern winging down the phone-line. 'I won't let you down, Miranda. I promise.'

After doing her research, Emily knew why her husband had chosen Lech for his winter retreat—the townsfolk were so used to visiting royalty no one paid the slightest attention to one more prince arriving for the winter sports. She realised now that any type of anonymity was preferable to none.

It wouldn't take her long to pack a suitcase, book a flight—

She swung around in surprise when the doorbell rang. She wasn't expecting anyone and, apart from kicking off her high-heeled shoes, she hadn't even changed her clothes after the final meeting with her clients. Checking her appearance in the mirror, she pulled a face and made a vain attempt to capture some of her long hair into the slide at the back of her head. Reaching the door, she opened it and gasped.

'Alessandro! Wh—?'

'May I come in?'

'Yes, of course. But—' Her bewildered gaze followed him across the wide expanse of floor to the picture windows, where he turned and stood looking around him, the corners of his mouth pressing up in an appreciative grin.

'This is very nice,' he said, looking around the apartment.

'Thank you,' she said. Shutting the door, Emily leaned back against it. Her heart-rate had gone into orbit...she needed a minute. No, a minute wasn't nearly long enough, she realised, staring at her husband.

His charcoal-grey vicuña overcoat had been left open to reveal a black V-neck cashmere sweater and black trousers, and his inky-black hair in its customary off-duty disarray fell over familiar dark gold eyes—eyes that were presently trained on her with amused speculation.

'I don't understand—I was just e-mailing you—'

'And you presumed I was in Ferara?'

She could see he was trying not to smile. 'Well, yes. I wanted to share the good news with you the moment I found out myself.' Even as she spoke the words it was as if a double helping of conscience had reared up to mock her.

'Good to know you were thinking about me,' Alessandro commented, slanting her a look.

He didn't miss a thing, she realised edgily, moving away from the door.

'I was just around the corner in my hotel at the time,' Alessandro said, clearly trying to put her at her ease. 'What about Lech? Are you packed?'

'I haven't booked a seat yet.'

'Booked a seat?'

It took a whole new mind-set to deal with Alessandro, Emily reminded herself. Of course he would have flown to England in his own jet. 'You came for me?' she said hesitantly.

'Looks like it,' he agreed dryly.

'Can you give me half an hour? Here—let me take that for you,' she said as he began to shrug off his overcoat. 'Can I get you anything while you wait? A drink?'

'Just get ready,' he said. 'I'll wait.'

'Wait out here, then,' she suggested, opening the window to the balcony. 'It's got a fabulous view, and—'

He caught her to him as she went past, dragging her close and shutting her up with a long, deep kiss that wiped her mind clean of everything but him. But even as she softened against him he gently but very firmly pushed her away.

'Go,' he whispered. 'We have a non-negotiable take-off slot. It's nearly Christmas—or had you forgotten?'

Alessandro took her through a sumptuous wood-panelled entrance hall into a quaint reception area decorated in typical Austrian alpine style, with red gingham curtains edged with heavy ecru lace. Garlands of dried flowers hung on the walls, and in a huge stone grate a roaring log fire acted like a magnet to the people clustered around, exchanging tall stories from their day on the slopes.

There wasn't a photographer in sight, Emily noticed with relief as she watched her husband complete the formalities and return to her side with a huge old-fashioned carved wooden key-fob.

'When we get to the room I suggest you take a bath,' he said as they strolled through the hotel to the guests' accommodation. 'It's too late to sort out skis for you tonight, and mine are already here. So we'll take it easy—have dinner, chat…'

Chat. Emily nodded and smiled, but her insides were churning. There would be no more running away from the truth now. But at least he was giving her time to prepare.

As he propelled her into the lift Alessandro's hands were around her waist. His touch was electrifying. And suddenly all Emily knew, all she could think of, was that she wanted him…

'Are we going to eat in the restaurant or our room?' she asked as he pressed the button for their floor.

As an attempt to kick-start the logical side of her brain it was a pretty pathetic gambit—and she knew it—but with Alessandro so close, and no one else around, it was all she could manage.

'Why, Principessa,' he murmured softly, letting his

hands slip down slowly over her thighs as the lift began to rise, 'are you hoping to seduce me?'

Resisting the temptation to lean back into him, Emily made a soft, double-barrelled sound of denial. And when he moved to drag her close she turned to face him, warning him off with her eyes. 'We have things to discuss,' she said, realising uncomfortably that he didn't know the half of it.

'Of course,' he agreed, with a small mocking bow.

But she could see the dark, smouldering desire in his eyes and the arrogant twist to his lips that proved he was remembering other occasions when the secrets between them had lain dormant and could not douse their passion.

She was relieved when the lift slowed at their floor. The atmosphere in the confined space had grown so thick with sexual tension she could feel herself drowning in it—and losing all sense of what she had come to do...to say to him. But when he stopped outside one of the heavy oak doors he rested his hand on the wall, trapping her.

'We have to share, I'm afraid. I could only get one suite because—'

'It's Christmas?' she supplied crisply, channelling all her apprehension into one snippy remark.

But he wouldn't be provoked, only stared at her lazily, forcing Emily to wonder how long she could remain immune to his unique scent...sandalwood, musk...man. And his slow smile was producing a sensory overload that made her want to drag him into the room and to hell with everything else.

But if he was in the mood for playing games... 'As we still have issues to resolve, I hope there's more than one bed in the suite?'

'Didn't I just say we'd have to share?'

'A suite...you said we had to share a suite. You didn't say anything about sharing a bed.' How come that had come out in a provocative murmur, sparing him the scolding she had intended?

'Why shouldn't we share a bed? After all, we are man and wife.'

'I hope for your sake the sofa's comfy,' Emily said, fighting to keep her voice steady as she took the key from his hand.

Just as she had feared, when she opened the door one large bed dominated the room. Spying her luggage in one corner, she hurried over to it and picked up the smallest bag. 'See you after my bath, Alessandro—'

The heel of his hand shot out, slamming into the bathroom door as she tried to close it.

'Perhaps I'd better warn you—these doors don't lock.'

'I'm sure I can trust you to be a gentleman.' Their faces were so close she could have kissed him. But, giving the door one final push, she almost sank to her knees with relief when Alessandro allowed it to close.

Inside the privacy of the marble-clad bathroom, Emily let out a long, shaky breath. With every hour that passed it became harder to tell Alessandro about the baby. She stabbed a furious glance at herself in the mirrored wall. Just when had she become such a coward? If she couldn't face up to it by the time she'd had her bath she didn't have anything to offer him—or their unborn child. It would be better for all of them if she took the next flight out of Austria…

Dinner was conducted with every outward show of restraint, whilst inwardly fires raged inside the two people facing each other across the cosy country-style table.

There was nothing remotely cosy about the workings of Emily's mind as she forked up the last scrap of home-made *sachertorte*, but she managed to hide her angst behind enthusiasm for the food.

'I've never tasted a better chocolate cake in all my life,'

she said, as if they were two friends on a casual outing. 'If I stayed here for long I'd be huge.'

'You have put on a little weight,' Alessandro commented, slanting her a look as he laid down his own fork with his own cake half-eaten. And she looked better for it, he thought. She looked like some luscious fruit that was ripe and ready for eating. He swiped the linen napkin across his lips to hide his smile at his mind's meanderings. 'Not that it's a bad thing—in my opinion the extra weight suits you.'

Emily remained silent. She hadn't noticed any changes to her body—not yet. She hadn't weighed herself for a while, but...'

'Have you finished?' Alessandro said, easing his position on the carved wooden chair. 'I thought we'd have coffee sent up to the room. That way we can talk in private.'

'Fine,' Emily said quickly. She wanted to confide in him—tell him everything—and this was the best opportunity there'd been. She was already moving to her feet before Alessandro realised she meant to go right away.

'OK, OK,' he said with amusement, reaching the door a pace in front of her to open it. 'I get the message.'

Emily turned to him as they stepped into the lift. 'Do you, Alessandro?'

'I think so.'

And this time when he dragged her close she hadn't the will to resist.

Binding her hands around his neck, Emily dragged him to her with a harsh, unguarded sound of need, opening her mouth against his lips, begging for possession.

His kisses weren't enough. But as her hands flew to the buckle on his belt he dragged them away. Ramming her into the corner of the lift, he kept her wedged there while he reached across to push the lever that would stop the antiquated contraption between floors. Then, wrenching up her slither of a skirt with one hand, he tugged off her tiny lace thong with the other.

Swinging her up, he wrapped her legs around his waist and, supporting her buttocks in hands grown firm and demanding, he entered her in one thrusting stroke, pausing only to utter a contented groan as the moist heat of her body enveloped him completely. Then, pounding into her, he answered her calls for more, increasing speed and force until she let out a long, grateful, wavering cry as the violent spasms engulfed her in sensation.

'And that's just the appetiser,' he murmured, nuzzling his face into her hair as he lowered her to the ground. 'Now get dressed,' he added sternly, bending to scoop up her discarded clothing. 'It wouldn't do for the Princess of Ferara to be seen without her knickers.'

This wasn't quite how she had pictured their first confrontation, Emily realised. But it wasn't easy to resist, when Alessandro could make her laugh at the most inappropriate moments…make her feel happy, and safe, and desired.

He hit the start lever while she struggled into her clothes. And when they reached their sumptuous suite, he slammed the door shut behind them with one hand and dragged her against him roughly with the other.

'One bed OK for you now?' he demanded huskily.

'Bed, floor, lift…' Emily breathed seductively against his mouth. 'It's all the same to me, *mi amor*.'

As he backed her towards the fluffy cream sheepskin rug in front of the roaring log fire she almost forgot what had driven her from the restaurant at such speed. But, sensing her minute mood-shift, Alessandro drew to a halt in the middle of the room.

'Coffee? Talk? Or…?'

Or would be nice, Emily thought, wavering a little, still reeling from the aftershocks of his attentions in the lift. But her rational mind insisted they couldn't go on like this. She had to tell him…tell him now.

'Coffee, please,' she managed.

'Sure?'

'No. Yes. I—'

'Coffee it is,' Alessandro said, as if nothing untoward had occurred between them since leaving the restaurant. Releasing her to switch on some subdued lighting, he poured out two cups from the coffee tray that had been left for them some time during their extended journey between floors.

How to begin? Emily wondered, murmuring thanks as she took the cup and saucer from him.

'So. What do you want to do about these baby issues? The contract?' he prompted. 'I presume that's what all this is about?'

Emily sank down onto a small leather sofa to one side of the inglenook fireplace, stunned into silence by his remark. There were no *baby issues*. There was only a small and very vulnerable child, growing a little more inside her each day.

CHAPTER ELEVEN

THE phrase *baby issues* would not have offended her so deeply had she not been pregnant with Alessandro's baby, Emily realised. Impending motherhood had already imbued her with an overwhelming desire to protect their unborn child from everything—even the most innocent remark. And she was sure Alessandro's remark was innocent. It hadn't taken her long to discover that pregnancy hormones equalled emotional incontinence, and right now she didn't trust herself to speak in case something irrational and angry burst from her mouth.

'Well, if you won't speak to me,' he said, butting into her thoughts, 'I don't know what else I can say.' Throwing up his hands in frustration, he crossed to the window, where he stood staring out at the ghostly shadow of the snow-capped mountain that loomed like a sentinel over the village at night.

And now he was angry—and her silence was to blame, Emily realised, sensing tension so thick in the air it hung like smog, keeping each of them isolated in their own lonely space. But how could she discuss their baby as if it was nothing more than a clause in a contract? She stared in dismay at the huge double bed that only seemed to mock her desire to resume normal relations with her husband.

'Alessandro—'

He turned and looked at her, his head slightly dipped and a furrow of concentration scoring a deep line between his eyes.

It was as if his vision cleared and he had time to study his wife properly for the first time in weeks, Alessandro realised. She looked so weary—exhausted, he amended. Why hadn't he noticed that before?

'Don't be angry,' Emily said softly. 'I really need to be with you tonight.'

His head jerked in surprised response, but he hid his feelings quickly. How had it come to this?

'Where else would you be?' he said gently, reaching out his hands. And when she took them he drew her into his arms.

He held her in his arms all night, dressed in the bizarre outfit it turned out was all she had brought with her—a long baggy tee shirt, with the logo showing only faintly on the front after too many washes, and a pair of stripy pyjama bottoms that trailed over her feet.

He had made no comment when she came out of the bathroom after her shower. And said nothing more when she climbed into the high, comfortable four-poster-bed and pulled the sheets up to her chin. He just climbed in after her, wearing a pair of boxer shorts for the sake of decency, rolled onto his back, and switched out the light.

He wasn't sure exactly when she edged towards him, only that she had...and he stroked the hair back from her brow and kissed her while she was sleeping, as she whimpered in his arms from some deep-seated despair.

He must have dropped off some time during the night, because he woke to find her at the window, staring out, peering from side to side as if there was something quite extraordinary happening outside.

Turning, as if she felt his waking presence as keenly as if he had spoken, she said,

'Alessandro, I think we're snowed in.'

Emily waited as he stretched and yawned noisily, then sat up and raked through his wayward black hair in a hopeless attempt to tame it.

Padding across the room to join her, he leaned his fists

on the windowsill and gazed out across what had become
in a few short hours a featureless snowscape.

'No chance of anyone leaving Lech today,' he murmured.

Where there had been pavements and cars and railings,
marking the banks of the river that wound its way through
the village, there was only a uniform blanket of deep white
snow.

'Hungry?' he said, not appearing too concerned by this
turn of events.

'A little,' Emily admitted, trying to ignore the fact that
her husband was naked, apart from his hip-skimming boxer
shorts, and standing very close.

'I'll ring down—have them send something up to us. I
feel lazy today. We might as well take it easy…after all,
we're not going anywhere.'

Emily moved away to put on some more logs and stoke
the dying embers of the fire. The fact that they had slept
in the same bed together and he hadn't attempted to make
love to her had left her feeling restless and uneasy. Was he
still angry with her? Maybe he didn't want her any more.
Maybe he was going to reinstate the celibacy clause in their
agreement. Maybe he would find that all too easy.

'How long do you think we're here for?' she said, pulling
herself together, knowing she sounded edgy, as if she didn't
want to be snowed in with him, when nothing could be
further from the truth.

But Alessandro seemed not to notice. He had the phone
in his hand and was gesturing for her to wait as he got
through to Room Service. He spoke rapidly in
German…something else she hadn't known about her husband, she realised, feeling panic sweep over her. The fact
was, she didn't know much about him at all.

'That's settled,' he said, replacing the receiver. 'Relax,
Emily. There's nothing we can do. We might just as well
settle back and enjoy the break. Why don't you stop prowl-

ing around the room? Go and have a nice long soak in the bath while we're waiting for breakfast to arrive.'

Did he want to put distance between them? Emily swallowed down the fear that had lodged in her throat. All her emotions seemed to be in turmoil—all the time; every little thing seemed to assume crisis proportions. 'How long?' she said again.

'Breakfast? Or—?'

'No, not breakfast,' she flashed back. 'You know what I'm talking about, Alessandro.'

'Do I, Emily?' he said. 'I know you're very prickly this morning, and over-sensitive. Is it something I've done—or not done?'

Her face flamed as the thought of what he had not done. And when she saw the faintly ironic shadow in his slanting amber gaze she knew for sure he was reading her mind.

'You seem to be in a great hurry to leave Lech,' he pressed. 'Do you have an urgent appointment to keep elsewhere?'

'No, of course not.' Emily's mind lurched back on track. 'I came here to be with you—to thank you properly for helping me with that case.'

Is that all? Alessandro thought as he snatched up his robe. Thrusting his arms into the sleeves, he threw her a cynical look. So, Emily only wanted to thank him for his help with her case? It was almost worse than being told she had only come for the sex. 'To answer to your question,' he said coolly, securing the belt, 'walking parties may be able to leave here quite soon with a local guide. Others, who are not quite so desperate to return to reality, can stay on at the hotel until the road down to Zurs is cleared.'

'Oh...' Emily said, peering distractedly out of the window.

'Which category of snowbound guest do you fall into, Emily?'

She moved back towards the fireplace, where the logs were well ablaze. 'I'm staying,' she said without hesitation.

'And we'll do what?'

Now it was Alessandro's turn to sound as if he was having difficulty reining in his feelings—as if he was determined that the emotional rollercoaster ride she had subjected him to had made its final run. It was time to build bridges between them, Emily realised, before the moment was lost for ever...

'I don't know,' she said, determined to find something that would bring them close again. 'Tell each other stories?'

His gaze narrowed thoughtfully, and then, to her relief, softened a little.

'For instance?'

'How about the one you never finished...the one about this ring,' she suggested, holding out her hand so that the central stone in the beautiful old piece of jewellery glowed like a drop of crimson blood in the firelight.

Their relationship was like a ball of wool that had become hopelessly tangled, Emily thought as he came to sit down on the sofa while she chose a spot on the rug. Telling each other stories wouldn't have been her first choice for Christmas Eve activities, but it was somewhere to start teasing out the knots.

'You reached the point where Caterina found the ring and believed it was a sign from Rodrigo,' she prompted.

'OK,' Alessandro said, settling back. 'So Caterina was forced to accept that her lover had drowned. But she decided she couldn't lock herself away in a religious community after all, and would live her life as Rodrigo would have wanted her to.'

'How could she know what he wanted?'

'Because that was the moment she realised she was pregnant with his child.'

Emily's glance flashed up, but there was no separate

agenda, she saw thankfully—he was only recounting a much-loved story.

'Caterina put Rodrigo's ring on her finger and returned to Ferara to fulfil her destiny. And every Princess of Ferara has worn the ring you have on your finger since that day.'

'That's the most romantic thing I ever heard,' Emily admitted, turning the ring around her finger so that the flames from the fire seemed to imbue it with life...or with challenge, maybe... And now it was her turn to come up with an equivalent tale. How would she begin? *Alessandro, I'm going to tell you the story of a baby*?

'I'm sure the history of that ring has been embellished over the years until it's little more than a fairytale,' Alessandro said, misreading the questions in her mind. 'Emily? Where are you going?'

'To have that bath you suggested.' To give herself time.

'You don't get out of telling your story that easily,' Alessandro warned. 'I'll order breakfast while you're reclining in bubbles, then it's your turn.'

Putting a CD on to play, Emily slipped the slim volume of poetry Alessandro had given to her, with the Christopher Marlowe rose from her wedding bouquet pressed inside it, between his jeans and jumper, where he was sure to find it, before heading for the bathroom.

'What are you doing?' he said suspiciously as she darted about the room.

'Nothing.'

'This music—?'

Her shoulders dropped with relief that the first part of her plan hadn't failed. 'Miranda's first commercial recording.'

'It's quite remarkable,' Alessandro murmured, remaining very still as he listened.

'It was brought out in time for Christmas. This is the first copy off the press. Miranda wanted you to have it...she signed it for you.' Hurrying to his side, Emily pressed the empty case into his hands. 'I suppose I should have wrapped it up—'

'No, this is perfect,' Alessandro insisted. And before she could get away he caught hold of her hands and raised them to his lips. 'Go and have your bath, Emily—and don't be long.'

The message in his eyes was unmistakable…irresistible. Emily held his gaze. Her heart was thundering in her chest. It was going to be all right. Everything was going to be all right…

'Do I have to?' she protested after her bath, when they were both sitting by the fire again. 'I'm fine with facts, but I'm absolutely hopeless at telling stories.'

'Then if you can't play the game,' Alessandro warned, 'you'll have to pay a forfeit.'

There was only a glint of humour in his eyes, but it was enough for Emily to feel as if the whole world had revolved on its axis and returned them to a moment in time before secrets had driven a wedge between them. 'A forfeit?'

'Certainly,' he murmured, in a voice that hovered between stern and seductive. Reaching towards her, he brushed a wayward strand of hair back from her face with one finger. 'And I get to choose what that forfeit should be.'

Emily's nerves were jangling with awareness.

She was acutely conscious of the crackling of the logs in the grate and the barely discernible patter of snow against the window as his hand moved to cup the back of her head and draw her close. As his warm, musky man-scent invaded the clean air she made no move to resist when he gathered her into his arms.

'Thank you for the rose,' he whispered against her lips, and even though his eyes were half closed Emily could see how bright they flared with passion, and with love.

'And for the gift of music. I can't think of a better Christmas present.'

'Except this,' she murmured seductively, drawing him down with her onto the soft rug in front of the fire. It felt like a homecoming, a long awaited return. She was lost from the moment his lips touched her body. And when his tongue began to work on her nipples there was no possibility of turning back.

Moving lower, Alessandro freed the fastenings on her jeans and took them down, together the tiny thong she was wearing. Naked now, Emily moved sinuously beneath him as he covered her waist and her belly with tiny teasing bites, before moving on to the insides of her thighs. Running her hands appreciatively over his back, she felt bereft when he left her briefly to tug off his clothes.

There was nothing wrong in having your husband make love to you, Emily reassured herself when something dark and unfathomable niggled at the back of her mind—nothing but the knowledge that you were really four months pregnant with his child and he didn't know yet! She pulled away as his kisses grew a lot more intimate.

'What?' he said, but there was already a hard look in his eyes—as if he knew, Emily saw apprehensively. But how could he know? 'You taste different.'

She was so thrown by the comment that it took her a few moments to rally her thoughts. 'Different?' she muttered.

'You heard what I said.'

The change in Alessandro's voice, in his mood, was frightening. Backing away, Emily sat up and hugged her knees to her chest. 'How do you mean, different?'

His eyes had narrowed and his gaze was calculating. 'I can't list the contributory factors like a recipe—'

'The *contributory factors*?' Emily demanded, reaching nervously for her clothes. 'Don't ever accuse *me* of lawyer-speak again!' Her attempt to lighten the mood skittered across the frigid silence between them, making no improvement. Stumbling awkwardly around, she pulled on her clothes. 'I should never have come,' she exclaimed when Alessandro made no response. 'I'm going to call down to Reception and find out when that guide will be leaving the village—'

'Put that down!'

One minute he was on the rug gazing up at her; the next he was standing beside her with the telephone in his hand.

'I think you owe me an explanation, Emily.'

'No—why—?' she said, backing away from the look in his eyes.

'I think you know. How many months pregnant are you, Emily? Why didn't you tell me the moment you found out?'

Emily's head spun and the ground seemed to come up to meet her. This was the very last thing she had wanted. The hurt in his voice jabbed at her mind like so many thorns.

'How long were you prepared to wait before you told me?'

'Stop!' She put her hands over her ears, as if she couldn't bear to hear another word. 'Please, Alessandro, stop firing questions at me. I can't think—'

'That's perfectly obvious.'

She glanced at him, then quickly looked away. Everything that had been between them minutes earlier had been replaced by an expression on his face that chilled her to the marrow. 'I'm sorry—'

'You set a great scene; I'll hand you that,' he said bitterly, swiping one angry hand across the back of his neck.'

'A scene? What do you mean?'

'The music, the poetry, the rose,' he flashed accusingly. 'I would have preferred honesty…and from the start. Why couldn't you just trust me?'

Silence swooped down between them, holding them

apart, until finally Alessandro said in a voice so low she could hardly be sure he spoke at all, 'It's my fault. That damnable clause in our country's constitution—I should have told you—'

'Stop it!' Her cry rang harshly round them after his murmured confession. 'I'm at fault, too, Alessandro,' Emily insisted desperately. 'But I was frightened—'

'Frightened?' He looked stunned. Wheeling away from her, he raked stiff fingers through his hair, and then stopped again, as if he hardly knew what he was doing. 'I can't stand this,' he admitted, shaking his head distractedly. 'I can't bear what's happening between us—and most of all I can't bear to think you were frightened of me.'

'I was never frightened of you,' Emily admitted softly. 'I was frightened of losing you…frightened of what it will mean to all of us…you, me, and especially our child…when that wretched contract comes to an end.'

'Contract!' He made a sound of disgust as he turned his face away. 'I should never have put my name to it in the first place.'

'We both entered into it in good faith,' Emily pointed out. 'We just didn't expect to have feelings get in the way of a business deal.'

'Can you ever forgive me?' he demanded tensely, staring at her as if his very life depended on her answer.

'Easily,' Emily said as she touched his arm. 'We've both made mistakes. Neither of us was prepared for how our feelings would grow. That contract was drawn up to satisfy our business instincts, not our emotions. I know I should never have left you…but when I found out about the clause in the constitution that demanded an heir before your father could abdicate I couldn't think straight—'

'And no wonder,' Alessandro admitted, very slowly drawing her into his arms, as if he needed to be certain she knew that was where she belonged. 'And now?'

'Now?'

'Can you think straight now?' he demanded softly.

'I hope so...I don't know.' She shrugged with exasperation. 'I'm just so—'

'Pregnant?' he supplied gently, a wry smile playing around his lips as he looked at her. 'This is the first time for you and the first time for me...and I am totally overwhelmed to know we are expecting a child. Your hormones must be in turmoil. Don't be so hard on yourself, Emily.'

As he dipped his head to kiss her Emily made herself pull back. 'Are you quite sure that marriage to a commoner is what you really want, Alessandro?'

'What on earth do you mean?' He drew his head back to stare at her in bemusement. 'How can you even ask me a question like that?'

'There must be so many women of noble birth who would jump at the chance—'

'And none of them is you.'

'But it can't have been easy for your father when you told him.'

Alessandro placed his finger over her lips. 'My father loves you, Emily.'

'You can trace your ancestors back thirty generations—'

'And half of them were warlords,' Alessandro broke in firmly. 'Brigands who snatched power from those weaker than themselves. They would be considered beyond the pale in today's society.'

'But still—'

'No, Emily,' he said firmly. 'Stop this right now. Did you know that Christopher Marlowe was the son of a shoemaker? No?' he said, staring at her intently. 'And yet he was a far greater prince than I. We quote his words more than four hundred years after his death. Who will remember my words?'

'You share your father's passion for Tudor playwrights,' Emily exclaimed, her face breaking into a smile as she relaxed at last.

'It would be impossible to live under the same roof as my father and not share his passions,' Alessandro admitted wryly. 'And one of his most profound, my love, is you.'

'And yet I've been so unreasonable—to both of you.'

'No,' Alessandro argued gently. 'You're a woman in love, a pregnant woman in love, and with a man you're still getting to know.'

'So, where do we go from here?' she said anxiously, scanning his face.

'That's the easy part,' he murmured, kissing her again.

When Alessandro insisted they should both dress for dinner that evening Emily didn't have the heart to refuse him, even though she expected the small, exclusive hotel festivities to be low-key.

The floor-length gown, packed into her suitcase at the last minute in a moment of whimsy, was of crimson silk, and emphasised the creamy whiteness of her skin. She felt particularly comfortable in it because it draped elegantly over her fuller figure. Leaving her hair to fall loosely around her shoulders, she wore the minimum of make-up— just some lip-gloss and soft grey eyeshadow to point up the brilliant jade-green of her eyes.

Wondering what Alessandro had planned, she found herself ready before him, and had to keep reminding herself that this was the man who loved her while she watched with naked appreciation as he dressed after his shower.

As he slipped into his dinner jacket, and made final adjustments to his hair in the mirror, he smiled back at her. 'I think it's time for your Christmas present,' he said, shooting her the type of look that always made her melt.

'But we've just got dressed—' She stopped at his amused glance of male awareness. The sound of his voice was enough to arouse her, she realised self-consciously. But he instead of moving towards her he made for the door.

'Alessandro?' Emily called after him anxiously. 'Where are you going?'

'I said it was time for your Christmas present now,' he reminded her. Removing what looked like a single sheet of paper from his jacket pocket, he left it on the oak dresser by the door. 'While I'm gone, you might like to cast your eyes over this,' he suggested. And then, before she had a chance to say a word, he left the room.

'Alessandro, wait—' Emily's heart gave a sickening lurch as she rushed towards the door. Swinging it open, she stared both ways down the corridor. But everything was silent. He was nowhere to be seen. Coming back into the room, she closed the door behind her. Biting her lip, she snatched up the sheet of paper and began to read.

Alessandro's bold pen-work leaped off the page at her, his blue ink resonating purposefully against the thick ivory-coloured sheet.

> *'Come live with me, and be my Love,*
> *And we will all the pleasures prove...*
> *If these delights thy mind may move! Then live with*
> *me, and be my Love.*

Two minds with but a single thought... When would she ever learn to trust him?

'Alessandro—' She whirled round as he came back into the room. 'I read the poem.'

'Did you like it?'

The confidence in his eyes thrilled her. 'Of course.' She wondered if they would ever make it down for dinner...

'So, I chose well?'

'How can you ask?'

'I apologise for leaving you so abruptly,' he said, crossing to her side. 'I just wanted to check everything was ready.'

'Ready?' The restaurant table, she surmised, imagining how busy the hotel would be on Christmas Eve.

'Yes. We have to go out onto the balcony.'

'The balcony?'

'Do you have a wrap? Here, take this.'

Before she could stop him, Alessandro had shrugged off his own jacket and was wrapping it around her shoulders.

'You'll freeze,' Emily said, looking at him with concern. 'And why the balcony?'

'Stop asking questions,' Alessandro said, snatching up another jacket from the chair. 'We'll miss everything.'

'What?'

But Alessandro was in no mood for conversation as he hurried her outside.

The balcony overlooking the immense, mountain peaks in front of them was beautifully lit, and there were heaters, strategically placed by the hotel, so that instead of feeling cold, as she had expected to, Emily felt positively cosy as she sank into the comforting warmth of Alessandro's jacket.

The particular balcony on which they were standing went right around the hotel, and more people were joining them, Emily noticed, trickling out of their rooms in twos and—

'Mum? Dad!' she gasped, seeing who it was. Bolting towards them, she gave them each a hug, laughing with surprise. Then, at her father's gentle prompting, she turned. 'Your Royal Highness—' Turning to Alessandro, she could only shake her head in speechless delight.

'Happy Christmas, my darling,' he whispered, drawing her close to plant a tender kiss on her lips. 'Look—' he said, including everyone as he gestured towards the mountain. 'They're about to start.'

'What…what's happening?' Emily demanded softly, looking for answers to Alessandro.

'Watch the top of the mountain,' Alessandro instructed, holding her in front of him as everyone else gathered round.

At first all Emily could see was a cluster of light, right at the top of the tallest peak. 'Where's Miranda?' she whispered, as her mother came to stand next to her at the front rail of the balcony.

'Listen,' Alessandro commanded, silencing everyone.

As she waited, Emily noticed that the whole village seemed to be out on the streets; people were standing on the wall by the river and on the parapet of the bridge to get a better look. But the silence was absolute as they all stood staring at the top of the mountain.

Emily jumped closer to Alessandro when she heard a cannon being fired, somewhere far away. The loud report echoed several times, fading with each repetition as the shots bounced off each majestic rockface in turn. As it fell completely silent again a haunting melody shimmered through the crisp mountain air.

'Miranda!' Her sister's playing was uniquely beautiful and Emily would have known it anywhere. Alessandro's hold around her waist tightened a little as he burrowed his face into her neck to give her a kiss of confirmation.

The limpid sound of the solo violin was completely suited to the magical occasion, and as the sound rose through the speakers judicially placed throughout the village a murmur arose from the crowds on the streets, and then applause.

As Alessandro pointed up towards the jagged peak again Emily could see that the tiny cluster of light at the top of the mountain had split up to form a chain, and was now beginning to stream down the slopes in a long, curling ribbon of light.

'The ski instructors—each holding a torch,' Alessandro explained, and the shimmering line took its cue from the waltz Miranda was playing and swung in giant rhythmical loops across the mountainside as they came down towards the village.

'It's magical!' Emily murmured, leaning back into

Alessandro. 'The best...the very best Christmas present I could ever have.'

'Don't speak too soon,' Alessandro murmured close to her ear, so that her whole body ached for him.

After the display they ate a light meal together. Miranda joined them, flushed and happy with success, and accompanied by a rather striking-looking man who, Emily learned, having won a gold medal in the downhill ski race at the Winter Olympics, had been granted the honour of leading the torchlight procession of skiers down the mountain.

When they had finished eating Alessandro led everyone back onto the balcony, to see a barrage of fireworks screaming into the night sky, illuminating the inky blackness with endless plumes of exploding light.

'Happy Christmas, *belissima*,' he murmured, as every clock in the village struck midnight.

'Happy Christmas, Alessandro,' Emily whispered in return, wondering if anyone in the world had ever been as happy as she was.

'Alessandro! Emily!'

Releasing their hold on each other, they turned to share their happiness with Alessandro's father.

'Tonight you have made an old man very happy,' he said, opening his arms wide to embrace them both. 'This—this is what I have wished for since our first meeting in the garden,' he added, turning to address Emily. 'I would gladly cede all the privileges life has granted me to see my son Alessandro as happy as he is now—with you, Emily. And to know,' he added archly, 'that for the very first time in his life he has met his match.'

Was that a wink? Emily wondered, laughing back. She was so happy. 'I will do my best to keep things that way,' she promised, matching his conspiratorial tone.

'I know you will,' the elderly Prince declared confidently. 'And as for you, Alessandro—' He turned to face his son. 'You are a very lucky man. And now...' He turned around to draw Emily's family into the conversation. 'I think it's time we left these two lovebirds alone. I would be honoured if you would all join me in my suite for a nightcap before we retire to bed.'

Giving her mother and father a warm kiss each, Emily saved a special hug for Miranda, taking the chance to murmur, 'I like him,' when she sensed Miranda's handsome new conquest was uppermost in her twin's mind. Embracing Alessandro's father, she kissed him on both cheeks and whispered, 'Thank you for everything...and thank you especially for Alessandro.'

With a last squeeze, he released her back into the arms of her husband.

'Goodnight to you both, and a happy Christmas to everyone.' With one last expansive gesture he led Emily's family away.

Under protection of the darkness Alessandro's lips brushed lightly against Emily's neck, and then moved on to her cheek, her mouth, always light, almost testing—as if they were on a first date. The thought excited her, and she turned her face up to him to whisper, 'Don't stop.'

'You're very forward, Principessa,' he growled softly. 'Do you think we had better go inside?'

Emily's limbs felt as if they had turned into molten honey as he swept her into his arms and carried her back into their suite.

Glimpsing her reflection in the mirror at the side of the bed, she watched Alessandro release the hooks on the back of her dress. As his hands moved lower he began to kiss the back of her neck and her shoulders, until she was leaning into him, sighing with pleasure. The jewelled pins in her hair made it seem scattered with stars, and he released them so that the ebony waves tumbled over her shoulders. Her breasts were creamy against the crimson silk bodice, the shadow of her cleavage deep and dark—

'Stop looking in the mirror,' he murmured. 'I want all your attention on me.'

'That's not so hard,' Emily admitted softly as the dress fell away and he eased it over her hips.

'Beautiful,' he murmured, looking at her admiringly as his hands moved to cup her breasts. 'I should like to keep you here for ever.'

'I should have to leave the bedroom some time,' Emily teased, but she gasped as his thumb-pads stroked firmly against her nipples.

'Don't worry, I would never stop my wife doing the job she loves,' he insisted, his gold eyes darkening to sepia as he observed her arousal. 'But not tonight,' he continued softly, sternly. 'I have never wished to narrow your horizons, Emily...only to broaden them.' And then, allowing her to sink back onto the soft pillows, he stood up and pulled off his clothes.

She was definitely ready to have her horizons broadened again, Emily thought, watching him strip. A familiar lethargy was already invading her limbs, and before he even touched her shafts of sensation were streaming through her body. As he lay down beside her she feared she was about to discover if it was possible to climax from anticipation alone.

Coming closer, he caressed her ear with his lips, moving on to nibble the tender lobe. And all the while his warm breath fanned her pulse, making her long for the firmer touch of his hands, a touch he knew just how long to deny her. Then his weight was controlling her, his hands positioning her, until she could do no more than submit—a licence he made full use of until she lay calm and sated in his arms once again.

And later, much later, when Alessandro was tracing the gently curving swell of her belly with awe, he murmured, 'No more separation for us, Emily—ever. When you have a case in London we will move Court over there, so that I can be with you…the baby, too, of course,' he said, a smile coming to his face as he looked at her. 'We will buy a suitable property. I don't see a problem.'

'I'm sure you don't,' Emily said, smiling as she ran her nail-tips gently through his tousled hair, making him gasp aloud with pleasure at her touch. 'But when have you ever seen a problem that you couldn't solve, Alessandro? I don't believe a problem ever existed that could defeat you.'

'I almost met my match with you, Emily,' he admitted wryly. 'That is, of course, until I found the perfect way of dealing with you…'

She sucked in a swift breath as he entered her again, smoothly and firmly, filling her completely.

'I can't argue—' She couldn't speak. Pleasure had stolen her words away. And then his lips and tongue claimed her mouth, finally completing the task.

Could there be more happiness in all the world than this? Emily wondered late on Christmas morning, when Alessandro swung out of bed and left her briefly.

'Another Christmas present,' he explained, coming back to her side. 'And this time it's for both of us.'

'What is it?' she said excitedly.

'This,' Alessandro said, as he held out an official-looking document.

When she went to take it from him he only shook his head, and then, very slowly and deliberately, began to tear it into tiny pieces.

'What are you doing?' she asked in surprise.

'Something I should have done months ago. That is what I think of our contract.' Turning around, he dropped the tiny scraps of paper into the wastebin by the side of the bed. 'Now it can never come between us again,' he said, coming back to stretch out beside her. Drawing her into his arms, he murmured, 'I love you, Emily—my wife, my only love, mother of my child—my children,' he corrected himself with a long, lazy smile.'

'And I love you, too, Alessandro,' Emily said as she wrapped her arms around him and snuggled into his chest. 'With all my heart.'

'So,' he murmured slumberously, 'will you live with me and be my love, Emily?'

'I will,' she whispered, taking hold of his hand and placing it against her belly to feel their baby's first forceful kicks.

PRINCE VORONOV'S VIRGIN

LYNN RAYE HARRIS

*To Mom, who took me to St. Petersburg and
Moscow many years ago, and who has always
been fascinated with all things Russian.*

USA Today bestselling author **Lynn Raye Harris**
burst onto the scene when she won a writing contest
held by Mills & Boon. The prize was an editor for a
year – but only six months later, Lynn sold her first
novel. A former finalist for the Romance Writers
of America's Golden Heart Award, Lynn lives in
Alabama with her handsome husband and two
crazy cats. Her stories have been called 'exceptional
and emotional', 'intense' and 'sizzling'. You can
visit her at www.lynnrayeharris.com

CHAPTER ONE

THE SCREAM THAT SPLIT the night arrowed down Alexei Voronov's spine like a river of ice water. His senses throttled into high alert. A light snow fell steadily, dusting the cobblestones of Red Square. To the right, the Kremlin wall bordered the square. At the far end, the Spassky Tower, with its giant clock like Big Ben in London, stood out like a beacon, as did the colorful onion domes of St. Basil's nearby.

But the hour was late, and there was no movement in the square.

Until the scream echoed again.

Alexei swore. He'd been standing in the shadows of the Russian museum, waiting for his contact to arrive, but he couldn't ignore the cry. Though it was probably a fight in one of the nearby clubs, a woman screaming bloody murder while her man fought for her honor, he had to act. It was going to cost him valuable information since his contact wouldn't wait around once he discovered Alexei wasn't there.

Then again, he'd been waiting for the last half hour and the man was already fifteen minutes late. In truth, Alexei had begun to wonder if the other man had changed his mind.

It was possible.

If Alexei's adversary had got wind of his intentions, he might have paid the informant more. Though Alexei had been about to pay him a fortune. Still, he couldn't stand around and wait while a woman needed help.

Just his damned luck to be cursed with a nobility gene, even at the expense of his own best interests. He was ruthless in everything he did—except when someone was in physical danger.

Across the square from the Kremlin, the GUM department store shone brightly. Alexei started in that direction but stopped when he heard a noise. Footsteps? The echo in the empty square made it difficult to pinpoint their direction.

Before he could figure it out, a woman bolted out of the darkness. He had no time to step out of her path. She plowed into him, nearly knocking them both to the pavement.

Alexei caught her close, steadied her as he took a step backward to brace himself. It was like trying to hold a jaguar. She made no noise, but she shoved against him with all her strength, her elbow darting up toward his face. Instinctively he deflected the blow, then spun her until her back was to him, clamping a hand tightly over her mouth.

He could feel the scream gathering in her throat as he dragged her hard against him. If he let go, she'd shatter his eardrums.

"If you scream again," he said very coolly in her ear, "whoever is chasing you will find you. And I won't get in the middle of your lovers' quarrel."

Why couldn't he, for once, stay out of it? It was later than the appointed time, but his informant could still arrive. A major business deal was at stake, not to mention years of working toward a single goal that was nearly within his grasp. Missing a meeting for the sake of what was most likely a drunken spat was not part of the plan. He could turn around now and be back to the museum in a few strides.

The woman's voice was muffled as she tried to shake her head. It occurred to him she might be a tourist. There were many tourists in Moscow these days, unlike in the old days when he was growing up. He repeated it in English, just in case.

He felt the sharp intake of her breath, knew he'd guessed right. He also spoke German, French and Polish, but English had seemed the most expedient choice since nearly everyone spoke it as a second language.

"I won't hurt you," he said. "But if you scream, I will let him have you. Understand?"

She gave a quick nod as he turned her in his arms again. Her smoky eyes shimmered in the reflected light of the store. Her jacket hood had fallen back, revealing dark hair caught in a thick ponytail. Her features were fine, delicate, though the elbow she'd aimed at his head had been anything but weak. She was strong, this woman. Strong and delicate at once.

Alexei pulled his hand away from her mouth. Her expression was wary but she didn't scream.

"Please help me," she blurted, wrapping her arms around herself to ward off the late April chill. "Don't let them take me."

American.

He shouldn't be surprised, and yet something about her was wholly unexpected. Such as what an American woman who spoke no Russian was doing alone in Red Square at nearly one in the morning.

Don't get involved, Alexei.

He shoved the voice aside and concentrated on her. "Don't let who take you? The authorities? If you've done something illegal, I can't help you."

"No," she said, casting her gaze behind her before turning to him again. "It's nothing like that. I'm looking for my sister and—"

Angry shouts rang through the square. She didn't wait for his answer; she simply bolted into the night as if shot from a cannon. Alexei caught her in three strides, clamping a hand over her arm and spinning her around.

"This way," he said, hauling her toward the department store.

"It's too bright. They'll see us."

"Precisely."

Boots clomped over the cobbles, coming toward them. They had only seconds before the men made it down the hill. The slick snow was hindering them, but not much. Alexei shoved the girl back against one of the huge plate windows. She made a sound of protest.

"Put your legs around me."

Her eyebrows shot toward her hairline. "Let me go! You aren't trying to help at all—"

"Your choice, *maya krasavitsa,*" he said, stepping away. "Good luck."

"No, wait," she cried out as he started down the sidewalk. When he stopped, she let out a harsh breath. "Okay, I'll do it your way."

Alexei gave her a smile he knew was anything but friendly. "*Speciba.* We will pretend to be lovers, yes? Put your legs around me," he said as he crowded her against the window and pulled her hair free of its confinement. She wrapped her arms around his neck, obeying without argument this time. Alexei cupped her thighs, pushed into the cradle of her hips. His coat was long and hid their bodies from view. If they did this right, anyone seeing them would think they were having sex.

The American bit back a soft moan as he pushed harder against her most sensitive spot. The sound crashed through his veins like a shot of vodka. No matter how he willed it otherwise, his body was reacting.

Chert poberi.

She was small, soft and she smelled like summer in the

Urals—a hint of flowers, sunshine and cool water. Anger flashed through him. Her scent made him remember, made him feel. He didn't like feeling. He had no room for feeling.

Feeling made you weak, had the power to break you.

"Kiss me," he growled as the footsteps pounded closer. "And make it believable."

Paige blinked up at the dark stranger holding her so intimately. My God, how had she found herself in this mess? She should have gone straight to Chad the instant Emma came up missing. But she'd thought her sister had simply forgotten the time. And Paige wasn't about to disrupt her boss's evening when he'd been kind enough to allow her to bring Emma along on this trip in the first place.

Chad Russell was one of Dallas's most eligible bachelors. He was cool, handsome and wealthy. And she was his secretary. Or at least she was for this trip, since his executive secretary wasn't allowed to fly longer than three hours at a time per her doctor's orders. Mavis had a clotting disorder that could be fatal if she spent a lot of time on planes, so Paige had gotten this assignment when Chad had to choose a secretary for the trip.

She'd been thrilled, and determined to do the best job possible since he'd chosen her over some of the other secretaries with more experience. No, Chad had enough to worry about without also taking on the problem of his junior secretary's younger sister. He was here to close a major deal, not to track down an irresponsible twenty-one-year-old.

And Paige was here to prove she could handle more responsibility and that she was an asset to Russell Tech.

Lately she'd even thought Chad might be interested in her as more than just an employee. She'd tried not to read anything into his actions, but he'd taken her to lunch twice—and he'd asked about her personal life, about her sister, about many things other than work. Her heart had pounded the whole time. Chad was everything she'd ever thought attractive in a man. She'd had a small crush on him since the first moment he'd walked into the office and smiled at her nearly two years ago.

Until now she'd never thought it was anything more than futile.

Tonight, she'd let her feelings get in the way of her common sense. She should have followed her instincts and asked for Chad's help. But she was so accustomed to solving her own problems that she'd dismissed her uneasiness and was determined to find Emma on her own. And now she was kicking herself for it.

"There is no time to waste," the stranger growled.

His voice was deep, rich, the rolling of the vowels across his tongue a thing of beauty. His accent wasn't heavy, but it was distinctly Russian.

Paige's heart flipped in her chest as he squeezed her tighter. She had to find Emma. But first she had to survive the next few minutes. And to do that, she feared she had to do as he asked. What other choice was there? The men she'd run from outnumbered them. If they caught her, she might not escape a second time.

Not that she really knew what they wanted. She'd wandered too far from the hotel, gotten lost and stumbled into a group of men who'd frightened her. They'd been drinking, and they'd not been too willing to help. Or not without a price. She shuddered as she thought of the blond giant with the meaty hands who'd told her in thick Russian that he'd help her if she would kiss him.

Then he'd laughed, and the others had joined in. The sound was ugly and made the hair on her arms prickle. But it wasn't until he'd grabbed her that she'd screamed. She'd bought herself a little time with the well-aimed kick to his groin. While the others scrambled to help him, she'd run.

Why she now believed *this* man was truly trying to help her, she wasn't sure. But she was positive he was—or at least he was the lesser of two evils, if the way her senses were reeling was any indication. The simple contact of body on body, of his groin pressed intimately to hers in spite of the layers of clothing between them, had her heart thundering, her nerve endings tingling.

She wanted to know who he was, why he was helping her, but there was no time to ask. The stranger's ice-gray eyes gazed down at her, urging her to comply. The heavy clomp of boots on the cobbles grew louder.

In an instant, Paige closed her eyes and fused her lips to his. She decided at the last second that she would keep her mouth closed. There was no reason to truly kiss him, was there? The appearance of it would surely be enough to fool these men.

But the stranger wouldn't allow it. His tongue slid along the seam of her lips. She gasped at the heat and surprise of the movement.

That little gasp was all he needed to slip his tongue into her mouth. Her heart hammered as he kissed her with such expertise that her knees would have buckled had she been standing.

He tasted like brandy and mint, so masculine and strong, and she was shocked at the languidness stealing across her senses. He wasn't Chad, wasn't the man she'd fantasized about for the past two years—but she wanted to lose herself in his embrace, wanted to see what kind of magic he could make if they were alone together and naked.

Except she hadn't the first clue *how* to make magic with a man, truth be told. In the last eight years, she'd had exactly one sexual experience—and that hadn't been anything to write home about. Becoming a single parent to a sister when you were only eighteen, and then working your way through school and trying to support a household, didn't leave much time for dating or building relationships.

But not one of the handful of kisses she'd ever experienced had been anything like this. *This* kiss was incredible. And it did things to her insides. She felt liquid and hot. Like the fireworks bursting in her body had turned into a single living flame.

Paige felt heat and passion so strongly that it shocked her. How could she be so responsive at a time like this?

The man growled low in his throat, squeezed her tighter to him as the kiss slid over the edge.

Paige wasn't herself. It was the only explanation. She was no longer a dull secretary working for a man she could never have, no longer the responsible older sister who took care of everything. She was hot, sensual, and completely in charge of her destiny. She was living a life of international intrigue and danger, an exciting life filled with passion and amazing men who spoke Russian-accented English and kissed the living daylights out of her.

Voices sounded close by, bringing her back to reality. And then a wolf-whistle. Paige's heart dived into her stomach.

"Don't be frightened," the stranger whispered against the column of her throat as he maneuvered her face away from the side the men were on. "They will go soon."

She trembled in answer, though it wasn't from fear as his mouth glided near her ear again.

"What is your name?"

It startled her, that question. He was pressed against her so intimately, his lips moving across her skin as if they'd been born to do so, the ridge of an impressive erection riding the crease in her thighs, and he didn't even know her name. If the situation weren't so insane, she'd have laughed.

He flexed his hips and sensation bolted through her. If he kept doing that, oh…

"Your name," he said against her cheekbone.

"Paige," she said in the instant before his mouth claimed hers again.

The whistles grew louder, and then a voice said something sharp and they stopped. The voice said something again, louder and sharper. She felt the stranger's muscles tighten.

The other man spoke in Russian, a question by the way he left the statement hanging at the end. The truth hit her like a blast of icy water. He was questioning *them*. Paige's breath drew in sharply.

"Moan," the stranger said against her lips.

The word was so foreign to her, so heavy with meaning. His accent scraped over the word, made it seem both harder and sexier than anything she'd ever heard in her life.

He squeezed her thighs hard, and she realized they were in danger, that he knew it, too. Somehow, the fact he was aware of the danger made it seem bigger, more real. They were completely outnumbered. If these men realized who she was, if they decided to finish what they'd started, the stranger would be no help against so many.

Paige pulled her mouth from his, buried her face against his neck and let out the best moan she could. The sound was weak, unconvincing.

"Louder," he said in her ear, his hips flexing once more against her center.

Sensation caught, held, spun her in its grip as he ground against her. The moan that left her lips this time was very real. His mouth sought hers again. His kiss was warm, hard and demanding. Paige threaded her fingers in the hair at his nape, toyed with the soft edge of the fur cap he wore.

With the pressure of his body centered on her most sensitive spot, he drove her toward something she'd never actually experienced with a man. They were clothed, and yet she was about to splinter apart.

She'd been so deprived and now—oh now the floodgates had been opened. They weren't even naked, weren't really intimate in any way, and she felt so much.

She moaned again, gasping as his hand cupped her breast through her shirt. His thumb slid over her nipple; he made a noise when he realized it was a hard little point. The sound of his voice rocked her, kicked up her senses.

Unbelievably she was almost there, almost to that peak of sensation. She felt wicked, hot and utterly desperate.

It was wrong, wrong, and yet—

The stranger tore his mouth from hers and put distance between them. He still supported her, but they were no longer so tightly pressed together. He looked completely unaffected by what had just happened while she was hot and cold and frustrated all at once.

And then she remembered. Her gaze shot over his shoulder as confusion gave way to panic. He'd decided to give her up, decided she wasn't worth helping—

"They are gone," he said. He eased her legs down his hips until she was standing. Released from his grip, she felt so cold all of a sudden. She wrapped her arms around her body. Her teeth started to chatter softly, but she couldn't seem to stop.

"Thank you," she said, strangely disappointed that she hadn't tumbled over that peak after all. Her body still hummed with the aftereffects of too much adrenaline, too much thwarted pleasure.

"*Ne ze chto.* Now we must go."

Paige blinked up at him, looking at him fully for the first time—and nearly sank to the cold ground in shock. He was a stunning man. Hollywood handsome in a way that screamed bad boy, playboy. Except he wasn't a boy at all. It struck her how incongruous those terms were to describe a man like him.

She'd been so focused before, so scared, that she'd barely registered any details about him.

Now, she took them in. Every last incredible line. Beneath his cap, he had dark thick hair that was probably brown but looked black in the lights, and the kind of nose and cheekbones that artists had been sculpting out of marble for hundreds of years. His lips were full, sensual, his jaw strong. He watched her with glacial eyes that missed nothing.

And he'd just told her they needed to leave. Together.

Paige backed up a step, suddenly confused and wary. She'd made too many mistakes already. She'd come this far from her hotel without a plan, and nearly been assaulted. Going anywhere with this man was out of the question, no matter how much she might owe him for helping her.

"I appreciate your help, and I'd be happy to pay you, but if you think I'm going somewhere with you to finish—"

His expression grew absolutely stony. "You think too highly of yourself, Paige. And you will come with me now if you wish to avoid a repeat scenario. Those men could return to the square in five minutes, when they've realized you didn't go into the subway or any of the open clubs."

"I'll return to my hotel. It's just down the street—"

"It's not safe."

"My boss is there and he can help—"

"No," he cut in. "It will be safer if you come with me now."

The slow burn of anger began in her belly. Who was he to tell her what to do? And what did he mean it wasn't safe? It had to be safer than going with him! "I appreciate your help, but my sister is *missing* and I think Chad is the only one who can help me—"

He took a step closer, every inch of him suddenly on alert. "Chad? Chad Russell is your boss?"

Paige bit her lip, uncertain whether this was a good or a bad sign. "You know Chad?"

His laugh was not precisely friendly. "Indeed, I know Chad Russell, *maya krasavitsa*. And I know that you had better come with me now, if you want to survive this night."

Paige shivered. Something in his tone made her want to back away. "I'm not sure that's a good idea," she said.

He glared at her until she was certain he would grab her bodily and force her to go whether she wanted to or not. But then he shrugged. "It is your life. Do what you wish."

"But why? Why isn't it safe?" she demanded, her heart racing.

His mouth twisted disdainfully. "The streets are not safe at night, as you have so recently discovered. This is true of many big cities, I understand."

She felt like he was mocking her, and yet there was some sense to what he said. Would she walk the streets of downtown Dallas alone at night? Definitely not.

"I can pay you to take me back to the hotel."

His bark of laughter was not what she expected. Her face burned, as if she'd insulted him somehow and embarrassed herself in the process. God, what a strange night!

"Come with me, or go your own way. The choice is yours." He didn't wait for her to reply. He simply turned and started down the hill in the direction the men had gone. Paige chewed her lip, shivering and wondering what in the hell she should do now.

Maybe she could make it back alone, assuming she didn't get lost again. Her hotel was through the square and down the road that ran along the Moscow River. It was a long walk. Cold. Dark.

She would run. She could make it in ten minutes if she hurried. Maybe Emma had already returned. If not, Chad was there to help.

The sound of male voices, speaking in Russian, filtered to her on the night air. Their speech was loud and punctuated with laughter. She didn't know if it was the same men who'd tried to grab her, but could she risk it?

Paige pressed the heels of her hands to her temples. Oh, God, what was she doing here? Why had she thought she could handle this alone? She didn't speak the language, and sometimes didn't even understand the thickly accented English that was spoken to her. Her eyes strained to see the figure of the man disappearing into the night. She understood him.

But he was a stranger. How could she go anywhere with a man she didn't know?

The Russian voices grew louder as they moved closer to where she still stood in front of the department store. Given a choice between meeting up with these men, or going with the man who'd helped her, she realized the truth: there was no choice.

Paige broke into a run.

CHAPTER TWO

ALEXEI POURED SCOTCH into a tumbler and handed it to the woman sitting so forlornly on his couch. The walk through the cold city streets had chilled her, he was certain, but a stiff drink would bring her around. And then he would find out why she'd been in Red Square at the precise time he'd been supposed to meet with his informant. Considering she was one of Chad Russell's employees, it was quite a coincidence.

He did not believe in coincidences. Hard work and sacrifice had gotten him where he was today, not belief in mystical concurrences. If he'd left his life up to luck and circumstance, he'd probably be lying in a crypt with the rest of his family.

She accepted the glass without looking and took a big drink. Then she coughed. "That's horrible!"

Alexei sipped his own scotch, enjoying the notes of caramel and oak as it slid down his throat. The fifty-year-old single malt was perfect. And so was her performance. She definitely knew how to play the innocent.

His mouth twisted in disdain.

Like his father before him, Chad Russell had always believed he could ruin Voronov Exploration if he threw enough money at the right people. He hadn't yet succeeded, nor would he.

Alexei would die before he would lose the next round in their epic battle. Whoever could convince Pyotr Valishnikov to sell his Baltic and Siberian holdings first would reap a huge reward—and effectively leave the other company in the metaphorical dust. This deal was the culmination of everything Alexei had ever worked for. With the stroke of a pen, Valishnikov could give him the power to finally crush Russell Tech once and for all.

Then Katerina would be avenged. It was all that mattered.

Alexei studied the woman on his couch.

Was she here to dig up information about his plans? If so, she would be sorely disappointed. But if she was supposed to distract him enough to let down his guard, she wasn't doing the best job of it. She was beautiful, though in an unstudied way. He'd known many beautiful women over the years, but this one seemed quite unaware of her beauty. She hadn't once tried to fix her hair or asked to see a mirror so she could primp and preen. Her makeup was so understated as to be practically nonexistent.

And she seemed to be in shock, which was why he'd given her the scotch.

As he watched, she reached into one of the pockets of her very unstylish coat and pulled out a pair of glasses. Then she glanced up at him and shrugged as she put them on.

"I can see pretty well without them, but I get headaches if I go too long." She dropped her gaze to the glass in her hand. "They fogged up when I went outside and I just never put them back on."

"What were you doing in Red Square alone?"

She looked up at him again, her dark eyes shiny with unshed tears. Once more, he got that little kick in the gut he'd felt earlier when he'd breathed in her scent. His sister'd had dark eyes like those. Dark, haunting eyes that he couldn't escape, no matter how successful he became or how much he tried to put the past behind him.

"I don't even know your name," she said numbly.

"Alexei," he replied. He did not doubt that she knew exactly who he was. Perhaps he should have taken her up on her offer to return her to her hotel. He hadn't believed it was genuine at the time, nor did he now. But what would she have done if he'd said yes? That would have caused a bit of consternation, he was certain. When he'd first told her she needed to come with him, before he'd known who she was, he'd had every intention of driving her back to her hotel once he'd reached his apartment.

Afterward, it had seemed unnecessary—not to mention counterintuitive to her plan. He wondered why she'd even told him she worked for Chad Russell in the first place.

"Alexei," she repeated.

"*Da*. Now tell me about your sister."

He would play her game. For now.

Panic threaded into those smoky eyes. She took another swig of scotch, coughed. If she was acting, she was doing a fine job of it.

"Emma's twenty-one, as of yesterday. She's nothing like me. She's tall and blonde, and she likes to have fun and go shopping. She went on a guided tour this afternoon while I worked to prepare Chad's papers for his meeting tomorrow. I ate dinner in Chad's suite while we worked, and stayed with him until about eight-thirty. I had a text from Emma around eight, telling me she would be in the hotel bar for a while. She wasn't in our room when I got back, but I didn't think anything of it until she didn't return by eleven. I tried calling her, but she never answered."

The twinge of feeling he got when he thought of this woman with Russell surprised him. Because he doubted very much that she'd simply been *working* with her boss all that time. A beautiful woman like her with a man like Russell?

He'd lay odds they'd been doing far more than going over paperwork.

She plunked the tumbler on the table and stood. But she must have gotten up too quickly because the color drained from her face and she sank back down again. Then she put a hand to her head.

"I don't usually drink alcohol," she said more to herself than to him. She looked up again, her eyes slightly glazed. How could anyone get drunk on two gulps of scotch? "I have to find her," she whispered.

"I will find her for you," Alexei said smoothly. Let her believe her plan was working. "You looked for her in this bar?"

She clasped both hands in her lap, her knuckles whitening. "Yes. I asked if anyone had seen her, but they claimed not to remember."

"So you decided to wander alone through Red Square at midnight?"

Her eyes were huge and liquid. "It was stupid, I know. But I thought she couldn't have gone far, thought maybe she was outside. And then someone said there was another bar, so I went there. Each place I went was farther than the last until I found myself in the square and those men started bothering me."

"Where is your cell phone?"

She patted her coat, came up empty. "I think I dropped it when they grabbed me."

Alexei took his phone from his jacket and handed it to her. "Try to call your sister."

She punched in a few numbers. He could hear the error message on the other end as she handed the phone back, her expression a mixture of frustration and fear. "I don't know how to dial it from a foreign number."

"Tell me the number." He punched it in while she recited

it, adding the proper codes, then handed the phone back when it began to ring. Her face screwed up while she concentrated, as if she were willing her sister—assuming there really was a sister—to answer.

It didn't work, however, because she gave the phone back to him a moment later, her expression crumpling.

Alexei dialed another number. After issuing instructions to his head of personal security, he hung up.

"Why don't you give me your coat? I will turn on the fire to warm you."

"I really should be going," she said, her pretty bow mouth drawing his attention as her teeth scraped her bottom lip worriedly.

Alexei tried very hard to ignore the arrow of arousal that shot straight to his groin. She'd been uncertain earlier, but she'd warmed up to their kiss, coming alive beneath his touch. It had been everything he could do to push her away when all he'd wanted was to sample the rest of her. To see if the fire in that kiss would translate to the bedroom.

Odd, when she wasn't his usual type of woman. He liked glamorous women, effortlessly feminine women who wore their confidence like a second skin. Paige was neither glamorous nor confident, though she was definitely feminine. *Authentic* was the word that came to mind—though of course that couldn't be the case when she was working for Chad Russell. She was simply a very good actress.

"It is safer to remain here," he said. "In case those men are looking for you."

She blinked. "How could that be? They don't know me—"

"Your phone."

Her eyes widened. "I hadn't thought of that. I still don't know why they'd care." She shook her head suddenly. "But they wouldn't. And I need to find my sister, so I should go back—"

"I will find your sister, I promise." He said it impatiently, since she couldn't really want to leave yet, but she didn't seem to notice.

She blinked at him, her eyes adorably owlish behind her glasses. "Do you really think you can find her?"

He nodded. "You are in Russia, *maya krasavitsa,* and I am Russian. I guarantee I will find her before your Chad could do so."

Real hope kindled in the depths of those eyes. It made him wonder, for an instant, if he was wrong about her motives for being here.

That is exactly what you are supposed to think.

He shoved the thought aside, but not before he pictured another set of eyes gazing at him with hope. *Katerina, I'm sorry...*

A cold hand gripped his, pulling him back to the present. He didn't mind the cold. It was the touch of her skin that surprised him. The jolt must have surprised her as well, because she quickly pulled away.

"Thank you, Alexei," she said in that soft, breathy voice that reminded him of film stars of the 1940s. "You have been very kind. I don't know what would have happened if you hadn't been there."

If the whole scenario hadn't been a setup, then he knew exactly what could have happened—and it wasn't pretty.

"You must never go out alone at night in a strange city where you do not speak the language or understand the culture." He said it rather harshly, he thought, but she merely nodded.

"You're right, of course." She sank back against the cushions and closed her eyes. When she didn't open them again, he grew concerned. A moment later, her jaw dropped open and a soft snore escaped.

Alexei stood there for a moment in disbelief. Tossing back the rest of his scotch, he decided to turn the lights down and leave her where she was. If she were here to spy, she'd be up in no time. All he had to do was wait and see.

Paige was warm and cozy. Something soft nestled against her cheek as she stirred. She smiled, sighing as she burrowed deeper beneath the cover. The hotel bed was comfortable, but it felt different tonight than it had the night before. Firmer. And why was she still wearing her clothes?

A tendril of unease twisted through her. Something wasn't right. Her eyes popped open—a second later, she bolted upright. Her gaze darted around the room, but nothing was familiar.

Where was she?

Her surroundings were luxurious—the couch she lay on was covered in silk brocade, oil paintings adorned the walls and the cover she'd been snuggling into was made out of some kind of fur.

A fire burned softly in the grate, the only sound in the room. Paige stood, wrapping the blanket around her though she was still fully clothed, and turned in a circle. She didn't have a watch, and she'd lost her cell phone in the square. She had no idea what time it was, or whether Emma had been found.

How had she managed to fall asleep when she was so worried?

"Alexei?"

She started walking toward a hallway directly behind her. It might be late, but she couldn't simply sit on the couch and wait until morning. She had to know if Alexei had found Emma.

The thought of her enigmatic rescuer sent a wave of a

different kind of heat rolling over her. She'd been wary when he'd first told her she needed to go with him, but once they arrived at his apartment, she'd realized he had money. This apartment was in one of the old Baroque buildings that had withstood time, several wars and a revolution. It was also furnished with expensive paintings, antiques and woven rugs.

And he knew Chad, though she still didn't know how he did, come to think of it.

But she'd relaxed a little then. Surely he did not need to lure poor American women back to his apartment for evil purposes. No doubt women fell all over a man who looked like he did. Add in the money, and you had a sure recipe for success.

No, Alexei did not need to bring her here in order to have his wicked way with her. He'd kissed her because it was necessary, not because he was attracted to her.

Paige lifted her chin. Nor was she attracted to him. He was a handsome man, no doubt, but he wasn't Chad. Chad was tall, blond, Texan, bigger than life. Everything she'd ever dreamed about when she was a girl growing up in tiny Atkinsville, Texas.

She knew that Chad taking her to lunch—and picking her to accompany him on this trip—might not mean anything, but a girl could dream. Though he usually dated underwear models, actresses and beauty queens, he wasn't seeing anyone just now. She knew because she was the one who usually got the task of ordering the flowers and making the dinner reservations. There had been none of those for over a month now.

Not that it meant anything, she reminded herself, when he'd been working nonstop on this Russian deal.

A lamp burned in one of the rooms off the hallway. Paige pushed the door all the way open. "Alexei?"

There was no answer, but she stepped inside to be sure he wasn't there anyway. The room was an office, with floor to ceiling bookcases, a desk and filing cabinets. A computer stood on the desk, and a printer sat idle nearby. There was an Italian leather couch on one wall, and a couple of chairs facing it.

But no one was inside. She turned to leave, biting off a scream as a man stepped through the door.

"Looking for something?"

Paige put a hand to her racing heart. "You scared me."

"Apparently," he said, though there was no amusement in his voice.

"I was looking for you."

One dark eyebrow arched. "Really? Why?"

Paige swallowed. He stood before her in jeans and an un-buttoned white shirt, as if he'd hurriedly pulled it on. His feet were bare, and his hair was mussed. She resolutely focused on his face instead of the naked skin of his chest and abdomen. Or the shadowed indentations of muscle and sinew.

"I'm sorry if I woke you. But I have no idea what time it is. If Emma returned to our room by now, she'll be worried. I really should go…" Her voice tapered off as she realized she was babbling.

"Your sister is not in your room."

Paige felt her heart skip a painful beat. She took a step toward him, thought better of it and clutched the blanket tighter instead. "How do you know? Do you know where she is?"

"*Da*. She is safe, Paige. You have nothing to worry about."

Relief threatened to buckle her knees.

Alexei reached for her as she swayed, caught her in a strong grip. Then he ushered her to the couch and sat her down. "You are quite good at this," he murmured.

Paige blinked up at him. "I'm sorry?"

He turned away and went over to a cabinet close by, returned with a glass and thrust it toward her.

Paige held up her hand as her stomach rebelled. "Not again—"

"It is water."

She took the glass and drank, thankful because her mouth was suddenly so dry. Her head felt light, and her heart thundered in her chest. She'd promised Mama that she'd take good care of Emma. Her sister had only been thirteen when their mother died, and Paige had done her best. If Emma was a bit spoiled, a bit irresponsible, it was Paige's fault for indulging her.

She'd been trying to make up for the lack of parents, but she hadn't done the best job. Tonight, she thought she'd failed utterly. To know that Emma was safe filled her with a profound sense of relief.

"Where is she?"

"She is with Chad Russell, as you very well know."

"Oh thank God," Paige breathed. Though what made him think she knew where Emma was?

Before she could ask, Alexei's cool silver gaze pierced her. "Why are you here?"

Paige blinked. "I was looking for you—"

"No, I mean why are you here, in my home?"

It took her a moment to formulate an answer. "Because you told me I had to come with you."

"Yes, but *why* did you do so? What did you hope to find? Is Russell so desperate he would send a secretary to spy on me?"

Confusion crashed through her. And a thread of simmering anger.

"Why would I want to spy on you? I don't even know you!" She set the glass aside and stood, tilting her chin up. It

was simply a show of bravado since she was shaking inside
her skin. But she'd learned at an early age to bluff her way
through the rough spots when necessary. Or, as her mother
used to say, *never let them see you sweat.* She'd had plenty of
practice when Child Services had come calling to see if she
was capable of taking care of her sister or if Emma needed
to go into foster care instead.

"Stop pretending you don't know who I am," he commanded.

Paige stomped her foot. It was childish, she knew, but it
was instinctive. She couldn't stop herself whenever she was
angry or nervous—though anger was not the dominant emotion at the moment.

"You are Alexei, a man I met in Red Square, who helped
me when I was in trouble. You obviously have money, and
you knew who Chad was as soon as I mentioned him. But I
have no idea who you are."

It was a troubling thought, not to know the man who
seemed to know so much about you.

He closed the distance between them, slipped an arm
around her waist beneath the blanket. His fingers traced her
jaw, slid into the hair at her nape. "You are a fascinating
woman, Paige. No wonder Russell chose you for this task.
Or did you volunteer?"

With a tug, she was flush against him. The blanket fell
away as she let it go to press her hands against his chest. Paige
closed her eyes. His *naked* chest.

His skin was hot beneath her hands, silky and hard, and
she longed to stroke it.

Stop it. How could she possibly find him sexy at a time
like this?

"Let me go," she breathed.

"Before you've done what you came to do?"

"I didn't come here to do *anything*."

"What did Russell offer you?"

"I don't know what you're talking about!"

"Were you supposed to seduce me? Supposed to leave me sated and exhausted in bed while you went through my papers?" His head dipped toward her. "Because I have to say, Paige, that I am very disappointed in your technique thus far. But I find I am quite willing to allow you to complete your mission."

She knew she should pull away when his lips touched hers, but it was physically impossible. Not because he held her too tightly, but because her body was zinging with sparks that she didn't want to end.

His tongue slipped into her mouth, and she met him stroke for stroke. He smelled so good, like spice and a cold winter night, yet he was as hot as a volcanic eruption. His skin sizzled into her where she touched him with her bare hands. She wanted to slip the shirt from his shoulders, wanted to see if his skin tasted as good as it felt.

His hands slid into her hair, tugged her head back. His mouth left hers, forged a trail of fire along her jaw, the column of her throat.

Her head fell to one side, giving him greater access. He made a sound of approval, and she opened her eyes—just for a moment—and found herself staring at the most erotic scene she'd ever personally experienced. A mirror on the opposite wall caught their reflection, shone it back at her.

It was like a scene out of a movie. A gorgeous man held a woman in his embrace, a woman whose dark hair flowed wildly over her shoulders, whose eyes sparkled with passion as the man's mouth moved across her skin.

It was exotic and beautiful.

And she wasn't supposed to be the woman in the scene. This man didn't care for her. He thought Chad had sent her here to seduce him, for God's sake—which was a laugh in itself—and she had no idea *who* he really was.

Paige's hands curled into fists against his hard chest.

And then she pushed. "Stop. Please stop."

Amazingly he did. Alexei's eyes were hot, glittering as he straightened to his full height and glared down at her. He was even taller than Chad, broader, and he did things to her insides—

Stop thinking about it.

Paige closed her eyes, took a step back. Her clothes were intact, but she felt as if he'd undressed her, as if he knew all her secrets.

A ridiculous feeling, really. He might know her name, and he might know she was Chad's secretary, but he did not know *her*.

"I want to go back to my hotel," she said with as much dignity as she could summon. "Chad has a very important meeting tomorrow, and I have to be there. He needs me. And Emma will be wondering where I am by now."

Alexei shoved a hand through his thick hair—black, not brown, she realized. "You will not be going anywhere tonight."

"I want to see my sister," she insisted. "You have no right to keep me here."

His gaze sharpened. "Your sister is busy, Paige. I doubt she will want to be disturbed. Though perhaps you did not know you were sharing your lover with her?"

Everything inside her went cold and still. "My lover?" she said numbly.

"You never give up the pretense, do you?"

She ignored him, her mind beginning to work overtime. Emma and Chad? They'd met once or twice when Emma had come to the office, but Chad hadn't shown any particular interest in her sister.

Or had he?

She remembered Emma's flirtatious giggle, Chad's mega-watt smile, Emma's declaration later that night that Chad was probably amazing in bed. She'd thought the same thing herself, but she figured she'd never know.

She just hadn't realized that Emma might actually find out.

Chad had suggested she bring Emma along on this trip when Paige expressed disappointment she would be gone for her sister's twenty-first birthday. She'd thought he was being kind. She'd refused at first until he insisted it would be fine, that he wouldn't hear of them being separated for Emma's birthday.

And now this.

Paige put a hand on the bookcase to steady herself. Rage, disappointment, betrayal—they whirled inside her like a hurricane, spinning her in a vortex of emotion. She'd thought he was interested in her, when all along it had been Emma! She'd been so stupid, so blind.

Chad and Emma. Her boss and her sister. Making love while she searched the icy Moscow streets in a panic. Making love while she nearly got assaulted by a group of drunken men.

Her sister making love with the man *she* wanted, the man she'd secretly been in love with forever.

Tears pressed against the backs of her eyes. She would not let them fall, not now. Not here, not in front of Alexei.

"Paige," he said, taking her arm.

She jerked away and hugged her arms tightly around her body. "Leave me alone."

"I apologize if this news hurts you."

She speared him with a glare. A blurry glare, since her eyes were swimming in moisture. "You don't care, so spare me your insincerity. Besides, how do I know you're telling the truth? How could you possibly have found Emma if she's in Chad's room?"

What if he'd made the whole thing up? Though why he would do so, she couldn't say, but surely it was a possibility.

"My head of security used to work for the secret police," he replied softly. "Yuri knows people, and he knows how to get things done. But I can certainly prove where your sister is if you wish. My men have audio of her with—"

"Stop," she blurted, turning away, her body trembling with anger and pain. Her intuition had told her all along he was telling the truth, which was why she'd reacted, but that hadn't stopped her from grasping at straws. The last thing she wanted to hear was Chad and Emma whispering together in bed. Or worse.

Before she realized what Alexei was about to do, he wrapped her in his embrace, his hand pressing against the back of her head so that her cheek was flush against his bare chest. Briefly she considered struggling—but gave up the idea as his other hand rhythmically rubbed her back.

It'd been a long time since anyone had comforted her. She was always the one doing the comforting, the one who'd sacrificed everything to raise her little sister, never complaining when Emma got the best of everything. Paige had been proud that her hard work enabled Emma to have a normal life, that Emma was able to be a cheerleader and a homecoming queen and a beautiful, successful young woman with a bright future.

She had done that for Emma, and she'd been happy to do so.

But why did Emma have to get *everything?*

On the heels of jealousy, guilt rode hard. Who was Paige to deny her sister anything? Paige had been practically an adult when their mother died. Emma was the one who'd grown up without a loving mother. Paige had done everything for her, but a sister wasn't the same as a mother, no matter how hard she tried.

A tear spilled free, and then another, until finally Paige was curling her hands into Alexei's shirt as the first heartbroken sob escaped her. After that, it was easy to cry. She'd held the tears in for so long. She hadn't cried since her mother's funeral, had believed that tears made her weak.

Now, it felt good to let it all out. Cleansing. The man holding her never stopped rubbing her back, never made a move to pull away and leave her alone. Selfishly she clung to him and cried for all the years she'd lost.

While she cried herself out, she made a decision. From now on, Paige would no longer neglect her own happiness for that of others. When she wanted something, she would not deny herself. She was through denying herself.

It was a new day for Paige Barnes. And she knew just how to prove it.

CHAPTER THREE

ALEXEI SENSED THE change in her before she acted. One minute she was sobbing her heart out, the next she was standing on tiptoe and pulling him down for another kiss.

He was tempted. More than tempted. Alexei let her kiss him, fighting his reaction as her lips moved tentatively over his. She tasted like salt and sadness, and he wanted nothing more than to take that sadness away. It was his fatal flaw, this desire to protect and comfort those in need. He'd spent years fighting for his family, years that had taken their toll.

But there was nothing he could do for this woman. Though it would be so easy to take what she offered, so easy to sweep her into his arms and carry her to his room, he wasn't going to do it.

She wasn't kissing him because she wanted *him*. She was doing this to prove something to herself. And he didn't feel like being the conduit through which she tried to vanquish her anger and disappointment.

Her reaction to his news about her sister and Russell had not been what he'd expected. He'd set her up in his mind as a cold, calculating woman on a mission for her lover. He'd not stopped to think that maybe she really had been worried, or that she didn't know her sister wasn't missing but was instead sneaking off to Chad Russell's room.

Alexei didn't like the way her tears had made him feel, the

way her sweet vulnerability just now—the tentative kiss, the hint of desperation—struck a nerve inside him.

She brought memories crashing into his head that he tried to shove away. Memories of a pale, sad woman lying in a hospital bed, her lips cracked and dry, a lone tear sliding down her cheek as she whispered that she loved him.

The last person on this earth who loved him had died because he wasn't able to save her, because even though he was a prince, he'd been poor and broken and couldn't afford to buy the best leukemia treatments money could buy. After Katerina's death, he'd vowed on her memory that he would not be poor for the rest of his life. And he would strike back at the cold-blooded man who'd stripped them of everything before he'd returned to America with the rights to the land their mother had sold, and the rich oil and gas deposits beneath.

Tim Russell had left them with nothing, and though it would have taken only a fraction of the wealth he'd amassed from their land to help Katerina, he'd refused. Alexei had scraped together the money to fly to Dallas and beg for his sister's life, but he'd been met with cold disdain. He still remembered standing in Russell's office, high over the Dallas skyline, and being both awed and sickened by the wealth on display. He'd wanted that life for his family, and it had made him sick to think it might have been theirs had this man not stolen it from them.

Once Katerina had died, Alexei had found the initiative to start Voronov Exploration with nothing more than bravado and a geological engineering degree from Moscow University. He'd burned with a passion to regain everything that had been lost and to destroy the Russells in the process.

It had taken years, but he was at the pinnacle of his success now—and victory over the Russells was within his grasp. If he could turn back time, he would save his sister from the cancer that had eaten her strength and her life. He would give back all the money and give up the idea of vengeance if it was possible to have another chance.

But there was no going back. Ever. Life moved forward, no matter how much money you had. It hadn't helped Tim Russell when his time had come, and it wouldn't help his son when Alexei finally gained control of Russell Tech.

Alexei gripped Paige's arms, gently, and set her away from him. She sucked in a breath, and for a moment he thought she might start to cry again. Instead she wrapped her arms around her waist and stared up at him, her eyes huge pools of hurt.

He couldn't help but feel sympathy for her. Those tears had been real, regardless of her reasons for being here in the first place.

And maybe, just maybe, he could turn her anger and sadness at Chad Russell to his advantage. She was his secretary; she knew sensitive information about his business.

Information Alexei could use.

"You don't really want to do this," he said softly. "You are hurt and sad and you want to make it go away. I understand this. But tomorrow, you would have regrets."

She shrugged one shoulder, as if to say it mattered not at all to her. Yet he knew it mattered a great deal with that single movement.

"It's okay if you don't want to m-make love," she said, casting her eyes toward the floor when she said *make love*, as if it embarrassed her to say the words.

Now why did that hint of innocence spike the heat in his blood?

"Paige," he said, waiting until she looked at him again before he continued, "I think you need to get some sleep. Tomorrow, everything will look brighter."

How many times had he told that lie to Katerina? They'd

both known it was a lie, but it was a fiction they'd counted on to get them through the hard times.

"I have to be back at the hotel by eight," she said numbly. "Cha—my boss has an important meeting to attend."

Alexei couldn't stop himself from reaching out and tucking a wisp of hair behind her ear. He was the good guy here and he planned to make her see it. "*Da,* I know this."

She frowned. "I really wish you would tell me how you know these things."

He smiled as tenderly as he could. It was a risk, but if he wasn't truthful with her, she wouldn't trust him. And he wanted her trust now that Russell had broken it. It was vital to the new plan he was formulating.

"Because his meeting is with me."

Her eyes grew big. For the first time since he'd met her, he truly believed she had no idea who he was. His sense of purpose redoubled. He would destroy Russell Tech when he was through, thanks to this woman.

"You are Mr. Valishnikov?"

He shook his head. "I am the other V."

If anything, her eyes grew bigger. Her fingers flew to her mouth, pressed against her lips. When her hand dropped away, her face was pale.

"Oh my God," she said. "You're Prince Voronov."

It was snowing as the Mercedes moved through the city. Fat flakes that ghosted down and gathered on the pavement. Paige stared wide-eyed out the window. She'd never seen so much snow in her life, and it was April! Dallas was balmy this time of year, and Atkinsville, on the Gulf Coast where she'd grown up, had always been temperate.

She wanted to turn to the man sitting beside her, to thank him for taking her back to the hotel so early when the meeting wasn't for another two and a half hours, but she couldn't look at him.

Alexei Voronov. A *prince*. She'd been kissing a prince. Trying to seduce him when her feelings were hurt, and he'd turned her down flat. Of course he had! Not only was he a Russian prince, but he was also gorgeous on top of that. Not at all the sort of man to be interested in her.

Paige's face grew hot as she thought about how he'd kissed her in Red Square, the way his body ground against hers, the way she'd nearly splintered apart simply from the delicious pressure.

A game, she reminded herself. *A necessary act to save them both.*

But the man who'd rescued her wasn't just any prince. He was Prince Voronov—and Chad seemed to hate him. According to Chad, Prince Voronov was determined to absorb Russell Tech into his vast operations—which he would be in a prime position to do if he acquired Valishnikov's land.

If he succeeded in his quest, Russell Tech would cease to exist.

Jobs would be lost, people displaced—including herself. She wasn't unemployable, but in this current economic climate, how long would it take to find a new job? And how would she make her rent and utilities until then?

Worse, would she find new work in time to make Emma's tuition payment next semester?

Last night, she'd had plenty of time to think as she'd tossed and turned in the guest room Alexei had shown her to, and she'd realized that though she was hurt, it wasn't Emma's fault at all. Paige had never said she had a crush on Chad, and it wasn't fair to be mad at Emma. Her sister couldn't help being beautiful and vivacious; of course Chad had been attracted to her!

"You are very quiet, Paige."

She turned her head slowly, steeling herself to meet Alexei's gaze. Would she still see pity in his eyes? It was nothing but wishful thinking to hope he'd forgotten how she'd thrown herself at him after he'd told her about Chad and Emma. She wanted to sink into the leather cushions and disappear, but since that wasn't happening, she forced herself to be cool under pressure.

"I'm just thinking," she said. "We don't get snow in April where I'm from."

His smile made her heart thump. "Ah yes, it is quite tropical where you live."

"I wouldn't say tropical."

He shrugged. "Compared to Moscow?"

Paige swallowed. He was too handsome, this man. Too easy to look at. She found herself wondering what it would have been like if he hadn't pushed her away.

Mind-blowing, no doubt.

"I see your point."

"You should see my home in St. Petersburg," he continued. "It is an old estate dating back several hundred years in my family. The snow is pristine, undisturbed. There are wolves that howl during the night, and the stars shine so brightly you cannot believe. It is perfect for a *troika* ride."

She had a vision from a movie, of a couple bundled under a fur and riding through the snow in a sleigh with jingling bells. It seemed so romantic, though of course he hadn't mentioned it for that reason.

"That sounds lovely," she replied.

"Perhaps I will show it to you someday," he said, and her heart thumped harder.

Was he flirting with her?

Impossible. A man like him dated movie stars and models, not plain secretaries who were so pitiful they could only admire a man from afar.

"I don't see how," she replied truthfully, "though it's a nice thought. We are leaving in a few days, and St. Petersburg is not on our itinerary."

His gaze glittered strangely. "Do you intend to take your lover back after what he did?"

Shock zapped her like an electrical current. "Chad Russell is my boss, not my lover."

"Is that so?"

She thrust her chin forward. "Yes, it is."

He laced his fingers between hers, brought her hand to his mouth. She was too stunned to pull away as his lips touched the back of her hand. "Then that is really too bad for him, isn't it? But it's excellent for me."

When he released her, she clamped her hands together in her lap. Her skin still tingled from his touch. "I don't know why," she said as the blood roared in her ears. "You had your chance last night and you didn't take it."

Had she really just said that to him?

His laugh was not what she expected. "When I take you, *maya krasavitsa,* it will not be as you cry over another man."

Her face flamed. "I wasn't crying over Chad."

His expression said he didn't believe it. She turned her head to watch the snow again. Damn him for seeing so deeply into her. Her shattered romantic fantasy hadn't been the only thing she'd cried over, but she wasn't planning to share everything about her life with this man in order to correct his impression.

He was nothing to her, in spite of the heat of attraction she felt. After he dropped her off, she would never talk to him again.

"I think perhaps you are in love with Chad Russell," he said from behind her, "even if he is not your lover. And I think you are bitterly disappointed to learn he has chosen your sister over you."

Paige whirled, both stunned and furious. "You have no idea what you're talking about!"

"I am not a blind man, Paige."

Her breath stabbed in her chest. Was she that transparent? Had Chad always known it, too? Was that why he'd taken her to lunch? To try to let her down easily?

My God.

"Leave me alone, Prince Voronov," she said coldly. "I appreciate your help, but that doesn't give you the right to pick my life apart for your amusement. You don't know *anything* about me, so save your rude speculation."

The car drew to a halt, but she couldn't seem to look away from the man staring so intently back at her. His icy gray eyes weren't cold like she expected—they were hot, boring beneath her skin.

"Then I apologize," he said after what seemed an eternity of them staring at each other in silence. "I would never want to hurt you."

The door swung open and she realized they were at the hotel, that a valet waited for her to exit. But everything in the car was surreal, and she found it hard to break away. The next time she saw this man, it would be at a meeting of corporate bigwigs. He would not notice her—nor did she want him to.

If Chad knew she'd spent the night with Prince Alexei Voronov, even though it was innocent, he'd go through the roof.

And she'd definitely be out of a job.

"Thank you for your help," she said again. She felt like a broken recording, but what else could she say? Paige tried her best to smile as if she wasn't still raw inside. "I suppose this is goodbye then."

Alexei's smile was wolfish. "Ah, but this is not goodbye,

is it? We will see each other again, Paige Barnes. We will see a lot of each other, I promise you."

Paige hurried from the car and dashed inside the hotel lobby without looking back. Her skin was hot, in spite of the frigid weather, and she stripped off her coat in the elevator as it sped to her floor.

Why did Alexei Voronov rattle her so much? Yes, they'd skipped a few steps with that meeting in Red Square, but a kiss was a kiss. Wasn't it?

Paige's ears were hot. No, it definitely wasn't. That kiss had been molten hot, and so had the kisses later, in his apartment.

That didn't make the kisses extraordinary, however. And, really, how would she know? She had very little to base it on.

Paige fished her key from her coat and slipped into the room she shared with Emma. A pang of feeling pierced her heart, but she pushed it aside. So what if Emma was with Chad? Paige was so over it.

"Oh my God, where have you been? I've been so worried!"

Paige stopped dead in the midst of trying to close the door silently, in case Emma was in bed after all, and turned very slowly to face her sister.

Emma's pretty face was lined with worry. Paige's heart squeezed in her chest.

"I'm sorry, Emma. I couldn't sleep and went for a walk." The lie slipped from her tongue with ease, but guilt followed in its wake. She didn't like lying to her sister, but it was easier than explaining what had really happened.

And safer, too, since Emma could be a chatterbox. She would innocently let slip the information that Paige had been with the evil head of Voronov Exploration, and that would be the end of Paige Barnes's career at Russell Tech. She'd be on the next plane home with her tail tucked between her legs and no reference to find a new job.

She couldn't even think about the potential repercussions to Emma and her budding romance, if that's what it was, with Chad.

Emma tossed her glorious blond hair, her face shifting into a pout that Paige knew only too well. "You could have left a note."

"Why would I do that?" Paige asked. "You never wake up before eight anyway."

Emma had the grace to look sheepish. "Well, I did today. And you weren't here. I was about to call Chad to help me find you."

Déjà vu. Paige casually laid her coat over the back of the couch in their suite, thanking her lucky stars she'd returned when she did. The last thing she needed was Chad trying to find *her*.

"I'm here now, so you can stop worrying."

"You're wearing the same clothes as yesterday," Emma pointed out.

Paige felt her face grow hot. "I put them back on when I woke up. Now I'm going to shower and get ready for the meeting." She was almost to the bedroom door when she stopped and turned back. "You didn't come home last night, Emma. Where were *you?*"

Emma's face split into a grin. Typical of her sister that she wouldn't see a parallel between her actions and Paige's. It simply didn't occur to her that Paige might have panicked when *she* hadn't returned. She expected Paige to always be there for her, but she didn't seem to think it was a two-way street.

"I was with someone," Emma said. "And I think I'm in love."

Paige forced herself to remain calm even though her heart

was pounding a million miles an hour. "That's fast," she said. "You can hardly know this man."

"Oh, Paige," Emma said, her face glowing with happiness. "I wasn't going to tell you just yet, because I knew you'd worry, but it's Chad."

Paige blinked. "You're in love with Chad? But you barely know him—"

"I've been seeing him for a month."

Paige sank onto the closest chair. A month. One month of lies, obfuscations and going behind her back. No wonder Chad hadn't needed her to send flowers or make reservations.

And she was beginning to understand why he'd taken her for lunch.

"I had no idea," she said numbly.

Emma came over and knelt before her, took both of Paige's hands in her long-fingered elegant ones. "I'm sorry, but Chad thought you might be upset if you knew. We wanted to keep it a secret until we knew how we felt about each other."

Paige's hands were so cold inside Emma's warm ones. One sister had all the life and heat while the other was cold and empty. It didn't seem fair. "Isn't a month awfully quick to know if you love someone or not?"

Emma's smile said that it clearly was not. "Sometimes you just *know*."

In spite of her pain, it warmed Paige to see her sister so happy. She'd always wanted the best for Emma. Though there were only five years between them, she often felt more like Emma's mother than her sister.

But Emma's beatific smile worried her, too. Paige squeezed her hands. "I've worked for Chad Russell for two years, Emma. He dates a lot of women."

"I know that. But he loves me. He wants to marry me."

Her heart was splintering into a million jagged pieces around her. She hadn't realized until that moment that she'd been living for Emma. What would she do when Emma was gone?

And what should she say now? Emma was looking at her so hopefully, but all Paige could do was worry. Was Chad serious? Would he really put aside his playboy ways and make her sister happy? Or was he merely leading Emma along with no intention of marrying her? He was so rich. He moved in different social circles, circles that Emma had never been in before. Was this real, or was it simply another affair?

"Have you set a date?"

Emma shook her head as she stood. "When we get back to Dallas, we'll start discussing it. He's just so worried with this deal right now."

Paige's heart flipped. But whether it was from her misgivings about Chad's true intentions or about the deal that held Russell Tech's future in the balance, she wasn't sure. Because when she thought of the reason they were here in Moscow, she also thought of Alexei. He'd helped her when she needed it, held her while she cried, and kissed her so expertly that she'd practically begged him to take her to his bed—though of course she hadn't done it right since he had not complied.

But he wasn't just any man. He was Prince Voronov, and he was out to destroy Russell Tech. If he succeeded, then he also destroyed Chad and Emma's possibility of a happy future together.

Paige stood and hugged her sister tight. "I'm glad you're so happy and I hope Chad realizes how lucky he is to have you. Because if he doesn't," she continued, pushing Emma back to look at her, "I'll castrate him."

Emma laughed and hugged her back. "Don't worry about me," she said fiercely. "I'll do it myself if necessary."

"I have no doubt you will. And now," Paige said, "I need to get ready for this meeting."

As she stripped out of her clothes and stepped beneath

the shower, she couldn't shake a sense of impending doom. She was still reeling from Emma's news, and her heart still smarted, but that wasn't the problem at all.

No, it was Prince Voronov who spiked her anxiety. Because she'd realized in the car, when he'd seen through her masks, that he was a very dangerous man.

And not just to Russell Tech, but to her. In spite of her wish it were otherwise, her veins already bubbled in anticipation of seeing him again. The best thing he could do would be to ignore her.

But she knew he wouldn't do so. What she didn't know was why that knowledge made her happy.

CHAPTER FOUR

THE TENSION IN THE conference room wasn't surprising. But the tension coming from Paige Barnes was. Alexei watched her while Chad Russell spewed on and on in near flawless Russian. Since Paige didn't understand a word that was said until Chad turned and told her to write something down in English, she spent a lot of time staring at her lap.

Alexei willed her to look at him, but she did not. He hadn't been able to stop thinking about her since she'd dashed from his car this morning. She was an odd woman; beautiful, but completely unaware of her beauty.

And innocent. That's what compelled him. She reminded him of Katerina in a way. Katerina had only been seventeen when she'd died, and to the last she'd had that sweet air of innocence. Cancer and poverty had not been able to take it away.

Thinking of Katerina brought his gaze back to Chad Russell. It had been nearly fifteen years since Katerina's death. Chad could not be blamed for his father's cruelty, true, but Chad seemed to have shouldered the mantle of dislike his father'd had for the Voronov family. Alexei hadn't understood until that single moment so many years ago when he'd stood before Tim Russell why the man had hated them. And though he'd known it was likely Russell's son would follow in his father's footsteps, Alexei still found it difficult to believe.

Chad Russell was half Voronov, after all.

Still, it made what Alexei had to do that much easier. If Chad had been likable, or friendly in any way, Alexei might have let it color his desire to destroy Russell Tech. He glanced at Paige again. Regrettable that he would need to use her in his quest, but he would make sure she was handsomely rewarded in the end. He shoved away the twinge of conscience that threatened to badger him and focused on the discussion.

Alexei watched his first cousin gesticulate in an attempt to impress Valishnikov with his plans and ideas for the Siberian land and Baltic oil wells. Chad might be half Russian, but that wouldn't be enough to convince the old man sitting so stoically across the table. Though Chad's mother—Alexei's Aunt Elena—had clearly taught him the language, Chad's father had made certain his son was one hundred percent American.

And Pyotr Valishnikov was old enough to remember what it was like to hate and distrust Americans.

Worse, Chad looked every bit the American oilman stereotype. While he'd worn a dark suit, he also sported cowboy boots and a white Stetson that now sat on the table beside him. It was the wrong impression to make on this man.

Valishnikov raised his hand suddenly to indicate he wanted silence. Chad sputtered to a halt.

"I will consider your proposals," the old man said. "*Both* of your proposals. Now if you will excuse me, I have another meeting to attend."

He levered his bulk out of the chair and, followed by his contingent of managers and accountants, he exited the room.

Alexei noted Chad's reaction with interest. He seemed to fold in on himself, just for a moment, before shooting a glare at Alexei and squaring his jaw in a belligerent gesture.

"It seems as if you will be spending more time than you

bargained for in our fair country," Alexei said in English as he rose from his seat. "Perhaps you should take some time to sightsee. St. Petersburg is particularly lovely this time of year."

Just as he'd hoped, Paige's head snapped up. Her smoky eyes were huge in her face. Her glasses had fallen down the bridge of her nose and she pushed them back up with a finger.

He wanted to kiss the tip of that pert nose. The thought startled him. He could not afford to feel such romantic nonsense. She was a woman, an attractive woman, and she very possibly had information he needed. That was his sole reason for being interested in her.

"I'm not going to St. Petersburg, Prince Voronov." Chad sneered. "I'm staying right here until this deal is in the bag."

"You will not win."

Hatred oozed from the other man. "Don't be too sure of that." He turned to the woman sitting behind him. "Gather everything and meet me in the lobby. I have a phone call to make."

"Alone at last," Alexei said once Chad had stormed out of the conference room like a Texas whirlwind.

Paige crossed to the table, doing her best to give him the cold shoulder. "You shouldn't be talking to me," she said as she started to stack papers into neat piles. He did not miss that her fingers trembled.

"Why not? I like talking to you." Oddly enough, he truly did. He shouldn't, but she was refreshing in a way the women he usually dated were not. Still, he would not allow anything—not even her relative innocence—to interfere with his plan to ply her for information.

Her gaze snapped to his, then dropped again. A tinge of pink stained her cheeks. He liked that about her. Her long dark hair was gathered in a ponytail, and she wore a conservative black pantsuit with a high-collared white shirt. The suit fit her well enough, but she looked like a penguin.

A penguin he wanted to unwrap. She was too staid, too stuffy. It would be a pleasure to strip her of her businesslike formality, to see the sensual woman he'd glimpsed last night when he'd kissed her in the square. Her glasses slipped down her nose as she worked. She took a moment to shove them up again before continuing with her sorting.

"I work for Chad Russell," she said, "and I'd like to keep my job, if you don't mind. So please don't talk to me."

"Why is talking to you a bad thing?" he asked, moving around the table until he stood next to her. Until he could breathe in her summery scent.

Were those peaches he smelled? Unbidden, the thought she should be dressed in warm vibrant colors like summertime filtered into his mind. Though white suited her, like snow covering a pure landscape, it did not do so when overwhelmed by so much black.

So prim, this woman. She would be a challenge, perhaps. He liked challenges, relished them. Especially when they were unexpected.

She stopped what she was doing and turned toward him. He didn't miss the movement of her throat as she swallowed heavily. Her fingers shook where they rested on a pile of papers in midsort.

"Because I don't like lying to my boss, and because I don't want him to ask me anything about you—why I was talking to you, what I think of you—anything. Because talking to you tangles me in a web of lies, and I'm no good at it."

Alexei laid his hand over hers on the papers. He affected her. And he definitely planned to use it to his advantage, to romance her, to romance any information out of her that

he could get. In war, he took no prisoners, eschewed no
tactics.

He pushed aside a stab of guilt as he caressed the back of
her hand. "Have dinner with me tonight."

Her jaw dropped. "Are you insane? Didn't you hear a thing
I said? I can't have dinner with you!"

"Chad doesn't have to know," Alexei said, giving her hand
a tug until she was flush against him. He had a sudden desperate urge to feel the warm softness of her body pressed against
him again. To drown in her soft scent and softer skin.

When she tried to pull away, he tightened his grip.

"Let me go," she said quietly, her eyes downcast.

And though he didn't want to do it, though he wanted to
kiss her into compliance, he did as she asked. She immediately stepped away and put her arms around her body.

Frustration sawed into him. "I admire your loyalty to your
boss, Paige, but does he also command your personal life? Is
he allowed to tell you whom you may or may not see?"

A shadow crossed her face. "Of course not. But this is
complicated. You're the enemy."

Alexei couldn't contain a sharp laugh. He was indeed, but
he didn't want her to think so.

"You *are*," she insisted, frowning. "To Chad, you are. And
I work for him." She took a deep breath, let it out in a long
sigh. "Besides that, he's asked my sister to marry him."

Alexei stopped laughing. Paige swiped a hand beneath her
nose and turned to the papers once more. Clearly she was hurt
by this new development. And he didn't like seeing her hurt.
The change in her expression was like watching dark clouds
blotting out the sun. It bothered him.

Watching her with Chad today, he could tell there was
no relationship between them, no spark. It had made him
absurdly happy. Yet now she was sad, and he didn't like it.

"I'm sorry, Paige."

She shrugged. "For what? This is a very good thing. My sister is very happy."

"Are you?"

Her shoulders seemed to slump. Just as quickly, she straightened and turned to look at him with pride on her face. "Yes, I am. Emma is beautiful and amazing and she deserves a man like Chad."

"And what do you deserve?"

Her lower lip trembled before her teeth stopped it. "I wish you wouldn't do that," she said very softly.

"Do what? I am asking you a question, such as one friend asks another."

"You aren't my friend."

He pressed his advantage. "Not yet. But I could be."

She shook her head. "Don't say things you don't mean, Prince Voronov. It's impossible, and you know it."

"Call me Alexei. And I can tell you what you deserve," he continued. He knew what she needed to hear. She was a woman who didn't believe in herself, and he was a man who was very good at saying the right things. She looked at him hopefully. He wondered if she knew she'd done so.

"You deserve to laugh," he said quietly, seriously. "You deserve to do something for yourself instead of always doing for others. You deserve happiness, Paige, and you deserve to stop worrying about everything and let someone else worry for you. You deserve flowers every day, candlelight dinners and a man who wants you very much. You deserve everything your sister has, and more."

Her eyes glistened. Her mouth dropped open, shut again, and he knew he'd hit the mark. Another spear of guilt shot through him. He didn't want to like her, didn't want to feel pleased that he'd moved her. He did what was necessary to avenge his family; he had no room for remorse.

"What makes you think I don't do anything for myself?

A few hours acquaintance hardly qualifies you as an expert on me."

She was defensive, and he didn't blame her. He'd gone deep and it had to sting.

"You are an open book, Paige Barnes. I am simply reading what is written for all to see."

Her dark eyes were wounded, as if he'd exposed the soft underbelly of her vulnerability with just a few words.

"I—I—" Whatever she was about to say was lost as her jaw snapped shut and she whirled away from him. Opening the briefcase, she shoved all the papers inside, no longer interested in order or neatness.

Alexei cursed inwardly as she jammed the lid shut and locked it. He'd gone too far, spooked her.

"I have to go," she said without looking at him again. "Chad's waiting for me."

Before he could stop her, she bolted from the room. For the second time today, Paige Barnes had run away from him.

Paige threw down her pen and pushed back from the desk in her room. How could she work when all she could think of was Alexei Voronov telling her she deserved happiness and love?

Of course he hadn't meant *he* was the man who was going to give her those things, but she'd felt as if she must look so pitifully grateful, so hopeful, that she'd reacted defensively. And when he'd called her an open book, it too eerily echoed her own thoughts. She'd suddenly felt the urgent need to escape before she embarrassed herself any further.

She was a strong woman. She'd been strong all her life, and she'd taken care of herself and her sister since their mother had died. She'd sacrificed and scraped, and she was independent and moderately successful. So why did she dissolve into a puddle of mush around a man she barely knew? Why did he make her feel so vulnerable?

A glance at her watch told her it was nearly four in the afternoon. It felt earlier since the sun usually set so late here in the spring and summer—though you wouldn't know it was spring with the snow outside. But her stomach growled and she realized she hadn't eaten since grabbing a pastry and coffee this morning before going to the meeting. She thought about ordering room service, but decided that going to the hotel restaurant was a better idea.

She'd locked herself inside since she'd returned a few hours ago, and it was time to get out, among people. Perhaps then she would stop thinking so much about one Russian prince.

Chad and Emma were off somewhere, and would be spending their free time together for the rest of the time they were here. Now that Paige knew about the relationship, there was no need to keep up the pretense. Chad had apologized to her on the ride to the meeting this morning. He'd wanted to tell her, he'd said, but he hadn't been sure she would approve.

She'd admitted that she wouldn't have, and—without a care for possible job ramifications—had told him that if he hurt her sister, she'd gut him. He hadn't fired her, as she'd half expected, but had instead assured her that he loved Emma and would never hurt her.

While they were at the meeting, Emma had moved her suitcases to Chad's room.

Which left Paige alone and feeling kind of blue. Though Emma was in college, she'd continued to live at home. Paige was accustomed to having someone there. Of course she'd taken business trips before, and of course she'd stayed alone. But this trip seemed so different, and Emma's absence so final, that it bothered her more than she'd thought it would.

Paige hadn't changed out of her suit earlier, so she grabbed her jacket and took the elevator down to the lobby. Fifteen minutes later, she was seated in a corner booth and contemplating the English menu a waiter had brought.

"Don't order the *borscht*," a deep voice said. Her head snapped up, her gaze colliding with icy gray eyes. Her pulse shot skyward.

He slid into the booth seat opposite her. "Everyone who comes to Russia orders *borscht,* but there is far more to our cuisine than cabbage."

"What are you doing here?" Paige demanded. "Go away before you get me in trouble!"

"Do not worry, Paige. No one will see you talking to me."

"You don't know that," she insisted. "What if Chad gets hungry? What if he comes in here?"

He shrugged. It infuriated her the way he so casually dismissed her fears. He was rich, and he didn't have to worry about losing his job. But she had so much more to worry about than her job now that Chad was planning to marry her sister. She would *not* cause problems between them.

"You should have agreed to come to dinner with me. Then we would not be here, but elsewhere."

Paige gritted her teeth. "Go away."

He leaned back against the cushions and shot her an arrogant grin. "Only if you go with me."

Her heart leaped into double time. "I'm not going with you, Alexei."

"Then I will stay with you," he said, reaching for the menu.

She held it tight, refusing to let go.

"This is a nice hotel," he said, "but it caters to tourists. Wouldn't you like to try real Russian food? See more than the inside of your room and the airport?"

"I've already been to Red Square," she said primly.

His grin could have melted an iceberg. "I have fond memories of your trip to Red Square."

Paige tried not to blush, though she could feel the heat creeping into her cheeks. For once in her life, she wished she'd slept around more. Then she wouldn't be so affected by Alexei Voronov's wicked grin.

"You didn't really come here to make me go to dinner with you," she said, trying to interject some reality back into the situation.

"No. I had to meet with someone. But I saw you enter the restaurant, and I couldn't pass up the opportunity to see you again."

"Stop saying things like that."

"Why not? You are a beautiful woman, and I wanted to see you."

No one had ever called her beautiful. She was passably pretty, but she was too plain to be beautiful. Fashion confused her, makeup was a mystery that she'd only partially solved— blush, lipgloss and mascara usage were pretty simple—and her hair was so long and thick that she usually just ended up with a ponytail. Emma tried to get her to wear trendier clothes, but she never felt quite right in them. Emma's style was wrong for Paige, and since she didn't really know how to find her own, she settled for business suits and jeans. It was a safe wardrobe. Conservative.

"I can see you do not believe me," Alexei continued. "This shocks me, Paige."

She lifted her chin a notch while she clutched the menu between her hands. "I don't trust you, Prince Voronov. You have an ulterior motive."

His face split into another of those jaw-dropping grins. "How well you know me already," he purred. "I do have an ulterior motive." Then he leaned forward and caught one of her hands in his. "The motive is that I want you to come with me now. I promise Chad will never know. He may speak Russian, but he does not know this place like I do. He will not venture beyond the more trendy districts."

"And you want to take me somewhere that isn't trendy?" She pulled her hand away, though her heart continued to beat overtime. "I'm not sure if I should be insulted or relieved."

Oh my God, she was bantering with him.

His sensual mouth curved, showing impossibly white teeth. "I would take you to the finest restaurant in the city, if you would allow me. But since you will not, I want to take you somewhere even better."

"Better than the finest restaurant in the city? That doesn't seem possible, now does it?"

"It is very possible, I assure you. You have only to say yes, and you will find out. Come with me now, Paige."

She liked talking to him. He took away the loneliness, and he made her insides churn with excitement. Warmth flowed through her like she'd submerged in a hot bath. It made her languid and less uncertain.

Was it truly wrong to consider going to dinner with him? Chad and Emma were very likely locked in their suite, ordering room service and making love. Why couldn't she see the city and enjoy herself for a while? What was the harm in that?

"I can't," she said, a hint of desperation creeping into her voice. Because she wanted to go. She wanted to spend more time with this man who told her she was beautiful. He made her feel like she was someone special, even if it were an illusion. It was a new feeling and she liked it way too much.

"That is Chad Russell talking," he said disdainfully. "I want to hear what Paige Barnes wants."

Paige closed her eyes. She wanted to see the city, and she wanted to have dinner with a handsome man who gave her compliments. "It's too complicated. I shouldn't go."

"What is complicated about eating together?"

But why couldn't she have an evening of fun? Emma was with Chad, and they were so happy with each other that they wouldn't notice if Paige went out for a few hours. So long as the restaurant was far from the hotel and not a place likely to be frequented by tourists, what was the harm? She'd already spent the night with this man. It couldn't get any worse than that.

Besides, what had happened to her vow to live for herself, to do what Paige wanted for a change?

"Yes," she breathed before she could change her mind. "I'll go to dinner with you."

"Speciba," Alexei said as he slid from the seat and grabbed her hand. He tossed some bills down on the table, though she'd ordered nothing yet, and tugged her toward the exit.

"Wait, I need my coat," she said, pulling against him. She hadn't expected them to move so fast once she'd agreed. She'd thought she would have time to run up to her room and get her coat at the very least.

"I will buy you a coat," he replied.

"I can't let you do that."

"Of course you can." He dragged her into one of the shops in the lobby, picked out a long white coat made of the finest cashmere and wrapped her in it while the shopgirl oohed and ahhed.

"Alexei—"

"Quiet, Paige."

Next he selected a fur cap, like the one he'd worn last night, though in white, a snowy scarf and matching gloves made of the finest kid. Then he took a credit card from the breast pocket of his jacket and handed it to the cashier before Paige could insist on paying for it herself.

A moment later and he was hustling her out the lobby doors and into a long black limousine.

"I want to pay you for everything," she said as the car started to roll down the driveway.

"I will not take your money. Consider it a gift."

"I insist, Alexei." She folded her arms and stared at him, daring him to argue. How could she accept a gift so fine? She could not be indebted to him. Dinner was one thing, but a cashmere coat that must have cost at least five hundred dollars?

"Very well," he said easily. "We will set up a payment plan. One hundred of your U.S. dollars a month for the next sixty months…"

Paige blinked. "Six thousand dollars? You spent six thousand dollars?"

He reached out and tipped a finger under her chin. Her mouth snapped closed as she realized her jaw had been hanging open.

"*Da,* but you needed a coat."

She started to shrug out of the garment, but he stopped her.

"Don't be a fool, Paige. It pleases me to buy this for you. You do not need to pay me."

She looked away as, ridiculously, her eyes filled with tears. When was the last time she'd gotten a gift for no reason whatsoever? Not since before her mother died. Mama had loved surprising her daughters with small trinkets—until she had the accident and every penny they had went toward her care.

Paige couldn't accept such an extravagant gift from this man. It wasn't right. "I'll give everything back when you return me to the hotel."

Alexei swore in Russian. Or so she assumed by the expression on his face. "Very well," he said, stony-faced. "Whatever pleases you, Paige Barnes."

And now she felt ungrateful. She'd hurt his feelings, and it bothered her. She was Southern—and like all Southern women, she'd been inculcated with graciousness and sensitivity to others' feelings from birth. She'd failed miserably just now.

Paige touched his sleeve. "Thank you for the coat, Alexei. It was kind of you."

He swung around to look at her, his brows drawn down over his remarkable eyes. Why did he have to be so breathtaking?

"I do not understand you, Paige."

She blew out a breath. The air in the car was warm, and she was feeling toasty and comfortable. "I'm not sure I understand myself," she said with a shaky smile. "But I'm sorry I was rude."

He waved a hand, as if dismissing the last few minutes from his mind. "And I am sorry if I made you uncomfortable. It was not my intention."

Paige's gaze dropped. She twisted her fingers together in her lap. "I have to admit I'm uncomfortable simply being with you," she said. "I don't want to cause any trouble."

"There will be no trouble."

"If I were your employee, and you saw me with Chad, would you be angry?"

"Truthfully? Yes. But," he said before she could interject anything, "I would not fire you simply because of that. Far better to keep you close."

She frowned. "Really? Why?"

He leaned in as if he were imparting a secret. "Because you might know things that could be valuable to my enemies."

Her stomach bottomed out. "You'd be mistaken," she said softly. "I don't know anything. And even if I did, I wouldn't tell you. If that's why you've gone to all this trouble, you're wasting your time."

Alexei grinned, and her insides melted in spite of her wish

not to react. "Such a little *teegr,* Paige. This is why I like you. You are loyal, even when he has hurt you deeply."

She twisted her fingers together in her lap. "I'm not hurt. I was simply surprised. And concerned for my sister."

"Your sister is old enough to take care of herself, don't you think?"

Paige frowned. He didn't understand, and she couldn't really explain it. "That's not the point. I feel responsible for her, and I love her. I won't let anyone hurt her."

"Of course you love her," he said. "But you are not responsible for her."

"You don't know anything about us," she protested. "It's easy for you to sit there and pronounce judgment, but until you've walked a mile in my shoes, you have no right to tell me how to feel."

He took one of her hands in his, rubbed stomach-flipping circles in her palm. "I am not telling you how to feel. But a twenty-one-year-old makes her own decisions. You are not responsible for what she chooses."

Her breath left her on a long sigh. "I know. But you don't stop worrying about someone just because they become an adult. I raised Emma. In some ways, she's like my child."

She'd never said that aloud to anyone, she realized. It was shocking to voice it to this man she barely knew. Of course people back in Atkinsville knew she'd raised Emma after their mother's death, but Paige had never told anyone how truly hard it had been. To open up would have been to admit she needed help—which might have led to Child Services intervening.

"Ah, Paige, this makes so much sense now."

"What makes sense?" The circles in her palm continued. Her body was softening, melting, her core liquefying beneath his touch. My God.

"Why you feel so responsible, why you would sacrifice your own happiness for hers."

"I didn't say that. Emma doesn't need me to be unhappy just so she can be happy."

His eyes were sympathetic, understanding. "You must have been very young when you had to become her mother."

"Eighteen," she said.

"It was difficult for you, yes?"

Paige sighed. Why was she telling him this? And yet it felt somewhat comforting to do so. Like her tears the other night, it was cleansing to finally let it out. "Of course. I was still a kid myself and I didn't always know what to do. I didn't get everything right."

"Yet you did enough. She is grown and independent. You must allow her to sink or swim on her own."

"I appreciate what you're saying, but you have no idea—"

"I had a sister," he said very suddenly, his eyes shadowed. "She was three years younger than I. I protected her fiercely, Paige. But I could not save her in the end. I only wish she'd lived long enough to be able to drive me insane with her choices." He squeezed her hand then. "Celebrate your sister's ability to do so, and stand by her when she falls—but do not ever feel as if you must cease to live your life in order to always be there for her."

Paige couldn't speak. Shock—and fear—had frozen her vocal cords. How did he see inside her like this? How did he *know* what her fears were, and what she'd given up over the years without her actually telling him the details? It was disconcerting.

And yet she also ached for him. For the loss that clearly still affected him. She wanted to say she was sorry, wanted to ask what had happened, but before she could find her voice again, his phone rang.

"You will please excuse me, I must take this," he said, frowning at the display. Paige nodded—but she needn't have bothered because he was already talking.

He spent the next thirty minutes on the phone as the car glided through the city. The farther they drove from the hotel, the more Paige started to wonder if she'd made a mistake. She usually deliberated before she made decisions. She did not act on impulse.

Until now.

She'd signed on for a nice, authentic dinner in a real Russian restaurant with a man who fascinated her. She'd not expected to have her soul bared to him, or to experience the chink in her heart when she'd realized he'd also lost someone he loved.

It was supposed to be *dinner*. Nice, simple, easy.

But the car kept moving farther and farther from the city center. They passed from the densely packed buildings of Moscow into the outskirts before rolling along a congested highway. She wanted to ask Alexei where they were, but he was still on the phone.

When they took an exit and made a turn, she suddenly realized they were approaching an airport. Her stomach dropped to her toes. Though it didn't look like the same airport she'd flown into only a couple of days ago, it was still a large facility with a lot of traffic.

"It is *Sheremetyevo*," Alexei said, as if he'd been reading her mind. He tucked his phone away. "You probably flew into *Domodedovo*, which is south of the city."

Paige tried not to panic. "Yes, but what are we doing here?"

"I am taking you to dinner, *maya krasavitsa*." His expression said it was obvious.

"At the airport?"

"No," he said as the car hesitated for a moment at a security gate. The chauffeur exchanged a few words with the guards, and then they were through. A couple of minutes later the car came to a halt. The door opened and Alexei stepped out, then held out a hand for her. When she emerged, she realized they were standing in front of a hangar where a jet was slowly taxiing out into the open. The whine of the engines was loud, the wind whipping her clothes and making her wish she'd changed into jeans and boots instead of her business suit and kitten heels. In spite of the gorgeous coat, the wind went up her pant legs and chilled her from the inside out.

Alexei leaned into the car and grabbed the shopping bag with the accessories.

"Alexei," she shouted over the noise as he placed the hat on her head and wrapped the scarf around her neck, "I can't get on an airplane with you! This is insane!"

He didn't let go of her hand, instead tugging her into the curve of his body and wrapping an arm around her to keep her from getting too chilled.

"It is a short flight, Paige. I'll have you back by midnight, I promise. Put these in your pockets," he said, handing her the gloves.

Her pulse skidded like an out of control ice skater. What had she gotten herself into? Agreeing to go to a restaurant with him was one thing, but getting onto a plane?

"I can't," she said, shaking her head frantically. They both knew she wasn't talking about the gloves.

He turned her and put both hands on her shoulders. Then he leaned down until his face was only inches from hers.

"You trusted me last night," he said, his voice soothing in spite of the fact he had to practically shout. "I'm asking you to trust me again."

CHAPTER FIVE

HE WOULDN'T TELL HER where they were going, yet she'd still gotten onto the plane with him. Paige shook her head at her own folly, wondering what on earth had happened to her good sense. It had taken less than an hour for the plane to land at a different airport, but instead of getting into a car, they'd boarded a helicopter.

It wasn't her first helicopter ride, but it was certainly the most luxurious. The inside of the craft looked like a custom yacht, all white leather and sleek wood. Beside her, Alexei was on the phone. He'd taken at least six calls since she'd climbed into the car with him outside the hotel.

But then, that's what multimillionaire—or billionaire—tycoons did. They made deals over the phone, bought and sold entire companies and transferred millions of dollars, or rubles as the case may be, with aplomb.

It was a world far outside her realm, in spite of the last few days as Chad's executive secretary.

Alexei tucked the phone back into his pocket. "I am sorry for the interruptions," he said.

Paige shrugged. "It's okay," she replied. "There's a lot at stake."

His gaze sharpened as he studied her. "Yes, there is. And I intend to win, Paige."

A shiver skidded through her. She hadn't been referring to

any one deal in particular, but clearly the Valishnikov acquisition was the subject of his many calls. Apprehension was a tight ball in her stomach as she thought of her boss back in Moscow. "So does Chad."

He looked out the window behind her as the helicopter began to bank. "Look."

She turned to where he'd pointed, her breath catching in her throat. She felt him move behind her on the luxurious leather bench, felt his solid body pressing against hers. It was intimate, casual, but she burned nonetheless.

Below, the land unfolded itself in a crystalline white blanket. A rich green and white palace sat in the center of the covering. Six massive white columns fronted the building, and ornate friezes clad in gold surrounded each of the myriad windows across the three-level facing. The domes of a small church nearby were a muted gold, though she imagined they would glint in the sun, while white trees reached with bare arms to the dull sky.

Alexei's arm was on her shoulder, his cheek near her other ear as he leaned in and pointed. "It is the Voronov Palace," he said, "built in the early eighteenth century. Look there, at the fountain. It was a gift from Tsar Peter the Great."

The fountain in the front courtyard seemed made of gold, its cherubs and mythical creatures frozen in time, waiting for some sign only they knew in order to step down from their perches and frolic in the courtyard.

The Voronov Palace was fairy tale beautiful, and she felt completely out of her depth being here. She'd been raised in a two-bedroom house with a tiny kitchen and a postage-stamp lawn. Hardly comparable.

The helicopter made another pass, then began to hover before gliding softly down, its rotors lessening in speed until they were on the ground and a man opened the door and smiled at them. He said something in Russian. Alexei answered before turning and taking her hand in his.

Then they were stepping out of the craft and hurrying along a path that had been cleared of snow until they reached the house. Alexei led her inside a grand entry where Paige came to an abrupt stop, her head tilting back and her jaw dropping open.

The entry was vast, its gilt and alabaster walls rising to a dome that was painted all around with a scene from the bible. Three large crystal chandeliers were suspended from different points of the dome. The glittering crystals threw light into every nook and corner of the fresco, which gleamed with rich golds, deep blues, and vibrant reds.

"It's the Adoration of the Madonna," she said in wonder. Mama'd had a print of a religious scene similar to this one on the wall in their living room. Paige had been so accustomed to it that she'd lost the ability to see it with fresh eyes when she was still quite young.

But this was like seeing it again for the first time—though clearly this painting was far better. Not to mention *real*. Still, odd as it seemed, it gave her that wistful feeling of home.

"Da."

She looked at Alexei, blinking back tears. For a moment, she'd forgotten he was there. What must it be like to live with this kind of beauty every day of your life?

He came to her, his gaze filled with concern. "What is wrong, Paige? You are safe with me, I promise you."

It was too late to hide her reaction now. She gave him a watery smile, embarrassment creeping through her. "It's silly," she said, swiping her fingers beneath her eyes. "I always cry in art galleries. There's just something about the ethereal beauty of old paintings that gets to me. It's like the painter's soul is inside, if that makes sense. It's just so wondrous."

It was true, and yet she knew it was more than the beauty

of this painting making her cry. It was that connection to the past, discovered in such an unusual place, that made her more emotional than she might have otherwise been.

Alexei wiped away a tear that slipped down her cheek. His handsome face was gentler than she'd ever seen it. "You are very refreshing, Paige Barnes. I do not think I've ever met a woman who cries in art galleries, though this is hardly a gallery."

She managed a soft laugh. Hardly a gallery? Who was he kidding? "Well, I've only been inside three in my life, not including this place, so maybe it's not a phenomenon so much as the newness of the experience. I might grow positively callous with time."

He smiled. "I doubt that. And I think I had better not take you into the portrait gallery. You'll never be able to eat dinner with your nose closed from crying."

"Maybe after dinner then?" How could she not want to see portraits of his ancestors?

"After dinner is a surprise." He took her hand and pulled her to his side. "Now come, if I'm not mistaken, a delicious meal awaits us in the library."

"The library?" she said as they moved deeper into the house.

"The formal dining room is vast, whereas the library is far more cozy."

If cozy was a two-story room the size of a small department store, then yes, this room was cozy, Paige thought, as Alexei ushered her into a book-lined space with a giant fireplace burning at one end. A round table was set near the fire with crystal, china and snowy-white linens. A trio of uniformed servants stood to one side, near a cart from which glorious smells wafted.

Alexei took her coat and hat and handed them to one of the servants. Then he piled his own on top and came to pull out a chair for her. Paige sank into the worn leather, wondering how many Voronov princes and princesses had used this very chair she was sitting on.

Alexei took the chair opposite, and the food began to arrive. There were meat dishes, steamy dumplings, fragrant vegetables and black bread. A dish of black caviar in ice sat to one side, along with flat pancakes she knew were called *blini*. One of the servants opened a bottle of white wine and poured it into their glasses. Paige started to ask for water as well, but Alexei said something in Russian and a glass of water appeared at her place setting immediately after.

The waiters filtered out of the room and they were suddenly alone. Alexei lifted his wineglass. "To a fine evening of good food and great company."

Paige clinked glasses with him. She took a small sip of the wine, surprised to find it light and refreshing, and smiled back at him. Her pulse thrummed, and she wondered how she would get through this evening when suddenly she couldn't think of a single thing to say.

It was completely unreal, what was happening to her. She'd been whisked away from Moscow by a Russian prince, flown on his private plane to St. Petersburg and now she was sitting in the beautiful library of his ancestral home and eating a romantic dinner with him. These things happened in movies, or to beautiful models and actresses, but not to hardworking career women like her.

She thought of Chad and Emma, and pushed away a spear of guilt that notched into her breastbone.

"You are enjoying the *pelmeni?*" Alexei asked.

"Everything is wonderful. But which dish is *pelmeni?*"

"The dumplings. The filling is a mixture of beef, lamb, pork and spices."

Paige stabbed another. "It tastes amazing. You were right there's more to Russian food than cabbage."

He followed the fork from her plate to her mouth, his gaze lingering while she chewed. She was beginning to feel self-conscious, but then he looked down at his own plate and resumed eating.

"They were my sister's favorite," he said. "It is a recipe from the Urals. My mother made them for us quite often."

"I'm sorry that your sister is no longer with you," she said carefully. And then she wanted to smack herself. Could she have sounded any stiffer? Any more uncomfortable?

"It has been many, many years," he replied. "But thank you."

When he didn't say anything else, she felt duty-bound to change the subject. Another tenet of the Southern creed: *never make folks uncomfortable, and never talk about upsetting subjects.*

"My mother cooked a mean Southern-fried chicken," she said lightly. "That was my favorite growing up."

He looked at her with interest. "But not any longer?"

Paige shook her head. "Not since I learned about cholesterol and heart disease. And not since I lost ten pounds once I gave up fried foods."

Though she'd probably still be eating Mama's chicken if Mama were alive to make it.

"I have never had this Southern-fried chicken before."

"If you ever come to Texas, I'll make it for you." Polite chitchat was the hallmark of Southern manners. She didn't expect he would truly come, but she felt obligated to say it.

He grinned. "Perhaps I will plan a visit."

Paige took another sip of her wine. After tonight, the last thing she needed was for this man to come to Texas and see her meager little house. Nor was he likely to do so, really. He was simply being polite in return.

"Your home is lovely," she said. "It must have been amazing growing up here."

His expression clouded, but then he shrugged. "I did not grow up here, *maya krasavitsa*. My father died when I was five, and my mother was forced to leave with my sister and me. We were, as you say, persona non grata."

She felt she should drop it, and yet she found she could not. "That seems so unfair. Shouldn't your mother have inherited the property when your father died?"

He took a sip of his wine. "You would think so, but no. Times were hard back then, and Mama did not have, shall we say, the right connections. There were those who very much wanted her gone."

"But you are here now," she said, trying to recover from her mistake.

"It took many years, but yes, I managed to buy the property back." His ice-gray eyes glittered with an emotion she could not identify. Hate? Rage? Fear?

Before she could figure it out, his mask slipped back into place. Once more he was the handsome, solicitous Russian prince.

She stabbed her fork into a pile of greens. "Where does your mother live now?"

The seriousness never left his expression. She began to get a bad feeling that she'd somehow blundered again.

"She is in the church you saw when we arrived. As are my sister and my father. I moved my mother and sister here to join him when I took possession."

Paige felt her stomach drop. She set the fork down. He'd gotten the family home back, but his family wasn't here to enjoy it with him. "I'm so sorry, Alexei. I shouldn't have asked—"

"How could you know?" He reached for her hand across the table. "They have all been gone a very long time now. But they are where they should be, in the family crypt, and I am happy I could give that to them."

She squeezed his hand, her heart going out to him. Though it was no consolation, she wanted him to know that she understood. "My mother died eight years ago."

"I am very sorry for your loss."

She shook her head. She was messing everything up, failing in her efforts to comfort him. Turning the conversation to oneself at a time like this was unforgivably rude—and not at all what she'd intended. "I didn't tell you because I wanted sympathy. I just wanted you to know that I understood what it's like to be alone."

He looked surprised, but he quickly hid it. "You have Emma."

She swallowed. "Yes, but not for much longer."

He lifted her hand and kissed it. "You will always have her, Paige. She is still your sister."

Paige's throat felt tight. He'd lost his sister, and she was complaining about hers moving out and getting married? What was wrong with her? "Goodness, how did we end up talking about me when we were talking about you?"

"I like learning about you," he said.

"I'd rather talk about you."

"What do you wish to know?" he asked, leaning back in his chair. His black hair gleamed in the firelight as he focused on her. Her thoughts began to stray, but the hint of a grin on his face brought her back to the present.

Paige's pulse ticked up. There was one thing she wanted to know most of all, but she hardly dared ask. Then again, why shouldn't she? She'd already strayed outside the bounds of polite conversation. "Why are you being so nice to me, Alexei?"

If she thought he would be put off guard by her question, she was wrong. He smiled lazily, his gaze glittering as he looked at her. "You have to ask after last night?"

She wanted to believe him, but she was too practical to do so.

"If you want information, you're wasting your time. Until this trip, I was a junior secretary. Chad only picked me to come because of my sister."

Saying it aloud hurt, but it was the truth. Chad had chosen her for this trip because of Emma. Because they didn't want to be apart, and without Mavis, he needed a secretary anyway. It had been the perfect cover. It was embarrassing to admit to anyone, much less to a man as successful as Alexei Voronov.

But she would not have him believe she knew things she did not. If he took her back to Moscow right this instant, then so be it. At least she would know what his true motive had been.

"Does that anger you?"

His question took her by surprise. It wasn't what she'd expected out of him, but she decided to answer honestly. "Yes, but that's life, isn't it? I'm still good at what I do, and this trip is still an opportunity. Provided you don't acquire the land and close Russell Tech for good."

He looked very dark, very dangerous in that moment—as if his masks had all been stripped away and only the essence remained. A dark, cold, cruel essence.

"*When* I win, I will not close Russell Tech," he said. "I will absorb it."

Her temples throbbed with the beginnings of a headache, and she felt hot in her itchy wool-blend suit. *You started it,* she reminded herself.

"Chad says you would destroy the company and we'd all be out of work."

Alexei made a noise. "Chad is wrong. Though there will be some reorganizing, you would still have a job, Paige.

You would simply be working for me instead of for Chad Russell."

It was his cold certainty, his arrogant assumption about her that made her say what she did next.

"*If* you win, I'll look for another job."

How could he imagine she would want to work for him? It wasn't because of the animosity between him and Chad, or the repercussions to Russell Tech, though of course those things bothered her.

No, it was because of this, tonight. Because he gave every appearance of liking her and then spoke of her working for him as if tonight had never happened.

But what has *happened, Paige?*

Aside from the extravagance of his method, he'd done nothing more than take her to dinner. Yes, he'd kissed her last night, but she didn't fool herself it'd meant anything. Everything about last night had been outside the realm of normal, from the kiss in Red Square to the kisses in his apartment later.

"Why would you not want to work for me?" he demanded.

She laid her napkin on the table, her appetite gone. There was another reason, a more important reason than her wounded pride. And she had no problem telling him what it was.

"If you ruin Chad, then you ruin my sister's happiness. I can't work for the man who hurts Emma. She's done nothing to deserve it."

Alexei could only stare. She bristled like a wild Siberian tiger, her eyes sparkling in challenge, her creamy skin golden in the firelight. He should tell her she was foolish, but instead he wanted to drag her into his arms and kiss her.

No, he wanted to do more than that. He wanted to strip that ugly suit from her body and bury himself inside her. The urge was overwhelming, surprising.

Alexei stood abruptly, before he acted upon his impulse. She tilted her head back, a shadow of alarm crossing her features before she veiled it.

It bothered him, the way she sometimes looked at him like he was a great Russian bear planning to devour her whole. Like he was a character in a Dostoevsky novel, a human personification of impartial evil.

Perhaps he was.

But he had reason. And he would not crumble now, not when victory was so close. Not when she was here, and he wanted her. He'd told himself he wanted to find out what she knew about Chad's business, but he was beginning to believe the truth was a bit more complicated.

That his need for her was based on more than expedience.

He wanted her, but he hadn't expected to like her. She'd surprised him with how interesting she truly was. She was a woman who appreciated beauty so deeply it made her cry, and who protected her sister with a fierceness he could well understand. And she was loyal, steadfastly so, in spite of the insult she'd been dealt by the two people she'd come to Russia with.

He tried not to think of what he planned to do as yet another betrayal of her trust when she'd already suffered so many. He did what he must.

It was *necessary*. Some promises went deeper than any misgivings he might have. Her sister might be hurt if Chad lost his business, but she would recover. And Paige would recover as well. This was not a life or death situation.

He had to be ruthless. He was too close to his goals not to be. Katerina deserved it. His mother deserved it. Tim Russell had cost them everything, and Alexei wouldn't be finished until he'd stripped everything from Tim's son and wife.

He would not allow this one intriguing woman to divert his focus.

"Nevertheless, you will have a job should you want it. Now come," he said, offering her his hand as he shoved away any thoughts of taking her back to Moscow immediately. "This is no time to talk about business."

"Where are we going?"

"It is a surprise."

She still glared at him, her color high in her cheeks, but he held his hand steady and waited. He didn't think she would accept, but then she sighed and placed her small hand in his. The touch of her skin sent a shock of desire coursing through him. He tried to push it away, but the feeling was too strong.

A shudder rippled down his spine. He could not let her go now even if he wanted to.

She rose in a fluid movement to stand at his side. He was hyperaware of her, could feel her breath ghosting in and out of her lungs, her blood flowing through her veins, her answering desire thickening and burgeoning inside her body.

Her color was still high, but he knew it was for a different reason now. It gratified him, this knowledge that she wanted him, even while it made him feel as if he were imprisoned behind bars—because he could not act on it, not yet.

But he would as soon as the moment was right.

Instead he drew her to the window and stepped back so she could see. Outside, in the snow that was beginning to sparkle as the sun sank beneath the cloud cover and shot its last rays over the icy landscape, three horses were hitched side by side to a *troika*. A groomsman stood at their heads, holding them in place, while another checked the traces on the sled.

He heard the intake of her breath, the little gasp of wonder, and he took advantage of her change in mood to press in closer. To settle his hands on her shoulders and lean down to nuzzle her ear.

"As promised," he whispered, his lips finding and nibbling her tender earlobe. He allowed himself that much because he could not stop. Soon, very soon, he would take her to his bed.

Her only answer was a shudder.

CHAPTER SIX

THE AIR SMELLED CRISP and clean, and Paige couldn't help but laugh as the *troika* glided over the snow. The horses snorted and tossed their heads, the bells and tassels shaking with their movements as Alexei drove them down a lane beneath trees covered in white.

"It's glorious," she said. "Thank you so much."

"It would be a shame to come all this way and not experience it, *da?*"

She was bundled in her new coat, with the fur hat pulled down over her head and tickling her skin where it touched. She was warm, and yet a shiver of excitement arced over her body. Paige pulled the thick blanket that lay across their legs higher.

"Are you cold?"

"Not at all," she replied.

He looked concerned. "If you are cold, we will return to the palace. You have only to say so."

Paige touched his sleeve. "Not yet, Alexei," she said. "I don't want it to end so soon."

He smiled down at her. "Then we will keep going."

Truthfully, once he'd stood up from the table, she'd thought the evening was over. And she'd believed it was probably best that way, no matter how her heart pinched at the thought.

Because what on earth was she doing? This man was a

prince, he lived in a palace and he was trying to destroy her boss's—soon to be brother-in-law's—company. She had no business being here, no business enjoying her time with him.

It was wrong.

Yet here she was, sitting beside him in a sleigh, gliding across a darkening landscape that was lit by the fat moon hanging low in the sky. The cloud cover of earlier hadn't dissipated, but it had lessened enough that the moon shone brightly so long as it was close to the horizon. Another couple of hours, and the light would be gone as the moon rose into the high clouds.

It was romantic, being out here like this, something she would remember for as long as she lived. She did not regret this moment, even if she felt guilty for enjoying it.

After a few minutes more, Alexei pulled the horses to a stop in a clearing on a small rise.

"If the weather were normal for this time of year, we wouldn't be able to do this," he said to her. "But we had a late snowstorm."

"I'm glad it snowed," she replied, smiling up at him.

He touched a gloved hand to her cheek. She shivered, but not from cold. No, when Alexei touched her, it was like a furnace fired up in her belly. Every part of her felt hot. She remembered his lips on her ear, and her skin glowed. She'd almost turned in his arms, almost told him to forget the *troika* and take her to bed instead.

Fortunately she'd shocked herself so much with the idea that she had not acted upon it.

"Perhaps the snow came for you," he said softly.

A blast of heat sizzled through her core. Any second, she'd need to rip off her coat and hat and let the frigid air chill her skin. He leaned toward her, his head dipping lower. She was wrong to want him, and yet everything about this moment was magical.

She stretched up to meet him—

And gasped as a mournful howl split the night.

"Wolves," Alexei said. "There aren't as many as there used to be, but they still come at night."

"Shouldn't we go?" Another howl sounded in the distance and one of the horses snorted. Bells tinkled musically.

"There is nothing to fear. We are not too far from the palace, and I am armed."

Paige squinted into the remote landscape. The snow went as far as the eye could see, but no shapes moved upon it. Still, the animals were close. "They sound hungry."

"Yes, but there is prey here. Wild boar and goats will feed their bellies."

"I'm not certain I find that reassuring." She looked up to find him watching her with an odd expression. "What is it, Alexei?"

"You look as if you belong here," he said. "I knew white would suit you instead of black. The coat, the hat. Your cheeks are red, your eyes bright and your lips…" His gaze dropped to her mouth. "Your lips need kissing."

"Alexei," she began. The rest was lost as his mouth came down on hers.

She knew she should stop him, but she simply wasn't capable of it. She *wanted* his kiss, wanted his touch. He groaned low in his throat as their tongues tangled. One arm came around her, pulled her in close, while his other held the reins. Paige grasped his lapels, tilted her head back as she pressed herself closer to him.

She let him pillage her mouth, her heart pounding so hard in her chest she was certain he could feel it. This was the kiss in the square, but bumped up a few thousand degrees. She felt as if she'd known him forever, as if she'd been destined to arrive at this very moment *forever*.

Everything about kissing Alexei felt right, though it should not.

It most definitely should *not*.

But she was caught in the grip of new feelings, of the excitement and danger of kissing this dark, hard man.

Paige threaded a gloved hand into the hair at his nape, let the other slip beneath his coat to wander over the hard muscles of his chest. He made a sound of approval. And then his lips left hers, trailed hot kisses along her jaw to her ear.

"Alexei," she breathed, his name turning to frost as he sought her lips again. Whatever she'd been about to say was lost as he kissed her into a quivering bundle of nerve endings and sexual excitement.

"You are so beautiful. I want you, Paige," he said. "Now. Tonight."

Their mouths fused once more, and her spirit soared. Whatever the past, whatever the future—*this* moment was right. She couldn't have him forever, but she could have him right now. And why not? She deserved her own slice of happiness, for however long it lasted.

A little voice inside her head tried to interject reason, but she refused to listen. She'd been listening to that little voice for the last eight years, and it hadn't gotten her anything but loneliness and heartache.

"Yes," she said between kisses. "Yes."

The ride back to the palace took no time at all. Alexei turned the horses and gave them rein until the *troika* was whisking across the snow at a smart pace. Behind them the wolves howled, but in the sled, Paige felt safe and warm. Soon they were gliding into the courtyard, and then Alexei was handing the reins to a groom and lifting her from the sleigh.

They raced into the house like a couple of children, Alexei holding her hand and tugging her up the grand staircase. She felt like a princess in her white coat and fur hat, and she laughed when Alexei threw open a door and pulled her inside. Then he was slamming the door, his fingers flying over the buttons of her coat as he walked her backward.

"I have wanted to get you out of this uptight suit since I first saw you this morning," he said, his voice hot and sexy as he slipped the coat from her shoulders and tossed it aside. The hat and scarf followed, and she tugged off her gloves so she could feel his skin beneath her fingertips.

This morning. Was it really only this morning that they'd faced each other in a boardroom? Paige extinguished the thought before she could dwell on it. She knew who she was with, and she knew why it was wrong.

But she didn't want to stop. She wanted to race recklessly forward, before sense caught up with her. She wanted to feel *alive* for one night, wanted to feel the passion and power of a man moving inside her.

This man.

It was only once, only tonight. Tomorrow, she would go back to being staid Paige Barnes, efficient secretary.

Alexei got out of his coat before she could do it for him, and then he started to work on the buttons of her blouse. Paige slipped his shirt from his waistband and ran her hands beneath, finally touching his hot skin.

He flinched, laughing. "Your hands are cold."

"So are yours," she said when he slipped a finger beneath the edge of her bra. But she was too hot to care. His touch soothed the sizzle, gave her hope he would quench this fire before the evening was through.

Crazy, crazy, crazy.

She could hear the chant in her head, but she didn't want to listen to it. There would be plenty of time for self-recrimination later. Now, she only wanted to feel how good it could be with him.

Alexei's mouth sought hers as he slid the blouse from her shoulders. Paige met him eagerly, arching into his touch like a cat. *Don't think; just feel.*

He broke away and ripped his shirt over his head, then kissed her again, his hands sliding to the waistband of her trousers. A cold shot of fear darted through her, threatening to douse her ardor.

Should she explain that she was inexperienced? That she'd only done this once before, and she wasn't even sure if it counted?

But if she did, would he stop? She couldn't stand the idea that her inexperience might make the difference in whether or not he found her desirable, so she didn't say anything.

Another moment, and her pants were gone, sliding down her legs to pool at her feet before she stepped out of them.

The heat in Alexei's eyes was so intense she felt scorched from the contact. He spoke in Russian, exotic words she had no hope of understanding. She started to fold her arms beneath her breasts, but he stopped her.

"I would have never guessed that you had naughty undergarments beneath that suit."

Paige blushed. "They aren't naughty. They're just lacy."

And maybe a little bit racy. Her bra was white lace, fairly staid, but she'd worn a thong beneath her pants because it left no panty line.

Alexei made a spinning motion with his finger. She turned in an awkward circle before facing him again.

"You are very beautiful, Paige."

Part of her wanted to tell him to stop saying it, that she wasn't beautiful at all, but another part wanted to believe every word.

"You have too many clothes on," she said, unable to bear

his scrutiny a moment more while he was still partially clothed.

"Then help me to lose them."

She reached for his belt buckle, slipped it open. His bare chest radiated so much heat she thought she would burn. Last night, she'd seen the shadows of muscle and sinew beneath his open shirt, but that hadn't prepared her for the sight of him. He was broad-shouldered, beautifully made, with tight muscle and silky skin. Heart in her throat, Paige tugged his zipper down.

He took over, shedding his trousers until he stood before her completely naked. Paige swallowed a bubble of apprehension. He was magnificent, tall and broad, with clearly defined stomach muscles, and a dark, sexy arrow of hair pointing a trail down his abdomen.

"Do you like what you see?" he murmured, and Paige's gaze snapped to his. She'd been staring at his penis, hadn't she? But he was hard, ready for her—and clearly unembarrassed by his state of arousal.

Oh, God.

Paige felt as if she were stuck to the floor. She didn't know how she was supposed to act now. What would a sophisticated woman do? Would she go to him, wrap her arms around him and purr in his ear? Or would she shed her underwear and drape herself artfully across the bed?

Thankfully Alexei had no such problem deciding what to do. Sweeping her up, he carried her to the bed and laid her down. She could hardly process the luxury of her surroundings—the bed was canopied, gilded, and draped with thick, rich velvet. Inside the canopy dome, someone had painted a scene of a man and woman in a *troika,* the horses stretched out as they flew across a snowy landscape.

"You are trembling," he said as he came down beside her on the crisp cotton sheets. "Do I frighten you?"

"No, but it's been a long time," she admitted.

It was true, in a way. It *had* been a long time since she'd lost her virginity to a guy from her accounting class. Bob, who drank too much, botched the job and never called again. She'd always imagined it was out of embarrassment rather than because of anything she'd done.

Now she was beginning to worry that she might have been wrong.

"Then we will take our time," Alexei said, removing her glasses and placing them on the nightstand. "I can imagine nothing more pleasurable."

His mouth came down on hers, and her body melted by degrees. When Alexei kissed her, she felt that she would do anything he asked. It must be true, considering that she was naked in his bed and more than four hundred miles away from where she was supposed to be.

Except that he hadn't kissed her at all tonight until they'd gone on the *troika* ride. Everything that she'd done up to that point was her own doing, not a result of coercion.

Nor was this, she admitted to herself.

Alexei reached beneath her, found the catch to her bra and unsnapped it. Then he tugged it off and tossed it aside before cupping her breasts in his hands and kissing first one nipple and then the other while she squirmed beneath him.

"You are most sensitive," he murmured against her flesh. "I like you this way."

When his lips closed over her nipple, sweetly sucking it into a hard point, Paige gasped and arched her back. He obliged her by sucking harder.

"You like this," he said. Goose bumps rose on her flesh where his hot tongue left a wet trail to her other breast. Then he was repeating the motions again and again, sucking each of her nipples until she thought she would scream from the pure pleasure of it.

"Alexei," she gasped. "I don't want to go slow anymore!"

She was burning up, aching for him in ways she'd never experienced.

He chuckled. "Patience, sweet one. We have plenty of time." He kissed her stomach, rolled his tongue around her belly button and then traced a line across the top of her thong. "This is very sexy underwear, Paige Barnes. You make me wonder what other surprises you have in store."

And then he pushed her panties down her hips until she had no barriers left. Her breath caught in her throat.

She thought she was prepared for what he did next, but how could you be prepared for a thing you'd never experienced?

Alexei pushed her legs open, teased her with hot kisses along the insides of her thighs—but when he spread her wide and touched her with his tongue, Paige couldn't suppress the little scream that escaped. She thought she would literally fly apart.

Her entire body was on fire. Her hair tingled. And Alexei's mouth did things to her that no man had ever done. She wanted it to last forever—

But it was over in a matter of seconds as her body reached an impossibly high peak, and then dove into a free fall. Paige cried out, gasping and sobbing for breath during the long journey to the bottom.

The experience was intense, amazing, far more than she'd ever dreamed.

Yet still it wasn't over.

She thought Alexei would enter her body now, but he brought her to the peak once more with his mouth, and, when she thought she couldn't possibly take any more, he did it a third time.

She was wrung-out, sated, her body quivering with pleasure—and still she craved more.

"Please, Alexei," she said as he moved away from her. "Don't go."

His laugh was deep, sexy. "I'm not leaving, Paige. Not for a long time."

He reached into the table beside the bed, and then he was rolling on a condom and settling himself over top of her. She wrapped her legs around him, knowing instinctively that this was what she was supposed to do. He kissed her sweetly while he entered her body, moving forward on a long, slow glide that made her moan.

The pleasure took her breath away, even while the size and feel of him was almost too much. There was a moment of pain, a sharp sensation of tearing—and then he was inside her fully, his body throbbing in the very core of her.

"You should have told me," he gasped out.

When she opened her eyes, the expression on his face tore her heart in two. He looked lost, alone—confused, as if he'd expected one thing and gotten another.

Paige's heart dropped. "Told you what? Have I done something wrong?"

"You're a virgin." He seemed angry, intense.

Shock momentarily stole her voice. "I can't be."

He groaned as she moved beneath him. "Trust me, you are. *Were.*"

"I've been with one man. He, um…" She could feel her face turning red as she struggled to say it. "He barely started before he was finished."

Meaning he'd started to enter her body, and then stiffened as his climax hit him. Her first sexual experience had been over before it ever really began. Which meant he'd not taken her virginity as she'd always thought. He'd only started the job. Alexei had just now completed it.

Alexei's expression changed, grew fierce suddenly. But it wasn't the kind of fierce that scared her. Or at least not in a bad way. No, it was an intense, possessive, determined kind of look that said he wasn't about to quit until they were completely, thoroughly finished.

"My God, Paige," he said. "Just when I think you cannot surprise me any more than you already have."

His mouth came down on hers, hot, possessive. She relaxed into his kiss for only a moment before he set her body on fire with his own. He was gloriously hard, moving, his body showing no signs of being done.

Her heart soared. This was really happening, they were really making love—it wasn't going to end with him apologizing, grabbing his clothes, leaving her alone and wondering what the hell had just happened.

She couldn't think of anything but him as the wave caught her and tossed her higher than she'd ever been.

She learned very quickly how to shift her hips up to meet him, how to open herself to him, and how to prolong her pleasure and stave off the inevitable—but only for so long, because Alexei was relentless, driving her toward a completion more intense than any she'd experienced before now.

When her orgasm hit her this time, she couldn't hold back the scream that had pooled at the base of her throat. Vaguely she was aware that he followed her over the edge. Moments later he rolled over, taking her with him until she was lying on top of him, his body still buried deep inside hers.

Instinctively she knew that nothing would ever be the same again.

CHAPTER SEVEN

NOTHING HAD GONE the way he'd expected. Alexei lay beneath her, wondering what in the hell had just happened to him. Everything had spiraled out of control the instant he'd kissed her in the sleigh. He had not meant to move so fast.

He'd intended a slower seduction, perhaps unfolding over the next few days. And he'd intended to get inside her head, to have her open up to him and trust him before they went to bed.

He'd intended, bastard that he was, to make her think he was falling for her. Paige Barnes was the kind of woman who should be eating out of his hand.

And yet she was not. Nor did she seem likely to.

Which, paradoxically, might explain this intense attraction he felt toward her. She was so much more than he'd expected, and every moment he spent with her only increased his fascination.

My God, she'd still been a virgin. He hadn't counted on that at all. Guilt stabbed him in the gut. She'd trusted him enough to give him her virginity, and all he'd intended was to take advantage of her.

But how could he have known? He'd entered her so easily that he'd barely noticed the slight resistance until he'd broken through it. Then he'd been blown away.

She'd turned the tables on him with her sweet innocence

and earthy sexuality. The contrast between the two fascinated him. Compelled him. Even before he'd known she was still a virgin, he'd wanted her like he couldn't remember ever wanting another woman in recent memory.

Or ever?

Alexei closed his eyes. No, of course not. He must have wanted another woman this badly. What about Fermina, the supermodel? She'd had the longest legs he'd ever seen.

But, no. She'd been delightful, not compelling.

He ran through a succession of women in his head. None conjured up more than pleasant memories. None conjured up violent need that spiraled out of his control.

Perhaps it was the excitement of making love to Chad Russell's secretary, of taking something from under his cousin's nose that the man had been too ignorant to see for himself.

But, no, it wasn't that, either.

Paige's warm body was limp, her breathing even, and he knew she'd fallen asleep. He wanted to sleep as well, but he could not. He was still inside her, still hard, but he needed to withdraw while the condom was still tight.

Except that he didn't want to move. He wanted to lie here, sated and content, and enjoy the warm woman in his bed. He wanted to enjoy the companionship with her, however brief.

Paige knew what it was like to lose family too soon. It was a connection they shared. Another reason everything about this night seemed so strange to him. He didn't usually share details about his family with the women he dated.

Hell, he didn't usually share details of his life and family with *anyone*. He'd learned that life wasn't fair, and that you couldn't trust another soul with the burdens of yours. No one was what he or she seemed. Everyone had an agenda of some sort.

And his was to destroy the Russells.

Not that he'd told her much, but he'd said more than he usually did. In the instant when he'd told her that his family was in the crypt, he'd felt a wall of loneliness pushing down on him that he hadn't experienced in a very long time. Somehow, she'd recognized it. He'd wanted to open up to her even more in that moment, but he'd stopped himself from doing so.

She did something to him, something he did not like. She made him long for things he'd forgotten, and feel remorse for things he could not help if he were to avenge his family. He had no room for sentimentality, no room for tender feelings of any kind.

A glance at the bedside clock told him it was nearly ten. A few more minutes, and he would wake her—though part of him wanted to keep her in his bed all night, to slide into her body in the dark hours before dawn, to lose himself.

But he would not. The sooner he returned her to Moscow, the better.

The sharp, insistent ringing of a cell phone startled Paige into wakefulness. Beside her, Alexei whipped back the covers and shot from the bed. His phone was still clipped onto his trousers, but he managed to grab it before it stopped ringing.

"Da?" he barked.

Paige sat up, her body protesting the movement. Though she wanted to stay snuggled into bed, where it was warm, it was time to return to reality.

Reality for her was not a naked billionaire pacing the room and barking into his phone in a language she didn't understand.

She took the opportunity, while he wasn't paying attention, to slip from the bed and start collecting her clothes. It took a few moments to locate her underwear, but when she had everything she darted into the attached bathroom.

Paige leaned back against the closed door, blinking in

disbelief. Yet another beautiful, fairy-tale room. Though at least there were modern fixtures—a shower, toilet and claw-foot bathtub with jets. Clearly Alexei had upgraded a few things.

She wondered why he and his mother and sister had been sent away from this place, but she'd hardly been able to ask. What must it have been like to be so young and to not only lose your father, but to also find yourself thrown out of your home? How had his poor mother handled everything with two young children to look after?

Paige felt a pang of emotion for the woman lying in the church crypt. And for the man who seemed so in control and detached when he spoke of his family, yet who was so alive and full of fire. A fire that had nearly incinerated them both when he'd focused it on her.

She set her clothes on a tufted bench and turned on the water in the sink so she could wash her face.

And did a double take at the woman staring at her in the mirror. My God, was that her?

Her hair was mussed, of course, but it was her face that shocked her. Her lips were red, swollen from kissing, and her eyes were lazy, sensual. Her mascara had smeared, but instead of looking like a Gothic vampire, it made her look tousled. Like she was a sex goddess who'd been making love all night long.

She took a step back, let her gaze wander down her body. Her skin glowed. She looked happy. Pretty. Was that what sexual satisfaction did to a person?

If so, she'd certainly missed out on a lot. She could barely process that she'd technically still been a virgin. She was slightly sore, but not so much so that her body didn't leap at the idea of doing it all again.

A sharp rap sounded on the door and she jumped. "Yes?"

"We must go, Paige," Alexei said. "The helicopter is waiting."

His voice was impersonal, sharp, and her stomach dropped. Whatever she'd expected after tonight, the indifference in his voice hadn't been it. Hadn't they just shared something beautiful? And, more than their bodies, hadn't they shared a bit of their souls with each other?

It had certainly felt like it, especially when he'd insisted on pointing out to her that she'd been living for Emma and it was time to stop. Or when he'd told her with such stark pain in his gaze that his family was buried in the crypt.

"I'm coming," she said, stiffening her resolve. She would not let him know how far out of her depth she was, how much this night meant to her. He was already behaving as if it was over, so she would do the same. Time to return to their proper roles as wary strangers.

She could do that. She *would* do that.

Paige hurriedly washed her face and got dressed. She hadn't been able to find the elastic that she'd held her ponytail back with, so she did the best she could with her unruly hair before opening the door.

Alexei stood in the middle of the room, talking on his phone once more. He was fully dressed—in different clothes, naturally, which made her feel rather cheap and, well, transitory. He did not look up when she walked into the room, and her heart squeezed into a painful knot.

What had she expected? She'd known what she was getting into when she'd said yes.

He finally glanced over at her, something flashing across his face before he looked away again. She picked up her coat and stood waiting. He motioned her to the door, opening it for her, then following once she'd gone through. She stepped back to let him take the lead. He didn't look at her while he walked down the hallway and descended the stairs.

Paige's skin was hot, but for a different reason than when they'd burst up these steps earlier. Then, she'd been giddy with excitement. Now, she felt like a prostitute he'd picked up on the street. He'd brought her home for a quick screw and now he was done with her.

She lifted her chin, determined not to let him see how much his indifference hurt and confused her. She hadn't expected a declaration of true love, but she'd thought they would at least act like two people who'd shared something intimate together.

They stopped at the door they'd entered earlier. Alexei put his phone away and donned the coat he'd been carrying. Paige did the same, settling the hat into place and wrapping the scarf around her neck. Stuffing her hands into her pockets, she realized she'd forgotten the gloves. But she wasn't going back for them.

There was no time anyway.

The man who'd greeted them earlier stood by the ornately carved door. He and Alexei spoke briefly, and then he was opening the door as Alexei turned and took her by the elbow.

"Watch your step," Alexei said as they emerged into the frigid night air.

"*Spokojnoj Nochi,*" the man called out before shutting the huge door behind them.

The *whop-whop-whop* of the helicopter rotors sounded nearby, as well as a scratching sound that she realized was the top layer of snow being disturbed in the vortex.

When they were safely onboard, the craft lifted into the air and banked to the right. Paige stared down at the ghostly shadow of the Voronov Palace, huge and hulking on the pristine snow. She half expected the ground to open up and swallow it whole, like a sacred location that disappeared after you'd completed a quest.

Twenty minutes later, they were boarding Alexei's private jet. Alexei hadn't spoken a word to her since he'd told her to watch her step. Instead he'd been on the phone, on his computer, his concentration intense and undivided. A flight attendant came over and asked if she would like something to drink.

"No, thank you," she replied. After the woman left, Paige tried to close her eyes and rest. It was nearly eleven-thirty, and though she had no idea what Chad's plans were for tomorrow, she had to get up and be ready in case he needed her to do something.

Hot guilt sizzled through her like a brand. She'd been reckless, and now she was regretting the impulse. The man she'd risked her job for had been ignoring her almost since the moment he'd found his release in her body.

It stung her pride, and yet she'd gone into it with eyes wide-open. She had no one to blame but herself.

She was aware of the moment he snapped his computer closed. Aware of the dark, powerful energy radiating from him as his voice went silent. Presumably he was finished with his call.

He said something that sounded like an order. When the flight attendant answered, Paige knew she'd guessed right.

A minute later something popped. It almost sounded like a gun. Paige sat up ramrod straight, her eyes darting to Alexei. He held a glass of champagne, his smile devilish as he lifted it in her direction.

"Madam," a soft voice said, and Paige realized the flight attendant was holding out a glass for her. She took it before looking to Alexei again.

His face had been transformed once more, and her heart thumped against her chest. He was so handsome, so sexy. And so lonely, she thought.

No. She would not feel empathy for him, not now.

"What are we drinking to?" she said as coolly as she could manage. Two could play this game.

"Triumph," he replied before taking a long swallow.

Paige's blood froze in her veins. She set the glass down. "What are you saying?"

But she knew. Oh, God, she knew.

"Chad Russell is broke, is he not? This was his last chance to salvage his company." He took another sip of champagne while her heart refused to beat. "His financiers have pulled out of the deal."

Chad would be destroyed. And Emma's happiness along with him. Paige was halfway out of her seat—to do what she didn't know—before Alexei's cruel laugh stopped her.

"Ah yes, you did know something, though you claimed you did not. I can see it written on your face."

Hatred broke the ice in her veins, pumped hot blood into her heart. She'd known the deal was life or death to Chad, but she hadn't known the extent of it. "Then I guess we both lied. This was all a game, wasn't it? You only pretended to want me."

He stretched like a cat before rising from his seat and coming over to plop down into the plush club chair next to hers. "Ah, no," he said, his gray gaze slipping over her, "I did not pretend. I think that should be clear based on what we shared tonight."

Outrage and self-loathing were a vile stew inside her. How had she fallen for this? How? "You brought me here to seduce me. You arranged the nice dinner, the *troika*—"

She broke off, unable to continue. She'd let herself go, let herself enjoy and believe—for a short time—that a prince could be interested in a dull secretary.

What a joke.

"*Da,* I arranged it all," he said matter-of-factly. "But that does not mean I didn't enjoy it."

She turned away from him. Evil man. Worst of all, she'd actually felt something with him. The wonder and beauty of what he'd done to her, the intensity of her response—it was more than she'd ever experienced before.

And now the memory was ruined.

"Come, Paige, do not act so hurt. This was war. You and I both knew it."

She collected her emotions, turned back to him. "Don't drag me down to your level. I'm nothing like you. I don't use people."

"Are you not? I seem to remember that you were the one who wanted me to make love to you last night in my apartment." He tipped a finger under her chin when she would have turned away again, held her steady while his hot eyes bored into her. "You wanted to use me to forget what Chad had done to you."

Her conscience burned with the truth of what he was saying. And yet it wasn't the same at all. "I told you that Chad and I weren't involved. He didn't do *anything* to me."

"But you wanted him to," Alexei said. "You wanted *him* to be the man who made love to you."

"No," she breathed—and yet he'd stated the truth. She'd thought she'd wanted her boss as her lover, thought he was the perfect man. But she knew, after tonight, that she couldn't have done with Chad what she'd done with Alexei.

"Deny it all you like," he said. "But we both know the truth."

"Why do you hate him so much?" she asked.

A shadow crossed his features. "Who said anything about hate? This is business."

Paige shook her head. "No, it's more than that. I saw the way you looked at him today."

"Perhaps you should ask him," Alexei said, his jaw tightening. She got the impression he'd said more than he intended with that short sentence.

"I can't do that and you know it."

He set the empty champagne glass down on the table in front of them and stood. "You can do anything you wish, *maya krasavitsa*. As of tomorrow, you will no longer be working for Chad Russell."

"I won't work for you, either," she blurted.

He scoffed. "Don't be stupid, Paige. You need the money."

Though fear made her pulse throb in her temples, she knew she couldn't work for Alexei Voronov. It was the one thing she could do for herself, the one way to reclaim her self-respect. After a night of self-indulgent folly, she could stand firm on this one thing.

"I'd rather clean toilets for a living before working for a man I hate."

He bent over her chair, cupping his hands on either side of her face before she could stop him. His mouth claimed hers in a hard, dominant kiss. Fury whipped through her with tornado strength and she clamped her lips tight against his. He answered her by gripping her jaw hard enough to force her mouth open.

And then he was inside, kissing her with the heat and strength of earlier. When she bit down on his tongue, he laughed and clamped his fingers around her jaw again until she released him.

The kiss turned explosive, with him bending her back in the seat and her taking as much as he could give. Never again would she be meek or easily manipulated.

This was an angry kiss, a kiss of war, but a hot kiss nonetheless. When he broke away, she whimpered in response before she could stop herself.

But she wasn't the only one affected. His eyes were wild

as he gazed down at her, hot and dark and full of need. He thrust a hand through his dark hair, pulled in a deep breath.

And then he was collected once more, staring down at her with such coolness that she shivered. "Oh, yes, Paige Barnes," he threw at her, "you definitely hate me. If we had more time, I would show you exactly how much."

CHAPTER EIGHT

One month later...

PAIGE HIT THE alarm, flopping back into bed with a groggy sigh. Six o'clock seemed to come earlier and earlier each morning. For the past two weeks, she'd had such trouble waking up. It wasn't jet lag; they'd returned to Dallas a month ago, and she'd been over the jet lag within a few days.

But she'd gotten more and more tired with each passing day, as if she needed a shot of caffeine straight to her veins to get her moving. She drank coffee every morning, but by noon she was dragging again. By the time she got home, she was ready for bed.

Nothing had been right since she'd left Russia. She'd started a new job at a downtown law firm just last week, thanks to Mavis, who'd recently taken a job there because she'd also refused to work for Alexei after spending so many years with Chad and his father. The pay, at least for Paige, wasn't as good as it had been at Russell Tech, but she'd gone over her budget and figured out how to pay all her bills and stay in the same house she'd been renting for the past three years.

It was tight, but it worked.

Somehow, Paige managed to haul herself from the bed and throw on her robe. Before she could hit the shower, she needed a cup of coffee.

"You look like hell," Emma said when she entered the kitchen.

"Thanks," Paige replied as she grabbed a mug and filled it.

She didn't bother to tell Emma that she looked like hell, too. For a different reason, of course. Since they'd returned to Texas, she'd barely seen Chad. He was off in Alaska, trying to drum up business with some of his father's old acquaintances. He'd poured his personal fortune into Russell Tech over the last few years. When the company went broke, he had, too.

There was no question of a wedding anytime soon. Paige secretly added *if ever,* though it hurt her to do so. Emma tried to be brave, but Paige heard her crying at night sometimes. She hated Alexei Voronov for many things, but for that most of all.

Paige took a sip of coffee, waiting for the pleasurable little jolt. But the flavor turned her stomach instead. She set the cup back down, frowning. "What are you doing up so early?"

Emma's brows drew together as she studied Paige. "I have final exams today. Are you sick?"

Paige put her hands to either side of her head. She'd asked herself that question every day. "I don't know."

"You look pale. Maybe you should stay home."

"I can't. I'm too new and I don't have any sick leave yet."

"But you're not well. I'm sure they'll work something out. If you want, I'll call Mavis for you."

Paige waved a hand. "No, don't do that. I'll be fine as soon as I shower."

But when she stood beneath the hot spray, she didn't feel better at all; she felt ill. Her stomach heaved, and before she could get to the toilet, she was sick. Since there was nothing in her stomach, it was over quickly.

Maybe Emma was right. Maybe she'd caught something

at work, though no one seemed to be sick at Fennell, Brown, and Ramirez.

Paige finished her shower, dragged on a pair of dark slacks and a powder-blue top and headed for work without attempting to eat breakfast since food was impossible.

The morning passed torturously. Paige tried to eat one of the doughnuts Mavis had brought in, but the first bite shot bile up into her throat. She ran to the toilet three times and threw up twice, though she'd eaten nothing at all.

The third time she returned to her desk, Mavis was frowning at her.

"You look like death warmed over, sugar," the older woman said. "Are you feeling okay?"

Paige settled into her chair very carefully. The document she'd been working on was still open on her computer, the cursor blinking at her accusingly.

"I think I must have eaten something bad," she said, taking a sip of her bottled water.

Mavis shoved a pencil in her steel-gray hair. Mavis's hair was a good five inches tall, having been teased and sprayed to within an inch of its life. Paige had often wondered if Mavis got home at the end of the day and discovered bits of flotsam she'd shoved in there during work. Stray pencils, an eraser, correction tape.

Mavis's face scrunched in concentration. "Could be, but seems like you'd be a lot sicker a whole lot quicker, if you know what I mean." She tilted her head to the side. "This has been going on for a while. Can you keep anything down?"

"Not this morning."

"Any other symptoms?"

"I've been tired a lot, but I think it must be leftover jet lag or something. I can hardly get out of bed in the morning."

The corners of Mavis's eyes crinkled as she screwed her

face up even tighter. "Now, darlin', you don't have a boyfriend or anything do you?"

Paige shook her head. "You know I don't."

"I thought so, sweetie, but things could have changed."

"Why do you ask?"

"Well, if you did, I'd be wanting to know when you'd last had your period. Because if it'd been a while, you might want to pee on a stick."

"Pee on a stick?" *Oh, dear God.*

Mavis mistook her statement for an actual question. "Honey, I'm talking about a pregnancy test," she said in her syrupy accent, drawing the word *test* into two syllables. "But since it can't be that, maybe you should go to the doctor and see if you got that swine flu or something. Though you sure do remind me of my daughter when she was pregnant with the twins. Poor girl couldn't keep a thing down for weeks. Slept all the time, too."

A frisson of icy fear danced down Paige's spine. It wasn't possible. Alexei had used a condom, and they'd only had sex once. There was no way she was pregnant!

But her brain was working overtime, doing the math, and she realized it'd been a while since her last period. She just didn't know how long. For that, she'd have to dig into her purse and check her pocket calendar. She always noted the date since it seemed to be the first thing the doctor's office wanted to know each time she went in for an appointment. Didn't matter what the appointment was for, they always wanted to know the answer.

The phone rang and Mavis answered it, sparing Paige from continuing the conversation. She opened a desk drawer and quickly located her calendar in the bottom of her purse. Flipping back, she found the date and counted forward.

Six weeks.

But that didn't mean anything. Stress could delay ovulation, which meant her period could start any day really. Paige closed her eyes and took a deep breath. Surely that's all it was. Stress, and a stomach bug.

But she knew she would worry until her period showed up. More worry meant more stress. More stress meant more delay, which meant no period.

The only way to ease her mind was to stop at the drugstore on the way home tonight.

Unbelievable.

She put the calendar away with shaky hands and tried to concentrate on the document. Half an hour later, kindly Mr. Ramirez emerged from his office and ordered her to go home.

She wanted to argue, but the truth was she just wanted to go curl up on the couch with the remote. When Mr. Ramirez assured her she would be paid for the hours she would miss, Paige logged off her computer and gathered her things.

By the time she got home, she felt better. But the package in her hand had the power to change everything.

She slipped the pregnancy test out of the bag and stared at it. Her heart hammered. Was this really necessary? Was it possible?

Anything was possible, she supposed. Practically, she was just ruling out a possibility, however remote, so she could focus on what might actually be wrong. When the test came out negative, she would call her doctor and schedule an appointment. Maybe she was allergic to something, or maybe she'd picked up a strange virus in Russia.

Twenty minutes later, after she read the instructions twice, Paige peed in a cup and inserted the stick—she didn't want any mistakes—and then removed it after the appropriate amount of time. While the stick did its magic, she crossed to the kitchen and peered inside the fridge. Her stomach was growling now, and she felt like she could eat something without getting sick.

Grabbing a yogurt, she popped the top and dipped her spoon inside before returning to where she'd laid the stick on the bathroom counter. It hadn't been more than a minute, but the digital window had an answer.

The spoon clattered into the sink as her fingers lost the ability to hold it.

Pregnant.

Paige snatched up the test and held it closer. Maybe there was a glare on her glasses that was obscuring the *not*. But the window was very clear.

Oh, God, she was pregnant! With a Russian prince's baby. It didn't seem real, didn't seem possible.

Yet the test did not lie. Paige made it to the couch before she sank into a boneless heap. What now?

She pressed her hand to her abdomen. Was there really a little life in there? A baby who was half her and half Alexei?

Her mind threw out possibilities in dizzying succession. She could terminate the pregnancy and no one would ever know. She could carry the baby to term and give it up for adoption. Or she could keep her baby.

Her fingers clenched reflexively. Already, she felt protective. And she knew what she was going to do. She *wanted* this baby with a fierceness that surprised her. She would keep her child, and she would raise him or her alone. It would be tough, especially now, but she knew what tough was. She already had experience with working herself to the bone to provide for a child.

So this would be a new experience, starting from the earliest moments of life, but she would adapt.

What about Alexei?

Paige chewed her lip. Should she try to get in contact

with him? Tell him about his child? Her mind rebelled at the thought. He was a cold, cruel man who'd pretended to be something he was not.

He'd pretended to be kind and solicitous, and he'd pretended an interest in her for the sole purpose of using her for information. When he no longer needed that information, he'd discarded her like yesterday's garbage. And he'd made no effort to get in contact since. He'd managed to find Emma when she was in Chad's hotel room, so Paige had no illusions about his ability to find her in Dallas if he so chose. He just didn't want to find her.

In fact, though it hurt to know, he probably gave her no thought whatsoever. Since the second he'd dropped her off at her hotel, he'd erased her from his mind.

She knew because she'd seen a photo of him at a Hollywood movie premiere recently. He'd been escorting a gorgeous starlet who'd clung to his arm and smiled at him as if he were the center of the universe.

Paige had quickly shoved aside the pang of jealousy she'd felt. The starlet would find out soon enough how cruel Alexei could be. He might seem like a prize to be coveted, but he certainly was not.

She thought of her sister, and her hatred for Alexei simmered.

No, she would not try to contact him. He'd made it clear what his feelings about their night together had been. It was one night that he'd already forgotten, and she was the one who would have to deal with the consequences.

Alexei told himself that he simply wanted to return the gloves she'd left behind. And the coat, scarf and hat that she'd posted to him before she left Russia. He'd been angry when he'd opened the box and realized what was inside.

Yet he should have expected it. Paige was proud and

stubborn and it would be just like her to try to have the last word.

He'd wondered why she'd only kept the gloves, but it wasn't until he'd returned to St. Petersburg the following weekend that he'd found them lying neatly on the nightstand and realized what had happened. A maid must have put them there, because he remembered quite vividly how Paige had stripped them off and thrown them aside so she could touch him.

Alexei closed his eyes. *So she could touch him.*

He could remember, even now, the sizzle of her skin against his, the heat and passion that had threatened to incinerate him. He remembered wanting to be inside her with an urgency that had surprised him with its intensity.

He hadn't been with a woman since that night. He'd thought about it. He'd even gone out with a beautiful actress recently, but the night ended when he took her back to her apartment and left her at the door with a chaste kiss.

She simply hadn't excited him.

Paige had. Paige Barnes, who wore dull suits and glasses and who'd kissed him like she needed his touch in order to survive.

He'd wanted to see her again, but he'd resisted the impulse. Now that he was in Dallas to explore his latest acquisition, he didn't have to wait. He would see her and he would return the damn coat he'd bought her.

Russell Tech was finally his, and though he'd thought he would take great pleasure in entering those hallowed offices as the owner rather than as a supplicant begging for his sister's life, it hadn't been as sweet as he'd thought it would be. For a moment, as he'd stood in that office where Tim Russell had refused to help him and gazed out on the Dallas skyline, he'd felt emptier inside than he ever had before.

Why?

The limo he'd hired drove him from his hotel through the

outskirts of Dallas and into a suburban neighborhood with small bungalows and green lawns. Paige had kept her word and left Russell Tech, but he knew she worked at a law firm and he knew she would be home by now. He'd thought about going to her office, but decided it was better they see each other in private.

What would she say when she saw him again? Would he see a flash of that sweet desire she'd never quite been able to hide? Or would she now look at him with abject hatred? He wanted the former and hoped, for her sake, it was the latter.

Because, though he shouldn't still want her, he did. As much as he would find the experience of bedding her pleasurable, he had nothing else to give her. He'd already taken enough from her. He would not take more, even if he couldn't quite stop himself from delivering the coat in person.

Finally the car pulled to a halt in front of a brown house with a covered porch. It was a cute home. Cozy. The grass was manicured, but not too much so. The flower beds weren't overflowing with plants, though they were neat and clean. It was as if someone cared about the garden, but didn't have a lot of time to fuss over it.

Alexei grabbed the garment bag he'd brought and strode to the door. He rang the bell and waited. A gray-haired woman in a pink housedress stood on the front porch next door, staring at him. He gave her a smile, which only seemed to fluster her. She hurried inside, but he didn't miss the curtain inching back on the window facing Paige's house.

Finally the mint-green door swung open. He wasn't sure what he'd expected to happen when he saw her again, but the immediate rush of blood to his groin was certainly not it.

"Hello, Paige," he said softly, his gaze slipping down her body. She was dressed in a pair of shorts that showed her lovely long legs, and a tank top that clung to her generous breasts. Her dark hair was pulled back in the usual ponytail.

But her face did not look happy at all. Her eyes shot daggers at him and her lips were pinched at the corners. "Nice to see you, too."

"What are you doing here?" she demanded.

He held up the garment bag. "Returning your coat."

Her fingers were bloodless where they clamped the door. "I don't want it, Prince Voronov. Thank you for coming by, but please leave."

"Ah, so we are back to that now. How formal and polite you are, Paige, considering what we've done to each other."

He loved the blush staining her cheeks. So innocent, and so sensual all at once. That's what he remembered, what he craved.

"I—" She turned green. If he hadn't been looking at her, he wouldn't have believed it. "Excuse me," she said, turning and bolting into the house.

Alexei walked into the entry and closed the door behind him. He tossed the garment bag on a chair and followed the sounds of retching to the small bath in the hall.

"Paige? What is wrong? Do you need a doctor?"

"No," she said miserably, her voice loud and clear through the closed door. "I'll feel better when you leave. So get out. And take the coat with you!"

"As you wish," he said, though he had no intention of doing so. Instead he retreated to the tiny kitchen nearby and sat on a bar stool to wait. The kitchen opened into a small living room furnished with an oversize couch, a couple of chairs, and a television. It wasn't sumptuous by any stretch, and yet he found himself drawn to the homey feel.

After his father had died, he'd lived in a house not much bigger than this. His mother had tried to make it homey, but they didn't have much to live on. All she'd gotten when his father died was a small sum of money and some land everyone had thought was worthless. He'd loved their land as a child.

They might not have had much money, but he and Katerina had played for hours in the woods and creeks. They'd fished, hunted and climbed the trees like monkeys.

They'd been happy, in spite of their lack. Kids didn't care, so long as they were loved and had enough food to eat.

More than anything, he'd wanted to give his mother back the lifestyle she'd had when she'd been a princess in a fairy-tale palace. He'd worked tirelessly, but his true success came too late.

Now that he had his family palace back, and homes in several countries, none of them gave him that feeling of comfort he wanted, that feeling he remembered from his childhood. This house had that feeling. Two minutes inside its interior and he knew the feeling was here.

Home. It was more than simply furniture or belongings. It was an indefinable *feeling*. His heart longed for it, and yet it was something he'd been denied for many years now.

And would continue to be denied. He was accustomed to it, even if he sometimes longed for it more than anything else. When you didn't care for anyone or anything, didn't have that feeling of home, it couldn't be taken away from you. He knew from bitter experience it was better that way.

The bathroom door opened and Paige staggered out. When she saw him, she froze.

"You said you were leaving."

"I lied."

She came into the kitchen and grabbed a bottle of water out of the refrigerator. After she'd twisted off the top and took a gulp, she speared him with a glare. "You're good at that, aren't you?"

"I never lied to you, Paige."

"No, you just didn't tell me the truth," she snapped. Leaning against the counter, she took another sip of water as she eyed him.

"Actually I did," he said coolly. "I told you why I would keep you close if you worked for me."

She snorted. "I understood what you meant, but it wasn't the truth exactly. The truth would have been, 'Paige, I'm not really attracted to you, but I'd like you to think I am so you'll spill secrets about Chad's business. Then I'll steal his company and put you all out of work.'"

Her dark eyes were full of emotion. The anger and hatred he expected. But the fear?

Why should she fear him?

"I did not steal anything, Paige. What I did was acquire a failing company. And my attraction to you was not a lie."

She put a hand to her head, massaging her right temple. "Fine, you didn't steal anything and you really were attracted to me. I believe you. Now will you please go?"

He frowned as he watched her. "You need to sit down."

"I will once you've left."

"I'm not leaving just yet. Come, sit on the couch."

Her eyes were wide. "It's a way of life for you, isn't it? You just show up, snap your fingers and expect people to do your bidding. Well, I have news for you, mister—this is *my* home and no one jumps to your tune here. If you don't get out, I'm calling the police."

"If you sit down, I'll go." Her threat to call the police meant nothing to him, but clearly his presence agitated her. He'd done what he came to do. His body hummed with frustrated desire, but he tamped it down and ignored it. There was no reason to stay any longer than he already had. There was nothing for him here. Nothing for either of them.

"Fine," she said, coming around the counter and shuffling into the living room. She sank onto the couch, sighing almost wearily.

"You need a doctor," Alexei said, frowning. She still looked green and she was shaking.

"No, I'm fine." She bit her lip as she looked away. "I had the flu recently and I'm still recovering."

"Very well," he said. "Then I will leave you now. I left the coat on the chair in your foyer. Do what you wish with it, but do not send it back to me."

The phone on the counter began to ring, but Paige ignored it. Her head was tilted back, her eyes closed. She had a hand over her abdomen, and her skin was pale. He didn't want to go when she seemed sick, but she did not want him here.

He turned and strode down the small hallway. The answering machine kicked on. Paige's breathy voice asked the caller to leave a message. Did the woman have any idea she sounded like a phone sex advertisement?

The instant a cheery voice began to speak, Paige made a sound he'd never heard before. A sound of sheer panic. He could hear her lever herself up off the couch.

But she wasn't quite fast enough.

"This is Dr. Fitzgerald's office calling to confirm Paige Barnes's first ultrasound appointment for tomorrow at 1:00 p.m. You'll need to bring—"

Paige felt light-headed as she finished the call and put the receiver down. When the phone started ringing, she'd just been too tired to get up and answer it. All she wanted was for Alexei to go. She hadn't thought of her OB-GYN's office calling to remind her about an appointment she'd only made yesterday afternoon. Did they really think she could forget it in so short a time?

She looked up, knowing what she would see and afraid at the same time.

Alexei had come back down the hall. No, he had loomed back down the hall and now stood hulking nearby. His ice-gray eyes gleamed, his brows drawing down, his nostrils flaring as he stared at her.

"Why do you need an ultrasound, Paige?" He sounded cool, deadly, and a shiver dripped down her spine.

She thought about lying. But she couldn't think of a single reason anyone got an ultrasound other than pregnancy. She knew there had to be other reasons, but they escaped her.

She thrust her chin higher. Time to brazen it out. "Why do women usually get ultrasounds, Prince Voronov?"

What did it matter if she told him? He'd been cold enough to stage an elaborate seduction for the possibility of information that could benefit his precious company—and to hell with other people's lives and feelings—so why would he care about one tiny baby?

His eyes narrowed and she knew he was remembering, scrolling through the events of that night like it was a film he could view frame by frame. "You cannot be pregnant."

Oh, the arrogant bastard! "Why not? Because it wasn't part of the plan?" She tossed her head. "I assure you I *can*. But don't worry, I don't expect anything from you."

He didn't say anything for a full minute. Then he grabbed her by the shoulders and pulled her close, his face twisting in rage. And something else?

"You're lying. You cannot be pregnant with my child. We used protection."

Paige stared at him defiantly. "Of course I can't, because the great Prince Alexei Voronov has declared it impossible. So let me go and get the hell out of my house. We don't need you."

A wave of nausea hit her like a rogue wave storming the shore. She tried not to show it, tried so hard to be fierce and strong so he would just go away. But if the expression on his face was any indication, it didn't work.

"Paige, what's wrong? Tell me what's wrong."

She tried to jerk away, but it was like trying to escape iron manacles. "I'm pregnant, damn you, and if you don't let me go right this instant I'll throw up on your nice suit!"

He released her and she turned to dash for the bathroom, barely reaching the toilet in time. She could hear him behind her. She wanted to shut the door, shut him out, but she didn't have the strength.

Her hair lifted away and she realized he was holding her ponytail, keeping it out of the way while she retched. She was thankful for the gesture, and scared at the same time. Because it made her remember the Alexei who'd taken her for a *troika* ride, the haunted man who'd told her about his family lying in the crypt with such sadness in his eyes. The kind Alexei. The one she could have loved if he were real and not a careful construct.

But wasn't part of that construct really him?

Stop.

She just wanted him to leave her and never come back again. Seeing him hurt. It made her think of every moment they'd ever spent together, of that incredible few hours in his bed when she'd felt so alive and so feminine. He'd been her first real lover, and everything about it had been magical and beautiful.

But it had all been a lie. He'd ruined Chad, ruined Emma's happiness in the process, and she hated him for it. How could she ever let herself think of him with anything but contempt?

Because he was the father of her child and she felt a connection to him through the child they shared. A deep, mysterious connection that would forever be between them.

Dear God, why *him* of all people?

When she finished throwing up, when he helped her up and swooped her into his arms and carried her to the couch, she had no idea what would happen next. She expected nothing, yet she had to admit that she was relieved he'd come and relieved she'd told him the truth. She'd done the right thing. Mama would be proud of her for that, at least.

Emma was likely to never speak to her again, however. Since Paige had learned she was pregnant yesterday, she'd been dreading telling her sister. She'd certainly never intended to reveal who the father was, but she was afraid that choice had now been taken away.

"You need a doctor," Alexei said, whipping his phone from his pocket.

She was too tired to fight him. "This is normal, Alexei. Pregnant women get sick. Not all of them, but apparently I'm one. Lucky me," she finished on a whisper.

His eyes were hard, his expression determined. "You will need a doctor for the flight."

Alarm bells sounded in her head. "What flight? I'm not going anywhere. I have work to do, Emma's coming home in a couple of hours and we're watching a movie together on television tonight."

His handsome face was an impersonal mask. "I am leaving for St. Petersburg in two days. You are coming with me."

Paige tried to get up, but her stomach roiled in response. "I'm not going anywhere with you! My life is here."

"Not any longer. If this baby is truly mine, then your life is with me."

CHAPTER NINE

THE VORONOV PALACE was exactly as she'd last seen it, except that it was perhaps more beautiful now that spring had arrived. She'd never thought to see this place again. She'd certainly never thought to return as the new mistress of the manor. She glanced again at the three-carat rock on her right ring finger—Russians wore their rings on the opposite finger—and her insides squeezed tight.

She was married. To a prince.

And everything about this marriage was broken and wrong.

Paige let Alexei help her from the helicopter, then snatched her hand away as soon as she could do so. He showed no emotion at the defiant gesture. He'd been as cold as stone since the moment he'd informed her that she was coming to Russia with him.

She'd threatened to call the police, threatened to scream bloody murder, threatened him with any number of impotent gestures that he'd shrugged off as if they were nothing more than annoyances.

Which they had been. The all-powerful Prince Voronov could and would do whatever he wanted to do. Including ordering her life as if he had a right to do so. She'd been determined to resist, but he'd undercut all her protests with a single promise.

He'd promised to take care of Emma's future. Her tuition would be paid in full, and he'd buy her an apartment of her own—or the house they were living in if she wanted it. Emma would never have to worry for money again.

Paige had trembled at the choice, but she'd known what she was going to do from the moment he said it. She told herself that she hadn't refused because she was afraid of what the alternative would be. If Alexei could be gracious when he got his way, she imagined he would be formidable when he did not. She had only to think of what had happened to Chad and Russell Tech to know it was true.

So long as she lived, she would never forget Emma's face when her sister returned home that evening and saw Alexei in their house. She hadn't known who he was, but when he'd introduced himself, she'd recoiled as if he were evil incarnate.

And when Paige explained that she was pregnant, and the baby was Alexei's, she'd thought her sister would never get over the shock of betrayal. Emma began to cry, begging Paige to tell her it was a joke, that it couldn't be true, that she would never have done something so stupid and so wrong as to sleep with Chad's nemesis.

Paige had tried to explain, but Emma refused to listen. And then she'd run to her room and slammed the door. Paige had turned to Alexei, her eyes blurring with tears, and asked him if he was satisfied.

He'd been like a marble statue, cold and unfeeling. She'd wanted to claw his eyes out, to make him feel *something*. He'd merely watched her with those rain-cold gray eyes, awaiting her answer.

The next two days had been a whirlwind. Alexei had arranged for her to have an ultrasound that afternoon. He'd sat in the exam room stony-faced and silent. Until the technician began the process. Then he'd leaned in close, watching the monitor as if he were searching for the secret to eternal youth or something equally as precious.

Paige hadn't known she could get so emotional over the sight of a little tiny sac that contained nothing that resembled a baby in the least. But she had. She'd been flooded with wonder, protectiveness and overwhelming love. She'd been too scared to glance at Alexei, so she'd focused resolutely on the screen as the technician made a series of clicks on the computer. Her eyes had filled with tears. She should be here with a man who loved her, holding his hand while they saw their baby for the first time instead of with a cold stranger who disliked her.

"You're six weeks and three days exactly," the technician had finally said.

Alexei's sharp intake of breath was audible. And then he'd asked if she was sure. The technician had gone on to explain that pregnancies were dated from the date of the last menstrual cycle rather than the date of conception, and that yes, Paige was exactly six weeks and three days—which meant the date of conception was right around the time they'd been together.

Paige had wanted to die of embarrassment. He'd sounded as if he weren't certain he was the father and needed confirmation, which she imagined had caused the technician to explain as she had. Paige had felt as if he'd come right out and said she was a slut who slept around and that she was trying to fob off someone else's child as his.

What should have been a beautiful moment was ruined by his cold-blooded arrogance. Yet when she'd gotten up from the table, he'd reached out to steady her. And then he'd kept his hand on her back the entire way out to the car. His touch burned her like a brand and, in spite of her wish it was not so, her body reacted to him. Hot need softened her inner core, made her long to turn and bury her head against his chest.

She had not done so, of course. How could she want love and comfort from the man who'd stolen those things from her in the first place? Her life had been just fine, if a little boring, before he came along. And now he'd taken her sister and her home away. Her life would never be the same. But for the sake of her child, she would endure.

When they entered the palace, the same man who'd greeted them on that night a few weeks ago was waiting. He and Alexei exchanged a few words, and then he bowed and left. Alexei turned to her.

"Vasily is preparing a room for you. If you wish to wait in the drawing room, he will come for you when it is finished."

Paige locked her hands in front of her body. She was surprised they weren't sharing a room, but also somewhat relieved. How could she share a bed with him, knowing that her body craved his? The entire time she'd been standing next to him at the government office in St. Petersburg where they'd married, her body had been humming with electricity, and her mind had thrown images of the night they'd shared into her head.

She'd been determined to resist his sweet seduction when the time came, because she'd never imagined it would not.

But his announcement preempted her. Alexei was indifferent to her. She should have realized it considering the impersonal way in which he'd married her. Instead of a beautiful dress, flowers, happiness and friends, she'd been married in a sterile office by a public official who spoke a language she didn't comprehend.

"I want to know what happens now, Alexei."

She couldn't stand the uncertainty. What was she supposed to do as his wife? Were they going to live together as a couple, or would he leave her here and continue his life as it had been? There were so many things she didn't know, so many worries. She felt very far from home, and very out of her element. She felt as if her life had been stolen from her. A cold shot of fear dripped into her belly at the thought.

His arctic eyes glittered with heat. "You will go wait in the drawing room. There will be hot tea and a small lunch, if you can stomach it."

She bit the inside of her lip to keep from reacting to the thought of food. Her queasiness was getting better since the doctor had prescribed antinausea medication, but she still reacted sometimes.

"That's not what I meant and you know it," she said softly.

"Yes, but I have business to attend to and no time for chit-chat. You made a deal, Paige. If you are finding it difficult to keep up with your end of the bargain, then perhaps you would like me to reiterate the consequences if you do not?"

Her temper sparked. "I understand full well what you are capable of, Prince Voronov. How could I not?"

"And what does this mean? Have I been anything but kind to you, Paige? Have I neglected you or left you behind to raise my child alone?"

She stamped her foot in frustration, uncaring what he thought about the gesture. "I would have been perfectly happy to raise my baby without you. I don't need anything from you."

For the first time since she'd opened the door and seen him on her porch, a flash of emotion crossed his features. He took a step toward her. She would have backed away, except that she suddenly knew what a trapped rabbit must feel like. Safer not to move.

"Oh, yes, you had no plans to tell me about my child, did you? You would let him go through life without a father, when I could give him so much more than you ever could."

She sucked in a breath. He looked angrier than she'd ever seen him. The corners of his mouth were white, and she suddenly knew that what he'd been battling for the past two days—the reason he'd barely spoken to her—was anger.

How did he manage to make her feel petty and mean when he was the one who'd dragged her halfway around the world with him? The one who'd ruined everything with his greed? God, how she wished she'd never met him!

She tilted her chin up. "I didn't think you'd want to know."

It wasn't a good defense, but it was the truth.

His laugh was not friendly. It was a broken sound that ended before it began. "Because you know so much about me."

He punctured her indignation like a balloon, and her heart suddenly ached at the emotion behind his words. She was supposed to hate him, and yet she hurt for him. She'd been wrong to consider keeping the baby a secret, but she truly had believed he wouldn't be interested.

"I know nothing about you, Alexei," she said. "But I'd like to."

She was surprised to find she meant it. He was the father of her child—her husband—and she wanted to know him. They'd shared a beautiful evening once, even if it had all been a sham. Though it hurt to think of how he'd used her, she knew this was a consequence he had not foreseen.

His mouth opened, and she found herself leaning forward, wondering what he would say. Would this be a rapprochement for them? A new beginning? She was surprised at how badly she wanted it to be. She could learn—they both could—to put their animosity behind them for the sake of their baby.

But then Alexei's jaw snapped closed. He pivoted and strode down the hall.

* * *

Alexei felt as if he'd been standing beneath an oilrig when it had suddenly, and without warning, crashed down on top of him. He'd gone to Texas to examine his new acquisition and returned home with a wife.

A wife.

And not only a wife. From the moment he'd heard the voice of a nurse inform Paige about her ultrasound appointment, he'd known what lay down the road he was traveling.

She'd been a virgin. She was pregnant. He'd gone back over the night in his head, and he'd remembered the one thing he'd tried to forget. He'd fallen asleep beneath her, their bodies still joined. When he'd awakened, the condom was loose. It didn't take a genius to figure out how she'd gotten pregnant.

He'd been careless, and now he was suffering the consequences.

Alexei put his head in his hands. He couldn't concentrate on the figures in front of him any longer. He did not want a wife. He did not want a child. He'd already lost the people he'd loved, and he had no room to care for anyone again. It was not a risk he'd ever planned to take.

But already he felt a burgeoning protectiveness toward the child she carried.

And toward her.

Chert poberi!

She was a thorn in his side. She looked at him with those wide, dark eyes, with her emotions on her sleeve, and he wanted to take her in his arms and tell her it would be okay.

But it wouldn't be okay.

How could he say it would? He'd said the same thing to Katerina, yet they had both known the truth. He would not do it again. He would not put his heart and soul on the line for life to crush. It was easier being alone. He understood how to be alone.

He did not understand how to be a husband and father.

Then why didn't you leave her in Dallas?

He did not know why, except that he could *not* do so. She was carrying his child. He'd thought the Voronov line, the direct paternal line, would probably die out with him since each year passed without him taking a wife. But Paige had changed everything.

On the long flight home, when she'd curled up in the center of the big bed in his suite, he'd wanted to lie with her. He'd wanted to curl behind her, to pull her into the protective curve of his body and spread his hand over her abdomen. He'd wanted to feel her breathing, smell her summery scent and sleep beside her.

He'd done none of those things, though the impulse had been overwhelming. The thought of doing them horrified him. What was happening to him? How could he let one small woman get beneath his skin like this?

Alexei got to his feet. There was only one answer. He had to leave. He had to go somewhere else, had to leave her here at the Voronov Palace where she would be safe. She would grow big with their baby, and he would make sure she had the best care available.

But he would be elsewhere, running his business and building his empire even bigger and better than before. He would visit from time to time, make sure she was thriving, but he would not stay for long. And he would never touch her again.

Because he was afraid, if he did, he'd never want to stop.

"I have to return to Moscow on business."

Paige's head snapped up. She'd gone for a walk on the vast grounds of the palace and found a stone bench beneath an arbor. It was peaceful, beautiful. A cascade of pink roses spilled down the arbor, their blooms sweet and profuse. It was a vastly different landscape from a month ago. It had gone from wintery wonderland to spring garden in a short amount of time.

The air still had a slight chill. She'd worn a sweater, but her hot Texas blood was beginning to cool in spite of it. She was accustomed to a far warmer climate.

"Hello, Alexei," she replied.

He loomed beneath the arbor, hands shoved into his trouser pockets, his broody face closed and dark. Her heart skipped a beat as she watched him. No matter how hard she tried, she couldn't help but remember shoving his shirt from his body and running her hands over all that smooth, hard muscle.

"I will be gone a few days, but you will have everything you need. And if you do not, you have only to tell Vasily and he will to it that you are taken care of."

Her heart had sped up while he talked. "You're leaving? So soon?"

She'd expected he would have to leave on business from time to time, but she hadn't expected it would happen within hours of their arrival. He was the only person she knew in this country. How could he leave her when everything about this situation was still so new? Who would she talk to? What would she do all day? She was used to working, used to taking care of herself. How was she supposed to do nothing at all?

She felt as if she were suffocating, as if she'd left one life where she'd been obligated to the needs of her sister only to step into another where she was at the whim of a man. A man who wouldn't want her if it weren't for the child in her body. Everything she'd ever wanted for herself, every dream and every scrap of independence, had been taken away from her by this enigmatic man.

And now he was leaving, as if it were nothing. As if she were nothing.

Alexei shrugged. "My business needs me."

"And you can't work from here for a few days? We've only just arrived."

He frowned down at her. "You cannot understand the pressures of my life."

Her spine stiffened. "Oh, really? I worked in the energy business for two years, Alexei. I understand the pressure that goes along with being a CEO. I did work for one, remember?"

He snorted. "But not a good one, *da?*"

Paige gritted her teeth. It was just like him to take a swipe at her ex-boss. "I like Chad. He was always good to me, he paid me very well, and he loves my sister."

"So you have forgotten his treatment of you."

Paige got to her feet. "His treatment? Chad never treated me wrongly, Alexei. I've told you that time and time again. In fact, I think he's treated me better than you have."

He took a step toward her, his brows drawing down. His face was a thundercloud. "He treated you so well that he lied to you about his affair with your sister. In fact, if I seem to remember, they *both* lied. And you put yourself in danger because of their lies."

"That's not what I was talking about," she said, her heart kicking up again.

"No, of course not. You forget that I helped you, that without me you would have been caught and abused by those men. But of course I am the one who has treated you wrongly."

Paige pulled a tendril of hair from her mouth where the wind had blown it. His gaze seemed to linger on her lips, his eyes darkening slightly before he looked away again.

"I thanked you for helping me that night. But you've not done a thing with my best interests in mind since. You've done what was best for *you*."

His gaze whipped back to her. "Do you think marrying

you was best for me? That bringing you here is what I wanted to do?"

If he'd stabbed her in the heart with a jagged knife, he could have hurt her no worse. She knew he didn't want her. But to hear it stated so starkly?

She would not cry. She didn't need him. *They* didn't need him.

"You made that choice, Alexei, not I. If you regret it so much, then why don't you let me go home?"

"You are home," he snapped. "For the sake of the child, you are where you belong."

She folded her arms beneath her breasts, shook off a chill. "I sometimes wish we'd never met."

Something flashed across his face, but it was gone too quickly for her to be sure what it was. "It is too late for that. We must deal with the consequences of our actions as best we can."

She blinked. "The consequences of our actions? Is that how you think of this baby?" As if she hadn't thought the same thing herself. But he said it so coldly, without even a hint of emotion. Did he love this baby, or did he just feel obligated?

"He is a consequence, is he not?" He took a step closer. She thought he would reach for her, but he just stood there with his hands shoved deep in his pockets, his rainy eyes gleaming with heat.

"He might be a she," she said softly. Because she couldn't think of anything else to say when he stood so close. She could smell the subtle spice of his skin, could feel the heat emanating from him. Suddenly she wanted to slip her arms around his waist, press her cheek to his hard chest. *Why?*

"It doesn't matter," he said. "This baby is a Voronov, a royal descendent of my line, and I *will* protect him—or *her*—with every last breath in my body."

Paige trembled. Not because he'd frightened her, but because he was so fierce and she believed he meant every word. He would never let harm come to their baby. He was an honorable man. She believed it to her core.

But he was not honorable in everything. And that's what she didn't understand.

"I want to know," she said, drawing in a deep breath to steady herself, "why you destroyed Russell Tech. I want to understand."

She *needed* to understand, because if she didn't, the guilt of what she had done would eat her alive. How could she be his wife if she felt guilty every time her body responded to him?

She didn't think he would answer her. He would think she didn't deserve an answer, or he would tell her it was simply business. He'd done that once before. She expected it, waited for it, yet she'd still had to ask.

His gray eyes took on a faraway cast, as if he were looking at some distant object she could not see.

And then he spoke, his gaze coming sharply into focus once more. What he said rocked her to the core.

"Tim Russell destroyed my family. He took everything, and he didn't stop until nothing was left."

CHAPTER TEN

PAIGE'S KNEES FELT weak so she sank onto the bench again. Or fell onto it maybe. Alexei's face was stark, raw with emotion. She hadn't expected it, and her heart went out to him, squeezed tight in her chest with sympathy.

But what if he was wrong? What if he'd misunderstood?

She quickly dismissed that thought as ridiculous. How could he misunderstand something so important? He truly believed it, regardless of what she thought.

"I'm sorry," she said, because she didn't know what else to say.

He turned, his face in profile to her, and stared out at the vast gardens. "My aunt was a ballet dancer with the Bolshoi. She met Tim Russell when she was on tour with the company in the United States. They married a short while later."

Paige couldn't have moved if she tried. Alexei's aunt had been married to Chad's father?

"But that means…"

"That Chad is my cousin, yes."

"I've met his mother," she said softly. "I had no idea she was Russian."

And Chad had never mentioned the family connection. Why not? He'd briefed her about his nemesis on the flight to Moscow, but he'd never once said that Alexei was his cousin.

But she'd only been an employee. Why would she need to know the personal side of their story? She didn't. Yet knowing he'd been romancing her sister at the same time, she felt oddly betrayed once again that he had not told her this information.

Would it have changed her reaction to Alexei? Would it have made her more cautious when he professed an interest in her? Perhaps she would have realized just how brutal this feud was and kept above the fray.

As if that were an excuse, she chided herself. She'd known that Chad and Alexei were business rivals and she'd still let herself be charmed. What would knowing the true relationship have possibly done to make it different?

"Did you not ever wonder where he learned to speak Russian?" Alexei asked.

"I assumed he learned it in college." She stared at her clasped hands on her lap, heat rising into her cheeks. Was there absolutely anything she'd not been deceived about?

"He learned it from his mother, just as he learned to hate us from her as well."

"But why?" she asked, unable to fathom what would make Elena Russell do such a thing. She'd thought Chad's mother was a bit standoffish, but she'd never thought the woman was rude or hateful. The few times she'd been in the office, she'd been nice enough. She just hadn't been overly friendly. Paige had chalked it up to reserve. Some people were just that way.

His expression was like granite. "My father's family believed my mother too lowborn to deserve the title of princess, and that created a rift between them and us. When my father died, it was my grandmother who turned us out. She should not have been able to do so, but she knew people in certain places and my mother did not."

Paige's heart throbbed with feeling. How could anyone

throw her grandchildren out into the cold, even if she didn't like their mother? It was monstrous, unfathomable.

"Where does Chad's father fit into this?" she asked.

"When he was expanding his operations, Elena suggested he go to my mother and try to purchase the bit of land she'd gotten on my father's death. By then, the majority of the family property had passed into state hands with the death of my grandmother. All that was left was what my mother had."

Paige shook her head. "I'm not sure I understand."

"We had nothing, Paige." Alexei shoved his fingers through his hair. "Nothing except our land, and not much of it either. Russell made promises to my mother in exchange for her selling to him. It should come as no surprise that he kept none of those promises," he finished, his jaw so hard she thought it might crack.

"But he paid you money, right? Didn't that help some?"

He snorted in disgust. "He paid far less than he would make when he developed it. And when he struck oil, he refused to share any of the profits as he'd promised. My mother was too trusting, and we ended up with less than nothing."

So Chad's father had bought Voronov land, promised to give them a share of profits, then disappeared with the money. She could understand why Alexei would dislike the Russells. But as successful as he now was, did he really need to embark on revenge simply to get back at Chad's family for what they'd done?

Tim Russell was dead, and Alexei was beyond rich now. She hurt for him, but she also hurt for Chad. They were both victims of one man's greed, and it didn't seem fair to either of them. They had so much in common, if only they could see it.

"I think I understand why you wanted to acquire Russell Tech," Paige said. "But Chad's father died a long time ago.

Could the two of you not leave this in the past? You're *family.*"

"*Nyet,*" Alexei spat. "Chad and his mother are nothing to me."

He ground his teeth together to keep from lashing out. How had he started on this trip down memory lane anyway? He had never, ever shared the details of what had happened so long ago with anyone.

And now he was spilling his guts to her as if they were two women gossiping about their lives. What was happening to him? He'd come out here to tell her he was leaving, because though he'd considered ordering the helicopter and simply going, he'd felt it was wrong to abandon her without an explanation.

Now he wished he'd done exactly that. He should have left and to hell with the rest.

She didn't understand, not really. He was surprised at how much he wanted her to. All he needed was to tell her the rest, to tell her about Katerina, and her lovely face would crease in sympathy. She might even get up and wrap her arms around him.

But he could not do it. He could not endure it if she touched him. And he found he couldn't speak the words about Katerina, couldn't say it aloud when he'd never done so before. No one knew that he'd gone to Dallas to beg for her life. No one knew that Tim Russell had laughed in his face and thrown him out. He'd been too humiliated to ever share it with anyone.

He would not start now.

"It is not as simple as that," he bit out.

"But what has Chad done to you?" she asked, her eyes shining with hope. As if she wanted him to see the error of his ways, wanted to play mediator and reunite him with the only branch of his family still living.

She'd boiled it down to a simple formula and she wanted

him to swallow the pill. It was so typically Paige that he would
have laughed if he weren't raging inside. She'd spent her life
pleasing people and did not see why everyone couldn't—or
wouldn't—do the same.

"Chad inherited his parents' dislike of me along with
Russell Tech. I assure you, had he been the one to close the
Valishnikov deal, our situations would be reversed."

"I don't doubt that, but it doesn't need to be this way. It only
takes one of you to change it. You should go to him, should
talk—"

"Stop," he ordered, his voice harsh and full of the hatred
he felt for the Russells. "Not everything can be fixed, Paige.
Nor should it."

He didn't like the way she looked at him, the way her lovely
dark eyes seemed so sad and disappointed and wary all at
once. Again, she made him feel like a great Russian bear,
ready to devour her whole and spit out the bones. It made
him angry. He might not have been completely honest with
her, but he'd never set out to harm her.

"You have no idea what you're talking about," he continued. "You think everything is simple, that a lifetime of
problems can be solved with a conversation. You think that
I need to forgive and forget, that I somehow need Chad and
Elena because we share DNA."

"I never said that," she protested. "But I don't understand
why you don't try. Someone has to make the first move."

"It will not be me," he said. "I don't need them. I don't
need anybody."

Her eyes shimmered with hurt. "Of course you don't. It's
much easier that way, isn't it? Needing people leaves you
vulnerable."

He was so stunned he couldn't speak. He'd dated many
women, but he'd never shared the details of his life with them.
And even if he had, he knew in his bones that none of them

would have seen what she had just now. She'd pierced the veil of his pride, of his loneliness, of his shield, and she'd stabbed into the soft heart of the matter.

It was easier not to need anyone. Easier not to love anyone. She saw through him, and he couldn't bear it a moment longer than he had to.

"I have to go now," he said stiffly. "There is much to be done before we are ready to develop Valishnikov's land. I will return as soon as I am able."

"Why can't I go with you? I don't know anyone here but you, and I don't want to be alone."

Her plea cut him to the bone. But he had to stand firm in this. He needed to get away from her until he could regain his perspective. "You will not be alone. Vasily is here, and the staff. There is much for you to do. You will need to learn Russian. When I return, there will be cocktail parties, dinners and evenings at the ballet and theater. You must learn to be a princess."

"Why can't I learn Russian in Moscow?"

"Because I wish you to learn it here."

Her expression fell just a little. "You don't really want me, do you, Alexei? You married me for the baby, just like you seduced me for information. *I* don't matter to you at all."

Isn't that what he wanted her to think? It was easier this way, easier than messy emotional entanglements. Not that he *was* emotionally entangled, but if he stood here and justified himself, if he tried to soothe her, he would only hurt her more. And he didn't want to do that.

When he found his voice, it was hard. Just like he needed it to be.

"You are my wife and the mother of my child. You are a princess, and wealthier than you have ever dreamed. What more could you possibly need from me?"

"What more indeed," she said, turning her head away to gaze into the distance just as he had earlier.

"I will return in a few days." He stood there a moment more, hesitating. For what reason, he did not know.

She waved a hand as if she were a queen dismissing a functionary. She did not look at him. "Fine. Have fun."

A few days turned into a week. A week turned into two. Paige had never felt so angry, so alone and so useless in her life. Alexei had dragged her to Russia, married her, and left her to rot in a gilded prison. This was not how she'd envisioned her life turning out. At only twenty-six, she'd thought she had a lifetime ahead of her to do what she wanted, to explore the world, to find a partner in life and get married. To have children.

Reflexively she pressed her hand to her abdomen. This child was the only wonderful thing about her relationship with Alexei.

But nothing about this life was normal. She'd left everything behind for the promise of financial security for her sister. But what about her needs? What about the baby? Would Alexei ever be more than a figurehead? Or would he simply leave phone messages and make vague promises about returning soon?

Paige had been deceived about so many things. Deceived about Chad and his relationship with Emma. Deceived about Alexei's true intentions when he'd first professed an interest in her. Deceived about the family connection between the man she worked for and the man she'd fallen into bed with.

Everything had been a deception. The only real thing in her life was this baby. Her fingers tightened over her belly. Sometimes she wondered if the baby was still there. How would she know? According to the doctor, she wouldn't show for some time, and she wouldn't feel movement for several more weeks.

"Please don't leave me, little one," she murmured. "You're all I have left."

The only person who would need her and love her was this baby. She hadn't heard from Emma since she'd left Texas two weeks ago. It tortured her to think that Emma might never forgive her.

And it angered her. Because she and Emma had been together so long and been through so much. How could her sister truly cut Paige from her life after all they'd been through? She knew Emma was angry, rightfully so, but Paige had to believe her sister would eventually pick up the phone or send an e-mail.

Because if she didn't believe it, she would never make it through the endless days and nights.

And the days literally were endless. This far north, it never got fully dark at night. As the solstice approached, the sky darkened to dusk, and the horizon stayed pink until the sun rose only a few short hours later. It was beautiful and magical, and yet there was no one to share it with.

Paige was more alone here than she'd ever been in the darkest, loneliest hours after her mother had died.

It was true there was a large staff at the Voronov Palace, but they were here to serve her, not to be her friend. Not that she hadn't tried to make friends, but Vasily frowned upon it. He was formal and structured. He bowed in her presence and called her "princess," no matter how odd it made her feel.

She did not feel like a princess, but he insisted on maintaining that level of formality and he insisted the staff do so as well. She'd been assigned a personal assistant, a cool young woman named Mariya whose job it was to transform her into a princess worthy of Alexei. So far, there had been daily Russian lessons, etiquette lessons and deportment lessons.

Today, Mariya had informed her, they were going on a shopping trip to St. Petersburg. Paige, who had never been comfortable shopping in her life, looked forward to the trip as if it were her favorite thing to do. Finally a chance to get out of the palace and see *something*.

The ride into town took about a half an hour. Mariya sat silent and respectful across from Paige in the limo, only speaking when Paige asked questions or commented on the sights. Another dark car led the way in front of them, with a following car behind them.

"Why do we need three cars?" Paige asked.

Mariya regarded her evenly. "It is security, your highness."

"Security?" She'd given up asking Mariya not to call her *your highness*. "Is it dangerous where we are going?"

Mariya's short blond hair didn't dare to move a millimeter when the woman shook her head. "You are a princess and your husband is very wealthy. Security is appropriate."

When they arrived on the Nevsky Prospekt, where all the couture boutiques were located, Mariya made Paige wait in the car while she had a security team check each store before they went inside. Once the men gave their okay—what manner of sinister things they expected in a clothing store, Paige had no idea—Mariya hustled Paige into the building.

Once inside, a team of women descended. Mariya conversed with them in Russian, and then Paige was whisked into the back of the shop and dress after dress was brought out for her inspection. Because she didn't know the first thing about fashion, she ended up saying they were all nice. Finally, Mariya gave a crisp order and several of the garments were taken away.

"Please try these on, Princess Voronova," she said.

Paige spent the next hour trying on clothes and shoes. When she emerged in a wine-colored silk gown, another woman was standing there, a frown fixed on her face. Mariya, Paige noted, seemed irritated.

"Princess Voronova, may I introduce you to the Countess Kozlova?"

"So this is the American that Alexei has married," the countess interjected with a sniff.

Something about the way the woman said Alexei's name sent a spear of jealousy through Paige's breastbone. That, and the other woman's appearance. The countess was blonde and groomed to within an inch of her life. She exuded elegance and poise, and she looked far more like the kind of woman Alexei should be with. She made Paige feel duller and frumpier than she ever had.

It surprised her, but the thought of Alexei with another woman had the power to make her crazy. He was still such a stranger to her, and yet she sometimes felt as if they were connected by more than just a baby.

She felt foolish for thinking so, when clearly he did not feel compelled to return to her side. For all she knew, he was living the single life in Moscow, sleeping with a different woman every night and never planning to return to his plain, pregnant wife.

"Ochen' priyatno," Paige said.

The countess's exotic eyes narrowed. *"Mnye tozhye."*

Paige knew it was the proper reply, yet she doubted very much the countess was actually pleased to meet her. The problem with learning Russian was that she couldn't understand inflections the way she would if the woman had replied in sarcastic English.

"You must come to my salon," the countess said. "There are many people who would like to meet you."

Paige didn't know what to say. She glanced at Mariya, but the woman was busy staring at her feet. Instinctively she was certain the Countess Kozlova did not like her. But she wasn't certain she could refuse an invitation. Would it reflect badly on Alexei? Did she care if it did?

Paige felt a slow flush creeping up her neck. For God's sake, the man had left her alone since they'd returned from Texas. He'd told her to learn how to be a princess, and then he'd abandoned her instead of helping her to learn the role himself. She was out of her element, out of her depth and growing more furious by the minute.

How dare he throw her into shark-infested waters to sink or swim on her own! How dare he drag her from her life and those she loved when he didn't want or need her!

Was this how she was going to live? Was this how she was going to be the best mother for her baby? By cowering and moping and waiting for instruction?

Something inside her snapped as she faced the woman watching her so confidently, one immaculately groomed eyebrow lifted in question. She felt as if the countess was mocking her, as if the world was mocking her.

And she was sick of her lack of control over her own life.

By God, from now on she would stop living like a hermit in a grand palace and immerse herself in the life and culture. Alexei wanted a princess? Then he would get one, though it might not be the one he wanted.

"Speciba," she replied, lifting her chin. "I would be pleased to attend."

The countess bared her teeth in a smile. "Very well. I will send the details to your social secretary, *da?* I *so* look forward to it, Princess."

Countess Kozlova lived in a grand town house located on one of the canals that crisscrossed St. Petersburg and gave it the nickname "Venice of the North." On the drive into town, Paige had begun to believe she'd made a mistake in agreeing to come to the countess's party. Mariya hadn't said a word, but Paige could feel her assistant's disapproval.

She'd steadfastly ignored it, just as Alexei had ignored her. Three days had passed since she'd gone shopping and met the countess, and Alexei had not called once. Though Paige had wanted to pull the covers over her head and pretend she'd not accepted the invitation, she'd known she could not do so. Instead, after consulting Mariya as to the type of party this was and what she was expected to wear, she'd chosen a white silk gown and tall, crystal-studded sandals that peeked from beneath the hem whenever she walked.

A maid twisted her hair up into an elegant French knot, and then Mariya had shown up with a selection of jewels that made Paige's breath catch in her chest. The diamonds, Mariya had informed her, had once belonged to a Romanov queen. As if the glittering jewels weren't enough, Mariya had also produced a tiara.

Paige had stared at herself in the mirror for several minutes, her eyes glassing over with tears. She looked elegant, like a princess should look. For the first time since she'd come to Russia, she felt as if she might actually learn to belong here.

Appropriately gowned and coiffed, Paige had set out on the journey into town, her heart thrumming like a bird in a cage. Now, as she stood in the glittering ballroom surrounded by men and women speaking Russian, she once more felt alone and isolated and completely out of her depth.

She should not have come. She should have contented herself with a book like she had so many other nights. Mariya was by her side to translate, but unless the woman sat behind her at dinner and told her which fork to use when, Paige would be lost. There hadn't been much use for this kind of complicated etiquette where she'd grown up.

"Ah, Princess Voronova," the countess said as she sauntered

up with her hand wrapped around a man's arm, "it is so nice to see you. I wish you to meet my brother, Yevgeny. He has admired you from afar and I have said I would introduce you."

Paige hoped her palms weren't sweating too badly as she held out her hand. "Pleased to meet you."

Yevgeny bowed over her hand as he placed a kiss on the back of it. "Very beautiful," he murmured. "Perhaps you will honor me with a dance?"

"I'm not much good at dancing, I'm afraid," Paige said.

"Nonsense."

"No, it's true. There wasn't much time for dancing back home."

"Home is Texas, no?" the countess said. She turned to her brother. "Alexei is so amusing. When I saw him in Moscow a few days ago, he told me he'd married an American girl with no money or connections. Were you a cowgirl, Princess Voronova?"

The blood pounded in Paige's temples. This woman had seen Alexei recently? Had talked with him? He had spoken to her of their relationship?

"You have me at a disadvantage, Countess," Paige said as coolly as she could. "I've heard nothing at all about you from my husband."

The countess laughed, her golden eyes sparkling with a hint of malice. "No, I rather doubt you have. It might not be good for marital felicity, no?"

Before Paige could manage a reply, the countess turned to her brother and gave him a playful little slap on the arm. "Yevgeny, do be good to the princess, will you? I have to speak with Mr. Kaminski."

"My sister is angry with you," Yevgeny said once the countess was gone.

Paige watched the woman move across the room, her hips

rolling sensually as she walked, the curve of her buttocks swaying with the kind of practiced grace that Paige knew she did not have. Men's heads turned to watch her progress.

"I don't know why. I've done nothing to her."

He took her arm and began to lead her around the crowd toward a door on the other side of the room. Paige didn't want to be rude, so she didn't protest. But when she glanced behind her for Mariya, the woman had disappeared.

"Ah, but you have done something," he said smoothly. "You have married Prince Voronov, which is a task she had set for herself after the count died."

"I imagine if Alexei had wanted to marry her, he would have done so. It's hardly my fault."

Yevgeny laughed. He was tall, blond and rather handsome. He was the kind of man she used to be attracted to, she thought wistfully. But since Alexei had come into her life, she seemed to only want dark, brooding men who ignored her.

Yevgeny appeared to be nice enough, in spite of his sister, and his English was good. For the first time in weeks, someone was talking to her as an equal. It'd been too long since she'd had a normal conversation with anyone—though this was hardly a normal conversation.

"Yes," Yevgeny said, "she had her chance to reel him in when they were lovers."

Paige stumbled, but Yevgeny righted her. "Sorry," she said. Alexei and the countess had been lovers? Were they lovers when he'd taken her to the Voronov Palace that night so many weeks ago? Her temples throbbed with the notion. She'd known Alexei wasn't celibate when they'd met, but she'd never considered he was involved with someone else at the time.

Yevgeny had guided her onto a terrace that overlooked a canal. The sky was pink with the setting sun that would never entirely disappear for the night. A boat glided along the canal while people stood at the railings, watching the city slide by.

Yevgeny's hand skimmed her arm. "No, it is I who am sorry. You did not know my sister and your husband were lovers, and I have blurted it out."

Paige subtly pulled away from him. She was beginning to doubt that he was nice after all. "It's not your fault."

"Yet I feel responsible."

Paige wrapped her arms around her torso and shook her head. "No, really, you shouldn't. I'm sure there are many women in Alexei's past."

"Are you cold?"

"A little," Paige admitted. "I'm not used to this climate."

Yevgeny shrugged out of his jacket. "Here, let me help you," he said as he stepped behind her to settle the coat on her shoulders. She felt she should refuse, and yet she didn't want to be rude when he was simply being solicitous.

But when his hands lingered on her shoulders before sliding down her arms, a thread of panic unwound in her belly. She started to turn and tell him she wanted to go back inside.

"Isn't this cozy?" a voice growled. Paige's head whipped around as the dark shape in the door coalesced into a tall man in a tuxedo.

Relief flooded her. "Alexei? What are you doing here?"

His gray eyes gleamed with suppressed fury as he stepped closer. "You were not expecting me, I take it?"

CHAPTER ELEVEN

ALEXEI WANTED TO KILL the man standing so close to his wife. Yevgeny Petrov shot him a malevolent grin over the top of Paige's head, but it was Paige who held Alexei's attention. She was radiant, more beautiful than he remembered, and he wanted her with a fierceness that clawed his insides into ribbons.

Not a day had gone by that he hadn't thought about her, but he'd stayed away because he'd believed it was best for them both. Now that he was here, however, he realized it had been a mistake. She was too lovely and too vulnerable to leave her alone with predators like Petrov circling around.

He closed the distance between them and yanked her from Yevgeny's grip. She stumbled against him and he caught her close, trapping her in the curve of his arm.

"Stay away from my wife," he growled.

"Then perhaps you should keep her close," Yevgeny said in Russian.

Alexei pulled the jacket from Paige's shoulders and threw it at the other man. "Get out of my sight, Petrov."

Yevgeny took his time shrugging into his jacket. Then he bowed to Paige. "It was lovely to meet you, Princess Voronova," he said in English.

"I enjoyed talking with you, too," she said in that slight

Texas drawl, all Southern politeness and grace. "Thank you for your kindness."

Alexei waited until Yevgeny had passed into the house before he turned Paige in his arms.

"You are never to be alone with that man again, do you understand?"

"I'm surprised you care," she flung at him, her brows two sharp slashes in her face as anger replaced the politeness.

"You are my wife," he ground out. "Of course I care."

She snorted. "Really? And here I'd thought I was simply your prisoner. Or is this how wives are treated in Russia?"

He hadn't expected her anger, hadn't expected her to challenge him. It surprised him, fueled the fire in his veins. He hauled her closer, his temper on a gossamer string. "We are leaving now," he growled. "And you will never set foot in this house again."

A flash of discomfort crossed her features. "You're holding me too tight. You'll leave bruises."

He immediately released her. The last thing he wanted to do was hurt her. He took a step back, raked a hand through his hair. He'd barely spent three minutes in her company and already she made him lose control.

But seeing her with Petrov had made him crazy. She was too good for a snake like Yevgeny Petrov.

Not only that, but she was also his wife. Pregnant with his child. His gaze slipped to her belly, but she looked the same as she had nearly three weeks ago.

But when he met her eyes again, he amended the thought. She did not look the same. She looked…elegant. Beautiful and ethereal—and brimming with temper.

He didn't like her this way.

Or, he did like it, but he didn't like everyone else seeing what he saw. His Paige wore dull suits and glasses. This Paige was gowned in pure white, like a virgin or an angel. The silk skimmed her curves like water flowing over a creek bed. Her dark hair was pinned up, showing the graceful curvature of her neck. He recognized, with a flash of surprise, the Voronov diamonds at her throat. The tiara she wore had once been his great-great-grandmother's.

His body throbbed with heat and desire. He wanted to sweep her up and take her from this place right now.

"Where are your glasses?" he demanded.

She looked at him like he'd lost his mind. Which, he feared, he had.

"I'm wearing contacts. Are you going to tell me what you're doing here, Alexei, and why you're acting so bossy?"

He took his jacket off and wrapped it around her, belatedly remembering that she'd been cold. He'd stood in the entry and watched her with Yevgeny for several minutes before he'd interrupted. He didn't know why, except that maybe he'd wanted to see how she would react. Now, he felt small and petty for having done so. Paige had been innocent when he'd made love to her, and though she'd harbored a crush on Chad Russell, she'd never acted upon it.

But he'd stood there, watching Petrov, who was more like Chad in type than he was, and wondering what she would do if the man tried to kiss her. Except that he'd been unable to let it go that far.

"I could ask the same of you."

She blinked. "Without the bossy part, I assume. And I was invited."

"So was I."

"Do you mean you didn't know I would be here tonight?"

"I knew," he clipped out. Because Mariya had called to inform him of the fact. And he'd raced from Moscow because he could not stay away. "But I want to know why you came."

She pulled his jacket around her body, covering the dress. "Because I'm bored, Alexei, and tired of being alone. Because someone invited me to a party, and I wanted to be out among people, where there was laughter and music and conversation. I married you for our baby and for my sister's future, but I didn't agree to be your prisoner."

An erotic image of her bound to his bed with silken ropes flashed into his mind.

"You are not a prisoner," he said.

She snorted. "No, but I might as well be. If I'd known we weren't going to make a life together for the sake of our baby, I could have stayed in Texas and you could just visit whenever you found yourself passing through."

"Your life is here now. With me."

She stomped her foot. He'd noticed she often did so when aggravated. For some reason, he found it amusing. But he did not dare to smile now that she was bristling like a cat.

"But my life *isn't* with you! It's in your palace, where everyone is so cold and formal and no one talks to me like I'm a normal person!" She slapped a hand against her chest. "But I *am* a normal person, Alexei. I'm not a princess, not an exalted being—I'm just Paige Barnes from Atkinsville, Texas, and I don't know how to be anyone else!"

He reached for her hand. He'd been handling this badly, and it was time to regroup.

She snatched it away and crossed her arms beneath her breasts. The movement lifted the creamy swells, drew his gaze. He wanted to touch her, wanted to strip her and explore every last inch of her glorious skin.

"You are Princess Paige Voronova, and I don't want you to be anyone else," he said.

Her eyes glittered. "That's not how it looks from where I'm standing," she said, her voice almost a whisper.

Alexei sensed a softening in her and reached for her again.

This time she did not resist as he pulled her gently closer. He tipped her chin up. He had to kiss her. It had been too long, and he was suddenly dying to do so. Dying to see if the flame inside him whipped higher, or if it was all his imagination.

He lowered his head slowly, waiting to see what she would do. For a moment, he thought she would reject him, but then her eyes closed and her mouth parted.

A fierce surge of possession went through him. He hadn't expected her to surrender. The gesture stunned him, humbled him. He did not deserve her surrender, but he would not reject it. Not this time.

He hovered above her mouth, not kissing her just yet, but letting his gaze brush over the cream of her skin, the long sweep of her lashes where they fanned against her cheeks, before finally settling on the lush pink of her lips.

She was in that moment the most desirable woman he'd ever known.

Her eyes fluttered open in question, but before she could speak and puncture the wonder of it, he crushed his mouth down on hers. He had not kissed her since the night he'd made love to her, and the moment their tongues met, he wondered why in God's name not.

She clutched the lapels of his tuxedo, opened herself to him while he plundered the depths of her lush mouth. Alexei surrendered to the feeling. He was through fighting her pull on him. It was ridiculous to do so when he couldn't even imagine touching another woman. She was a fever in his blood that would not be abated through deprivation.

Tonight, he was taking her to his bed and to hell with anything else.

Paige hardly recognized the man who hurried her to the waiting limo and climbed in beside her. With a sharp command to the driver, he hit the button for the privacy glass before turning to her.

Her heart raced, but whether it was from the look in his eyes or the way he'd kissed her, she wasn't certain.

"I want you," he said as he pushed her back on the long, plush seat and spread his body over hers. "It has been too long."

Paige swallowed as the hard lines of his body pressed into her soft curves. She ached with heat and need, and though part of her gibbered that she shouldn't fall into his arms so easily, she knew she was ultimately going to do so.

His lips found the tender skin of her neck, and she sighed helplessly. How could she reject this pleasure?

There was something about this man, something about the way she felt when he touched her, that she could not deny. He turned her inside out, made her skin seem too tight and thin to contain what she felt for him.

Was this what it felt like to be in love?

Love. The word cracked in her brain like thunder over the Gulf of Mexico. How many times had she cowered from the power of those sonorous blasts as a child? She wanted to cower now, to hide her head in the sand and make the noise go away.

Love.

She could not love him. She didn't know him well enough, even if her heart insisted that she knew everything she needed to know. He was driven and strong and he felt things deeply. And he'd made her his wife because he would never abandon his child.

But there was still the matter of his deception. He'd set out to seduce her with a goal in mind. He'd not actually asked her for information that night, but she told herself it was because he'd learned what he needed during his endless phone calls instead.

"You are thinking about something," he murmured against her cheek.

It surprised her that he knew. "Yes."

"Tell me what it is."

"I'm wondering why you're here."

"I'm here because you are my wife."

She settled her palm on his cheek because she could not help but do so. He turned into her hand, kissed her skin. "I want to believe that," she said.

"Then believe it."

Her pulse throbbed in her throat, her temples. "I can't."

His gaze clouded. "What is this all about, Paige?"

"What's it *about*? How can you ask me that? You know what it's about!"

He sat up with a sigh. She scrambled into a sitting position. Part of her was cursing herself for opening her mouth, and another part was urging her on.

"I wish to make love to you, and you wish to talk." He shoved his fingers through his hair. "Yet I suppose I deserve it."

"I haven't heard from you in three weeks," she said. "And now you're here, kissing me and scrambling my brain—"

"I scramble your brain?" He looked supremely satisfied.

She folded her arms as if to shield herself. "You know you do. If you didn't, I doubt we'd be here now. I would not be pregnant, and you wouldn't have had to marry me."

He was moving toward her again, sliding her back against the seat once more. "I am liking this idea that I make you forget yourself," he purred.

She put her hands against his shoulders, though she did not push him away. "You do, and now you're making me forget that I'm upset with you. You left me all alone in a strange country with no friends, not to mention dragging me from my home in the first place. And you tried to seduce information out of me."

He kissed her throat. "I did not try to seduce information out of you," he murmured. "I intended to do so, but I forgot all about it in my desire to bed you."

Her eyes closed and she bit back a moan. *Concentrate.* "Is that supposed to make me feel better?"

"I don't see why not." He flexed his hips against her, his glorious hardness pressing into her sensitive core. "This does not lie, *maya krasavitsa*. I wanted you then and I want you now. But I am sorry I hurt you."

"Are you really?"

He lifted his head and gazed down at her. The expression on his face was intense, solemn. "*Da,* I am. I should have never attempted to use your connection to Chad."

She couldn't say why precisely, but she believed him. She simply knew it in her soul that he meant what he said. Her heart swelled until she hurt from the intensity. "Thank you. It means a lot to hear you say it."

"I am not perfect, Paige, but I admit when I am wrong."

He lowered his head to kiss her again, but Paige braced a hand against his chest. "One more thing."

One eyebrow arched in question.

Paige swallowed. But she would not be stopped. She deserved to know. "I want to know what your relationship with the countess is."

He answered without hesitation. "She was my mistress very briefly, and that was quite some time ago."

"You were not with her when we were first together?"

"No."

"She said she saw you in Moscow recently. You told her about me."

He grinned, and her heart flipped. "And you would prefer I kept you a secret?"

"That's not what I meant."

"Countess Kozlova is a vain, shallow woman," he said. "She means nothing at all to me, and never has. Does this satisfy you?"

"I'm not sure," she said. "How do I know you're telling me the truth?"

He looked suddenly very serious. "Because the truth, Paige, is that I have not been with another woman since the night I was with you."

She was stunned into temporary speechlessness. "But— but...I saw you. That actress—"

He flexed his hips and sent a current of sensation arcing through her body. "She was quite disappointed, I assure you."

He lowered his head, his lips touching hers gently, a light skimming of flesh against flesh. "I have been unable to think of anything but that night we shared, the night we created a baby," he murmured. "There has been no one but you since that night."

Tears pressed against the backs of her eyes. It was so close to what she wanted to hear from him, and yet not close enough. But how could she reject him now? How could she say no when this was a beginning? It was possible, wasn't it, that they could build a relationship together if only they tried?

Suddenly she wanted more, wanted to feel if he was real and this moment not simply a figment of her imagination. Would she wake soon, hot and throbbing and disappointed?

She wasn't sure who deepened the kiss first, but it soon turned erotic, sizzling, a meeting of lips and tongues and teeth that was so deep and thorough Paige thought she might combust at any moment. And then his hand skimmed down her silk-clad form until he reached her ankle.

He caught her hem, inched her dress up, his fingers sliding

over her calf, along the inside of her knee, her thigh. Paige whimpered as his thumb brushed across the silk of her panties. Sparks of sensation ignited in her belly as moisture pooled between her thighs.

"Alexei—"

"No more words, Paige. Just feel. Just enjoy."

When he sat up and removed her panties, she could only hold her breath and wait for what he would do next. Did he truly intend to make love in the confines of the car as it moved through the city? The idea was wicked, exciting. She felt as if she should protest, and yet she craved his touch. She wanted to see what he would do next, wanted to feel every sensation he could give her. It'd been too long since she'd felt close to anyone, and she longed for the contact. Deprivation had made her reckless, she decided.

But when he slid his hands beneath her buttocks, she instinctively closed her legs. Was it modesty or fear? She wasn't certain. Without a word, Alexei eased her thighs open and settled between them. Paige held her breath, her heart thundering in her ears with anticipation.

The instant his mouth touched her hot center, her back arched off the seat and she gasped out his name.

He was relentless, bringing her to stunning climax again and again until she begged him to stop. Her body was so sensitized that she couldn't take any more.

But she wanted more. She wanted him, inside her, taking her to the heights of sensation with nothing but skin and heat between them.

She wanted him with a hunger she'd never imagined possible.

Alexei pulled her dress back down and settled into the seat beside her as if nothing had happened. She lay against the door frame, her chest heaving, her body singing, and felt disappointment seep through her that he had not continued.

"What about you?" she asked when she could manage to string two words together.

His silver eyes glittered, the corners of his delicious mouth turning up in a wicked grin. "Do not worry, *maya krasavitsa*, this night is far from over."

As if he'd planned it to the second, the car rolled to a stop. Paige sat up and smoothed her dress before the door could open. A moment later, the chauffer held the door while Alexei helped her out of the car.

"But this is a hotel," Paige said as they walked through the glass carousel into the soaring lobby.

"*Da*. I keep a suite here, for when I need to be in the city."

He led them over to a private elevator and slipped a card through the reader. When the door opened again, it was onto a suite decorated in sleek cherry and steel, sparkling glass and plush leather.

Alexei swept her into his arms and carried her over the threshold. It was romantic, but she told herself not to read anything into it. It was impatience, not romance, that had him carrying her into the bedroom and setting her on the floor before he located the hidden zipper at the side of her gown.

Their clothes disappeared in quick fashion, and then they were tumbling onto the bed and Alexei was thrusting into her body. There was nothing between them this time, no barrier, and the sensation was exquisite. His hard flesh fit her so perfectly that a tear slipped down her cheek.

It was only the second time they'd made love, and yet it felt as if they knew each other's bodies as intimately as lovers of a dozen years. They moved in tune, as a single entity, his thrusts matching hers, until the explosion that happened was so exquisite, so extraordinary, that they both cried out with the power of it.

Afterward, they lay tangled together, their bodies sweating, their breaths cooling their skin, and let their hands wander over each other.

"You are extraordinary," Alexei said sometime later.

Paige sighed contentedly. She didn't feel extraordinary. She felt…peaceful, as if she'd been swirling in a vortex and had finally landed on solid ground. "I feel very ordinary," she replied, yawning.

Alexei toyed with her nipples. Sharp, sweet sensation spiked through her, pooling in her core.

"Your breasts have grown bigger," he said softly.

"They are more sensitive, too."

"I had noticed this."

She pushed back until she could look him straight in the face. "How could you possibly know that? We don't exactly have a long history together."

"No, but what we do have is imprinted on my brain. I have a memory for these kinds of things."

"I'll just bet you do," Paige grumbled.

His brows drew down. "What does this mean?"

"It means that I wonder how well you remember what turns Countess Kozlova on."

He laughed suddenly, startling her. "Jealous, Paige? I have told you she means nothing to me."

"Of course I'm not jealous," she said, though the blush creeping beneath her skin gave away the lie.

Alexei's hand slid to her belly, caressing her. She imagined what it would feel like when she was bigger and the baby could kick in response.

He looked up, his silver eyes intense as they caught and held hers. "I have no desire for any woman but you."

Paige pulled the sheet up, shielding her body as if she could also shield her heart. It was what she wanted to hear from him, and yet it frightened her as well.

Alexei frowned. "What is the matter, Paige?"

"I'm just wondering when the fairy tale ends." Because it would. Just like the last time, the bottom would drop out and she'd find it had all been a lie.

"Don't fairy tales always have a happy ending?" he said lightly.

"Not if you're the wicked witch."

He laughed. "Surely you are not trying to tell me you're the wicked witch?"

Paige couldn't help but smile even as she tried to be serious. "Of course not. I was just trying to say that it all depends on your perspective. The fairy tale might not always end well."

In a quick movement, he stripped the sheet back and moved on top of her, his body hovering over hers, hard and warm and sexy. Paige's breath caught in her throat as her desire quickened inside her again.

"It's our fairy tale," he breathed, his mouth finding the hollow of her throat. "We get to write how it ends."

Paige arched her neck and moaned at the exquisite sensation of his lips moving over her collarbone, between her breasts. Her heart swelled for him, swelled with all she was beginning to feel. She wanted the fairy tale and she wanted the happy ending.

And she wanted tonight. She wanted him like this always, as starved for her as she was for him. She didn't want to think it could end, though she knew it could. But tonight she would not consider it.

He placed a reverent kiss on her stomach before working his way back up her torso. She could feel him between her legs, hard and ready, and her insides liquefied. How did he do this to her? How did he make her feel as if she could never get enough of him?

"You must tell me if it's too much, if you are too tired," he said.

Paige tilted her hips up, sliding her calves along his thighs to hug his waist. "Make love to me, Alexei."

When he entered her this time, it was without the urgency of before. He made love to her slowly, sweetly, taking her to the heights and then bringing her gently back to earth with the exquisite pressure of his body inside hers.

She hadn't known he could be so tender and in control, hadn't known it could be even more beautiful between them than it already had been. As she lay in his arms after, drifting into sleep, she feared her heart was already lost.

CHAPTER TWELVE

PAIGE RETURNED FROM a stroll on the grounds of the palace to find Alexei standing on the terrace, hands shoved in the pockets of the khakis he was wearing, lost in thought. She stopped beside the stone steps leading up to the terrace and watched him.

He was still so breathtaking, and he made her heart thrum with excitement just looking at him. His handsome face was in profile to her. He shoved a hand through his dark hair and lifted the drink he was holding with the other. She wanted to ask him what was wrong, but she sensed that he would not welcome the intrusion.

In the weeks since he'd burst into the Countess Kozlova's salon and whisked her away, they'd spent the days talking, making love, eating dinner on the terrace or beside the fire on cool evenings and taking small trips into town to see the sights.

He'd taken her for a cruise on the Neva River, shown her the Hermitage Museum and the Admiralty, St. Isaac's Cathedral, and the Peter and Paul Fortress on Zayachy Island, among other things. He'd explained that the spire of the St. Peter and Paul Cathedral was the tallest structure in the city, but when he'd asked if she wanted to go up on the viewing platform, she'd refused. Alexei had laughed and hugged her.

"I do not blame you, *lyubimaya moya*. It is very high."

They'd spent a few evenings at the ballet and opera, as he'd promised. Her Russian was getting better, though she could in no way be called fluent. But she'd enjoyed the opera regardless. Mariya had delivered librettos in English, and Paige had read them through before attending in the evening.

Watching Alexei now, she put a hand over her belly. She was nearly fourteen weeks along, and though she couldn't feel movement yet, they had seen their baby on the ultrasounds. It was too early to know if they were having a girl or a boy, but all she had to do was think of that little fist pumping in the air during the ultrasound, and she melted with love.

Paige was humbled by the love she felt for this child. She loved her sister, and she'd worked hard to make a good life for them both, but she'd never felt the kind of protective possessiveness she felt toward this baby growing inside her. It was an experience in a whole new realm.

She wanted to share what she was going through with Emma, but they were so far apart now—both literally and figuratively. Emma had finally e-mailed her, and they'd spoken on the phone several times, but the chill had not completely dissipated. In some ways, it made her angry, but in others she understood.

She'd done everything for Emma for the last eight years, and now she was halfway around the world, married to the man who'd destroyed Emma's fiancé. It was awkward, and yet it hurt her that Emma couldn't find it in herself to understand what Paige was going through. Her entire life had changed when she'd fallen pregnant with Alexei's child, and she was doing the best she could to make something good and lasting in her new life.

It wasn't what she'd once thought would happen to her, but each day she spent with Alexei, she knew it was the right thing. The fairy tale would end the way she wanted it to. She refused to let it happen any other way.

Once, when she'd spoken of her sister's lack of support to Alexei, he'd asked her why she wasn't angry that Emma's first thought the day Paige had told her the news was how it affected *her*.

"She did not ask how you were feeling, Paige, or if the baby was well."

"She was upset," Paige defended.

"Yes, but if the situation were reversed, you would have been more concerned for her welfare than for your own."

She'd known he was right, even if she couldn't admit it. And that's what hurt the most. Emma *had* been more concerned about herself—and still was, to a certain extent.

Paige pushed away the sadness that accompanied her thoughts of Emma and watched her husband in silence. A slow, steady warmth trickled into her veins. Her body always hummed when he was near. It was desire, yes, but she knew it was more than that.

Life with Alexei had been almost perfect these last weeks. He was attentive to her every need, gentle when she wanted it, and fierce when she needed him to be. He knew her so well, sometimes better than she knew herself. It was stunning, really.

One of his smiles had the power to rock her world to its very foundations. She woke up in his arms each morning, and fell asleep in them each night, and she couldn't imagine anywhere else she'd rather be. Couldn't imagine herself with any other man. Once, she'd thought Chad Russell was her ideal man. Now, she couldn't fathom that she ever had.

As her husband stood there so lost in thought, she felt a pang of sadness. No matter how wonderful their lovemaking, or how strong her desire to make him happy, she knew he kept a part of himself separate.

She'd known from the beginning, when she was trying so hard not to let her heart do something stupid and fall in love, that he had a core of loneliness he would not allow her to reach. It was his shield, his armor against the world.

She imagined breaking through it one day, imagined how it would be if he allowed himself to be completely free. She'd tried to talk to him about Chad and Elena a few times, but he shoved the conversation expertly aside each time. He didn't grow angry, the way he once had, but he also refused to allow it to take place.

Paige started up the steps, deciding that she'd spied on him long enough. He turned at the sound of her footsteps. His silver eyes, clouded with some emotion, cleared when he saw her.

"You have enjoyed your walk?" he asked.

She went to his side and leaned against the balustrade. "I did. It's quite refreshing to be able to enjoy a summer stroll without needing to shower and change afterward."

"It is very hot in Dallas now, isn't it?"

"Definitely. If I were there, I'd be inside with the AC cranked up on high and a glass of iced tea in my hand."

His smile was tender. "Don't let this weather fool you. We are located on the Gulf of Finland, so we do get hot and humid days during summer."

"I'll take a few days over several months," she said.

"Come, sit down and have some water." He took her hand and pulled her to the table. A crystal pitcher filled with sparkling water and sliced lemons sat on a cart beside it. He poured some into a goblet and handed it to her.

"Is everything okay, Alexei?" she asked after the silence stretched out between them.

He turned back to her, seeming to hesitate before speaking. She thought he would tell her that nothing was wrong, but he said, "Today is the fifteenth anniversary of my sister's death."

A little pang of feeling pierced her heart. He hadn't spoken of his sister since the first night when they'd eaten dinner together. Did this mean he was opening up to her? Or was she reading too much into it?

Her heart wanted to think he was beginning to feel for her the way she felt for him, but her head was more cautious.

"I'm sorry, Alexei. Do you want to talk about it?"

A gentle breeze stirred, blowing a napkin open where it lay on the table. Paige folded it over again and waited.

"Katerina had leukemia," he finally said. "She died because we couldn't afford the experimental treatment that might have saved her."

Her heart pinched. "I'm so sorry. That must have been hard for you and your mother."

"There was only me. My mother had advanced Alzheimer's by this time. She never knew what happened. She followed Katerina into the grave three years later. I am the only one left to remember any of them."

"There is still your aunt," she offered. She knew it was a risk, but she wanted him to realize that he really wasn't alone in this world. That he had the power to change things for them all. People made mistakes, but no one remained static over the years. His aunt might regret the way she'd felt about his mother now that she was older.

Alexei's face grew hard, closed off, and she knew she'd made a mistake.

Paige simply couldn't imagine cutting herself off from all her living family the way he had. She needed Emma, not just because they were sisters, but also because she saw her mother's beauty and grace in her sister's smile. Families were living reminders of those who had gone before.

But he did not see things the same as she did, and it saddened her.

"There is no possibility of reconciliation, Paige."

Stop right now, don't say it. But she couldn't leave it without stating the truth.

"Tim Russell is dead. Why let what he did stand between you and your family?"

"They are *not* my family." Alexei's voice cracked between them like a whip. Then he closed his eyes for a moment. "I'm sorry," he said when he opened them again. "It's not your fault."

Paige stood and went to him, wrapping her arms around his waist and burying her head against his chest. She couldn't stand to see him hurt, and she couldn't stand when she caused it by picking at his wounds. "I'm sorry, too. I didn't mean to hurt you."

Just when she thought he might push her away, his arms came around her and he squeezed her tight. "I know this."

"I just want to understand, Alexei." She wanted to understand so many things: why he was so adamant, why he couldn't let go of the past, why he kept himself closed in—and why, in spite of everything, she'd fallen in love with him.

His chest rumbled against her ear. "There is nothing to understand. It simply is."

Alexei couldn't sleep. Beside him, Paige's even breathing told him she'd had no such problem. Outside, the sky was white, but he had no idea what time it was. It could be midnight or it could be 3:00 a.m. They were in the middle of the *Beliye Nochi,* or White Nights, that St. Petersburg was famous for.

He pushed the covers back and got up, padding naked to the window to pull the thick curtains back and gaze at the sky.

Katerina had died on a night like this, when the sun never set and the world seemed bright and filled with eternal summer.

But there was no eternal summer, for Katerina or for

anyone. There was only a short season between dark, frozen, barren ones.

It scared him, that knowledge. It was why he'd refused to grow close to anyone else after the passing of his family. You couldn't hurt when you didn't care.

But Paige had taken that comfort away from him. Though he'd tried not to let it happen, she had grown important to him. He'd known when he'd returned to her side that night so many weeks ago that he was taking a chance. That once he touched her, he would not be able to let go.

She was all he needed. Paige and the baby. He did not need to reach out to Chad and Elena, though she wanted him to do so.

He only needed her. And he needed to explain to her why he could not cross that chasm, and why he'd had to destroy Russell Tech. The real reason, not the partial one he'd already told her. He wanted her to understand, and he wanted at last to tell another living person what he'd never said before. He *needed* to do so.

"Alexei?"

He turned to find her pushed up on one elbow, squinting toward the window. He let the curtain fall. "I'm sorry I woke you."

"No, it's fine. Please open the curtain again." She climbed from the bed and donned a robe while he did as she asked. She came to his side, yawning, and slipped an arm around his waist. "I'd heard about this, but it's hard to believe it never gets dark until you see it. It's the most amazing thing."

He was looking at the top of her dark head, her thick hair mussed from sleep and lovemaking, when she gazed up at him. "No, you are," he said softly.

She smiled, and his world lit from within. "You always know the right thing to say."

"Do I?"

"You must. You talked me into kissing you when I didn't know you, and you kept right on talking me into things until we ended up here."

"Perhaps I should have gone into politics."

Her smile grew more radiant, if that were possible. "It's probable we'd have world peace right this instant if you had."

Alexei grew serious. "I don't always know the right thing to say, *angel moy*."

"Perhaps not, but I'd wager you usually do."

If only that were true.

"When Katerina was dying, I went to Dallas," he said quickly, before he could change his mind.

The arm she'd wrapped around his waist tightened, as if she knew what he was about to say. She could not know, but he loved the way she sensed his turmoil. It comforted him, gave him the strength to continue.

"I went to see Tim Russell. I asked for his help, Paige. But he would not give it. He told me the Voronovs were dead to his wife, and therefore dead to him."

Her eyes glistened. "Oh, Alexei, I'm so sorry."

"She died in agony, because I could not save her. I tried, but I couldn't."

"It's not your fault," she said fiercely. Tears rolled down her cheeks now, and he cursed himself for making her cry. Why had he burdened her with this? He'd wanted to share it, but now that he had, he wished he could take it back. Anything to return the smile to her face.

"I've never told anyone what happened," he said thickly. "I didn't tell Katerina. It would have done her no good."

"You've carried this around by yourself for fifteen years? Oh, Alexei." She shook her head. "Why are you so stubborn?"

He blinked. Stubborn? Was he? "I had no reason to tell anyone, *lyubimaya moya*. This is not stubbornness."

She turned to him, put her hands on either side of his face. "But it is. You can't keep this kind of thing inside. It eats at you if you do. It's not healthy."

He put his hands over hers. "I'm not keeping it inside anymore, am I? You know—and now you know why I can never forgive the Russells. They took far more than land and money."

She lifted herself on tiptoe and pressed her mouth to his. He tasted the salt of her tears, and it sliced him open deep inside, both the knowledge he'd made her cry and the fact she was crying for him.

When she pulled back, her beautiful face was sad. He wanted to take her back to bed and make her forget everything he'd just told her. Why had he done it? And why did he feel as if a weight had been lifted now that he'd done so?

"You have to let this go," she said softly. "It's killing you."

He knew what she meant and he stiffened. "No, it has given me purpose. It has driven me to be what I am now." He spread his arms wide, encompassing their plush surroundings. "Without that purpose, I might not have any of this. And though I would trade it all for Katerina's life in a minute, I would not change what I have done to get here. Or what I will continue to do to keep this empire for you and our child."

"I don't want it at the expense of *you*," she cried. "Nothing is as important as—"

She stood there with wide eyes, her bottom lip trembling.

His heart thumped. "As important as what, Paige?"

"As you are to me," she finally said. "I love you, Alexei. Surely you know that by now."

His chest hurt. Absolutely hurt. Her words filled the empty

corners of his soul, made him ache with the sweetness and pain of it. She wasn't the first woman to say those words to him, and yet something about them coming from her was different.

Why?

A thread of panic began to unwind in his gut. How could he allow this to happen? Objectively he could say he needed her. That being with her made him happier than he'd been in a very long time. That hearing these words from her completed a missing part of him.

But emotionally he couldn't face the truth of it. Because need and love meant loss and pain and uncertainty. He'd vowed never to allow someone else's existence to determine his happiness. He knew from bitter experience that it would not turn out well.

"Aren't you going to say anything?" she asked, and he realized he'd remained silent too long. She searched his face, and though he wasn't certain what he saw there, he knew it wasn't what she wanted because the weight of sorrow bracketed her mouth once more.

"What do you wish me to say?" As if he didn't know. But he couldn't do it, couldn't tell her something that he feared would swallow him whole if he said it. The words wouldn't come—and he wasn't sure he wanted them to.

She clutched her robe tighter around her body. "Nothing, Alexei. Nothing at all."

"You need to sleep," he said gruffly. Because he'd hurt her again, and because he hated doing so. "The baby needs you to be healthy."

She flinched as if he'd hit her. "The baby. Yes, of course." Her hand had settled over her abdomen.

He didn't know what to say. It was within his power to reverse this. To tell her what she wanted to hear and to make her smile again. But it was impossible to do so.

She walked over to the bed and shed her robe. He followed, turning her in his arms and hauling her close before she could lie down again. Her body was stiff with rejection and he thought, for a moment, it would kill him.

"I'm tired," she said softly, her voice heavy with emotion.

He held her for a moment longer, his heart thumping in his breast like a trapped eagle beating its wings against a cage. He knew what he needed to say, what would make everything right again—

He let her go. And then, because he deserved the torture, he spent the rest of the night beside her, not touching her, knowing she was lying as far from him as she could possibly get without falling out of the bed.

When Paige woke the next morning, Alexei was gone. It wasn't the first morning she'd awakened and he wasn't there, but this morning was different. She knew it in her bones. After last night, after her stupidity in confessing her love to him, she'd known he would be gone.

But part of her had hoped he wouldn't be. She'd let her emotions get the best of her, when he'd told her with such pain in his voice about his sister and about Chad's father's cruelty to them. She'd hated Tim Russell for him in that moment.

She'd understood, in a way she'd have never thought possible, what had driven him to ruin Russell Tech. And it horrified her, feeling those emotions. If it horrified her after feeling it for only a few minutes, what must it be like to live with that feeling for fifteen years?

She'd wanted him to understand how damaging those emotions were, but she hadn't meant to tell him she loved him. Not yet. It was too new, too fragile, and she'd feared he didn't feel the same way. They'd had a wonderful few weeks together, but that wasn't enough to build a lifetime of love on.

Paige groaned as she stood in front of the mirror, brushing her hair. The look on his face when she'd told him she loved him—oh, God. You'd have thought she'd told him the world was ending tomorrow at noon he'd looked so horrified.

He didn't love her, didn't need her. He'd married her for the baby, and he enjoyed the sex. Sometimes, he even enjoyed the companionship.

But why had he told her about the dark things in his life if he didn't care?

Paige dropped the brush and whirled from the mirror before she drove herself insane. She didn't understand anything about the man she'd married. Just when she thought she did, he stunned her with the evidence that she'd had it all wrong. When he'd told her she needed to sleep for the sake of the baby, she'd felt like he'd slapped her. She'd been stunned, hurt and numb.

When he'd tried to hold her, she'd wanted to be in his arms—and yet she'd known she couldn't survive it. She'd hated the way they'd ended last night. She'd hated lying on the edge of the bed, aching for him to touch her and knowing he would not once she'd rejected him. Knowing that she would fall apart if he did so. Because he didn't love her, and she loved him desperately.

And now he was gone and she was cursing herself for spilling her love so carelessly. If she'd said nothing, they would have continued the way they had been.

But, she asked herself angrily, was that enough? Didn't she deserve more?

She emerged into their suite to find a maid setting the table outside on the terrace with a full breakfast. She wasn't sure she was all that hungry, but for the baby's sake she knew she needed to eat.

"Dobroye Utro," she said to the woman, who curtsied and

returned the greeting before picking up her tray and hurrying away.

A cream envelope lay beside her plate. She picked it up and sliced it open with a butter knife. She already knew what it was. The only mystery was how he would phrase the need for his absence.

Have to go into Moscow this morning. Will return tonight.
Alexei

She stared toward the Gulf of Finland in the distance, her insides churning with a riot of love, pain and fury. The morning sunshine sparkled on the water like millions of winking diamonds. Would one night turn into two? Would it become a week, and then a month, and then two months before she saw him again? Had she chased him away with her naive declaration?

Because how could a man like Alexei love her? He was handsome, successful and utterly ruthless with his enemies. He'd married her out of a sense of duty, nothing more. No matter what he said to the contrary, he belonged with a woman like the Countess Kozlova—someone elegant and accustomed to his world.

No. That was ridiculous. She was being emotional and stupid and, worse, indulging in self-pity. Paige crumpled the envelope in her fist before she set it on the table and smoothed it flat again.

There was a fluttering in her stomach, so soft and light that she ignored it at first. And then it happened again. It felt like a tiny bird, like a butterfly. She realized with a sense of wonder that it was her baby moving.

Her resolve hardened. No more self-pity. No more waiting on the sidelines for Alexei to figure out how he felt.

Because she was worthy of love, and she was worthy of this man. And she was not about to let him evade her this time.

CHAPTER THIRTEEN

It hadn't been easy to get to Moscow, but Paige had refused to take no for an answer. First, she'd ordered a car to go shopping—without Mariya there, she'd managed to get away without a security detail. Then she'd made the driver take her to the airport where she'd found an English-speaking ticket agent—in truth, they all seemed to speak English—and bought a ticket to Moscow on the earliest flight she could get.

She had a bit of difficulty finding a driver to take her to Voronov Exploration's headquarters, but she finally managed that as well. Now, she sat in the limo speeding into Moscow and wondered if she'd gone too far.

Alexei would be furious. Her heart had been racing since she'd begun the journey, and now her stomach was upset as well. A sharp pang sliced beneath her kidney, nearly doubling her over. She should have eaten something more than a boiled egg and a glass of milk.

When the driver pulled in front of the soaring glass and steel building in the Presnensky district, Paige counted out the rubles from her purse and stepped onto the sidewalk. The noise of the city was somewhat jarring after she'd spent so many quiet weeks in the country. Cars shot by, the older ones belching fumes, and men and women hurried up and down the sidewalks, talking on cell phones, gesturing wildly as they strode along. She remembered that life, though it seemed like a distant memory now. Once, she'd been the one in a suit and tennis shoes, rushing down the sidewalk with a tray of coffee she'd picked up at the nearest Starbucks.

She didn't miss the economic uncertainty of that life, but she did miss Mavis and the other friends she'd made at work. Even Mr. Ramirez, who she'd barely known. He'd been so kind to her when she was new and ill, before she found out she was pregnant. He'd paid her the hours, as he'd said he would, but when she cashed the check, she sent that portion back since she hadn't earned it.

She missed that life in some ways, the one where she mattered to people and where they valued her. She wanted Alexei to value her. But if he did not, if he would not, she was better off in Dallas, sitting in her cubicle and struggling to make ends meet. At least her life would be her own. Though it pained her to think it, she knew she had the strength. She loved Alexei, but if he did not—or would not—love her, then she would insist on making her own choices instead of meekly waiting in St. Petersburg for him to return.

Paige went into the sleek lobby and marched up to the front desk. A woman with a headset looked up, smiled briefly and then continued talking on the phone. When she finally finished, she asked what she could do to help.

"I'm here to see Prince Voronov," Paige said.

Even the woman's frown was friendly. "I am afraid that is not possible, madam. His schedule is booked solid today. If you would care to make an appointment?"

"No, I would not. I am his wife, and I want to see him now, please." She tried so hard to be cool and collected, but her stomach was burning and she realized now how ridiculous it seemed for a woman to march into the lobby and claim to be Alexei's wife. If she truly were his wife, wouldn't she know where to go and how to find him? Wouldn't she at least have his cell phone number?

The woman smiled the bland, noncommittal smile of an efficient receptionist. "Please wait over there," she said, gesturing to a row of low bench seats along one glass wall.

Paige started to argue, but what good would it do? Instead she marched over and sank onto the white leather bench as gracefully as she could manage. She was beginning to wish she'd stayed in St. Petersburg. At least she could lie in bed and wait for this queasiness to go away.

She didn't know how long she waited, but she knew before he arrived that he'd come for her. There was an electric disturbance in the air, the crackle and snap of fury that preceded him like a wave.

And then he was in the lobby, striding toward her, his face dark and hard.

"Are you out of your mind?" he snapped, the words cracking through the air like a whip.

"Maybe I am," she said. She wanted to get up and jab her finger into his chest, to demand to know why he'd left, but she didn't have the energy.

She'd come here to be strong, to demand he not withdraw from the life they'd been building. She'd come here to assert herself and fight for her husband.

But now she was tired and aching and she just wanted to lie down and sleep. Perhaps she'd picked up a summer cold, or eaten something bad.

He reached for her. "Come, I'm sending you to my apartment. When I'm finished here, I'll join you."

"Fine," she said, though she wasn't sure she believed him. He would board a plane to St. Petersburg and leave her here, she was certain. Anything to get away from her.

Even with his hand on her elbow, it was a struggle to stand. It took her a moment to realize that she was wet, that she must have sat in someone's spilled drink. Why hadn't she noticed when she first sat down?

"Alexei," she started to say.

But the color drained from his face until he was as white as the bench seat. "My God, Paige," he croaked.

She followed his gaze downward as warmth spread along her legs. It took her a moment to understand the meaning of the small drops of red on the floor between her feet. When she did, a cracked scream wrenched from her suddenly dry throat.

It was all his fault. He'd been a fool, an ass, an arrogant un-feeling brute. Alexei shoved trembling fingers through his hair. Why had he left her like that? Why hadn't he realized it was the wrong thing to do? Why hadn't he brought her with him? He'd intended to go back tonight, but if he were honest with himself, he knew he'd have found a reason not to.

Why?

Because he was a coward. Because he didn't want to face his feelings and fears. He was very good at running from emotions he didn't want to feel. He'd been doing it for years, subsisting on hate and ambition, and it had finally taken its toll.

Not only on him, but also on Paige and their child.

In that moment when he'd seen the blood on the seat and floor, he'd believed his world had come crashing down around him. He'd thought he was losing her, and he'd offered up everything he had—every ruble, every ounce of success, *everything*—if only God would listen to his plea and spare her life.

Someone had listened, because she was fine. She and the baby both. Relief had made him so weak he couldn't stand when the doctor gave him the news. The bleeding was stabi-lized, and there had been no contractions, which was a good sign. The doctor said she could go home, but she was on strict bed rest for the next month.

A nurse came and told him he could go into Paige's room now. Alexei pushed open the door to find Paige sitting on the bed, dressed in the clothes he'd had sent over for her, her hands clenched in her lap.

His throat closed up. "You look pale, *lyubimaya moya.*"

"I'm sorry, Alexei," she said, her eyes red and swollen from crying. "I put our baby in danger and I can never forgive myself—"

Her voice broke and he went and wrapped his arms around her, tucked her head against his chest. His heart raced as he stroked the glorious, fragrant silk of her hair. "Do not cry, Paige. It's bad for the baby."

She made a strangled sound against him. He felt the reverberations through his body and knew that, once more, he'd said the wrong thing.

"It's bad for you, too," he amended. "Please don't do anything that's bad for you."

She clutched his shirt as she took deep, steadying breaths. "No, of course. You're right. I have to be careful, for both of us."

"For all of us."

They stayed like that for a long time, with him stroking her hair, and her holding tight to him.

"I didn't want you to stay away," she said softly. "That's why I followed you to Moscow. I don't want to do this alone, Alexei. I want what we've had for the past few weeks."

He couldn't speak, could only hold her close and comfort himself with the rhythmic rise and fall of her chest. She was alive, breathing.

She pushed away from him. He let her go, uncertain of what she wanted from him and unwilling to upset her again.

She looked so beautiful sitting there, so pale and fragile, that he wanted to pull her into his arms again and never let go.

"No, that's not true," she said, shaking her head, and his heart dropped. She'd decided that she didn't love him, that she didn't need or want him after all. It was his punishment for what he'd put her through, for his stubbornness and inability to see the truth.

"Tell me what you want and it is yours," he said. Even if she wanted to leave him, he would do his utmost to allow her to go. Whatever it took to make her happy.

Her expression grew suddenly fierce. "I want *more*, Alexei. I want you to feel what I feel. I don't want to live with a man who doesn't love me. I've spent my adult life pleasing others, and I'm ready for someone to please *me*. It's my turn to have it all. And if you can't give that to me, then I want to know it. Because, though I love you, I won't stay in your palace and your bed and hope that one day you'll love me, too."

She was so fierce, his wife. So amazing and fierce and wonderful. And he would do anything to make her happy. *Anything.*

The feeling sweeping through him was so strong that his vision narrowed, as if he would collapse if he didn't give it voice. "I love you," he said. But the words sounded choked, rusted through. "I love you," he said again, stronger this time.

She looked hopeful. And then, just as quickly, hope faded. "You're just saying it because you know I want to hear it."

He couldn't blame her for thinking such a thing. She knew him to be ruthless and determined, willing to use her for information, willing to do whatever it took to win. Why wouldn't he say the words he knew she wanted to hear if it benefited him to do so?

He had to make her believe, had to prove to her how hard this was for him and how utterly certain he was that it was right. Alexei dropped to his knees in front of her. Her eyes widened as he clasped her hands in his. Then he bent until his forehead touched her knees.

"I'm no good at this," he said, his heart feeling like a dead weight in his chest. "I don't know how to tell you that you are the most important thing to me, that I was dead inside until you crashed into my life. I don't know how to say the right words, Paige. *Ti nuzhna mne, ya tebya lyublyu.* That is all I have, all I know."

"What did you say to me?" she asked, her voice soft and thready.

He looked up, his gaze clashing with hers. "I said that I need you, that I love you."

"I want to believe you, but so much has happened, Alexei." Her smoky eyes were sad, haunted.

"For you," he vowed, "I will go to see Chad and Elena."

She withdrew her hand from his grip, smoothed it along his jaw. "Oh, Alexei." Her eyes filled with new tears. It gave him hope like he'd never had before. "I want you to see them because *you* want to, because *you* believe it will enrich your life to do so, but not because it's something you think I expect of you."

He understood what she was saying, and yet he knew that it was right. That he wanted to do this for himself as much as for her and their child.

"I've had time to consider many things these past few hours," he told her. "When I thought I might lose you, I realized how closed off I have become, how alone. I thought you and the baby would be enough for me—and you are—but I also realized that you are right. I have hated the Russells for fifteen years, and I believed they hated me. Perhaps they still do. But I'm tired of hating. I have no more use for it."

He drew in a breath, more certain of this than he'd ever been. "I will see them, Paige, because you have convinced me it is the right thing to do. And I will know, once I've done so, that no matter what happens, I made the effort."

"You really mean it," she said wonderingly.

"*Da*, I do."

"But why do you love me *now*," she said, as if she still couldn't fathom that he could truly be in love with her. "If you are simply trying to keep me happy until the baby comes, I'd rather you didn't. I don't want to be lied to."

Alexei got to his feet. This part was easy, comparatively speaking. "I understand why you are skeptical," he said. He spread a hand along her jaw, cupped her lovely face as he skimmed his thumb over her cheek, her soft brow. "But, Paige, I have been drawn to you from the first moment I met you. You are unlike anyone I've ever known. You are so fierce and strong, yet you don't seem to always know it. You are uncertain of yourself sometimes, uncertain of your beauty and appeal, and you have the kindest heart of anyone I know. You cry over art, you laugh like an angel, and you'd fight to the death to protect those you love."

The tears were flowing down her cheeks now, and he wiped them away with his thumbs. "Shh, please don't cry, Paige. It breaks my heart when you cry."

"I can't help it," she said, shaking her head.

"I love you, Paige, and it terrifies me to say this. Because everyone I've ever loved has left me, and I've had to carry on without them, missing them, knowing I failed to do all I could for them. I don't wish to fail you, Paige, or to live without you. I need you too much."

She wrapped her arms around him and hugged him tight. "I love you, Alexei. So much. And I don't believe we need to be scared of love. We have to take what it gives us and be happy. If we do that, we can't fail. Just as you didn't fail Katerina. She knew you loved her, and though I know you wish she had lived, it's not your fault she didn't. It really, truly isn't. I want you to believe that."

He smiled at her, his heart opening so wide it hurt. The love was overwhelming once he let it in, and the fear faded by degrees until all it could do was sit in a corner and look out at the unfolding scene. Fear would always be there, he knew, but it wasn't the biggest thing in the room anymore.

"I will try to believe it, *lyubimaya moya*. For you."

"No," she said fiercely. "For you."

"Yes," he said. "For me." Because she was right. Because she knew him so well, and loved him so much, and because he wasn't afraid to face his fear any longer.

Dallas in winter was far more pleasant than St. Petersburg. The temperatures were mild compared to the subzero temperatures of Russia. And yet Paige missed Russia, too. She missed the huge, elegant Voronov Palace and she missed the winter *troika* rides. But they would return in the early spring, when snow was still on the ground and the weather was not so severe.

"The baby is asleep," Emma announced as she returned from the room where she'd taken little Katerina for a nap.

"She's a good baby," Paige said. "She hardly fusses at all."

Emma sat down on the couch beside her. "She is so perfect, Paige. You are very lucky."

Paige smiled. She *was* lucky. Lucky to have her wonderful baby and lucky to have a husband she adored. A husband who bought her a house in Dallas and moved them there for the winter because he knew she was homesick.

The house he'd bought for them wasn't as vast as Paige had feared it might be, because she'd begged him to find something approximating normal. And he had. They'd found a gorgeous classical architecture house in the historic district that she absolutely loved. The trees would be huge and shady in summer and the front porch ran the full length of the home. There was plenty of room for furniture and sitting out in the evenings when the weather warmed a little bit more.

She'd had to explain the Southern tradition of sitting out on the front porch and greeting neighbors to Alexei. He hadn't exactly understood the necessity, but he'd kissed her and told her that whatever she wanted, he would get for her.

Emma glanced toward the patio. "Are they still out there?"

Paige laughed. "Yes. I believe Chad is explaining how to smoke a whole hog in a pit." She'd heard them talking when she'd gone into the kitchen to refresh her drink.

Emma rolled her eyes. "They're supposed to be grilling steaks. How did that happen?"

"I'm not sure, but Chad seems determined to teach Alexei what it means to be a true Texan. Barbecue is high on the list, it would seem."

In the last eight months, Alexei had made good on his promise to contact Chad and Elena. He and Chad were slowly building a relationship, though it couldn't be called easy or smooth by any means. Unfortunately Elena was a bitter woman who would probably carry her disapproval of Alexei and his mother to her grave. Alexei did not seem to care, which was a relief to Paige even if it hurt her that the woman couldn't acknowledge her nephew.

Chad, however, seemed eager to get to know his cousin once he'd gotten over the shock of Alexei actually offering an olive branch. Alexei hadn't told Chad what his father had done, nor would he. Paige understood, and though she already loved Alexei to distraction, that single act of nobility and selflessness made her so proud to be his wife.

He was a good, good man.

"Chad told me that Alexei offered him a position overseeing

the American branch of his operations," Emma said, twisting a lock of her long hair as she did so.

"I believe the man who'd been in the position retired recently," Paige replied. "And Chad has the experience."

"Thank you for talking him into it," Emma said. "It means a lot to us both."

"I didn't talk him into anything, Emma. And Alexei would do nothing to harm his business. If he offered the job to Chad, then he believes Chad is right for the position."

Emma stretched, grinning. "Whatever. I don't care so long as it means we can finally be married."

Just then, the men came back into the house, speaking rapidly in a combination of Russian and English. Chad carried a platter of steaks in one hand and a beer in the other. Alexei was loaded down with grilling implements that he dumped into the sink.

They spent the evening eating, talking and laughing together like a group of old friends. Paige glanced over at Alexei, loving the way he was so animated and open, the way he seemed to truly take pleasure in Chad's company. It was a far cry from the way the two men had once looked at each other across a table.

Later, while Chad and Emma carried the dishes into the kitchen, Alexei turned to her. His expression changed, became possessive and sensual as his hungry gaze slipped over her. Her insides liquefied, softened. She wanted him as much, if not more, than she ever had. When he looked at her like that, like she was everything in the world to him, she melted.

He leaned toward her, kissed her softly—much more softly than she would have liked when she was absolutely on fire for him.

"Thank you," he said.

She wrapped her arms around his neck, unwilling to let him go just yet. "For what?"

"For making my life so much more than I ever thought possible."

Her heart swelled with love and longing. "I'm not done yet," she murmured. "I have a lot more to show you. Starting as soon as our guests have left."

His grin was feral, hot and sexy. "I look forward to it," he growled. "Because I have a few things to show you as well."

Paige laughed. "Bring it on, big boy."

Hours later, when Paige lay in bed exhausted and happy, she knew she would never, ever tire of life with this man.

"I love you," she whispered against his hot, damp skin.

He kissed her shoulder, her throat, her lips. *"Ya tebya lyublyu,"* he replied. "More than you will ever know."

And then he showed her again, without words, how much he loved her.

THE AMALFI BRIDE

ANN MAJOR

Ann Major lives in Texas with her husband of many years and is the mother of three grown children. She has a master's degree from Texas A&M at Kingsville, and is a former English teacher. She is a founding board member of the Romance Writers of America and a frequent speaker at writers' groups.

Ann loves to write—she considers her ability to do so a gift. Her hobbies include hiking in the mountains, sailing, ocean kayaking, traveling and playing the piano. But most of all, she enjoys her family. Visit her website at www.annmajor.com.

One

Amalfi, Italy

Her last few days in paradise…so many sights, so little time left to see them. So, what was she doing here…in a bar…wasting her valuable time…lacking the will to hike or to tour one more cathedral or villa? Flirting with a dangerous stranger?

Oh, my God! I'm not flirting with him.

It was late July and warm in the open-air bar, although not nearly as warm as it would be back in Texas. Regina Tomei grabbed her glass of chardonnay and sipped too much, too hastily, spilling a few drops on her chin and neck. Quickly she dabbed at the dribbles with her napkin.

Her lengthy list of cathedrals and the notes she'd written about the Greek ruins fell to the floor. She didn't bother to pick them up. Instead, she stole another quick glance at the tall, dark stranger leaning against the bar across the room.

Who had said, "I can resist anything but temptation?"

The man instantly stopped talking to his short, plump friend and lifted his bottle of beer in a mock salute to her.

Oh, my God! Not again!

He took a slow, long pull from the bottle. Then his gaze touched her throat and lips. She gasped. Involuntarily, her hand with the napkin went to her mouth and then to the hollow of her throat, where her pulse was racing.

The heat of her own fingertips made her imagine his big hands and his lips upon her flesh. She began to perspire, so she fanned herself with the damp napkin.

Then, realizing what she was doing, Regina seized the ornate golden cross around her neck and held on for dear life. She'd bought the necklace from Illusions, an opulent shop she'd discovered tucked away in an alley of charming Ravello near her hotel.

Sightseeing and shopping were her hobbies; not barhopping, not flirting with strange men in foreign lands.

Run!

The man took another pull on his bottle and then stared at the gardenia in her hair. Before she could stop herself, she grazed the velvet petals with a stray fingertip.

Do not touch, signorina, *or the petals will turn brown.*

Regina picked up her camera and set it on her little table. Agitated, her hands flew to her lap, where she clasped them and her napkin, but not for long.

She looked up again, straight at her Adonis. Was it only her imagination, or did his blue eyes blaze with the same intensity as the sapphire Gulf of Salerno behind him? Was she the cause of all that fire?

Heat washed over her and, at her blush, he smiled.

Mortified and yet thrilled, too, she picked up her camera and pretended she found her light meter fascinating.

His friend observed all with a raffish grin and then, as if bored, hugged Adonis goodbye.

Oh, my God! The short guy was leaving! He would have to pass by her table!

She buried her face in her hands to avoid conversation, and he chuckled as he passed.

Somehow, the friend's departure seemed significant.

Not wanting to think about that, she concentrated on the glittering rings of condensation on the ceramic table from her wineglass.

Rule number one: smart women traveling alone in foreign countries do not pick up strange men, no matter how handsome or friendly or desirable they seem. In particular, women don't pick them up in a bar, even one with whitewashed walls, cascading bougainvillea and lots of sunshine and tourists.

She told herself to grab her camera, get up and walk away! No! Run! She should run like she had last night. She had no idea what sort of person he was.

What if he was a gigolo or, worse, a serial killer?

Her mind returned to the G-word.

A gigolo? Was the blond fellow a pimp? Did gigolos even have pimps? She could write a brief on what she didn't know about gigolos and their business plans.

Regina frowned as she remembered the older woman with the platinum hair, loud makeup and trailing orange veils with whom she'd seen him yesterday in the red Maserati convertible. The woman had caught Regina's attention because she'd spotted the car in front of Illusions earlier.

The driver had been the same elderly shopkeeper who'd sold her the cross, the sentimental little painting of the black-haired boy playing in the sand, the scandalous pink-and-black lace underwear she was wearing now, her skimpy new dress and, of course, the darling white sandals to match.

Yesterday afternoon, when the older lady had dropped him off at the beach near the mooring of the immense white yacht called *Simonetta,* Regina hadn't thought much about her kissing his dark cheeks so many times. Nor had she wondered why the older lady had been so reluctant to let him go. When the woman had spotted Regina watching them, she'd recognized her and had waved, beaming. When he'd looked at Regina, he'd acted startled and had broken off the embrace.

Suddenly, the little scene took on a darker, more lurid meaning. A gigolo?

And what about that diamond the size of an ice cube on the finger of the regal, middle-aged woman in the black Ferrari with him today? She, too, had driven him to the same beach and had kissed his cheeks almost as ardently as the other, older woman. Only the second woman had had a more commanding air, summoning him back to the Ferrari twice.

Now, the stranger's eyes on Regina's bare skin felt like fire. She wished she'd put on something that was more *her*.

Regina's usual attire back in Austin, Texas, tended to be dull, predictable suits that covered her up, which were appropriate when a young woman was an attorney and made her living in courtrooms.

How ironic that his elderly mistress or client, or whoever the woman was, had sold Regina her revealing white sundress. The same woman had talked her into taking the clips out of her hair, too.

"You very lovely, *signorina*. With wavy hair down. You need flower in your hair. Special flower from magic bush. Then you get boyfriend for sure. Come. I show you."

Was it so obvious Regina had no lover? No boyfriend?

With orange veils trailing behind a body that was still voluptuous and hidden bells jingling, the woman had led Regina out of the shop down a cobblestone path to a courtyard with a marble statue of Cupid and a thick bush ablaze with gardenias.

"This bush blooms all year. Pick one every day you are here, if you like. And I promise, a miracle will happen. *Prometto*." Her dark blue eyes had twinkled like a fairy godmother's.

Delighted, Regina had picked one yesterday. Then, this morning, she had gone back for another.

The gulf had a mirror finish; the sinking sun was turning to apricot the villas and hotels that perched precariously on the cliffs. Soon the coast would be magically suffused by the soft, slow twilight she'd come to love.

For as long as she could remember, Regina had wanted to visit the Amalfi Coast. Leaning down, she picked up her list of sights and notes. She should be admiring the mountains trembling steeply above the sea instead of devouring a man who could be a sexual professional.

You probably couldn't even afford him.

Oh, my God!

If he *was* a gigolo, *he* obviously thought she could afford him. Why else was he eating her up with his dark blue eyes?

Her throat went so dry that she gulped more chardonnay.

Gigolos were losers who preyed on older, lonely women; definitely not part of her life plan. She should be shocked to the core by her train of thought.

Afford him? She should indict him!

In Austin, she had a reputation for being prim and proper and…and well, bossy. Not that she was. Nobody, not even her family, understood how strongly she had to focus to accomplish her goals.

"You're a control freak and frigid!" Bobby had accused after she'd stunned them both, herself and him, by rejecting his marriage proposal.

"Please, let's don't get ugly," she'd said.

"Give me my ring!" He'd bruised her finger when he'd tried to pull it off. "Even though you chased me for a whole damn year, you probably did me a helluva favor."

"I chased you? I gave you my card at a party because I wanted to work for your father's firm."

"Just my luck! He hired you! You may be a good lawyer, but you're one lousy lay." He shoved his chair back and slammed out of the door of their favorite sushi restaurant, leaving her alone with a huge wooden serving dish filled with eels and shrimp and caviar, zero appetite, and the bill.

A lousy lay? Okay, so, yes, she had faked an orgasm or two. But only to make him happy.

What if a talented gigolo was able to teach a motivated student a few naughty tricks and make her sexier in bed?

Susana, her flaky, younger sister had tried to console her. "You're going after the wrong type. I never liked Bobby anyway.

Who wouldn't have to fake orgasms with a man who never thought about anything but billable hours? Just a word though, maybe you should try being more intuitive. And maybe you shouldn't boss guys around so much."

Susana, a housewife, who'd stolen Joe, the one man Regina had loved, had had the gall to give *her* advice. How had Susana, a college dropout, become the successful sister?

Hello! Susana had given their folks three darling grandchildren.

"I'm not *that* bossy."

"Well, don't let your boyfriends see all those lists you make."

"I just like to get things done," Regina grumbled aloud to the voices in her head as she crumpled another napkin and wiped the condensation rings on her table.

Intuitive?

She was sitting as far as she possibly could from the sexual professional, if that was indeed what he was. Too aware of his satiny black hair and flirty eyes, she tidied up her table, slipping a fresh napkin under her wineglass. Still, just knowing he was over there, alone now, had her pulse beating like a war drum.

Most of her girlfriends had shocked her by sleeping with strangers at least once, and then describing their sexual misadventures in vivid detail over long lunches. But that lifestyle hadn't been for Regina. She'd always known she'd wanted to love and marry a respectable professional man, and she'd accepted dates only from men who met her criteria. She had a long list of criteria.

But the instant she'd seen this stranger, who should be unappealing to her, her world had shifted. It was as if the real Regina had gone into hibernation, as if Austin were a remote planet on the other side of a galaxy far, far away.

Intuitive. Dangerous word.

If ever a man was the antithesis of the ambitious, Type-A individuals the real Regina always chased, this G-word guy was it.

Obviously, Adonis was all looks and no substance. Still, his broad-shouldered body seemed made of sculpted teak, with muscles that rivaled Michelangelo's *David.* What well-educated girl didn't appreciate a masterpiece? But could he read without moving his beautiful, carved lips?

Like all Italians, he wore clothes that fit perfectly. Hello! Why didn't she care whether or not he had a brain? A soul?

She was too entranced by the shallow stuff to dwell on deeper matters. His white shirt was open to his waist, revealing a lean, washboard abdomen. Some fierce mating instinct made her want to tear off his shirt and his ripped, faded jeans, to lick his warm, sun-caressed skin and have him do the same to her. *Yes!*

Despite the balmy July sea air, she thought of him naked. The idea of tasting him had her so hot she lifted her icy glass of chardonnay to her lips. Rethinking the more-alcohol move, she brought the cool glass to her warm cheek and then placed it against her forehead.

Would his babies be as gorgeous as he was?

Babies? The thought broadsided her. For a long moment she stared into her wineglass. Suddenly, dazzling golden images of a beautiful little boy and a darling little girl materialized, both with thick heads of shiny, black-satin hair, splashing in a backyard pool.

She swirled the wine in her glass so violently a few drops splashed her wrist. When he smiled, she blushed again.

A baby. His baby? No way!

What about E-321, which she'd learned about thanks to her friend Lucy? The sperm from a donor whose profile was so perfect Regina had bought the last eight vials of it from the sperm bank?

Hello, is the real Regina alive and well? The Regina who knows one doesn't buy sperm and then sleep around?

Okay, so she hadn't shown up on the day of her appointment for insemination.

But after Bobby, she had had a life-changing epiphany.

Baby first. Finding Mr. Right, second.

Time was running out for her to meet Mr. Right, date him, plan a wedding and get pregnant—in the proper order.

So, why not reverse the order of things?

Why not become a single mother of choice first and find her soul mate later?

So, how did one find the perfect father? Her best friend Lucy, who was now pregnant by sperm donor E-321, had been full of advice. After lots of research, Regina had decided E-321 was the right donor for her, too. Lucy and Regina's children would be half-siblings. Regina had told her family that she and Lucy and their babies would almost be a real family.

"You've got a real family!" her father had thundered. "This is your fault, Sabrina!" It was his habit to blame everything, good and bad, on Regina's mother. "You shouldn't have let her read all the time! Or run around with liberals like Lucy. I don't want to even think about those college loans I'm still paying off."

Although his temper hadn't won the day, he'd slumped into a scowling sulk and had remained glued to the television set whenever he was home over the next few days, refusing to speak to anybody, even his adored Sabrina.

Desperate, her mother had called an hour before Regina's insemination appointment.

"You're making Constantin unhappy. He's never gone quiet on me like this. Not in thirty years. It's summer. Take a vacation. When was the last time you took a vacation? Go to Italy. See your Nana before you do this crazy thing, eh, Cara."

Her mama always called her Cara, which was short for Carina, Regina's middle name.

"You can't control everything, Cara. In Italy, people let life happen. Susana fell in love. You will, too."

Yes, with Joe. I was in love with him! Susana stole him right out from under me. Why doesn't anybody, especially you, Mama, ever remember that Joe was mine first?

Regina covered her eyes for a long moment. Then she opened them to a line of ceramic pots overflowing and ablaze with geraniums, to terraces and umbrellas drenched in coppery light, and to him.

Two girls beside him were batting their lashes at him and looking winsome, but he had eyes only for Regina.

He looked at her with such longing, Regina felt a physical ache to simply get up and go to him, to press herself against him, to run her fingers through his hair, to touch him everywhere. To get to it. To do it somewhere nearby, any private place.

She wanted to lie under his lean, hard body on a soft mattress with sea breezes whispering over their glued-together, sweaty bodies. She wanted everything, all things, unnamable things, unimagined things from him.

I don't know his name. He hasn't even spoken to me and I want to make love to him like an animal.

Still, she knew his voice was low and deep and thick with amusement, because she'd heard him talking to the girls at the table next to his earlier.

In her real life across the Atlantic Ocean, she would have wanted to know where Adonis had gone to school, what were his life plans, who was his family. But this half-naked girl with the gardenia in her hair felt more than thought.

She was beginning to become a little scared. It was as if vital pieces of her being were rushing toward him and he was claiming all as his due. The hunger to be in his arms, to kiss him, to taste him, to know passion, real passion, maybe for the first time in her life, kept intensifying.

So, if he were a G-word guy, did that mean he could be hers…for a night? If she was willing to meet his price? Or did he just service a privileged few?

Blood rushed from her head.

But what about those eight precious vials of E-321's you-know-what stored at the sperm bank? What about E-321's picture and profile taped to her fridge? What about Lucy—brilliant, well-meaning Lucy—and their plan to raise their children together as siblings?

A sexy stranger was not for a health nut and control freak like Regina, either! She might catch something.

No. Something told her she wouldn't.

Maybe she'd gone without sex for too long. Maybe it was the voluptuous, naked statues dotting the landscape and decorating the palazzos all over Italy that had her hormones hot to conceive the old-fashioned way.

Regina believed sex was for committed relationships and marriage. Period.

What about for procreation? whispered the hormones. *You're thirty-three and single and nearly too old.*

You should be married, whispered another voice. All her life, Regina had been known for her brains, her old-fashioned morals, her perfectionism, her goal-setting abilities, and her quick decisions. What if she let herself go just this once?

Her lips parted. She nudged her skirt above her knee and waited for life to happen. How exactly did one go about hiring a gigolo anyway—*if he was a gigolo?*

Was there some secret signal? Should she lift her skirt even higher? Or maybe lower her lashes and wink seductively? Or should she walk over to the bar, open her purse and show him the money? Or should she just sit here and wait for him to make *the move,* whatever that was?

Last night he'd followed her into this same bar. Only, when he'd started to flirt, she'd run out and hidden behind some chestnut trees. He'd rushed outside and looked for her while she'd held her breath, frantic he'd find her. Finally, he'd given up and kayaked out to *Simonetta,* the mega yacht moored some distance from shore, where he must have spent the night.

With a woman? A client? The older lady in veils? Her thoughts made Regina feel slightly nauseated.

One moment, the object of her affections was leaning back against the bar, sipping his beer while studying the magnificent white yacht with a rather keen interest. The next, his gaze swept the room and fastened on her again.

She met his eyes. With a fingertip, she teased her skirt higher. Her lips parted. Spellbound, dry-throated, she did not look away.

His gold necklace flashed with the last of the sun's rays. A gift from a client? From the woman in the Ferrari? Or the one on the yacht? How many women were there? She had a prejudice against guys who wore gold necklaces.

Did one tip a gigolo? Would he tell her the rules? As an attorney, she had a natural interest in all contracts.

When he kept staring at her, the two girls giggled at the little table near his and then glanced at her, too knowingly. Doubtless, they were locals and knew his profession and read her intentions.

Was she that obvious?

When the girls frowned, Regina felt her cheeks heat and her pulse race.

Maybe she should rethink this. When she tried to stand up to leave, her legs felt too weak to hold her. She sagged against her table. Then her waiter scurried over with an icy flute of sparkling champagne. He said something in rapid, nasal Italian, which was beyond her minimal knowledge of the language and pointed to her admirer at the bar. When she looked over, Adonis shifted his weight onto his right leg and beamed.

Her heart sped up even faster, and her lacy pink panties trimmed in black lace began to feel damp. She should run out to the taxi stand and hire somebody to take her up to the palazzo where she was staying. She would take a cold shower or a long swim in the pool and then a sleeping pill. She needed to think this through, form a plan.

Instead, she touched the stem of the flute he'd sent over with a manicured fingertip. When she threw back her head, her long brown hair flowing down her back, and began to sip, his mouth curved again. She smiled back just as boldly.

Instantly, he uncoiled his long body and strode across the bar, causing a ripple of conversation, as well as bursts of giggles from the girls near the bar. When he pulled out a plastic chair at Regina's table, Regina gulped the last of her champagne.

"Do you mind if I sit down?" His voice was deep and dark, faintly accented, surprisingly cultured. It was as perfect as the rest of him.

A well-educated gigolo?

"I—I should say yes. I should go…really…."

"Probably you are right." He smiled. "But you're following a dangerous impulse." He paused. "Just as I am."

Her heart thundered.

Up close, his dense lashes seemed even longer and darker.

Why did God give guys eyelashes like those? It wasn't fair. But then, life wasn't fair, was it? Or she would be married and have children, and her father would still love her best.

Adonis's gorgeous, broad-shouldered body towered over Regina, making her feel even more vulnerable.

If you were to have a daughter by him, the lucky child would surely be movie-star beautiful, whispered her sex-starved hormones.

"I will go, if you want me to," he said.

When he turned, a savage pain tore her heart. "No."

Her throat went even drier. Her acute need threw her off balance. She licked her lips but could say no more.

He sank down beside her and signaled the waiter. Without asking, he ordered more champagne.

Did he expect her to pay? Was that part of the contract?

When the champagne came, she gulped it again, which seemed to amuse him. "Do I scare you?"

"I scare me. I've never done anything like this before."

"Good. That's reassuring." He laughed. "You're perfectly safe," he said. "I promise, we won't do anything you don't want to do."

Far too many needs and emotions were on fire inside her for such a comment to reassure her.

He held up his hand to order another drink, but she put her fingers over his. And instantly, at that light touch of fingertip to fingertip, a surge of syrupy heat flooded her. When the waiter looked over, she shook her head wildly.

Her admirer turned her fingers over and brushed the back of her hand with a callused fingertip. His touch was gentle; lighting hot sparks along every nerve in her body.

She felt weak, sexual, sizzling. All he'd done was caress her hand. When he fingered the cross at her throat, she pulled back, afraid he'd sense the rapid pulse that pounded beneath it.

She'd never experimented with drugs, because addiction hadn't been part of her plan for success. But now she suddenly understood the concept of mindless addiction at a profound level.

He was lethal.

No. He was just a professional. He knew what he was doing.

That was all. He was good at his job. This was what he got paid for. Everything was under control. He wouldn't do anything unless she decided to hire him. He was after money. Billable hours. Like Bobby. That she understood. *Too well.*

It wasn't as if he felt what she felt. She was in no danger. She was in control.

She felt hot, and the cool breezes gusting up from the sparkling gulf did little to cool her.

"I'm Nico. Nico Romano," he whispered against her ear, stroking her hand with that seductive fingertip.

The way he said his name warmed her blood almost as much as his touch.

But was it his real name? Did gigolos have stage names as actors did or pseudonyms as writers did?

"But then you probably know who I am…or at least *what* I am," he said, his expression almost apologetic.

So she was right—he *was* a gigolo.

She blushed, liking his discretion about avoiding the G-word.

"Yes." She glanced away.

"There's no reason to let it bother you. I'm a man, just an ordinary man."

"If you say so." She felt shy, unsure, out of her depth.

"And you are?" he continued.

"Carina," she said in a rush, choosing her middle name for protection, to put distance between them. "My mother calls me Cara. Everybody else calls me—" She stopped, realizing she was about to start babbling, something she did when she was nervous.

"Cara," he breathed. "In our country your name means *beloved.* It suits you."

The air between them seemed to grow even hotter, if that were possible. Or maybe it was only she who was ablaze.

He was good. But how much did someone of his caliber cost? Not in the mood to ask and discover his price excessive, she put the all-important question off.

"Are you hungry?" he murmured. "Or would you prefer to go straight to your hotel?"

Did having dinner with him cost more? And what would the staff of her palazzo think when they saw her with him in the restaurant? Did he go there often?

"I ate a late lunch," she said.

"So did I," he murmured.

He leaned closer. He slid one hand around her waist. His other hand lifted her fingertips to his sensually curved mouth, and he kissed each long nail and fingertip, lingering a little on the tips of her nails. Then he stared into her eyes. Everything he did was infinitely gentle. Somehow, nothing he did seemed faked or practiced, and long after he'd let her fingers go, the pit of her stomach felt hollow.

When she lowered her hand to the ceramic table again, she sighed. Good. She wasn't ready for the serious kissing to start. Not in public, anyway.

He leaned closer and traced her mouth with his fingertip, flooding her with more erotic heat. His eyes followed the path of his finger. He swallowed hard. So did she. The girls, who were watching, giggled again.

"Che bella," he whispered, scooting his chair back a little.

He wasn't subtle. But what had she expected? He was a gigolo. Not to mention Italian. This was a business relationship. She should applaud his talent and his professionalism. Instead, she was so caught up in what he was doing it was hard to remember this wasn't real.

He held up his hand for the check. Before she could rummage in her purse, he threw a wad of euros on the table, cupped her elbow and escorted her out of the bar. She was acutely aware that, when he'd stood up, everybody stopped talking. Even the music stopped. When he turned at the door to wave to the bartender, a final burst of girlish giggles saluted them.

He'd paid, no doubt, for appearances' sake.

He was one classy gigolo.

Remembering the Maserati, and the Ferrari and the yacht, *Simonetta,* where he'd spent the night, she began to wonder if she had enough cash in her purse.

If she didn't, would he take a credit card or at least escort her to the nearest ATM if they finished at a late hour?

Then she remembered he was one classy gigolo.

Of course, he would!

Two

Regina stepped out of the shower, dried herself with a warm
towel and put on the hotel's thick, white fluffy robe as Nico had
suggested. Her damp hair felt heavy and soft about her shoulders as she left the bathroom. Picking up her cell phone, she
padded through the bedroom and then out onto her private belvedere to wait for Nico, who had left her suite to take a phone call.

Nico. She gulped in a breath of warm humid air. Trying not
to think about him and what they were about to do, she looked
down at the quaint town and its lush gardens. Nevertheless, her
hands were shaking as she punched in her friend Lucy's number
back in Austin.

Surely, heaven couldn't best Ravello. The jewel-like, medieval
village seemed to hang suspended from its mountainside over
the Amalfi Coast. The views from Regina's hotel, formerly a
fourteenth-century palazzo with crumbling, vine-covered walls
and Moorish arches, were breathtaking even now when the
shadows were lengthening.

Flowers perfumed the balmy sea breezes. The bees were gone,

and the church bells were ringing. Cliffs and villas alike seemed to tumble to a dark, turquoise sea.

Not that she was all that interested in the white yachts or *Simonetta* or the sparkling water or even the palazzos. She was too consumed with excitement and fear.

"Pick up, Lucy," she whispered, tapping a bare foot with impatience on the sun-warmed stones. She could hardly stand feeling so alone and uncertain.

"Pick up!"

Pacing while she waited, she spotted Nico four floors beneath her. He was also striding back and forth on a terrace near the aqua pool, looking just as impatient and upset as she felt.

Did he want to be with her, or did he hate his work and dread the time he'd be spending with her? Or was it his conversation that had him on edge?

She wished his phone hadn't rung. She wished he'd look up and wave reassuringly, but his dark head was bent over the phone, and he seemed so absorbed she wondered if he'd forgotten her existence.

His cell phone had buzzed just after he'd ordered champagne, strawberries and an assortment of cheeses, and had suggested they get into the hotel's white, fluffy bathrobes and enjoy a drink on her balcony. When he'd recognized the caller's name in the little blue window on his phone, he'd frowned. Then he'd cupped Regina's chin, kissed her on the forehead, and apologized because the call was too important to ignore. He'd answered the phone with a smile and endearments in Italian and had excused himself, which had made Regina curious about the caller's identity, and a little jealous.

Was it a woman? A client? Whoever it was, the call was very important to him.

Just as Regina was worrying that her attraction to Nico might be heading toward an obsession—something she'd never experienced before in her orderly, controlled life—Lucy finally answered, her voice breathless.

"Hi!"

Lucy was pregnant by the sperm donor who she and her partner Beth had agreed was a perfect fit for them. They had pictures of him and his *children,* future half siblings to their own much-wanted child, posted all over their apartment.

"You'll never believe where I am," Regina began.

She went to the closet, pulled out the painting of the little boy playing in the sand, then returned with it to her balcony.

"Italy!" Lucy answered.

"I mean—" Regina stared down at Nico again "—where in Italy? And you'll never guess what I'm doing...."

The little boy's painted hair shone like black satin, exactly as Nico's did.

"You probably just got through jogging and are about to treat yourself to some tomatoes and fat-free mozzarella while you make long lists of must-see tourist attractions for tomorrow."

"Ravello! Which is *the* best place ever. I don't think anybody has ever heard of fat-free cheese over here, either. Are you familiar with Maxfield Parrish's paintings?"

"I'm not sure."

"Ravello is like those paintings." Regina lowered her voice. "I've met a man."

"Those are the four most dangerous words any other woman could say...especially if he's an Italian. But then you're you, so he's probably smart, ambitious..."

"He's not! But don't worry, this isn't serious. He's absolutely gorgeous, the most gorgeous man I've ever seen. *But...*"

"But what? With you, when it comes to your men, there always has to be a *but.*"

For a long moment, Regina hesitated. She almost regretted calling Lucy.

"But? I'm waiting!"

"I—I think he might be a gigolo."

"You've got to be kidding."

Regina remained silent.

"That is such a cliché. And not a good one. Not for you! You've got to come home now! You've definitely been over there too long. You were supposed to relax, enjoy good food, art, pretty scenery, visit your grandmother in Tuscany…."

"I think the art may be part of the problem. The sculptures here are so erotic."

"Pay him and then drive straight to the airport," Lucy ordered.

"But he's so hot. I feel like I'm burning up."

"Did he slip something in your drink?"

"No!"

"Don't do it! This is all because Bobby said you were uptight and frigid and because you were pushing yourself at work way too hard. You don't have to prove you're a hottie in disguise. You don't! Now you know you called me because you wanted to hear the voice of reason."

No, Regina had called Lucy because she'd wanted to share something that felt important.

"I think I've been having doubts about E-321. I think Italy has made insemination just seem way too impersonal. I'm not *you*, you know. I can…be with a man."

"We talked about this, girlfriend. E-321 has gone through numerous screenings…. Use a condom with this Italian fellow if you don't come to your senses! What do you know about him except he's hot and that he charges gullible women like you a bundle for the pleasure of his body? I would think there would be plenty of free, horny Italians over there."

"Not like him."

Even three stories below her, Nico's tall, dark figure in jeans and a white shirt radiated power, assurance and masculinity. And something more.

When he looked up and smiled warmly, her breath caught in her throat.

She waved, as thrilled as a high-school girl with her first crush.

"I—I feel this weird, totally powerful connection to him."

"And you haven't even had your first orgasm! Not good. Run for your life! This is not a good thing."

"But it feels like a good thing."

"This is very, very bad."

Regina's cell phone began to beep. She saw Susana's name. Her flaky baby sister, who didn't have a digital gene in her body, never called her.

The name *Susana* flashed in bold blue.

"Oh, my God! Today's the day the twins are being christened. Susana's calling me! She's actually calling me—in Italy! I've gotta go! I totally forgot to call Susana!"

"One word! Airplane!"

"I'll call you right back."

"That sounds like a plan!"

Regina punched a button and took Susana's call. There was a loud wail on Susana's end, which meant either Regina's niece, Gina, who'd been named after her, or one of her twin nephews was unhappy.

"Hi, there," Regina said, feeling guilty. "How was the christening?"

"It's you! It's really you! Gina, she answered! I can't believe I really got you…on my fourth try even! All the way to Italy. Not that you know where that is, Gina, sweetie!"

"How's the christening going?"

"Everybody's here…except you."

Regina's guilt deepened.

"We're all out in the backyard. It's so hot. But you know Daddy. He had to grill. Mama's hovering to make sure he doesn't burn the steaks like he did last time. She keeps saying maybe you'll meet a man in Italy. She's still upset that you dumped Bobby. She hasn't given up on you meeting an Italian even though we all know that's not why you went. Don't tell her I told you, but she made me call you. She even dialed. She wants to know if the love bug has bitten."

Regina stared down at the extraordinarily good-looking man on the terrace and then swallowed. "Right."

"It has?"

"No!"

"She'll be so disappointed. She was sure Italy would do the trick."

Regina swallowed, her throat feeling extremely dry all of a sudden.

"Gosh, I miss you," Susana said. "Gina asks about you every single day. When are you coming home?"

"Three days."

"Gina's crying her head off. She wants you here. We all do. Especially since Daddy just said *the* most awful thing to her."

"What did he say?"

"I don't know what gets into him. I quote, 'Now that we've got two new cute baby boys, we don't need you anymore.'"

Oh! "He didn't! *Not again!*"

"Again?"

"Nothing."

Nothing…only…

Time whirled backward. Instantly, Regina was transported to the day when a darling, bald Susana had been brought home from the hospital in a flurry of parental excitement. Flushed with pride at being a big sister at last, three-year-old Regina had run to the baby carrier.

Her father had knelt, and she'd climbed into his lap and had thrown her arms around him.

They say you don't remember things when you're three, but they're wrong. His words had been like poisoned darts wounding her soul.

Now that I've got a new, cute daughter, I don't need you anymore.

Regina had backed away from him, and he'd picked up Susana. "Why don't we sing 'Rock-a-bye Baby'?"

Regina had raced to her own room and had hidden in her closet. Ever since, she'd been jealous of her sister and had doubted her father's love. Instead of abating with maturity, her dark feelings had grown more intense since Susana had married Joe and had given birth to her precious trio.

Her father didn't care about any of Regina's accomplishments. All he could talk about was Susana and the grandchildren. Not that Regina wasn't smitten by the children herself. Not that she didn't hate herself sometimes for feeling the way she did.

The green monster, especially when it involved a sister, had to be one of the most hatefully twisted feelings ever.

"Put Gina on," Regina whispered, biting her lips.

Gina's racking sobs got so loud Regina had to hold the phone away from her ear.

The poor, poor darling.

"Gina. It's Aunt Reggie. Listen to me, sweetheart. Papaw loves you. He was just teasing."

"I hate the baby brothers!"

Regina remembered all the times she'd felt as though she'd hated Susana just for being cute and petite and blond and adored, when Regina had been beanpole skinny in middle school. Not to mention flat-chested and too tall for all the boys.

"No, you're a good big sister. You love your little brothers. Dino and David need a good big sister. Papaw is being a bad Papaw! He does that sometimes. Everybody has a weak moment once in a while."

"Bad Papaw!"

"You're beautiful and adorable! Everybody loves you, darling. Especially me."

"And Pawpa?"

"And Pawpa," Regina said, even though she'd always secretly believed that once Susana had been born, he hadn't really needed his oldest daughter anymore.

"I love you, Aunt Reggie! Chocolate cake! Bye!"

"They're about to cut the cake," Susana said. "She's just like you when it comes to chocolate. Just like you in so many ways."

"You know I'm her biggest fan."

"I'm just glad I caught you."

"Me, too. Kiss all your darling children for me. I've missed them so much. I've bought two suitcases full of clothes and toys for them."

"Joe says hi."

Joe. Regina chewed on her bottom lip. What if Joe had married her? And she'd had children?

Susana hung up.

Her eyes misting, Regina couldn't stop thinking about her father and the hole he'd carved in her heart.

Now that I've got a new, cute daughter, I don't need you anymore.

For a long time, she stared at the dark gulf and the huge white yacht in the harbor.

Before Susana, her father had adored her. Regina had worked hard in an attempt to regain her number-one position in paradise. Always, always, she'd had to be a high-achiever, hoping against hope. But it hadn't worked.

Susana had been charming and flaky, *intuitive* as she put it, and so adorable that nobody minded her bad grades or lateness. They hadn't cared when she'd dropped out of college to marry Joe Hunt. Or even noticed that she'd stolen Joe from Regina, and Regina had been brokenhearted.

He'd been gifted, too. Law Review. Killer work ethic. He'd been *her* beloved boyfriend, but the moment he'd set eyes on Susana, the numerous things he'd had in common with Regina hadn't mattered anymore.

Too bad for Regina that Joe had been the only man she'd ever really loved.

Everybody in the family thought she was over him.

And she'd told herself constantly that she was. Just as she'd told herself that all her orgasms with Bobby had been real, too.

She didn't want to think about the fact that Nico was tall and dark and looked a little like Joe.

"Did you call Viola?"

Nico frowned. His mother, Principessa Donna Gloriana Lucia Romano—to mention only a few of her illustrious names and only one of her numerous titles—whose close friends called her Glory, was speaking Italian to him over his cell phone and quite rapidly, of course. Not that she liked Italian.

She'd been educated in Paris because her mother, Nico's grandmother, with whom Princess Gloriana was bitterly estranged, had had a French mother and had preferred all things French.

Both Nico's grandmother and mother loved the French language more than any other, but he preferred Italian or English, so his mother was humoring him. Because, as always, unlike Grand-mère, who wanted only his happiness, his ambitious mother wanted something from him.

"Not yet," he said.

"Nico, *tesorino,* why do you keep putting this off?"

"Maybe it's my gypsy blood."

She ignored his comment. She never liked being reminded that their original ancestor had been a gypsy king.

"You did promise to call the Principessa Donna Viola Eugenia di Frezano today when we lunched," she said. "You did say that you'd court her and that you'd ask for her hand in marriage as soon as possible."

"I did. And I will. You have instructed me as to my duty for my entire life. Have I ever failed in my duty?"

The silence between them was suddenly filled with tension.

"You know that the two families have already talked, that the marriage is practically arranged."

Of course, he knew. It would have already happened if he hadn't been dragging his feet—grieving. His heart was in the grave, as the saying went.

"You know that today marks…"

"I know," she said, trying to sound sympathetic. "But it's been two years."

His family and the family of his intended, Viola, were modern aristocrats with lineages dating back nearly a thousand years. Both families valued influence, power and money above all. Next, they counted culture, pedigree and tradition, not to mention titles—the grander and more illustrious, the better.

Nico's parents, who'd left much of his upbringing in the hands of countless nannies, tutors and chauffeurs, had taken the time to teach him and his sister that what really mattered was money, power and luxury, in that order. Personal wishes were to be sacrificed to strengthen the family.

A young man's dalliances with different types of women,

even actresses, were regarded as necessary, perhaps even a healthy diversion. Even after marriage, such playing around was tolerated, although not advisable.

But one did not marry just anyone.

"You're thirty-five," his mother reminded him again, just as she had this morning when they'd driven along the narrow roads high above the coastline. "It's time you settled down…again."

"I did settle down."

"She's dead. You're alive."

Was he? Every time the paparazzi caught him with another beautiful actress, the tabloids referred to him as the merry widower. But they didn't know about the guilt that tore at him over his treatment of Simonetta. How could they, when he'd been blind to what was in his heart until a month before Simonetta had died? At her death, love had overflowed inside him until he'd felt as though he were drowning.

"The *principessa* is very beautiful," his mother said.

"Like a jewel with icy fire."

"Without power and money, Nico, titles are meaningless. She has much to recommend her."

"So you've told me—countless times."

"You are a prince."

"A lamentable fact that overly complicates my life."

"With great privilege comes responsibility. You must marry well and behave responsibly to remain a prince. You must think of your children, of future generations. Our position has never been more fragile than it is in these modern times. Love, if one is lucky, comes after marriage. You loved Simonetta, didn't you?"

"I was lucky. Lightning will not strike twice in the same place." Annoyed by his mother, he drew a long breath. Somehow, he resisted the impulse to snap the phone shut. "Please, let's not talk about Simonetta."

"My poor *tesorino*."

His mother believed grief and all emotions were luxuries for people like them. After World War II, the Romanos had lost ten castles and nearly a million acres to the Russians. The family had prospered since the war by marrying well and diversifying their business interests. They had vast holdings in the Americas, many of which Nico managed.

Still, Viola's family had fared better in the past century and was much richer than his. His mother had begun courting Viola's parents at Simonetta's funeral.

"I understand that the match with Viola would be an exceedingly advantageous one for the family," he said. "But does everything really have to be about money?"

"Of course not, *tesorino*. But Viola is very beautiful, is she not? She is not an ogre. You will fall in love with her."

Nico frowned. As always, his mother had the worst possible timing. Because of Cara, he wished now he'd been more evasive on the subject of Viola when they'd lunched today at the family's summer palazzo.

He had no taste for marriage. It was too soon. Two hellish years ago he'd lost not only Simonetta but their unborn son, as well, when the brakes of her car had failed, and she and her chauffeur had plunged off the side of a cliff on the French Riviera.

His and Simonetta's marriage had been arranged, also, and because Nico had resented having to marry her, he hadn't realized he'd come to love her in the last months of her life.

Because of his willful stubbornness, their happiness had been too brief.

This time of year filled him with memories and regrets. He'd made her unhappy far longer than he'd made her happy. If only he could go back and make it up to her. But it was too late. His mother was right, in a way. Somehow, he had to find a way to move on.

Inadvertently, his gaze shot to the tall brunette standing high above him on her belvedere.

Guarda, che bella!

She was nothing like his shy, innocent Simonetta. Still, Cara was incredibly exciting. When Grand-mère, naughty Grand-mère, had dropped him off at the beach yesterday afternoon so he could take the tender out to his yacht, *Simonetta*, to brood, she'd pointed out the girl reading on the bench under the lemon trees. The instant Nico had seen Cara in that short sundress, she'd made him forget his grief. He'd changed his mind about going straight to his yacht.

Simonetta had been small and blond. Cara was tall, dark, more mature and self-assured. Or, at least, he'd thought so at first when she'd set down her book and taken off her glasses to study him.

He'd liked the way Cara's rich brown hair fell in glossy waves down her slim back. He'd liked the way her coffee-colored eyes burned him, even at a distance. The gardenia in her dark hair was more beautiful than a jewel.

She'd looked excited, as if she were mesmerized by him, too. Simonetta had been so shy in the beginning, so virginal in his bed that he'd found her sometimes childlike. Never had she looked at him with desire as blatant as Cara had shown, even in that first moment. Something told him he wouldn't have to waste time wooing this woman, that she was already his.

He'd imagined Cara had found out he was staying aboard *Simonetta* and had been waiting for him. He was used to being chased by celebrity hounds and aggressive fortune hunters, who were after his title and money and a few seconds of fame. Usually he avoided such women.

But Cara had made him forget, so he'd made an exception and had followed her into the bar when she'd run. He'd known he was right about her because she'd left her book on the bench for him to find and return, which he'd done. Then, much to his surprise, after smiling at him and blushing and taking her book, she'd run and vanished into thin air.

Now that he'd found her again, he was in no mood to dwell on his family responsibilities regarding Viola. He wanted to forget Simonetta and Viola. At least for tonight.

"Mother, I'll call you tomorrow," he said, aware that his voice lacked warmth.

"You won't forget to call Viola?"

"Ciao," he whispered, refusing to promise. He told her he loved her and hung up, even though he knew she would not be satisfied with that response.

Before she could call him back, he turned off his cell phone, slid it into his pocket and looked up at Cara again.

Her bright eyes touched his, lingering, her visual caress making him grow hot and hard. Even in her bulky robe, she looked full bosomed and slender hipped. Her dark hair swirled about her face. He'd always preferred blondes, but her rosy cheeks and the ripe lushness of her youthful, dark beauty made her look both innocent and as alluring to him as a siren singing from the fabled rocks.

Was she his siren? After all, this part of the coast was where Homer had placed the sirens whose songs lured men and made them forget their reason.

Was Cara naked underneath the robe? He guessed that she probably was. He looked at her and then looked some more. It was time to strip her of that bulky, unflattering garment and find out.

As he loped toward the elevator, Nico felt a wild stirring of desire. It alarmed him only a little that he was more powerfully attracted to her than he'd ever been to any other woman.

He was a prince. The blood of warriors who'd conquered lands, seizing anything and anyone they wanted, especially women, flowed in his veins. His ancestors had a history of discarding such prizes when they tired of them.

He wanted her. He would use her to forget the past and its sorrows, to forget the future, as well.

Tomorrow he would call his mother and promise to woo and wed the beautiful Viola.

Tonight belonged to Cara.

Three

Nico had a key, but he knocked before letting himself in. "Cara?"

His deep voice echoed in the tall-ceilinged bedroom. Then she ran in from the belvedere.

"Sorry about the call," he said, smiling because she was so lovely.

Cara hung back in the doorway. She was holding a rectangular frame, a painting, it appeared, which she set down on a chest. Flushing, she lashed the tie around her waist so that the robe fit more snugly.

"It's fine," she said. "I had a couple of calls to make, too." She pushed a long strand of brown hair behind her ear.

Oh, how adorable she was.

"I was out sightseeing all day and couldn't call my family earlier. I missed a christening."

When he saw the painting, his grandmother's painting, *his* painting, his brows shot together. Not for the first time, his grandmother had gone too far. With great effort he kept his face neutral.

"Christening?"

"My sister's twin boys."

He forced his attention from the painting. "So, how is Italy as a tourist destination?"

"Perfect." She swallowed. "I took an entire smart card full of pictures."

"Perfect. And soon to get better," he murmured, sliding a finger against the light switch, dimming the lights. "Good thing you can't take any more pictures."

"Oh, I have another smart card."

When she lingered by the French doors for a few more seconds, he regretted dimming the lights.

She was losing her nerve. He stepped soundlessly across the tile floor to her.

Her hesitation appealed to him. Aggressive women often annoyed him.

With the lights low, the room with its painted ceiling and gilt furniture was full of shadows. The last of the sunlight came from behind her, so he couldn't see her face clearly.

He didn't touch her at first, and neither of them spoke. But her dark eyes burned him and made him aware of the tension in his own body. He needed to take her to bed and make love to her as soon as possible.

Her eyes widened, and she scanned the room, as if seeking an avenue of escape. Afraid she might run, he gathered her into his arms.

"Mistake," she whispered, struggling to pull away. "This could be a huge mistake."

She was right. Especially for him.

What if she threatened to sell her story tomorrow about her night with the prince? He'd been blackmailed before. Not that the family hadn't hired people to deal with such matters.

"There's always a risk to everything, isn't there?" he asked, holding her tightly.

"I suppose. I'm not usually one for risks…with men."

"You miss a lot of good things, if you never take chances," he said, lowering his mouth to her cheek. When his lips nuzzled her hairline, she jumped as if his kiss shocked her.

"That's easy for you to say. The risk is mostly mine though. You do this all the time. With all kinds of women probably. It's what *you* do."

He tensed, not liking the reminder that she knew who he was and had had designs on him.

"You can't believe everything you read," he said, assuming she was referring to the tabloids. "My reputation has been wildly exaggerated."

She went still against him, and he was very aware of how her hips fit his, how the tips of her breasts touched his chest.

"Then you advertise…like an ordinary businessman?"

"Advertise?"

She squeezed her eyes shut and her hands were shaking. "I'm babbling. I do that when I'm nervous."

Clearly she was starstruck. He'd dealt with that before.

He needed to put her at ease. "I'm not really so different from you," he said. That wasn't entirely true, of course. A centuries-old lineage of privilege had a dulling effect on the human spirit. He was not allowed to surrender to his feelings all that often.

"But…"

He didn't want to argue. "I'm just man, and you're a woman. We find each other attractive." He feathered a kiss that was meant to reassure against her brow.

She jumped again.

"What could be more basic or more elemental or honest than a man and a woman and a night like this?" He kissed the tip of her nose, and she gasped.

"You know it's more complicated than that," she whispered.

He really didn't want to argue. Not when she was skittish and rigid in his arms.

He wanted to make love to her badly. She'd chased him and flirted with him for two evenings in a row. He'd thought about her last night for hours. He had to do something, so he kissed her full on the mouth.

She let out a sigh and then a harsh, uneven breath. Funny, how one taste of her was such a shock to his system.

When he deepened the kiss, she began to tremble, as if she were needy and ready, too. Good, she wasn't immune.

Still, after a kiss or two, she put her fists against his shoulders, and for a moment, he was afraid she intended to push him away. His mouth nibbled hers persuasively and she finally melted against him.

Slowly, ever so slowly, she relaxed her fingers and raised her arms around his neck. He felt wild with relief, and desire filled him when her mouth opened wider.

His tongue explored inside, teasing the tip of hers with his. When she let out another little sigh, sounding like a purr, he shuddered.

His heart sped up. She tasted sweet, and her skin was hot and soft, so hot he was mad, mad to have her. Had he ever been this mad for a woman? Still, remembering how nervous she was, he forced himself to hold her gently and to kiss her softly, lingeringly.

Her fingertips brushed the hair at his neck. "I've never done anything like this. I really don't know what's come over me. You see, I'm a planner."

"Me, too."

"And quite traditional."

"We have that in common, too," he whispered.

She smiled. "Are…are most of your women…regulars?"

"Regulars?" He didn't want to talk about other women.

"Women who are used to doing this sort of thing? Or are they like me? First-timers?"

"Why do you want to talk about other women?"

"Because I'm afraid," she admitted.

Suddenly, she seemed almost as shy and uncertain as Simonetta.

"Don't be."

"Let me go," she said suddenly.

He stroked her cheek, her throat, coaxing her with his lips and touch to stay in his arms. "As if I could—now. Cara…Cara…. *Tesorina. Ciccina.*"

Then he kissed her again, long and slowly, until she moaned.

Reluctantly, she pulled away. "So, do I get to be in charge? Do I get to tell you exactly what I want…if I decide to really do this?"

"What?"

What was going on here? One moment, she was as shy as a young doe. The next, she was the aggressor.

American women. They were taught to be so damned independent. Celebrity hound or not, he decided to humor her.

"I'm yours," he said in a light, teasing tone. "I'll do whatever you want."

"For how long?"

"All night," he said.

"What if I want you tomorrow, too?"

He thought about his mother and Viola. He could always say no to Cara tomorrow.

"That could be arranged."

"And the next day, too?"

He nodded even though he felt a strange, new tension building between them that he didn't understand.

"And the next? Both nights, too, of course?"

He was too hot for her to argue.

"I can pretty much clear my calendar. I might have to make a few phone calls though," he said, thinking of his mother. "Business obligations."

She blushed and grew thoughtful as her gaze raked him almost possessively. "I understand. Okay." The word came out like a small sigh, as if she'd been holding her breath. "It's a deal. And we'll stay in here for the most part, so people won't see us. I could see in the bar that you're well-known locally."

Not just locally, as surely she knew. "Whatever you want," he agreed.

"Then I'll do it. I can't believe I'm saying this!" Her coffee-colored gaze was intense. "Three nights. And two days. Then I fly home. So, we're settled on that?"

Again, he nodded, although he felt impatient with all this talk and ridiculous negotiating, not to mention a little concerned about how he would deal with his mother.

"And you'll really move in here, with me?"

"As I said—whatever you want."

"You're being most agreeable. I appreciate that."

"I try to please."

"I'm sure you do. I'm beginning to think I should have done something like this for myself a long time ago. I mean, most men are thinking about how a woman can please them…instead of the other way around."

Some painful emotion flickered in the depths of her dark eyes. She waited, as if she expected something more from him.

"How much?" she finally whispered.

He stared at her.

"I really would think you'd want to get that settled up front."

"How much what?" he asked, puzzled.

"Don't get me wrong. You are so sweet, so understanding about how difficult this is for me. And…and I like that. I like it a lot that you're so discreet and polite and you aren't pushy about the money. I mean, it's really sweet of you, especially since I'm a first-timer, and it makes me feel special or like we're almost friends or this is a real date or something sort of normal…instead of…what it really is. I mean, this is just one more thing about you that makes me feel so…so hot. In fact, I've never felt—" She stopped herself. "I'm sorry. I talk too much sometimes…when I'm nervous."

He'd never been so drawn to a woman, either. Why else was he being so patient with this endless, ridiculous, unfathomable conversation?

His lips barely moved. "Can't we talk later? If you feel hot and I feel hot, shouldn't we begin—"

"No. I really do have to know what you charge."

"Charge?"

For a moment longer he remained baffled, completely so, and then before she said anything else, the true meaning of her words slammed into him.

His grip on her waist tightened. "You think I'm a gigolo," he said softly.

"And, naturally, I want to know how much you charge for the sex?" Her whisper was raw, her face purple before she lowered her eyes.

She bit her lip savagely. "Do you charge by the hour?" She was fiddling with the sash of her thick robe like someone who was afraid she was in some sort of trouble. "Or do you charge for services? Do you take VISA or cash? I don't have all that much cash, so maybe we could go to an ATM later."

She was so embarrassed she couldn't meet his eyes, but when he couldn't think of any way to answer her, she continued fiddling with the sash. "I'm a lawyer, and I like to know what I'm getting into…I mean, when it comes to business."

An ATM!

"So the hell do I."

He let her go and then jerked away as if she'd slapped him. He strode to the minibar where he opened a little bottle and poured himself a Scotch and water. Studying the golden liquor in the lambent light, he opened a second bottle and splashed more Scotch into his glass. He didn't bother with ice.

She was watching him, shaken, her dark eyes wide and frightened.

"I didn't mean to insult you," she whispered. "I thought you'd want to talk about this."

"How exactly did you figure out…er…what I do for a living?"

"By watching you with those two older women. The ones who dropped you off. The way they kissed you."

His mother? His grandmother? His glance flew to the painting his grandmother had done of him when he'd been a child, visiting her for the first time. It was on the tip of his tongue to explain who the women actually were and who he was, when she went on.

"The Ferrari. The Maserati. Really, they gave it away. Not to mention the blonde's diamonds. I mean, her ring, it must be nine carats."

Ten. It had been in the family three hundred years.

He swirled the Scotch in his glass.

"The way they kissed you...like they adored you."

Did she know nothing about the Italian maternal instinct? He had always been his mother's favorite. His older sister had been pretty sweet about accepting that, most of the time. After all, he was her favorite, too.

"Your ragged clothes compared to hers."

He loved old, soft, worn clothes. They made him feel free, almost ordinary, not so burdened with who and what he was and all that was expected of him. Naturally, his mother wanted him in Armani.

"I see," he said. The Scotch burned his throat and set his stomach on fire. "And do you do this often—travel alone and hire gigolos?"

His gaze must have hardened, because she looked away. "No. I told you. Never. Never before! And probably never again! That's why I don't really know how to do this."

"Have you slept with other men in Italy? Men you met in your hotel or at restaurants?"

"No! I told you—you're the first."

The Scotch worked swiftly. He felt the beginnings of a much needed buzz. "So, you haven't read about me? You don't know who I..."

She studied him, her pretty face charmingly quizzical. "Maybe you do look a little familiar. Maybe I did see one of your ads or something, but magazines and papers are full of ads. I just look at the pictures in Italian magazines. Are you a really famous gigolo or something?"

He nearly choked on his Scotch. "You might be surprised at just how famous." He couldn't resist teasing her. "A gigolo to the stars."

God help him for what he was about to do, but he couldn't help himself.

"Then we definitely stay in my hotel."

"I could wear a disguise. I'm quite good at them, you know."

"I'm sure you have to be...in your line of work." She laughed nervously.

He smiled. He didn't want to play games, but this was obviously her fantasy and he wanted her more than ever. Maybe it was the Scotch, but her fantasy was beginning to turn him on, too. *A gigolo?* A professional who indulged a woman's secret desires?

"How much?" she said.

His lips tightened. Sober, he wouldn't have been able to endure this money talk or the fact that she thought he was a gigolo. But the liquor had mellowed him. Not to mention, he was hotter for her than ever.

"How much?"

"You are nothing if not persistent."

"I'm a lawyer."

He had a law degree and a business degree. "I know a thing or two about lawyers." They were pushy and bossy, traits he had not desired in his women—until her.

"Since it's so important to you, you decide," he said.

"I keep forgetting. You're the professional."

"Right." He eyed another little Scotch bottle and considered a third shot.

"Since you have all the experience, how could I possibly know what you're worth?"

"For you," he began, his voice deliberately husky as he stared into her eyes, "I'll make a special, one-time deal. Just for you. Pay whatever you feel like. The amount doesn't matter."

"Now? Or later?"

"Later. How will you know what I'm worth before you've sampled the merchandise?"

"You really are the sweetest gigolo ever."

"We are trained to please."

"You went to gigolo school?"

"Stop!" He really did have to have another drink to continue this idiotic conversation.

This time he threw ice cubes into his glass. Then he opened a third little bottle, poured the shot and downed it in a single gulp.

"One more thing—"

Hell. "What now?"

"I'm sort of a health nut…"

"You want me to use a condom? No problem."

"No…I…don't know how to say this."

"I'm sure you'll figure it out."

"I…I was wondering about Italy's health guidelines. I mean, for gigolos."

Oh, God.

Afraid he'd give himself away, he glanced out the window. "You may be assured…er…that I am extremely discerning about my women…er…I mean, my clients. Extremely discerning. I always use a condom. The very best grade, naturally. Then I go to the doctor every sixty days for a thorough examination. Blood tests. The works. I would go more often, if I thought it was necessary. My client list is extremely exclusive."

He set his glass down, determined to end this ridiculous conversation. "Do you need documents, or are you satisfied?"

"Not quite yet." She lowered her lashes and tried not to look at the bed. "But I'm sure I will be soon, now that we have all these obnoxious little business details out of the way."

"I've never had a complaint," he murmured drily.

Finally. He set down his glass and pulled her into his arms again. She closed her eyes.

Finally.

Four

Nico liked the way a faint tremor passed through Regina's body when his arm circled her shoulders and he cradled her close. He liked the way her pulse began to beat madly when he slipped his hand beneath her hair and pressed his mouth to her throat.

"I could still say no, pay you and call this crazy thing off," she whispered.

"But you don't want to do that, do you?"

"Not at all."

He lifted her fingers to his lips and kissed them one by one as he'd done at the bar. As he gently sucked their tips, she shuddered.

He slid a fingertip inside her robe and very slowly pushed it aside a fraction of an inch. "What do you want?" he murmured against her earlobe.

His hand coaxed the thick terry off her shoulder, and she gasped.

"You mean, I get to tell you what I want?"

"You hired me, remember. That was our agreement. I mean… er…bargain. Do you like it straight…or kinky?"

"Kinky? I…I…I'm not sure I know or want to know what you mean by that."

He laughed. "So what do you want?"

"I…I want you to undress me and then give me a massage and then maybe make love to me very, very slowly."

"I can't wait," he whispered.

He heard her breath catch even before his hand found the terry-cloth tie at her waist and he unthreaded it all the way. He slid the robe off her shoulders, and it tumbled in a heap to the tile floor.

"Pink bra, pink panties, edged with black lace," he murmured, cupping her breasts. "Nice."

"I bought them at Illusions," she said.

Grand-mère!

When his thumbs brushed her nipples through the black lace, her hands closed over him through his jeans.

"No, no," he murmured. "Let me do my job. After all, I am the…"

Again, he couldn't bring himself to use the graphic term for what she thought he was.

"Pleasure provider," she offered. Reluctantly her fingers, which had been seeking to fondle him through the soft denim, fell away.

Gathering her to him, he led her to the wall. "Pleasure provider?"

"Professional. Whatever term you prefer."

Her back was against the cool plaster as he knelt, at eye level with her belly. Using his hands, he spread her legs. Even before he began to kiss her navel, his tongue delving, she sighed. Then his callused palm began to stroke her from her waist to her ankle, gliding over her skin in slow caresses meant to tantalize.

"You're good," she gasped in a strangled tone.

"Thank you."

"Worth every penny."

On a low growl, his mouth followed the path of his rough palm, kissing her thighs, her calves, lifting her feet and sucking each bare toe. Then he did the same thing to the other leg. When he was done, his mouth lingered on her pink satin panties, on the area that covered the dark curls between her legs.

When a fingertip entered her, she clutched his head closer and let out a sob that made him groan.

"I want you so much," he said. Then he ripped her panties down and hauled her to bed.

As he settled himself on top of her, a knock sounded loudly against the outer door. "Room service," an impersonal voice called.

"Damn. Damn." He jerked free of her. "Who the hell ordered room service?"

"You." She giggled.

"Right."

"You said we had to have strawberries."

Sucking in a breath, he let her go. Then he picked up her robe and helped her into it.

"You stay here," he ordered.

"Tell him to add the tip to the bill."

"I think I can handle it."

She was still standing against the wall, clutching her robe to her body when he returned with the tray of food. His blue eyes were fierce and hot, his black curls damp against his brow.

"You look adorable," he said.

She bit her bottom lip. "Come back to bed."

"Sometimes it heightens pleasure to stop and start."

He carried the tray out to a shaded loggia and set it down. He plucked a bunch of purple grapes and went back to her. He nibbled half a grape and then shared the other half with her. It was sweet, yet tart.

"Did you really have a late lunch?" he murmured.

"No. I am…a little hungry, but I can wait."

"No, if you're hungry, let's eat now." He led her outside, pulled out her chair and seated her, placed a plate, napkin and silverware before her, and then opened a bottle of wine.

The evening was darkening rapidly. Birds settling in the nearby treetops twittered noisily. Delicate, fleecy clouds were lit up by the moon and the town's lights.

"We call clouds like that *pecorelle,* little sheep," he said.

"They look like they're on fire."

With another sigh, she breathed in the scent of the sea and flowers, as if she were, at last, relaxing in his presence.

"So, you're a lawyer?" he said.

"Yes."

"Do you like it?"

She seemed about to say yes and then stared at him, as if in wonder. "You know, I don't think I ever thought about how I feel about it until a couple of months ago. I just wanted to be successful."

"In what way?"

"Make A's in school. I wanted my parents to be proud of me. I wanted to live in the right neighborhood, have the right husband, and be acceptable to the right kind of people. So, I went to college and law school."

"I see."

"I suppose it's the same everywhere."

"And are you successful?"

"For a while, I thought so. I mean, I have everything I ever wanted. Only, it isn't like I thought it would be. My firm represents a lot of major corporations. Some of them do things I hate, such as pollute groundwater. I get paid handsomely to defend them. And even though I drive a nice car and have a nice house, lately I've been wondering if I'm still one of the good guys."

He nodded.

"Then there's my sister, who didn't even finish college. She's so happy. She's married, and she has three adorable children. My parents are prouder of her than they are of me, and maybe they should be. So, lately I've been wondering about my life, where it's going…where I want it to go."

"Do you want children?"

"Very much. I love my niece and nephews so much, you see."

"Boyfriend?"

"Not anymore."

He waited.

"What? You don't think I'd be here like this...I mean, with you...if I were serious about someone back home?"

"Some women come to Europe to play."

"I suppose you'd know about that."

He felt his mouth tighten.

"Sorry. I—I..." She drew a breath. "My last boyfriend, Bobby, asked me to marry him right before I came. I said no."

"Why?"

"Long story. I thought I wanted to marry him. But what I really wanted..." She stopped herself. "Why am I telling you, of all people, about my life?"

"Because I asked."

"Okay, I'm confused. Who isn't?"

He cut off a piece of cheese and placed it on a cracker. Then he offered it to her.

She bit into the cracker. "You know what's odd? I took two months off, which is unheard of at the firm, and came over here to think about my life. Only, this is the first time I've slowed down long enough to do it. Suddenly, I don't want to go home. I'm sick and tired of who I was there. It's like my real life is a weird dream that makes zero sense. I feel good, right now, right here, with you—which is crazy."

"I feel exactly the same way. It's incredibly easy being with you. Why is that, I wonder?"

He stared at her so long, she looked shyly away.

"I bet you tell that to all your clients."

Damn. "I don't," he said.

"I'm sorry," she whispered.

He sat back abruptly in his chair and took a long breath.

"Okay, I'm going to ask you a personal question," she said. "You don't have to answer. But in your real life, I mean, when you're not working as a gigolo..."

The word bit. He ran a hand through his hair.

"I mean...do gigolos ever fall in love?"

"Yes. I was married. I fell in love with my wife."

"Did you work while you were with her?"

"I was faithful to her in all ways, if that's what you're asking. Until she died."

"She died? Oh, I'm sorry."

"Two years ago today." He broke off, unable to go on.

When she reached for his hand, he gripped hers tightly.

"In a car wreck. She was pregnant. I didn't know about the baby until the doctor, who tried to save her, told me."

"I'm so, so very sorry," she whispered.

"We honeymooned in Ravello. I come here every year on the anniversary of her death. My grandmother lives here, so I visit her, too. She's been very worried about me. The rest of my family wants me to forget my wife, to think of the future."

"But you're not ready."

"My mother lost my father a few years ago. She didn't allow her grief to overwhelm her, so she doesn't understand me."

"I suppose everyone's different, or maybe it's different when you're younger. I guess when you're older, you've been through more. Hey, don't listen to me. I don't know what I'm talking about. Only, maybe you have a right to your feelings."

"I came here with my cousin to try to remember the good times. Only, my gra...er...my friend, my client, saw you and pointed you out to me."

He brought Regina's hand to his lips. "Your smile was so beautiful. For the first time since my wife's death, I feel almost at peace with the past, with her death. My mother keeps telling me that she's dead and I'm alive. I didn't really understand what she meant, until I saw you."

"I'm glad you're feeling better." She stroked his hand lightly. "Maybe you were lucky to have had her, even though her loss has been so painful. I'm almost jealous in a way. I don't think I've ever been truly in love. Not like that. In fact, before I came here, I was about to give up on men."

"I find that very difficult to believe."

"All my relationships, I mean the serious, real kind, not like this, always just fizzled out."

He continued to hold her hand, waiting.

"So that's why I'm here with you, I guess...a gigolo."

He felt a muscle tick along his jawline. "Do you have to keep harping on my...er...career?"

"I keep forgetting that it makes you uncomfortable."

The tension remained with him.

"I could never pay you enough for what you've done for me, and all we've done is talk," she said.

"They do say confession is good for the soul."

He got up and walked back into the bedroom. He stood before the chest where she'd propped the painting. Frowning, he lifted the picture.

"Do you like it?" she asked.

"Very much. It reminds me of a beach I once knew near my grandmother's house. It's always been quite wonderful being with her. She's been something of a black sheep and forbidden to me, by my mother. *Her* daughter. My mother is as proper as her mother was scandalous."

"Do they know that you're a gigolo?"

"No." He set the picture back down.

"Would they disapprove?"

"My grandmother approves of love, in all its many forms."

"You didn't include your mother in that last statement," Regina said.

"No."

They ate, and when they were done, Nico took her by the hand and led her to the bed. Slowly he removed her robe again. As it fell, her hand found the zipper of his jeans.

Suddenly she was tearing his clothes off and kissing him all over. He was huge. When he grew even larger, she laughed in delight.

"Cara, you're getting me so excited I can't remember your plan. Wasn't I supposed to massage you and make love to you slowly?"

"Forget my plan. I don't have a plan."

A rush of powerful feelings swept him. He took her in his arms and carried her to bed. Within seconds their bodies moved together in an ancient, timeless rhythm. When he entered her, he felt the most powerful, pleasurable connection to a woman in all his life.

For a long moment, he held her close, celebrating that first glorious wonder of being with her. Then his breath started coming in harsh, rapid gasps. He gripped her waist, pressing himself closer and plunged again and again.

"Faster," she murmured, her breathing as out of control as his. "Yes. Yes. Yes."

"I should slow down."

"No!" she whispered in a low, frantic tone. "Faster."

After they exploded together, she fell back against the bed, her body damp all over. He collapsed beside her, heavily exhausted.

"I'll never be able to stand or to walk again," she whispered. Then she began to laugh and to sob and to cling to him. "You're really, really good."

"You're incredible, *tesorina*."

"Does that mean we can do it again?"

Five

The thick black straps of the backpack cut into Regina's shoulders after their climb from the sea. The pack, which had felt light hours ago when they'd started their circuitous, uphill hike on a bougainvillea-shaded cobblestone path, felt as heavy as lead now. The dull pain throbbing in her lower back sharpened with every step.

Nico had offered to carry the pack. Why had she insisted on wearing it?

"Stop! I've got to rest." Her legs were shaking from the vertical climb, and she was gasping as she sank down against a low stone wall and stared at the breathtaking view of cliffs towering above the blue water. She pressed her hand into her spine.

"Didn't I tell you, you should let me carry this?" He lifted the backpack from her shoulders and set it on the dusty ground. "Do you want to go back to the hotel?"

"No." Not that going back to the hotel would be a bad thing.

After making love for hours and sleeping all night in each other's arms, she would surely have slept until noon if she hadn't heard him calling room service. After making the call, he'd rolled over and pulled her back into her arms, nuzzling her throat and lips with his mouth and tongue until she'd been fully awake.

"I can't let you waste your last few days and not tour the Amalfi Coast," he'd said.

"Waste?" She'd smiled up at him dreamily. "I'm not wasting them."

"Not if we hike. That was number one on your list."

"You read my list?"

"While you were sleeping." He'd smiled. "You'll never forgive yourself if you don't do what you came here to do."

"Oh, but I will. I assure you." She'd stroked his lower belly affectionately.

Room service had knocked just as he'd pulled her into his arms and had kicked off the sheets. He'd let her go, and they'd eaten and then dressed and prepared for this glorious if arduous hike.

"You were right," she said, speaking over the sudden barking of dogs in a village somewhere below them. "This is all so beautiful. Thank you. Thank you for making me come here."

"When you said you came here to hike the Sentieri degli Dei, I had no choice."

"The path of gods," she translated unnecessarily. "The guide book said it was steep, but the photographs were so extraordinary."

"Pictures can't really capture something like this, can they?" he said, his blue eyes on her face rather than the view. But then he'd seen it all before, she told herself. He lived here, didn't he? And gigolos probably weren't too keen on views.

Although she was deeply moved by the irresistible mountains and sea and had worked hard for this view, she couldn't stop staring at him. She pulled out her camera.

"So much beauty is dangerous," he murmured.

"Yes." She snapped a picture of him.

"You feel like you could fly into such a view and be part of it as you might in a dream." He brushed the tip of her nose with a fingertip and smiled.

Every moment with him had been perfect up to now. He'd served her breakfast in bed. He'd even sat on the bed, spoon-feeding her cereal with sugar and fresh raspberries. Never had she imagined that nibbling berries out of a man's hand could be such a sensual, magical experience.

The morning was sunny and picture-perfect, too. He'd organized everything—her, the hotel. He'd even told her what to wear and had bought her sunscreen in the gift shop. He'd had the hotel pack a huge lunch after their breakfast even though she'd protested that after two cups of raspberries—they had been too good to waste—she could never eat again.

Then with him directing her, rather bossily, she'd driven them to Nocelle, where they'd left her rented Fiat so that they could walk this trail that offered the most dramatic views of the rugged coastline.

She'd read that the walk to Praiano was four and a half hours and the return would be the same, so she'd protested when she'd realized his plan.

Nine hours of hiking.

Much as she liked to hike, she hadn't wanted to totally exhaust herself on the trail when they had so little time together.

"Don't worry." He'd placed the car keys under a rock behind the left, front tire. "A little genie will spirit your car to Praiano, so we can drive back from the end point of the trail."

"But my contract says I'm the only one who can drive."

"It will be okay." He'd lifted his cell phone to his ear.

"It will most definitely not be okay! The road was very narrow and windy. Your genie might wreck it."

"He is an excellent driver. Besides, this is Italy. He and I have many friends. Important people who will help. You understand, no?"

She would have argued, but he'd held up his hand. "*Scusa.* Massimo…" After that he'd turned away and had rattled incomprehensible Italian to this Massimo fellow.

Somehow, even though he was a gigolo, which meant technically she was the boss, she'd resisted the instinct to seize control. At the same time, she'd wondered if his many friends were rich women with important husbands, women who could pull strings for their gorgeous special pleasure provider, who made their pampered lives with dull husbands more bearable.

One night with him and Regina was feeling possessive of him, and as if she were losing control.

Not good.

Good thing she was leaving Ravello in a couple of days, or he might become a permanent addiction.

"Do you want some water?" he asked, still staring at her rather than the view, his question bringing her back to the present.

When she nodded, he uncapped his water bottle and offered it. When she was through sipping, he took the bottle and drank after her, as if their sharing the same bottle was the most natural thing in the world.

He slid the bottle into her backpack and lifted it onto his shoulders along with his own. He pulled out his camera and took a picture of her and the view. Then, of course, she had to take another one of him.

After that, they continued their walk and were rewarded with glimpses of ruins and an abandoned farmhouse and an ancient arch that once had led somewhere but now led nowhere. Of course, she had to photograph him again in front of the farmhouse and then the arch and had to have him photograph her in front of both settings, as well.

"You must send your pictures to me," he said, his manner so urgent and sincere she nodded.

She could almost believe this was a real date and that last night had been real, too; that they were beginning a genuine relationship that would be vitally important to both of them.

After they left the farmhouse, they came to an ancient convent filled with fading frescoes of saints. He charmed her by picking a bouquet of wild roses and olive branches. After giving her a rose, which she put in her hair, he knelt. His face grew serious as he said a silent prayer and left the saints the rest of the flowers as a humble offering.

When he stood again, he said, "If you are hungry, I know a perfect spot for a picnic."

"I could eat something."

"All right, then."

He led the way up another bougainvillea-shaded, cobblestone path that passed between the whitewashed buildings of a second deserted farmhouse, more charming than the first, and then through a lemon grove.

With every step the sun rose higher and became warmer on her back. The hike became more of a plod. She was breathless and perspiring long before they'd made their way up the hidden path and a nearly impassable cliff to a stone bench in the shade of an olive tree with stunning views of the mountains and sea.

"You're right. This is perfect," she said, still panting from the climb.

When she sank wearily down onto the bench, he came closer. Smiling down at her, he studied her so intently she almost stood up in the hopes that he might kiss her. But instead of doing as she wished, he lowered her backpack to the ground and rummaged in it.

Quickly, he got their boxed lunches out, sat down and spread their sandwiches, cheeses and wine between them on the stone bench. Then he deftly uncorked the wine bottle and poured two glasses of jewel-dark, red wine.

When he began to eat his sandwich in silence, she lifted a thick-crusted slab of bread to inspect hers. The mozzarella, grilled chicken, fresh basil and avocado smelled delicious.

Still, she was thirstier than she was hungry, so she sipped her wine rather too enthusiastically while he continued to eat his sandwich.

Their silence lengthened. The sun felt warmer. Not that his not talking felt the least bit awkward or the heat of the sun the least bit uncomfortable. No, it was one of those comfortable lulls that can happen between two people who are so completely at ease with each other that there is no need for idle conversation.

It was too perfect, being with him, both in bed and out of it.

He looked up at her and then at the view.

"Dolce color d'oriental zaffiro," he said.

"What?" She was beginning to love it when he spoke Italian.

"A gentle hue of Oriental sapphire." He smiled. "We Italians are quite attached to our *Divine Comedy.* I memorized big pieces of Dante's epic every year in school, and then again in university. We can all quote from it. Even my cousin, Massimo, can be quite eloquent."

"I'm afraid I read more *Cliff-Notes* than the *Divine Comedy* itself," she confessed.

"You missed something then. The great masters are usually worth reading."

A gigolo who quoted Dante and defended the great masters with passion?

"The line comes from 'Purgatory,' and it describes the sea-to-sky horizon when the Divine Poet emerged from the depths of Hell and came to the calm shores of Mount Purgatory."

"What can a girl who crammed for all her quizzes with *Cliff-Notes* possibly add to that?"

"Perhaps more than you think."

He smiled. Then he opened a sack of chips and offered them to her. Normally, she never ate chips. But the hotel had made these.

She took one and munched noisily as he grabbed one from the bag for himself.

The chip was pure grease and carb—and sinfully delicious. She glanced at his olive-toned hand holding his chip. Taking the hint, he fed her his chip.

Apparently, she was on a *sinfully-delicious* kick.

"How did you get started as a gigolo?"

He was swallowing a chip himself and choked so violently she began to pound his back.

He shot to his feet, and she began to beat on his shoulders. "I thought I made it clear I don't want to talk about my work." His manner was abrupt.

"Why are you so ashamed of it when you're so good at it?"

"Who wouldn't be?" he lashed. His eyes were hard and cold now.

"If you don't like it, why don't you stop? Do something else?"

"Believe me, I'm going to," he muttered. "The first chance I get."

"I could be your last customer."

"Believe me, you will be." He shot her a look filled with self-contempt. Then he knelt and began throwing things into his backpack. "Are you finished eating?"

She tried to swallow the last of her wine, but there was a painful lump in her throat. Was she so disgusting to him? Had he been acting last night? She remembered his passion, his tenderness. Closing her eyes, she fought tears.

For her, last night had been too wonderful to believe. Never had she felt so cherished or so special. Had it been awful for him? It must have been, and she couldn't bear the thought.

Obviously, gigolos had to be skilled actors to play the parts in whatever fantasy their clients demanded. If he'd been disgusted, his performance deserved an Oscar.

"I'm sorry if it was awful for you," she said in a broken whisper.

"Awful? What the hell are you talking about now?"

"Last night." She couldn't bear to look at him, so she was unaware of his expression. Pain cut her like a knife. "You found me disgusting."

Suddenly she felt his arms, tight and hard, pulling her against his muscular chest.

"Cara, Cara." His deep voice was infinitely soothing, his hands gentle now as he stroked her. His lips pressed lightly against her temple. "Disgusting? Last night was wonderful. I'm sorry I lost my temper. The last thing I ever want to do is make you unhappy."

"I feel the same way, even though you are a gigolo and I know you can't care about me as much as you act like you do."

"God!" He mashed her against his chest. "I hate this." He stroked her hair thoughtfully. "Cara, I...I'm afraid I haven't been entirely honest with you."

"How could you be? You were doing your job. But if your work is so repugnant, I relieve you from all obligations that we contracted for. I'll even pay you now for tonight, too, and for tomorrow, as well."

"I don't want your damn money."

"I refuse to take advantage of your generous—"

"Stop it, okay?"

For another long moment he held her close, his hands stroking her hair. He seemed to be struggling with something while she clung to him. Hating his anxiety and afraid of what he would say, she held on to him in a state of stupefied tension.

"I'm not a gigolo," he finally whispered, his low tone edgy.

She shook loose of his embrace and looked up at him. "You're not?"

"No. There. Now you know."

"You lied to me?"

"Yes. No!" He ran his hands through his hair. "Hell, I played along."

"Then who are you really?"

"Nico Romano."

"And your profession?"

"I'm…an international businessman."

"And those older women, who kissed you?"

He hesitated. "Relatives."

"That's it? You're telling the truth? The whole truth."

That muscle in his jawline quivered. He flushed. "Last night, I wanted you so much I think I would have said anything or done anything to have you. And nothing's changed. I still want you, maybe even more, if such a thing is possible."

"Me, too. Oh, me, too."

If she had an ounce of pride she would never have admitted her feelings to him so freely. Instead, she should have asked him about those older women in the fancy cars. Who exactly were they?

She'd slept with him. She had about a million questions, but when her gaze met his, his eyes burned with so much emotion she forgot everything except the simple joy of being with him now that she knew he hadn't been acting.

He hadn't been acting! She wasn't disgusting to him!

His arms tightened around her, and he buried his face in her hair. Soon she was lost, utterly lost to all reality. She wanted only this moment with him. Even before his lips claimed hers, she was aware of a wildly thrilling happiness.

When he began kissing her, the sinfully delicious chips and their sandwiches and wine were forgotten. Such passion could have only one ending. In the space of two kisses, they were both breathless.

"Farmhouse," he muttered on a ragged note.

She nodded as he began gathering their things, slinging them into his backpack, not caring that their sandwiches would be hopelessly crushed. Then he seized her hand. Together they ran stumbling, laughing back down the trail to the last deserted farmhouse.

Inside the musty-smelling building, he tossed their backpacks to the ground. Then he shoved her against the wall and leaned heavily into her. His mouth closed over hers again and devoured her lips.

Once again, the mysterious force that had drawn them together swept them up in its fierce tide. Their passion was like a wave that took charge of them, lifting them higher and higher and then shattering them against an unknown shore that was part of a strange, thrilling world they'd never known before and felt lost in.

The moist heat of his breath on her nipple through cotton made her heart skip. She was aching, dying for him as he pulled her T-shirt up and her jeans down. As eager as he was, she fumbled for his zipper. When she'd opened it and released him, her hand closed around him for a moment, every long inch of him, causing his breath to come ever more harshly. Then her hand fell away, and she stood on her tiptoes, arching herself toward him. He leaned closer, cupped her buttocks and plunged inside her.

Clinging to him, her nails dug into his back. He drove faster and faster until she began to weep. Then he shuddered and she quickly followed, and for a timeless moment they were joined in all ways, physically and emotionally.

Long seconds later, his black head slumped over hers. She felt herself falling back into herself, wondering once again what was happening to her. Sex had never been anything like this before.

"Cara, Cara...." His deep voice was infinitely tender. "If only..."

She was still gasping for every breath when he lowered his mouth to her throat and kissed the pulse beating madly there. Through her tears of exultation, she laughed a little, for she was so close to some edge, she was both happy and sad.

"I will never forget you." Clumsily, she wiped her eyes and then touched his cheek with her damp palm.

He pulled her close, kissed her tears away, then simply held her while the balmy sea breeze rustled the leaves of the lemon trees outside the farmhouse.

"Two days. That's all we have," he said in a tortured voice that indicated he never wanted to let her go.

"Two nights, too."

He began to kiss her throat again and then her lips, murmuring more Italian endearments that she didn't understand. And, as before, their desire built until the white heat of passion melted everything away once again, except the searing fact that they'd been made for each other.

Never again could she go to bed with another man without comparing him to Nico. Would she ever be able to fall in love again, to marry?

"And I wasn't even good at sex before," she said.

"I don't want to know about before," Nico said, his voice so harsh he would have frightened her if she had not felt exactly the same way.

Possessive.

Never before had she felt so completely possessive about a man. She wanted him to be hers, only hers, for the rest of her life.

But what good were such feelings when she was going home the day after tomorrow?

"I...I wish you were a gigolo!"

"No, you don't."

She pulled her jeans up and her shirt down. "Don't you see, I thought I was safe with you."

"Safe? With one of those guys?" He wasn't smiling as he arranged his own shirt and jeans.

"I couldn't possibly care about a gigolo. I just wanted..."

"Sex," he finished, his voice dark. "Something simple. I know, because all I wanted was to use you to forget my wife."

"But this is too much," she said.

"For me, too, but it is what it is."

His expression was growing gloomier by the second. She sensed in him a bleak determination to separate from the powerful force that had taken them both over, to separate from her. Forever. She half expected him to run down the trail.

Pain tore at her heart.

"Men always want to leave me," she said. "My sister says it's because I'm too bossy."

"Believe me, I'm used to bossy." When his lips curved in amusement, she wondered who had caused that smile. "I would never let you go if I had a choice."

"Are you engaged or something?"

He went still as death.

"Is that it?"

He didn't deny it.

"That's it. Oh, my God! You're engaged! And you're with me! You told me about your wife to win my sympathy. The real truth is that you're with me because you're having second thoughts about the woman you're about to marry."

"No!" But he looked away. *"Not exactly."*

"Yes."

"Listen to me. *I love you.*"

He looked so stunned by this admission, she almost believed him.

"No, you don't. So don't lie. You're going to marry some-body else."

The pain in his eyes cut her to the soul. "I didn't lie."

"You say you love me, but you're going to marry her? Is that the truth? Or not?"

He heaved in a breath. "Okay, if you'll let me explain, I'll tell you why."

"I don't need to hear any more!" She backed away from him, hating that, despite her anger, she still desired him. "You miserable, unholy skunk! You snake! And to think I was so touched by those flowers you left the saints." She yanked the flower he'd given her out of her hair and stomped on it. "What a miserable, insufferable piece of work you are. All men are skunks. Especially you!"

He stared at the mashed flower.

"How can you do that to *her?* She'll figure it out eventually. You'll break her heart. You know that, don't you?"

"No, I won't. Because she doesn't love me, either."

"Is she rich?"

His eyes narrowed.

Of course, she was rich. "So, you've got your cap set for a rich girl."

He didn't deny that, either.

"So that's it!"

He hung his head, his focus drifting toward the flower. "In a way you're right, I guess, although I wouldn't put it that way."

"Why not call a spade a spade?"

He reached for her. "Cara, it's not that simple."

"Sure it is! And don't ever touch me again! Don't you dare touch me, do you hear? Where's my Fiat? I want to go back to my hotel. Now!"

She would have run, but his hand snapped around her wrist. He caught her to him, his mouth closing over hers. The power of her will was no match for his desire, and again, despite everything she'd learned about him, his kisses flooded her with warm, pleasurable sensations.

She yanked free of him, and then she stopped, realizing a way she could hurt him, too.

"Why shouldn't I have one more for the road? Correction— for the long flight home? I wanted a gigolo. You want to know something? You're not all that different from what I thought you were. Bottom line—you're selling yourself."

"Shut up." His expression was both tortured and wild. "You don't know anything about my life, and maybe it's best you don't."

"I want you—gigolo."

"Have it your way."

Before she could protest, he ripped her jeans and panties down and pushed her against the wall again. Then he knelt in front of her in an attitude of worship and spread her legs.

"No! What are you doing?" She felt too intimately exposed.

His broad brown hands locked around her waist. "I want to remember you and this day for the rest of my life."

When the tip of his tongue touched her outer lips and then slid upward and then down with slow, thrilling strokes, her mouth went dry. Heat from his lips poured into all her secret feminine places. Lava washed up her spine, flowed into every cell, drenching her in flames. Even her heart could not remain unaffected from such fire, and the cold place in its center melted, too.

When his tongue flicked deeply inside her and then went still, every pore in her being felt sexually charged. Instead of feeling ashamed, she forgot herself and clawed the wall.

He was what she wanted, what she'd always wanted. Without knowing who she was or what she did, she began to twist and writhe against his lips and tongue. Crying out his name, she wept.

Sensing how near she was to climaxing, he gripped her bottom and hauled her against his mouth. His tongue plunged inside her again and again until she screamed in ecstasy.

As the explosion ripped through her, she sank her fingers into his hair and dug her nails into his scalp. She held on to him, the chaos of her emotions tearing her apart as the shattering experience consumed her.

When it was over, he jerked his head back, and she sagged against the cool wall. Then her knees collapsed and she slid down beside him.

She wanted to hate him. At the same time she wanted his mouth to lick her intimately forever.

"Oh, Lord," she whispered. "What have I done?"

Her heart was pounding and her hair was dripping with perspiration. She was afraid because she'd lost all control. Because somehow, some way, against her will, in less than twenty-four hours, he'd made her his forever.

"I hate you," she vowed softly, "for what you just did."

"You only wish you did."

"Then I wish I'd never met you."

"So do I. So the hell do I."

He clasped her chin tightly, forcing her to stare into his tortured blue eyes. "What gives you the high moral ground? You're the one who wanted your own personal stud and hired a gigolo. Well, maybe you just got him, Cara."

She gasped. Then she bristled with all sorts of self-righteous indignation that he'd so aptly pointed out she had no right to feel.

"When the hell are you going to figure out neither one of us is in control here?" he said, his tone gentler, his eyes softer. "This thing has us."

When he pulled her close, she shuddered, willing herself to resist him. But, as always, she was weak and needy, so she let him hold her. At the thought of their impossible relationship, her mood grew unbearably sad—and angry, too.

This was all his fault! It had to be!

Or was it? Somehow her needs and emotions were all mixed up. How could this have happened in such a short time? She'd left Austin to sort out her life, not for confusion like this.

"You're a bastard," she whispered. "A royal bastard."

"You don't know how right you are," he muttered.

She'd been right to want to control things, too. Leaving him, even though she knew he was marrying another woman for money, was going to break her as nothing else ever had.

"You're a bastard!" she repeated. "How can you look so sick at heart when I know you're slime? I want you out of my life— gone! I don't want to ever think about you again!"

"You think you have all the answers, don't you? Well, you don't! Before you go back to Austin, there's something I've got to show you!"

"Nothing you could say or do or show me could change the way I feel about you!"

"We'll see then, won't we?"

Six

"You can't drive my car. You're not on the contract."

Regina was in *lawyer* mode. Translation: she was in the mood to argue about anything.

Nico shot her a look before he unlocked the passenger door for her.

She glared at him and refused to get in.

"Suit yourself," he said. "It's a long walk back to Ravello." He strode around the front of the Fiat.

"You can't just drive off in my car and leave me here."

"Watch me." He got in and slammed his door hard. "I'm a bastard, remember!"

When he started the car, she jumped in and slammed hers, too, harder.

He adjusted the mirror and the seat, so that he had more leg room. "The road is dangerous. I know it and you don't."

She was about to protest when he shifted into reverse. Tires whirred in the dirt, spitting gravel.

"You scared the hell out of me this morning when you backed

up and we nearly got rear-ended. And it was so early, the road was almost empty."

"I had to back up for that bus," she muttered.

"One bus. There'll be traffic now. Besides, like I said, even with the road empty, you scared the hell out of me."

She'd scared the hell out of herself. Was it her fault that the road was so narrow two cars couldn't really fit side by side, not to mention trucks and buses?

"Besides, you grind the gears," he said.

Without another word, she buckled her seat belt. If only they hadn't quarreled. If only she didn't feel achingly heart-broken, she might have enjoyed the lovely views and sparkling afternoon.

By the way he drove, she knew he was as enraged as she was. He ignored the scenery, whipped around hairpin curves, tires screaming. He passed a motorcycle with mere inches to spare on her side where a three-foot stone wall was the only thing separating them from a sheer drop to the sea.

Amber sunshine in the trees and deepening shadows made the mountainside a sparkling fairy wonderland. Not that she could enjoy it as cafés, trucks, villas and other cars raced by them at a sickening speed. Far below, fishing boats seemed as small as children's toys, bobbing in secluded coves.

She stole a glance at Nico's hard, silent profile. How could she have ever thought he was a gigolo? He looked more like a warrior.

"Stop! Now! And let me drive before you smash us into the mountain!" she cried.

"No."

"You're driving like a maniac."

"I know what I'm doing." He spoke between clenched teeth.

He did seem to be skirting danger closely, not recklessly seeking it. She decided he knew what he was doing.

"If you have a wreck, my insurance won't pay," she told him.

"I'll pay."

"Right. With your rich wife's money."

His eyes narrowed on the road. "You're wrong about that."

He slammed his foot on the accelerator and drove even faster. She covered her eyes with her hands when the whirl of mountains, blue sea, and their mad race on the winding drive carved on the verge of an abyss was more than she could bear. She was, however, peering through her fingers when he whipped past the sign that pointed to the high road that wound up to Ravello.

Forgetting her fear, she turned on him. "Where are we going?"

He said only, "You'll see," as the car left the main road, traveled through a wooded hillside and began to climb.

"I want to go to my hotel."

His glance was quick and unsmiling. "Later. I told you that I had to show you something."

The Fiat snarled up a steep hill lined with cypress trees and towering hot-pink oleanders on one side and dazzling views of the sapphire Gulf of Salerno on the other. Finally, they reached a tall golden gate that surely stood on the top of the mountain.

"Where are we?" she whispered.

He wrenched the Fiat to a stop and spoke blistering Italian into a little box on his side of the car.

No sooner had he said his name than the gates whooshed open, revealing an immense, opulent, late-Gothic palazzo with Moorish curlicues. The grand palazzo looked out on a park of lush lawns and bright flower beds that had been carved out of the craggy mountainside. Although not all that large, the palazzo was gorgeous. Somehow, Regina knew that men of taste and immense wealth had created it.

"Where are we?" she repeated, both her curiosity and wonder expanding.

Wordlessly, he drove her inside. When the gates clanged behind them, she felt a momentary frisson of panic, terrified she might be trapped in the wonderland forever.

Then she caught her breath because, on closer inspection, the palazzo standing in its sea of green with cliffs on one side and the sea on the other was *so* beautiful. She had never been anywhere so beautiful.

"Where are we?"

"This is the Palazzo Romano." He spoke in a low, dead voice. His blue eyes regarded her warily. "It is one of my family's *many* ancestral palazzos. A favorite, in fact, even though it is really only a small country home for us."

"Now you're telling me you're rich?"

She scanned the high, pink walls of the palazzo perched on its cliff top promontory and felt eyes, unseen and unfriendly, watching her. She stiffened at the thought that she was being judged inferior in some way and was unwelcome here.

"You mean this is your future wife's home," she exclaimed.

"The Palazzo Romano will be her home. Yes. But only when she marries me."

The Palazzo Romano? Hadn't she read about it in her guide-book?

What? Was he telling the truth? Surely not.

He got out of the Fiat and went around to Regina's side and opened her door. When he put his hand on her arm, she didn't resist his help getting out.

"Look," she said, glancing up at the windows again and feeling cold all over. "I see. It's beautiful. Impressive even."

"I think most people would be impressed," he replied, his tone oddly distant. "The paparazzi certainly are."

He took her hand and pulled her through the gardens, which were vast and well tended. They passed a pool with a pair of swans, countless fountains and statuary before they drew to a stop in an ancient cloister.

"This is my favorite part of the house," he said.

"It's quite charming."

"I used to play here with my sister when I was a little boy."

Was he telling her the truth?

"My family has a palace in Florence that is filled with four hundred years of fabulous art. We have extensive vineyards outside of Florence, as well. In the centuries when the Romanos really counted, they were known by nothing more than their surname, like the other great families of Florence."

She took a deep breath. The warm air was sweet with the scent of flowers.

"It was only when we started losing power that we gained our titles," he continued.

He hadn't missed a beat. He certainly had his little story, if that's what it was, down pat.

"You're good," she said.

"The Romanos were made marquises quite late in their history, in 1750, when the Dukes of Lorraine started handing out dignities to win the support of the town's patrician establishment. At first, the family scorned the titles. Not too long afterward, we were made princes."

When he took her arm and led her out of the cloisters, the tall parapets and towers looming above her seemed even bigger and more intimidating. Again, she had the distinct feeling that she was unwelcome.

There was a formality and a perfection to everything. There wasn't a single weed in any of the flower beds, nor a wilted petal on any of the roses. And yet, no gardeners could be seen.

"Very impressive," she repeated, wondering if he really was a Romano. More likely, he was a poor relation, or maybe the son of one of the absent gardeners.

"I understand that you want to live in a palace. Lots of people do…even in the States, which is why we have MacMansions…." She caught herself. She was babbling.

When they rounded a curve in the gravel path and she saw her Fiat, she said, "Just take me to my hotel."

He stopped. "Listen to me. This is only one of my homes. *Now. It is mine now. Before my marriage.* Or rather, it is one of my family's many homes. It might interest you to know that it has been in the family seven hundred years."

She stared at him. Was he serious?

"Do you work for these people or something?" she asked gently.

"Oh, most definitely." He smiled, but his eyes were wary and cold. "If we went inside, you would be greeted with dozens of gilded chambers hung with tapestries and baroque chandeliers, not to mention paintings by the great masters, as well as paintings of my ancestors—who resemble me."

"Really? I'm sure it's all very lovely."

"The older woman you saw in the Maserati is my grandmother. Only don't ever tell her I said she was old. The blonde you saw me with is my mother, the Principessa Donna Gloriana Romano. My father, Principe Don Livio Carlo Romano, died five years ago. My mother wants me, his heir, to do my duty and marry the Principessa Donna Viola Eugenia di Frezano. In fact, my mother is insisting upon it. Yesterday, I gave her my word that I would call Viola, whose family is as eager for the marriage as mine. The paparazzi, not that they know anything, say I'm the most eligible bachelor in Europe."

She stared at his dark, patrician brow which was knit, at his aquiline nose, at his magnificent warrior's physique and felt an unpleasant jolt of recognition. He looked tough and arrogant enough to be a conquering prince of old. And he did look a little familiar.

"You're a prince? You're really a prince?" Regina searched his incredibly handsome face for some sign of triumph or conceit. Humility was all she saw.

"I wish to hell I wasn't," he said. "I wish to hell I could change who I am and follow the path of my heart, which would be a life with you, *tesorina*."

Tall, dark and handsome…and an Italian prince to boot. If only she were a princess, too, maybe her life could be a fairy tale.

But Viola was the princess in this fairy tale.

"Thank you for bringing me here," Regina said grimly.

"You must understand—I cannot betray my family."

"I do understand." Her heart was thundering, threatening to explode. "What I don't understand is why you didn't tell me the truth in the beginning."

"I'm sorry."

"Not good enough!"

"I know."

"All those people in the bar knew who you were?"

"Yes."

"Including those girls who were flirting with you?"

"Yes."

"You deliberately made a fool of me!"

"No. At first, I thought you knew. Later, I played along with your fantasy."

Her feet crunched noisily in the gravel as she strode to her car. She opened the passenger side door for herself. He got in behind the wheel.

"Are you all right?" he asked.

"Just take me home."

He started the Fiat. "You could stay…indefinitely," he said.

"In Italy?"

"With me."

"Are you asking me to be your mistress?"

He was gracious enough not to restate his intent.

"We could sleep together while you courted and married your princess?" Regina let out a long sigh and then a little scream. She banged the dashboard with her fists just as she'd banged on so many tables in courtrooms. Then she turned to him again.

"Ohhh! You think I'd settle for that? How could you even ask me such a thing?"

"I love you. I want you. It might be the only way."

"Haven't you got any principles?"

"I thought I did, until I met you."

"Do people like you, princes who live in palazzos, I mean, get everything they want, just because they want it?"

"No. They follow the rules. They are taught that all that matters is influence, power and money. They are taught to marry one of their own kind, so that they can perpetuate their families' titles, pedigrees and traditions on the solid foundations of their wedded fortunes. It's all exceedingly dull."

"Poor little rich prince, who must try to get richer and richer. I'm not going to feel sorry for you, you know."

"I'm not asking you to. I just want you to understand my

future engagement. Viola's family is richer than mine. The tax man is vicious. For a thousand years my family has lived here and in palazzos grander than this."

"And they want to be in them for another thousand?"

"Aristocrats do tend to take the long view. Unfortunately, my father lost quite a lot of money, so the family's future rests on my shoulders."

"Which fortunately are quite wide." She paused. "Okay. I see. I understand. I wish you the best. Now, will you take me to my hotel?"

"Just so you understand what is expected of me and why. If I don't marry Donna Viola, I betray my family."

"I said I understood. But that's it. Don't pretend you're a good guy. Not when you lied to me."

Thankfully he didn't remind her she'd thought she'd been hiring a gigolo.

When he started the car, the gates opened as if by magic. Again, she was aware of unfriendly eyes watching her depart.

"Like I said, at first, I thought you knew who I was, that maybe you were a fortune hunter," he said.

"That's so lame."

"It's happened before."

"American tourists recognize you and chase you?"

"Yes. The paparazzi chase me, too."

"And do you always accommodate them as you did me? The other women, I mean?"

He muttered something under his breath. Then he lifted his chin and stared at the road coldly. He drove back to her hotel silently and slowly, but somehow his carefulness stung her like a deliberate insult.

"Well, do you accommodate them?" she goaded.

He flinched. Good. She'd gotten to him.

"No," he said, grinding the word between his teeth. "Damn it, no!"

"Then why did you decide to go slumming with me?"

He jerked the car into a driveway on the side of the narrow

road just as a bus whipped past them so fast their little car rattled violently. Then he turned and pulled her roughly into his arms.

"I wanted you. I had to have you. I didn't care about anything else. I'd felt so horrible for so long and there you were—so sweet and adorable. I thought we'd have one night."

"Why is this happening?"

"Hell if I know why. Hell if I know. Do you think I wanted it to? Damn it, now I want a lifetime. And I can't have it."

Before she could say anything, his mouth came down on hers, searing, punishing. His large hands spanned the back of her waist, his palms burning through her thin cotton T-shirt as he pressed her curves against the hard contours of his body.

At the first taste of his lips, her anger left her. So did her pride. Her heart thudded slowly, painfully. Then her arms climbed his neck and hung on for dear life.

Yes, for dear life because he was life itself. Because he was everything.

She had no idea how long they sat there on the side of the road while trucks and buses roared past them. Finally, he got control of himself again and gave a hard jerk out of her arms only to gaze back at her in shock.

She was as thoroughly shaken as he. She saw that his hands trembled as he started the Fiat. Somehow that made her feel a little better. So, he wasn't a total bastard after all.

When he reached the hotel, he cut the engine. Before he could get out and come around to her side, she flung her door open and raced to the hotel. She'd left her key at the desk, so Nico was able to catch up to her at the elevator.

"Cara…"

"Go! Just go! Marry your princess! Or principessa! Do whatever! Be happy!"

She punched a golden button on the wall and two gold elevator doors opened. She stepped inside.

"Cara!"

The doors closed.

She punched the number to her floor. When she got out, she

stepped onto a belvedere and saw him three stories below talking to the same short, plump man she'd seen him with that first night. His cousin, Massimo, she thought. His genie.

They looked up and saw her. Nico's blue eyes blazed. His dark brows lifted.

A single glance was enough to cut her heart in two.

To hell with him!

She gave a little cry and ran to her room.

Seven

Nico paced *Simonetta*'s deck with a vengeance. Massimo watched him with exasperation and amusement while sipping Pinot Grigio. Then Nico saw a flash of white on shore.

He grabbed his binoculars and ran to the railing to stare at the slim brunette in a white sundress with a flower in her hair. She had suddenly materialized on the seaside bench as if she were a supernatural being.

"It's Cara."

Massimo laughed. "Naturally. You two are like a pair of brainless magnets in heat."

"Don't laugh, Cousin."

"The paparazzi will love this."

"They haven't been around much since *Simonetta*'s funeral. I've been too damn dull."

"Worse than dull. Dead."

Nico set down the binoculars and rushed to the stern of *Simonetta*. He hopped into his sleek, black tender and began throwing off the lines, which Massimo caught with one hand, careful not to spill his wine.

"Do you want a ride to shore?" Nico started the engine.

"No, thanks. She'll be gone in a day or two. I'll have you sulking and grieving all to myself soon enough."

"Don't remind me."

"So, enjoy and I'll kill the last of the Pinot."

Nico waved. Massimo held up his wineglass in a mock toast.

Two minutes later, Nico was striding up the beach. Cara saw him and got up slowly.

Again she was wearing a white gardenia, and the paleness of the flower made her dark hair and brows and wide, luminous eyes seem all the more dramatic. She looked so young, lovely, and vulnerable, he was thoroughly disconcerted.

"I'm weak," she said. "I couldn't bear my room alone, thinking that I would never see you again, knowing you were so near. I'm sorry about—"

"Don't." He took her hand, kissed her fingertips. "I understand completely. I'm just so glad you're here. I want to spend every free second I have with you."

For the rest of my life, he thought grimly.

"I don't want to think about the future," she said, her voice as desperate as his own emotions.

"Are you hungry?"

Her brilliant dark eyes lifted to his. "A cappuccino, maybe." He read her hunger for other things.

"I know the perfect place, and it has the best gelato in all of Italy."

"Really?" The excitement in her voice made his throat catch. She was looking at him, and it was easy to see her mind was not on sampling gelato.

"I'm something of a gelato addict," he murmured.

"I didn't know that. I'm glad to know that. Gelato, huh? That's all it takes to tempt you?" She squeezed his hand. "For me, it's chocolate."

He threaded his fingers through hers and led her to a nearby terrace restaurant on a cliff overlooking a tranquil cove. Under a canopy of dangling wisteria blossoms, he ordered cappuccinos and grilled calamari. Then more cappuccinos and a vanilla gelato for himself and a chocolate gelato for her, chocolate because she'd pointed to it and clapped like a child.

He liked watching her eat and drink while the gulls sailed above them and the wisteria stirred in the breeze.

"Would you like to go for a boat ride?" he asked as she licked the last bit of chocolate gelato off her spoon.

She stared at the blue water and then at him. "If you want to."

"I do."

"Okay then, yes." She laughed. "I want to. Very much."

Once they were in his tender and moving slowly away from the beach out into the glistening harbor, he said, "We can go fast or slow. Whatever you want."

"Fast," she said. "I want to fly."

"First, we see the yachts. Up close. They are quite impressive. But we have to go slow in the marina itself."

"Slow or fast. They're both good." She smiled, as delighted as a child with a new puppy, and he felt thrilled to be with her as they motored from yacht to yacht while he told her stories of the people who owned them.

When she pointed to villas and palazzos that dotted the hills, he told her their histories, as well. An hour or two sped by. The sun began to sink, the sky and sea exploding in brilliant color.

"People used to travel this coast only by boat," he said.

"After our nerve-racking drive, I can see why."

"Do you know how Amalfi got its name?" he asked.

"No."

"Hercules loved a nymph named Amalfi. When she died he buried her here because he thought this was the most beautiful place on earth. And then he named it after her."

"How romantic."

"I know a lovely sea cave that's even more romantic. We'll go there later. After the sun goes down."

Time seemed to evaporate when he was with her, and he felt complete. He cut the motor and they drifted on the slick gilded surface, holding each other tightly, until the sun sank and the light went out of the sky and sea.

As he stroked her hand, he thought about his family's palazzos that were filled with the portraits of generations of his ancestors.

"They remind us who we are and where we come from," his mother often said.

As a boy, Nico had stood under the massive gilt frames at length while his parents had told him about their ancestors' lives. "You resemble them," they'd said.

Outwardly, he resembled them. So why hadn't he ever felt he was one of them? Instead, he'd felt trapped by their traditions and their demands and most of all by their insatiable need for wealth.

Only with Cara, now in this little boat for the first time in his life, did he feel the easiness that comes when one is in tune with one's true self. Not even Simonetta had been able to free him of the life he'd been born to and its pressures.

He breathed in the sea air and pulled Cara closer. With her, he felt the possibility of discovery of a new kind of life. Which was absurd, of course.

He'd known from the first that their brief idyll couldn't last. He'd known his title and its responsibilities would be an insurmountable barrier. When the paparazzi discovered his yacht offshore, they'd start hounding him and thereby discover her, too.

Not wanting to dwell on the negatives, he motored to a sea cave where they removed their clothes and made love. Then he took her back to the marina. There he got his red Alpha Romeo, and they raced along a curving black ribbon of asphalt up to an exclusive nightclub on a mountaintop terrace, where he was known but would not be bothered. They danced and, in between dances, they held hands and sipped Pinot Grigio at a corner table in the moonlight.

"You can hear the traffic even up here," she marveled.

"Sound carries in the hills."

"You should have told me that when we were in that abandoned farmhouse."

Laughing, he caught her hand fiercely and kissed it. Under the big, quiet night at their private little table, they talked and talked, opening their souls and hearts so wide he wondered if he could ever close himself off to all emotion again.

"I could talk to you forever," he said.

"Why? Why is this happening?"

"You think everything happens for a reason? Not knowing the answer to that question is one of life's great mysteries."

She was a mystery he wanted to solve. He wanted to do everything with her in the short time they had left together. But of course, all too soon it was three in the morning and she was yawning.

"I'm boring you," he said.

"No, it's the wine. It makes me sleepy."

Taking her hand, he led her to the Alpha Romeo and drove her back to her hotel.

"I had a wonderful time," she said, as he helped her out of the car.

She seemed all right. Then a sob caught in her throat.

"What's wrong?" he whispered.

"Why do I need you so much?" she whispered.

His breath left his lungs on a shudder.

"I'm not usually such a crybaby." She brushed at her damp cheeks.

"Cara—"

Then she was in his arms. He had no idea how she got there, only that she belonged.

"I need to pack. But I—I need *you* more." She traced the shape of his face with loving fingertips. "How am I ever—"

When her hand trailed across his lips, he kissed them one by one.

She stared up at him for a long moment. Then she shut her eyes as if memorizing his features. He shut his eyes, too, and saw her lovely face behind his lids, every detail was perfect.

"I'm glad you took so many pictures," he said.

"Me, too." She spoke through more tears.

Even before she sprang forward a little and pressed her soft curves more tightly against his body, clinging to him, his arms clenched around her waist.

He remembered wishing he could bring Simonetta back to

life. Wishing for a second chance. Wishing that he could hold her just one more time.

How much harder would it be to let Cara go when he knew she was still alive in this world?

He pushed his hands under the straps of her sundress so violently a strap tore. He wanted to hold her, to bury himself in her warm flesh, to possess her so completely she could never bear to leave him.

"Not here," she pleaded in a soft, urgent voice.

His mouth found hers anyway.

"Someone might see," she insisted.

"Must you always take charge?" He kissed her hard.

She laughed a little. "You keep asking me that."

"And?" His own voice was rough.

"Only sometimes." She snuggled closer.

He buried his mouth against her breast and sucked at her nipple, tasting warm, salty-sweet woman, as well as wet, cotton sundress.

"Stop…before we can't," she pleaded. "Security might find us."

Or worse, the paparazzi.

Gulping in a savage breath, he set her aside. He raked his hair with his hands. Then he adjusted his collar and tucked his shirt back inside his jeans. He stepped back a few inches.

She straightened and stood a little stiffly, as if wary of him, too. When she turned and marched toward the hotel, her head held high, he tagged along behind her, his attention on the sexy sway of her cute butt.

When she went to the desk for her key, he waited by the elevator. She was coy and sedate and studiously proper in the lobby. When the elevator doors closed, whisking them upstairs, she stood as far from him as the small golden box with glass sides would allow. But when the doors opened on her floor, she gave a wild cry and chased him down the hall.

The moment they were inside her room, she shot the bolt and ran into his arms. Catching her, he cupped her chin and lifted her mouth to his.

In no mood for tenderness, she tore at his fly and then at the buttons of his shirt.

When a cool draft of air hit his naked chest, he laughed. Then he unzipped her sundress and watched it spill down her tiny waist and flaring hips to the glossy tiles. She kicked her sandals across the room. Then she sprang into his arms again, teasing him with her mouth and tongue, kissing his lips open, each hungry kiss promising and demanding more than her last.

Lifting her high, he let her slide down his body. She wrapped her legs around his waist, and he squeezed her tightly, holding her there for an infinite moment before carrying her to bed. It felt like long hours ago since he'd made love to her in the sea cave and had brought her to climax with his tongue.

She was slim and beautiful. Why did it keep amazing him that she felt perfect underneath him?

Her wide, dark eyes met his. When he smiled, her lips parted and those gorgeous eyes shone. She was like the moon and the sun, giving off light but reflecting his, too.

With his lips he touched her smooth forehead, her silken hair, her eyebrows, even her eyelashes. He wanted her babies, and the thought that he'd been born to a complicated life and couldn't have her or those babies caused a visceral pain near his heart.

She was leaving in little more than twenty-four hours. Suddenly, the urge to possess her now, this minute, forever, over-powered him.

"Cara. Oh, Cara." Forgetting himself, the love words he used as his hands roamed her body were Italian. He cupped her breasts, caressed her waist and thighs. Then he slid a finger inside and stroked her there, too. When he had her quivering and her breath almost stopped, his pulse raced out of control.

His mouth found her lips again, teasing her tongue with the tip of his, playing and sucking until her nails dug deep into his shoulders. Until she moaned.

"I want you so much," she murmured as she crawled under him. Her skin felt feverishly hot as her arms locked around his neck. He was on his knees, and her sleek body was open and ready beneath him. When his heavy sex touched her entrance, she gasped and then licked her lips. Without more foreplay, he plunged inside her. Buried to the hilt, he went still, his blood pounding in his temple. He wanted this moment to last forever.

She was slick, tight, wet. And hot, so hot.

And then she moved, and he went wild.

"Oh, Nico... Nico..."

He slammed into her again and again. Soon, he was driving faster and faster until she was screaming and he was out of control, fighting himself as he hurtled over the edge.

"Don't stop. Just take me with you."

Then she was crying and shuddering, too. He pounded into her two more times before he exploded.

They held on to each other. He caressed her hair and spoke Italian again, his heart making promises he could never keep while she said his name over and over again in the sweetest, throatiest whisper he'd ever heard.

When their heartbeats finally slowed, she ran her fingers through his damp hair.

He heard her muffled sob.

"I never cry," she said.

"You keep saying that."

"Only with you."

He clasped her fiercely. Damn it. Why had he been born Principe Don Nico Carlo Giovanni Romano? How could he watch her get on a plane and fly away?

She would marry someone else. Have another man's children.

But if he defied his mother and the rest of his family, and married Cara, such a union would be considered a disaster by everyone in his world—especially his mother.

His fist gripped a tangle of sheets as Cara continued to whisper love words in his ear. He wanted this night to last forever.

Their damp, hot bodies still joined, he fell asleep with her arms wrapping him loosely.

Eight

When Regina woke up hours later in Nico's arms, the damp sea air smelled of gardenia and felt cool against her skin. Silver moonlight washed the bed and him. She knew the exact moment his long lashes lifted drowsily and his eyes caught the light.

"Cara?" he whispered, nuzzling closer.

She fingered the ornate cross on her throat. "I'm right here, darling."

"Are you all right?"

"Better than all right." She touched his sex. "You're so big."

"They say size doesn't matter."

"*They* don't always know everything. Besides, that's hearsay."

When she sighed in contentment, he took her hands and kissed her fingers. She felt delicious, satiated, complete.

So, this was what love felt like. At least now she knew. Some people never found this kind of easiness or passion ever, although her happiness was made bittersweet by the knowledge that she had to leave him.

At least I have him now.

She touched his large maleness gently, just enough to make contact. She smiled possessively, and then yawned because his warmth had made her sleepy again. She went limp against him and soon was asleep once more. The next time she awoke, the sun had tinged the bedroom with slanting, pink radiance. Nico was already awake beside her, his expression tender, his dark eyes shining as he watched her.

Never had she felt more protected or cherished.

"How long have you been awake?" she whispered, feeling a little shy.

"A while. You're so beautiful."

"So are you," she said, running her hand down from his throat over his magnificent brown chest.

The sheet wrapped her waist, leaving her breasts exposed. She couldn't believe that lying naked beside him, even after all the sex, could feel so right, so easy.

"You don't seem all that grand. Shouldn't a prince be cruel and haughty?"

"You're right. I command you to make love to me all over again."

"I have to take a shower first."

"We could take one together," he whispered.

"All right." Using her knuckles, she stroked his rough, shadowed chin. "Why did I have to meet you the last two days I was here? Life isn't fair."

"Life never is." He closed his eyes, but not before she saw his pain.

She squeezed her eyes shut, too.

"I came to Italy to find myself. And I have. Only now when I go back…"

"What?"

Biting her lip, she shook her head, not ready to admit to him that she would be leaving a big piece of herself behind.

"Maybe this is better," she said brightly. "I'll always think I found the perfect love. I'll remember how passionate you were, yet gentle, and I'll compare you to all other men."

"Damn it. Do you think I want to hear about other men?"

"I'll never get annoyed with you for forgetting my birthday or our anniversary."

"As if I would. I plug important dates into my digital assistant. Which reminds me, what's your cell number?"

When she told him, he wrote it down on the hotel notepad by the telephone. He ripped off the page and then scribbled something on the next sheet.

"This is my private cell number…just in case you ever need me for anything."

"You'll never get impatient with me for keeping you waiting because I can't decide what earrings I should wear or because I've lost my keys. Did I ever tell you I lose my keys all the time? We won't fuss because I spend too much money on clothes or furniture. I like to shop—I think I told you that. I buy the most atrocious things at flea markets and garage sales—horrible purple sofas for a dollar with the stuffing coming out."

"Shut up."

"We can always imagine our children would have been perfect, dark-haired angels with enchanting dispositions, little prodigies who potty trained at one. And our sons will be…virile, athletic and great scholars."

He put a fingertip against her lips, and she stopped herself at last.

"Sorry, I'm babbling."

"How could your babies be anything other than darling little prodigies or our sons anything but pint-size studs?"

"You don't know what I was like as a kid," she teased.

"I was a bit of a handful myself. Two nannies were assigned to me."

"High-maintenance?"

"I'm an aristocrat. It comes with the territory."

"From having that supersize appendage?"

"Would you stop it with that? I was always scaling the castle walls, flying kites off them. After I nearly dived off a parapet to reach one kite I lost, I was confined to the nurseries and the gardens with my two nannies or with Tiberio."

"Tiberio?"

"I owe my life to my family's majordomo, Tiberio Abruzzi. I was awfully hard on all the antiques, too. By the time I was eighteen, every time I sat down, priceless brocade tore and fourteenth-century gilt wood shattered. Pieces were constantly having to be restored."

"I really had better take that shower."

"With me, remember?"

When she raced into the bath and turned on the hot water, he followed her inside the steamy, white-tiled cubicle.

When he closed the door, her nipples brushed his arm. She giggled because of the tightness of the space and the immense size of his dark body.

"There's no way to move without touching you."

He cupped her breasts, and she shivered.

"Exactly," he whispered, lowering his mouth and sucking each nipple until they were as hard as berries.

"You keep accusing me of being bossy. Now I have to live up to that. Stand against the wall, Your Highness."

When he stayed where he was, she placed her hand squarely against his chest and pushed him backward.

"Hell, nobody calls me that," he muttered.

"Spread your legs, Your Highness!"

When his legs moved apart, she sank to her knees and looked up at the coils of dark hair and at his other, impressive stuff, playfully, as warm water streamed over her head. Without a word, her hand circled his huge, erect organ.

"Definitely, it's Your Highness," she said.

He growled low in his throat.

"Maybe we should call you Your Bigness," she said as she buried her face against his groin. "Or Your Hugeness."

"I'm almost beginning to like Your Highness."

Then she began to lick him, up and down and all around. With every delicate stroke, he grew harder and tighter and bigger until, finally, he burst in her mouth.

He began to whisper to her in Italian.

"How I love it when you speak Italian."

"How I love it when you do the things you do."

Very tenderly he lifted her up. Encircling her with his arms, he held her close against his chest for a long time.

"Good thing the hotel is five star." He turned off the faucets and opened the shower door.

"What?" She felt as limp as a noodle as he toweled her off.

"The hot water never gets cold."

"I wouldn't think you, being a prince, would know anything about running out of hot water."

"Four-hundred-year-old castles leave a lot to be desired."

She brushed her teeth while he watched, which was kind of nice and almost as intimate as the sex. He observed her darken her brow with a pencil and put on mascara, too.

She opened her lipstick and whirled on him. "I'm going to mess up if you don't go."

When he didn't budge, she couldn't stop staring at His Bigness, which caused prickles of heat to climb her spine.

"I like knowing what you do in the morning to put yourself together," he said.

"I want you to think I'm a natural beauty."

He leaned against the doorjamb.

"Would you just go? Or at least put on a towel. My hand is shaking."

"Hot for me again?"

She forced her attention away from His Bigness.

"No! What I am is starved...for breakfast." And she was. Much to her surprise, she really was.

"So, you worked up an appetite."

"Why don't you be a good boy, *Your Highness,* and call room service? I want some of those delicious strawberries again and an omelet and more of those fabulous croissants with the gooey chocolate inside them. Can you see if they have hot chocolate, too?"

"*Bossy.* It's getting harder and harder to remember who's the blue blood."

He grabbed a towel off the rack, whipped it around his waist and wandered off to do her bidding, so that, at last, she could put on her lipstick and dress in peace.

She smiled when she heard his deep voice on the phone ordering coffee, omelets, berries, fresh orange juice and croissants.

"You're forgetting the hot chocolate," she yelled.

He laughed and ordered it for her.

How easy it was to imagine he would be with her every morning for the rest of her life.

The next few moments were filled with bliss and peace. He asked her what she wanted to do for the day. She handed him one of the long lists she'd made of the various possibilities.

He laughed. "We'd need two weeks."

"You pick," she whispered.

"I see you listed a sightseeing boat to view the coast. I'll take you out on *Simonetta*. You'll save money, and I'll have you all to myself."

She put a new smart card in her camera and snapped dozens of pictures of him wearing only a towel, and then, when he was dressed, more shots of him out on her balcony with the gulf and the mountains behind him.

He stole her camera and photographed her, too. Then she set the camera up on the railing and made the necessary adjustments so that it would photograph them together. But every time she tried to pose or get him to pose for the camera, he'd cup her breast or buttock and kiss her lips in such a way that the picture probably looked like she was swallowing his tongue.

"I'm not going to be able to show anyone my X-rated pictures."

"I want you to remember me." His mouth stretched lazily into a grin. "Like this!"

The flash went off as he put his mouth to her breast again.

When the expected knock sounded at the door, she jumped away from him like a startled wild thing. Not wanting the hotel waiter to see her erect nipple or the telltale damp spot on her sundress, she turned and began to rearrange her hair and the folds of her full skirt and let Nico stride to the door.

When he threw it open, she heard men, yelling questions.

"Prince Nico, who is she—"

When she turned, a dozen flashes whitened Nico's chiseled, tanned face.

He swore vividly in Italian or, at least, she imagined the harsh, rapid-fire bursts to be colorful curses.

With a little cry, she ran to him, hoping to protect him from the horde and their cameras, not realizing that her sudden appearance would energize the demons.

Like a spark set to gasoline, their roar was an explosion.

"Signorina—"

"Get back, you little fool!" Jumping in front of her, Nico slammed the door.

"Are you all right?" he demanded distractedly.

"F-fine."

She placed her hand gently on his arm.

Furious, he jerked free of her and strode to the phone and rang security.

"Paparazzi! Get someone up here! Fast! Get rid of them!"

Nine

The hot chocolate and omelets never came and were forgotten. Regina had lost her appetite, so what did it matter? Nothing mattered except that the paparazzi had found them and that Nico was upset.

If only he would stop pacing back and forth.

"Grab your things. I've got to get you out of here before these jackals swarm the gates."

"Haven't they already?"

"This is nothing," he said.

Too agitated to fold clothes and pack them with tissue, she opened drawers and dumped the contents into her suitcase.

"No," he said, pausing in the middle of the room. "On second thought, I'll send Massimo up to do this. We need to get you out of this mess, if we can."

When she tried to pick up one small suitcase, his hand covered hers, and he forced her to put it down.

"But—"

"Trust me. I'll take care of you. Massimo is on the family payroll."

Nico rang someone and rattled more high-speed, impatient Italian. She could catch only a word here and there, but she surmised, by his friendlier tone, that he'd called his cousin Massimo.

What had happened to the romantic mood after their shower? Suddenly her beloved Nico was not only a prince but a furious stranger.

She'd known him—what? All of two days.

He was an Italian prince who'd been indiscreet with a young woman. This probably wasn't the first time.

Why hadn't she thought of this before? What she felt for him was a once-in-a-lifetime experience. But how many times had this happened to him? How many other women had lost their hearts to him?

Who wouldn't fall for him? His looks, his manners, his elegance, his abilities in bed and on the dance floor; not to mention the title, the yacht and the palazzos. Or *his size.* For centuries, his kind had been groomed from birth to charm, rule and seduce.

He would forget her in a week, and then he would court and marry his princess and make blue-blooded babies with oversize ding-dongs. If Regina were wise, she would look at their little adventure as a unique vacation experience, something to chat about with her friend Lucy or her sister Susana over a lingering lunch. Maybe she could even brag a little about *the appendage.*

Regina bit her lip and swallowed hard. The day that had dawned like a golden dream now felt cold and empty.

Nico set the phone in its cradle. "I've arranged for a car and a driver. We leave by a private entrance in five minutes."

In less time than that, the phone rang again. When he hung up, he took her arm to lead the way. At the door, she stopped. Then she ran back and seized the painting of the little boy playing in the sand.

"Leave it," he said.

"I'll carry it on the plane."

Regina scanned the tapestries, paintings and antiques and tried to act as if she wasn't the least bit intimidated by the opulent grandeur of the beautiful salon. In truth, she felt like a naughty little girl who'd run away from a paid tour and had gotten lost in the grand palazzo and would be found and scolded for such mischief.

Where was Nico? Why didn't he come? Had he forgotten she even existed?

His regal mother in her silk designer suit and exquisite pearls had gone through the motions of behaving graciously to Regina, greeting the limousine with a frozen smile. She'd even extended an icy hand to Regina and had offered tea, which Regina had desired but politely refused, not wanting to put the princess to more trouble. The princess had pursed her lips. The next moment, Regina had been asked if she would be a dear and wait while the princess and Nico discussed "the situation" alone. When Regina had nodded, a tall, imperious man in a stiff, black suit that emphasized his height and gauntness, introduced to her as Tiberio Abruzzi, had whisked her out of the way and escorted her here.

Glancing at her watch every five seconds, Regina tried to sit as still as one of the marble statues. She really tried, but the brocade chair was stiff and she'd been here nearly an hour. And she didn't have a clue about what was going on.

Every time she turned toward the door, her gaze met Abruzzi's forbidding black eyes. His face was shaped like a skull, his skin white as a cadaver. Was he as old as the castle, or rather, the palazzo?

Definitely, he'd been ordered to watch her. Thus, she'd sat as still as she could for as long as she could with her hands folded neatly across her lap.

Then like a toddler restrained too long, she burst out of her chair. The ancient chair groaned, and when she began to pace the parquet floor, Abruzzi's brooding gaze followed her as it seemed the painted eyes of Nico's ancestors did, as well. Feeling self-conscious, she walked the length of the golden oak-and-porcelain-filled Gothic sitting room and then retraced her steps.

She stopped in front of a portrait of a staid, elderly man in red velvet, who had a particularly disquieting stare. A cardinal? One of Nico's predecessors? Had he been painted by one of the old masters? When she moved closer to inspect the artist's signature, Abruzzi stepped closer.

Warned, she jumped back from the painting, and like a shadow, he receded to his former place. Afraid that the glittering antique glass-and-gem-studded snuff boxes on all the little tables were worth a fortune, Regina steered clear of them as she continued walking.

Feeling trapped and out of place in such dazzling surroundings, she stepped to a tall window and looked out at the lush, sloping lawns. Two white swans gliding serenely on a dark pool caught her attention.

How she envied them their beautiful garden. Was it only yesterday that Nico had brought her here and told her who he really was and all that was expected of him?

Not wanting to dwell on any of that, she went back to her chair and sank down again onto the hard little cushion. No sooner had the spindly wooden legs made a cracking sound again than she wanted to spring to her feet once more.

Instead, she tilted her head back and stared up at the ornate ceiling, where a profusion of angels swirled in colorful, painted robes.

When had it been painted? What story had been in the artist's mind? Beneath the ceiling, a chandelier from a later period blazed like ten thousand diamonds. Not that she had the slightest idea what period that might be.

Nico had probably been taught from birth the value of all these items. No doubt he appreciated their artistic worth. He was accustomed to fine things, fine homes. He knew famous people.

The Nico she knew saluted girls in bars with his beer bottle, went dancing on mountaintops at midnight, made love in dark sea caves. That Nico laughed and was tender, and she thought he had shown her something of his secret, innermost self. But his real life, the ordinary, methodic rhythm of his days, was spent here.

His tall, reed-thin mother hadn't said a word about how unsuitable Regina was. She'd simply left her in this room with its priceless furniture and jeweled snuff boxes, and the room had spoken volumes.

Regina thought of her parents' cluttered, three-bedroom tract house with its framed prints and recliners. She was from ordinary, middle-class, all-American stock, and more fortunate than most. But an accident of birth had thrown Nico into an extraordinarily exalted position that she could never belong to or begin to understand.

Impossible relationships. My specialty, she thought.

Measured footsteps rang faintly from the hall. Hoping for Nico, Regina sprang to her feet just as his tall, sharp-featured mother glided inside. Regina tried to smile, but her lips wouldn't move. His mother, obviously more practiced than Regina, managed a tight little pursing at the edges of her mouth.

"I didn't do this on purpose," Regina stammered.

A draft of icy air gusted between them in the ensuing silence.

His mother's lips moved. "Still, I'm sure you must understand how difficult this is for the family."

"I'm sorry."

"Well, we'll have to carry on the best way we know how," the Principessa Donna Gloriana Lucia Romano said. "This, too, shall pass, as they say." Again the rigid lifting at the corners of her mouth. "At least the press doesn't know who you are, and if you don't tell them—"

Where was Nico?

"Surely you don't think that I would—"

The Principessa Donna Gloriana arched her brows. "Of course not," she said softly.

Clearly, Gloriana saw Regina as the enemy.

"Massimo has arranged a new airline ticket for you. First class. Tonight."

So, she was to be bought off with a first-class ticket.

"Thank you."

Gloriana nodded, her decorum flawless. Did Regina only

imagine that she had a keen talent for using her careful manners and her regal bearing as weapons? Never had Regina felt more common and uncouth, nor so entirely inappropriate for Nico.

"Where's Nico?" Regina asked, in a crushed voice she barely recognized.

"Right here," rang his deep, cold voice from the doorway. "Did my mother tell you that everything has been arranged?"

Feeling even more chilled by the coldness in his tone, Regina nodded.

"Mother, we'd better go," he said.

With a look of resignation, the *principessa* joined him in the doorway.

Regina wanted to run past both of them and make her escape, but, of course, some reporter would probably find her. Then she would only make more trouble.

With a little shrug, she forced herself to walk slowly toward them. Thrusting her chin upward, she imitated his mother's haughty carriage so exactly Nico smiled. As Regina's heels clicked on the parquet, like fingers tapping a keyboard, his mother frowned.

Unable to maintain her regal act, Regina laughed nervously and ran into Nico's arms. Even though his body felt stiff and wary, he hugged her tightly. His mother's expression grew arctic.

Inside the limousine, Regina slumped against the leather seat. When Nico got in after another lengthy conversation with his mother, he wrapped his arms around Regina.

"I thought it went fairly well," he said. "You held your own with her."

Had she? "My luggage?"

"In the boot."

The chauffeur slammed doors and started the engine.

"And Massimo?"

"He's driven on ahead. He'll meet us. I'm afraid he'll have to escort you inside once we arrive at your terminal."

"I understand." Of course, she didn't. She was merely trying to sound brave and act sophisticated.

"The last thing I want is for you to be hurt because you became caught up in my life and family's position and all its complications. I don't want your name dragged through the mud."

"I'll be fine. It could never have worked out. We come from different worlds. This only proves—"

"Cara. Oh, Cara… Sometimes I wonder if all the things that separate us aren't rather shallow in these modern times. If we simply pursued this relationship, wouldn't the fuss die down? I've been lucky at making money. So what if you don't have a title or a fortune?"

"And your mother? Would she move on?"

"It wouldn't be easy for her, not in the beginning, but then she wouldn't have a choice, would she? She has too many responsibilities to dwell on a single disappointment."

Regina tried to imagine sharing Christmases and Easters with such a formidable mother-in-law. What would they talk about or do together? What sort of grandmother would she make? What sort of expectations for her grandchildren would she impose on their mother, the commoner?

Nico held her while the big black car sped along the Amalfi Drive. The limousine swept past spectacular views of mountains and sea. Normally, Regina would have had her nose pressed against the glass window like a puppy. Today, she was too aware of Nico and the short time she had left with him. Burying her head against his shoulder, she snuggled closer. She loved him so much she ached.

"I just wish we'd had today to make more memories together," she said aloud.

"We have the backseat of the limousine."

She focused on the square shape of the driver's head and cap. "But the chauffeur…"

"For a lawyer, you don't get around much."

"I'm in Italy."

"That's not what I meant."

Nico pressed a button, and a little wall went up between them and the driver. Door locks snapped.

"The windows are tinted," Nico said. "Our privacy is complete, *tesorina*."

The next thing she knew she was flat on her back and naked beneath him, and, as always, the sex was much more than sex. Oh, the gifts to her soul he bestowed with every kiss.

Once they reached the airport, she would never see him again. To say they made the most of what little time they had left would not be saying nearly enough.

Ten

Massimo walked Regina through the airport and helped her with her electronic ticket and bags. On their way to security, they passed a newsstand. A close-up of Nico's angry face, his hands raised to shield Regina from the cameras leaped out at her. His name was splashed across the front pages of two tabloids in two-inch headlines.

Regina's heart sank. She approached a counter to buy a paper, but Massimo laid a warning hand on her shoulder. "Let me," he said.

After she'd boarded the plane, alone with her hoard of news-print, she devoured the photographs of all the beautiful women with whom Nico's name had been linked. So many women. Then Regina read the articles, and each story chipped away at her self-confidence. Had she really been so special to him?

In the past, she'd read about celebrities, but reading about Nico and seeing her own blurred picture was entirely different. If Nico's mother had made her feel totally unsuitable, the lurid coverage of his numerous romances reinforced that point for her on a deeper level. His other women were so beautiful, so famous.

Could she, who was so bad at love, possibly have held his attention for much longer?

Fame, status and glamour are supposed to bring status and happiness, not to threaten or diminish it. Regina's hands shook as she closed and refolded the newspapers.

The flight attendant came up and asked her if she would like a drink.

She shook her head and wiped at her eyes. "No, thank you."

"He's so darling, no?" the woman said, her gaze on Nico's picture. "Every woman in Italy…we all love him, and they say he has a big heart…." She leaned closer. "And a big *you-know-what* to love all the women in Italy, no? A flight attendant I know says she spent three days in Portofino with him once. And they never leave her hotel. They eat strawberries and chocolate and they drink champagne."

"Three days…lucky girl." Regina turned away. Her throat worked as she swallowed.

She wasn't crying.

She wasn't.

Nico sat with Viola, or rather as far as possible from her as he could, in the west wing of the palazzo, and thought that he'd never liked this grand room because the long French windows let in more shadow than sun. He looked past Viola's lovely blond head, past all the precious furniture and tapestries, to the simple glass door that led to the marble staircase, a dramatic and rather terrible renovation in the eighteenth century.

He had only to arise from the crescent-shaped sofa and fly to that door and then down those pale, stone stairs to escape this impossible interview that his mother had insisted upon as soon as he'd returned from Rome. He imagined streaking back to Rome on the autostrada in his red Alpha Romeo. He would be willing to fly any way he could, even coach, just so long as it got him to the States. To Austin, Texas.

His mother cleared her throat, and the sound snapped him back to his reality. For one final second, he saw Cara's face in his mind's eye, her dark hair, her dark, glistening eyes when he'd told her goodbye. At the vision, a jolt of white-hot pain hit him.

With an effort, Nico forced his attention to Viola.

Viola. Beautiful Viola. Marriage. Duty.

She was flushed and golden, but her beauty did not move him. Yes, she was as exquisitely formed as any of the cold marble masterpieces that graced the palazzo. When they married, heads would turn. The world would applaud them as a glittering, fairy-tale couple.

Viola smiled at him, a shy, uncertain smile. So, she was human after all. Too bad for her. Too bad for him. He did not want to hurt another woman.

His wife?

Dear God.

The mother of his children, his all-important heirs? He remembered Cara's perspiring, satiated body beneath his in the limousine, her shining eyes adoring him.

The shadows in the room darkened. He got up and strode to the windows, where he watched a pair of swans swimming together on their distant pool.

Swans mated for life. He found he could not tear his gaze from them.

His mother's chair creaked. She got up and led Viola to him.

Like a robot, he forced himself to turn and smile politely at the two women, to take Viola's hand. But instead of bringing the slender hand to his lips as he'd intended, he dropped it and turned back to watch the swans.

The glass door opened, and Tiberio announced that the photographers had arrived. His mother had told Nico earlier that pictures of him with Viola were necessary to quell the rumors about his mysterious romance.

"We must give the masses their fairy tale," she had said, the corner of her lips lifting. She didn't like the media, but she was not above manipulating the press any time it suited her interests.

Nico took Viola's hand in his again. "Shall we go?"

Watching, his mother smiled.

* * *

With a frown, Regina closed the file on her antique desk, then looked out the window of her lavish suite in the offices of Merrit, Riley & Whitt, her mind a world away. Seven stories beneath her, white diamonds danced on the emerald surface of Town Lake and flickered like silver medallions in the pecan trees. She saw a tall dark man on the red jogging trail, holding hands with a slim brunette who seemed to be looking up at him lovingly.

Regina squeezed her eyes shut and tried hard not to think about Nico.

She'd buried herself in work ever since she'd returned from Italy, her goal to forget Nico. But visions of his mouth, eyes and handsome dark face wouldn't vanish at her command. Now, she returned to her computer keyboard and saw that she'd received fifty-two e-mails in the two hours she'd spent reading the Hewit complaint. Most of them were from Black Boar.

Frowning again, she picked up the Hewit file. The complaint against Black Boar, an immense oil and gas drilling company that Regina's firm had represented on numerous previous occasions, seemed too legitimate to discard.

Rebecca Hewit had worked for Black Boar for twelve years. A methodical person, she'd carefully collected dozens of memos and documents that proved Black Boar was recklessly pouring carcinogenic toxins into a municipal water supply. While still on the job, Rebecca Hewit had told management to change its ways or she'd blow the whistle.

Black Boar had fired her. When Hewit didn't disappear quietly, Black Boar's corporate attorneys had made threatening calls. Rebecca Hewit had recorded them all. She'd spent the past six years collecting incriminating evidence, keeping a detailed diary, and printing and saving damaging e-mails.

Regina flipped through the formal complaint slowly. She even replayed one of the taped copies of a telephone threat. Black Boar's henchmen sounded rough, scary. Rebecca had grit. Maybe because her little girl had leukemia.

Just yesterday, Regina had watched her niece, Gina, play in her backyard kiddie pool, immersed in gallons of water.

Nobody except Black Boar executives and a few corrupt, local officials probably had any idea what Black Boar was up to.

Black Boar had to be stopped.

Not your job, sweetheart. You're on the other side. You're one of the bad guys.

Ever since middle school, Regina had known where she wanted to go. She'd made a plan, and she'd stuck to it. Valedictorian, National Merit Scholarship, Rice University, University of Texas Law School, Law Review. And those weren't all her honors.

Landing this job at Merrit, Riley & Whitt, the hottest firm in Austin, a year ago had been sweet. And she was still here, climbing the ladder, even dreaming that someday, maybe even before she was forty, she'd make partner.

The Hewit file burned her hand, and she dropped it.

Her plan didn't matter. None of the ambitions that had driven her so long mattered. She simply couldn't do this.

Why? What was wrong with her?

She was shaking when she picked up the file again, but when her hand finally steadied, she charged out of her office and down the hall to talk to Robert Riley, Sr., the man she'd once believed would be her father-in-law.

"I can't make Rebecca Hewit go away. I can't represent Black Boar."

Robert didn't open the file when she thrust it at him. He did listen patiently, at least, for nearly a full minute, before smiling paternally, indulgently.

"I don't like the way Italy affected you. You're different."

"Read the file."

"I don't need to. But you need to take a long lunch and think this over. Very carefully."

Not good.

She barged ahead with the rest of her speech anyway.

* * *

The sky was still ablaze in a magical way, as was the sea. But long shadows were creeping across the Amalfi shore.

Nico strode past the kiosk selling tabloids that ran front-page stories about his developing romance with Viola and saw only the beach and the empty bench under the lemon tree.

He stopped. He'd had a long day at the office, and he was tired and in no mood to see Viola.

He was still staring at Regina's bench when a woman in veils driving a red Maserati much too fast screeched to a stop behind him. She tapped her horn mischievously just to startle him.

"Damn." Nico spun on his heel. "Someday you'll give me a heart attack doing that."

"You won't be the first man. But never with a car." She winked at him. "Nico. My precious little love."

As always, his grandmother spoke to him in French. Since her mother had been French, it was her favorite language.

"Grand-mère," he said, smiling when he saw that the veils blowing about her papery, blue-veined skin were pink. "Aren't you too old for pink?"

She smiled wickedly, her face crinkling in all sorts of places it shouldn't have.

"Old. Awful word. Someday you'll know just how cruel it is. All my life people have tried to tell me how to live."

"Tried and failed."

"Thank goodness." She laughed. "I did listen to them when I was too young to know better…as you are now trying. And I failed. I think you have my genes."

How beautiful she still was, he thought, even if her skin, which had seen too much of the Mediterranean sun and had known the caresses of so many younger lovers, was as dry as parchment. Like a faded movie star, she had the painted brows and lips of another age, but beneath the makeup, her eyes were young and bright and shone with all the love for him that filled her generous heart.

"Get in," she commanded. "I've been trying to call you. Of

course, all your mother's dreadful people told me you weren't in. Gloriana even came to the phone and told me herself."

His mother, *her* daughter, did not approve of his relationship with his scandalous grandmother, the artist who'd divorced her royal prince, but doing so only after she'd done her duty and had produced heirs.

"So, my magic gardenia failed, and you gave up the beautiful American girl," she said as she sped along the narrow road, her focus on him instead of the traffic.

His eyes on the oncoming bus that was taking more than half of the road, he said nothing.

Fortunately, the bus stopped. *Grand-mère* swerved at the last second, too, missing it on her side and missing the low rock wall on his, but by mere inches. "I was hoping you wouldn't give her up," she said, not the least bit perturbed.

As soon as the danger was past, she was whipping around the curves again, tailgating within a millimeter, oblivious to everything except their conversation, as usual.

"*Grand-mère,* you should let me drive."

Her hands tightened possessively on the wheel. "I'll drive. Back to your girl...."

He made a silent vow to never get in *Grand-mère's* red death trap again unless he could drive. But he'd fight that battle on some other day.

"You know what my life is, what is expected," he said.

"Other people's expectations."

"The life I lead would have made her miserable."

"And you think she is happy without you?"

"Happier," he said. "Why did you sell her that painting of me, the painting you'd always promised me, and then point her out to me and tell me what you'd done? If you hadn't pointed her out—"

"A wicked little voice told me to do it, the same voice that tells me what to paint, what to buy for my shop, and who to love next. I am a slave to *the voice.*"

"It was wrong of you to meddle. Very wrong."

"Are you sure, my precious little love?"

"You've made us both unhappy. Viola, too."

"We make our own happiness in this world. The choice is yours, my love."

"No. I have a duty—"

"But are you suited to your duties and to this life any better than I was? I have watched you suffer these past two years. I only wanted you to be happy again. You don't have to give in to your mother. She was an extremely difficult child, you know. Quite dull. Never took to painting or anything the least bit interesting. Just sat in her corner and put beautiful clothes on her dolls. She isn't like you, you know. Do you remember how wild you were when you were little? You are meant to know grand passion, as I have. You will make Viola miserable."

"You shouldn't have meddled. It was a wicked voice."

"But I did. What is done is done. And cannot be undone. If it weren't for the wicked, life would be very dull, indeed."

She'd made a loop, and they were back at the beach and the lemon trees where she'd picked him up. She said goodbye and kissed him many times. He got out of the Maserati and strode toward his tender and tried to forget what she'd said.

A minute later, he was motoring toward his yacht. He secured the tender and jumped aboard *Simonetta*.

When he looked back at the beach, he remembered the night he'd brought Cara here.

Would she haunt him forever?

In his stateroom, he chose a bottle of his finest whiskey and poured himself half a glass. As he lifted the glass, his cell phone materialized in his other hand.

Who the hell did he intend to call? Massimo? No. Viola?

As he gulped from the glass, savoring its fire, he found Cara's saved number on his phone. Then he punched a button.

Not knowing what he'd say if she answered, only knowing that he had to hear her voice, he waited.

"Hello." Her voice, pure and sweet.

What the hell was all that background noise?

Babies were crying. Then a high-pitched, energetic voice chirped loudly, "Can I have another cookie, Aunt Reggie? Pl-e-e-e-e-z!"

He'd read somewhere that one three-year-old could make more noise than two hundred civilized adults.

"Just a minute, sweetheart. Sorry. So sorry about that! Hello! Hello!"

Even though she sounded like she was next door, he felt the ocean and all the distance between them.

"It's me. Nico. I had to know if you arrived home safely."

"I called Massimo weeks ago. Didn't he tell you?"

"Yes. I wanted to hear it from you."

"I'm okay." She sounded a little lost. "Working hard. Baby-sitting for my sister today. It's Saturday, you know."

Babies screamed. Then a toddler shouted, "Aunt Reggie. Aunt Reggie!"

"Oops! Oh, no! Not the whole plate of cookies, sweetheart! You will turn into a Teletubby if you eat all that! Nico, it's a circus here. Could you hang on a sec? I've got to go!"

Nico heard more noise and what sounded like a crash.

"Hello!" a little girl yelled merrily.

He heard telephone buttons being punched, no doubt by a stubby-fingered, little hand. Then the line went dead. The toddler had hung up on him.

Maybe it was for the best. Cara had her life. He had his.

He clenched a fist. Feeling bleak and empty, he lifted his glass and drained it. Lucky for him, the whiskey was real, its effects strong.

Or maybe not so lucky.

With his guard down, memories of Cara's face, body and smiles consumed him. He thought of the recent nights when he'd awakened stiff, hard and throbbing because of his hot, las-civious dreams in which she writhed beneath him or licked him all over with her tongue.

He stared at his phone, but instead of reaching for it again, he got up and poured a second shot of whiskey.

Eleven

David and Dino were both yelling at full volume from their cribs. Regina felt close to tears herself when Gina, who had grabbed the phone away from her to say hi to Nico, snapped it shut.

Was it only yesterday that Robert Riley, Sr., had echoed Donald Trump's favorite phrase?

You're fired!

What had Rebecca thought would happen when she'd sashayed into Robert Sr.'s office and tossed the Hewit complaint on his desk? After she'd insisted on voicing all of her reservations and objections about the case, he'd ordered coffee. As he stirred in sugar and cream, he'd *explained,* in the careful, softly modulated tones that one would use with a child, exactly how many hours the firm billed each year to Black Boar.

When she hadn't backed down, he'd fired her. Just like that. For the first time in her life, she had no plan.

What she did have was a large credit card bill from her trip to Italy and stacks of unpaid bills on her desk. She'd spent half the night on her computer, tweaking her résumé. But she was clueless about what kind of job she might want. What she did know was that as soon as she was near a pay phone, she'd make an anonymous call to Rebecca and recommend a more gifted attorney than the one she had now.

"Gina, why'd you hang up on him?"

Gina's eyes gleamed with mischief. Then she frowned, her chubby face twisting in innocence and confusion. When she cocked her head playfully, her rhinestone tiara toppled to one side.

She was wearing her blue satin princess costume, and Regina's dark Ray-Bans. Only the overlarge shades were upside down and hovering on the tip of her nose, about to fall off as the child bit off another chunk of chocolate chip cookie.

The babies' cries turned to screams in their cribs.

"You shouldn't have grabbed the phone. My friend will think I hung up on him."

Gina shrugged and chomped off more cookie. "We can call him back!" She threw up her hands.

"And no more cookies, young lady, for either one of us."

Clutching the remnants of her cookie, Gina raced to a far corner. When it came to chocolate chip cookies, Gina did not have a stop button.

The babies were still yelling and Regina was leaning down to pick up the tray and all the spilled cookies, when the doorbell rang.

Regina ran for the door and peeped through the window shade.

"Lucy!"

Regina flung the door open and hugged her radiant pregnant friend before allowing her to waddle across the threshold.

"Chocolate chip! My favorite!"

"Join the club."

Lucy plucked a cookie off the tray. "What's all the ruckus?"

"Thank goodness, you're here. I'm pretty overwhelmed. Watch Gina while I change the babies."

Lucy ran a hand through her short, spiky red hair. "There was an accident on Lamar. The traffic was horrible."

Gina smiled coyly at Lucy from her corner.

"What have you got there, Princess?"

Tina opened her mouth, displaying her tongue and chewed-up cookie.

"Are you a princess today?"

"Cinderella."

"My favorite fairy tale. Do you want me to read it to you?"

"I can read it myself."

Ten minutes later, each woman had a baby guzzling a bottle in her lap while Gina sat on the floor at their feet with her dolls and books, waiting to be read a story.

"I can't wait for mine to be born," Lucy said. "Babies are so sweet."

"But trouble. Lots of trouble."

"They're worth it." Lucy petted Dino's dark head. "Aren't you a cutie-pie?"

Now that the children were temporarily under control, Regina remembered Nico's aborted call and wondered if he was okay. She'd bought all the tabloids that had stories about his romance with Viola. Prince and princess: they sounded perfect for each other.

Why had he called her?

Don't think about him.

I can't help it.

Yes, you can. You can do anything you want to do.

You should start dating again.

Not until I find a new job.

She should never have risked her position by speaking so recklessly without another job. Just thinking about that depressed her. If only she had a plan.

Forget Nico. Get a job. Pay your bills. That's a plan.

"We've hardly talked since you got back from Italy," Lucy said.

"I've been busy…. Work." Technically, Regina was still earning a salary since she'd been given two weeks' severance.

"You never told me about the gigolo."

"He wasn't a gigolo."

"He was a real guy, huh? And you had a real date?"

"It's over."

"So-o?"

"I—I can't talk about him right now."

"That good, huh?"

"I hate the way you think you can see straight through me."

"The way I think…ha!"

"It was a dream. I woke up. I'm here, and he's there, and that's the end of it."

Lucy's eyebrows flew together. "I don't mean to criticize, but sometimes your devious lawyer mind is too smart for your britches."

"Quit!"

"Are you in love with him?"

"I said quit!"

Lucy wouldn't stop looking at her, so, of course, she saw Regina's telltale blush.

"That's it!"

"It wouldn't have worked. He's Italian."

"And what are you? Italian-American!"

"We're completely different, okay? Not possible!"

"Nothing is impossible," Lucy said. "Look at me. I finally got pregnant."

"You, you're a walking miracle."

"Your turn will come. So, if the gigolo-guy's a no-go, have you thought any more about E-321 and maybe having that little half brother or sister for my baby?"

Regina shook her head. "I'm not ready. Neither is my family. I've got some bills. Italy…" She thought about Nico and blurted, "I'm just not ready to have anyone else's baby."

"Anyone else's…? Hey!"

"I didn't mean that. I didn't mean what it sounded like."

Lucy lifted Dino to her shoulder to burp him. "Why won't you talk about this guy?"

"I just can't."

"You seem different somehow. I mean, after Italy. Was it *him?*"

"I wish people would stop saying that. People change. Maybe I matured."

Lucy shook her head.

Closing her eyes, Regina told herself she had to quit thinking about Nico all the time. She was home, back in her real world. Someday soon she had to rethink the E-321 issue. Her biological clock hadn't stopped ticking just because she'd chosen the wrong man.

Why had he called? Had he missed her a little? Was the gorgeous Viola as icy as his mother? Regina bit her lips. She hoped so.

No. If she truly loved him, she should want him to be happy. But she was human, okay? And humans aren't perfect, right? Nobody expected her to be a saint filled with noble virtues, did they?

Still, when she'd first come home, she'd buried herself in work to avoid her dark, selfish feelings.

Having finished eating every single cookie crumb off the floor, Gina ran to her and patted baby David with her chocolate-smeared fingertips.

"Gently," Regina cautioned. "And why don't you lick your fingers?"

When Gina bent over her fingers, her tiara fell off. Leaning down, Regina picked it up.

Gina snatched it and put it on and whirled, clapping and giggling, making Lucy and Regina laugh.

"When I grow up, can I be a real princess?"

"Of course you can, my darling," Regina whispered, her voice choked. "Come here, darling, so I can straighten your tiara again. All that twirling, it's hanging on your ear."

"Are you all right?" Lucy asked as Regina brushed at her eyes. Like Regina's sister Susana, Lucy was too intuitive sometimes. "I'm fine."

She didn't feel all that well, actually. The sweet baby smell was getting to her. Regina set David's bottle on the floor. Holding him close, intending to put him in his swing, she was instantly too dizzy to take a step.

Lucy's red hair and freckled face whirled amidst flashes of brilliance. Then the room became bright white and suffocatingly hot. Beads of perspiration popped out on her face. A band of iron circled her chest. Clutching David, she sank weakly back into her chair.

"Are you okay?" Lucy whispered, her low tone urgent.

The white flashes were still swirling as Gina ran to Regina and tugged at her arm. "What's the matter, Aunt Reggie?"

"I—I'm fine."

"You're as white as that wall behind you," Lucy said. "What's wrong?"

"I just feel a little faint. That's all. Busy week. I guess I stood up too quickly."

"Maybe you should see a doctor."

"I said I'm fine."

But later that night when Regina was eating warmed-over pizza while she further revised her résumé at her computer, the black font blurred sickeningly. Her head began to feel thick and funny, and her pulse sped up.

She spit out her pizza and pushed her white wine away. The pizza was spicy, the way she usually liked it, but much too spicy tonight. And the chilled wine, Nico's favorite, was so dry her mouth felt like cotton after one sip.

When bile climbed her throat, she ran to the kitchen and drank ice water.

Still queasy, she fell onto her bed without removing her jeans. Not that she could sleep. The next morning she woke up with raccoon circles under her eyes. Her skin was pale and clammy, and when she even thought about cooking oatmeal, she felt so sick again she had to lie back down.

As she lay on her back, she grabbed one of the celebrity magazines off her nightstand and studied Nico's picture and then Viola's. Bold headlines screamed. Prince and His Princess. Fairy-tale Marriage.

Their gorgeous faces began to spin.

Regina threw the magazine at the wall.

Suddenly overcome with an urge to retch, she got up and raced to the toilet, where she threw up disgusting chunks of undigested pizza. Her head was still over the bowl, when a life-changing thought occurred to her.

She hadn't had her period.

Not since Italy.

The phone rang. Still feeling weak, she crawled back to her bed, grabbed the receiver and flung herself on her rumpled sheets, belly up.

"Hi. You there? It's your mother. Say something, Cara, so I'll know you're alive!"

"M-Ma! Hi."

"It's Sunday. I'm calling about lunch. Joe's out of town, but Susana and the kids will be there."

Sunday lunch was a longstanding tradition.

"I'm sorry. I don't think so. I—I don't feel well. Nausea."

"Maybe you should see a doctor. You haven't been yourself. Not since Italy. Maybe you caught something over there."

Twelve

Pregnant.

A shocked Regina sat in the doctor's waiting room with her right hand cupped over her mouth. Her left hand was clutching the armrest of her chair as if it were a life preserver. Her stomach tightened, and she looked down at it and was surprised that it was still so flat.

Nico had used a condom every time, but the doctor had confirmed the results of the pregnancy test Regina had taken at home with more tests and a physical exam.

Nico. How would he react when she told him? And she *had* to tell him. Would he be pleased?

Was she pleased?

Yes. Or, at least, she would be when the shock wore off. For another long moment, unsure about whether or not she could stand, much less walk out to her car and drive, she simply sat there, adjusting to her new reality.

Pregnant. Nico's baby.

Baby first. Husband second.

Her plan.

Only she'd hadn't planned *this.* For one thing, a job had been a given. How could she raise a baby without a job?

And Nico. She thought about the lovely Viola and his plans to marry her as soon as possible. He had to be told immediately.

Biting her lips, Regina stared up at the ceiling. A baby. Nico's precious baby, but no job and no husband. And no Nico.

"Thank you," she whispered, even as she began to shake and feel scared at the same time. "Thank you. With your help, I can do this." *Somehow.*

When she finally felt strong enough to drive and was behind the wheel, her thoughts strayed back to Nico. She hated upsetting him, hated telling him over the phone. But this problem wasn't going away.

When she got to her house, she flipped on the television to CNN, muted the volume and then pulled her cell phone out of her purse. At the thought of calling Nico, what little confidence she had leaked out of her.

Sinking onto her couch in a daze, she punched in his number. Her heart began to beat faster with each ring.

"Ciao," he mumbled in a cranky, groggy voice.

"Oh, my God! *The time!*" She looked at her watch in horror.

"Nico, I'm sorry. It's five-thirty in the afternoon in Texas! I totally forgot it's twelve-thirty your time! I'm sorry! Sorry, sorry!"

She was still babbling when he said, "Viola?" And then louder, "Cara? Cara! Is it really you, *tesorina?*"

Did she only imagine that his deep voice had softened?

Viola's picture flashed on her television screen and was followed with a clip of Nico dining with her at a posh restaurant in Rome, holding her hand, smiling. There was a shot of them on his yacht.

Regina closed her eyes. Did he suck her fingertips, too? They did look perfect together.

"It's Regina."

"Regina?"

Her stomach knotted. He didn't even know her name.

"I mean Cara. Regina's my real name. I—I shouldn't have called. I'll call back at a better time."

"Cara! Wait!"

"I'll call back. Sleep well." She hung up. She shut her eyes again. "Sleep well, my darling."

Viola? He'd expected Viola.

How quickly we forget.

Wide-awake now and in a hellish mood because Cara had sounded so lost, Nico rang her back as fast as he could. When he got her voice mail, he cursed vividly.

She'd called him. Then she'd turned off her phone.

Women.

But she'd sounded scared. He had to talk to her, so he left a message, demanding that she call him at once.

He held the phone in his palm for an hour. When she didn't call, he began to feel crazed as the uncertainty in her tone grew in his mind. Something was wrong.

He called her again and again, leaving more messages demanding that she call him. Then he paced his gilded bedroom until two like a caged cat.

Her voice had sounded strange. He had to find out what was wrong, as soon as possible. Despite the late hour, he rang Massimo.

"Can this possibly wait? I'm in a bar. With the most gorgeous *signorina.*"

"Sorry to disturb you. You have to help me check up on Cara."

"Cara!" Massimo groaned.

"She called and hung up on me. Now she won't take my calls. I'm worried about her."

"She's fine," Massimo said, sounding bored and distracted. There was a lot of music and laughter in the background.

"I have to know that for sure."

"It's the middle of the night, and the *signorina* is touching me in places I won't discuss on a cell phone."

"It's not the middle of the night in Texas. Hire detectives.

Keep me and the family's name out of it. No scandal, but do whatever it takes."

"If she doesn't want to talk to you—"

"I don't give a damn about that. Call me as soon as you know something."

Nico hung up. Not that he'd quit trying to call her himself.

Not that she didn't consume his every thought that night and throughout the next day.

"When are you going to announce your engagement?"

Nico dropped his fork, looked up from his omelet and frowned at the regal woman sitting beneath her peach-colored umbrella just outside the pink walls of her favorite palazzo. His favorite, too.

He felt like he was in a prison, and his mother and the generations before her were his jailers. Her black silk suit fit her exquisite figure like a glove; her perfectly groomed hair gleamed like spun gold. Now that things were going her way she looked young and lovely and quite serene.

He wanted to stand up, seize control of his destiny and tell her what to do, which was the way he always acted in business. And in that arena, in the space of a decade, he'd made his family richer than they'd ever imagined. He'd done so by working hard and by following his gut instinct.

Why was it that, when it came to marriage and lineage, he let her run him?

Maybe because she had a thousand years of tradition on her side.

"Can't you think of something besides my marriage?" Nico said, his tone clipped.

He hadn't touched his omelet. Usually he ate a huge breakfast. Now he had no appetite.

He stood up and tossed his napkin down. "I have an early appointment."

"But, Nico, darling, you didn't eat anything."

When he saw the hurt on her face, he felt guilty. She was only doing what she'd been taught was the right thing to do, what the generations before her had believed to be right. Modern ideas of democracy and romantic love meant nothing to her.

"I apologize," he said. Then he stalked off the terrace and into the palazzo.

Later, at his office, he regretted his rudeness to her, but the mounting pressure about his romance with Viola, his mother's stubborn ambition for him in all arenas, and his genuine concern about Cara had him feeling disturbed.

He'd thought he could give her up. Damn it, he'd tried.

As the hours passed and he attended to his routine business duties and appointments with no further word from Massimo, he grew even edgier, snapping out commands, hanging up too abruptly on important people, even a French financial minister, whom he had to ring back with an apology.

At eleven that night, when he was beside himself, pacing in his bedroom, Massimo finally rang.

"You're not going to like this," his cousin said.

"Is Cara all right?"

Nico splashed Scotch into a crystal glass, waiting for an answer that didn't come.

"Damn it, Massimo? Is she?"

"Yes. And no."

Nico ground his teeth. "And?" He gulped the Scotch.

"She's pregnant. Saw the doctor yesterday."

Pregnant?

"Pregnant?" He began to cough and spit Scotch.

"Who's the lucky father?" His strangled voice was barely audible.

"Not sure. Apparently, before she met you, she told everybody she wanted to have a baby on her own, to be a single mother of choice."

"What the hell is that?"

"Some crazy American-women idea. Her parents weren't for it. Her father went into quite a sulk when he found out she'd bought eight vials of sperm from a sperm bank. So, she broke her appointment to be inseminated, took a leave of absence, and flew to Italy."

And tried to seduce a gigolo.

A hard band closed around Nico's lungs.

"Did she get pregnant in Italy? Or after Italy? How far along is she?"

"The detective couldn't say. He's happy to keep digging though. Likes the money. It was getting late, so I thought I should call—"

"Thanks. I'll let you know," Nico mumbled a few more questions. Then he jotted Cara's full name and address and all her phone numbers in a little black notebook and slammed his phone shut.

For a long moment, he stared at the phone numbers, not really seeing them as he considered calling one of them on the long shot she'd answer.

No, she was a lawyer. Better to show up without giving her any warning. That way she wouldn't have time to build up her defense.

Pregnant? Vials of sperm?

Had she known who he was and set him up?

He went to the tall window of his bedroom. In the moonlight, he could see the swans gliding peacefully together on their glimmering pond.

Was he the father? Why had she called him yesterday? To inform him? To blackmail him?

Had her parents pressured her into giving up on the sperm-donor idea? Had they talked her into getting pregnant the old-fashioned way? Had that been the real purpose of her vacation? Her real purpose in that bar?

How many men had she slept with before him?

He stared at the swans, his emotions tearing at him. How could he have let himself believe that at least for a short space of time, she'd cared about him for himself alone, cared enough to sacrifice her own feelings for the higher good of his family?

Hell. What a fool he was to have thought she might love him.

Wearily, he turned away from the swans. Their loyalty made him angry somehow. He had to banish all softness, all notions of enduring love and romance. He had a duty to his family. He also had a duty to his unborn child—if he had one.

Bottom line: was he the father?

He felt betrayal and something even worse.

Damn her to hell and back.

If Cara had manipulated him, if she intended to use this pregnancy to hurt his family, to use their child for financial gain…

He'd see her in Dante's inferno first.

Thirteen

Pregnant.

Regina smiled. She would have a baby to love, a baby who would be just hers, someone who couldn't abandon her, someone who would need her for a long, long time.

Nico had called her back, too. Again and again. But he'd sounded so urgent and upset she hadn't been able to force herself to return his calls.

She would; she even wanted to.

She'd been trying to work up her nerve to do just that. She sat on the couch listening to his messages again, each one colder than the last, while her lifelong feelings of abandonment resurfaced to make her think that perhaps he'd never really truly cared for her in the first place. She decided that maybe a nice, long bath would relax her and make calling him easier.

Pregnant. Nico's baby.

In her bathroom, she stripped and studied her breasts and stomach with a critical eye. Although she wasn't showing, she felt so totally changed. Already she loved this baby so much. And yet...

All her life she'd tried to be strong and independent. Now she felt just the opposite—one big reason she dreaded telling Nico about the baby. She didn't want him to think she expected anything from him, and still...

Truly, she wanted to reassure him that she was perfectly able to raise their child alone even though the very thought of doing so alarmed her.

He was her baby's father. And she loved him. And the baby would love him. It was stupid, idiotic, hormonal, whatever. But she felt a strange, new, wonderful vulnerability and at the same time, a crushing sense of dependency.

Their baby needed a mother *and* a father.

Hello! This is the modern world. What happened to the idea of being a single mother by choice?

Nico owed his family. There was no room in his complicated life for her. She knew that. Just as she knew she couldn't fit into his world any more than he could fit into hers.

But hormones don't listen to reason. Their siren song is more ancient and truer than any new social idea.

So, a conflicted Regina, the modern woman and the ancient, ran her tub full of water and then lay down to soak and hoped she'd relax.

Like a child, she batted at the bubbles floating on top of the water. Then she sang, as she always did, off-key. Finally, when she was hoarse, she soaped a leg and lifted her razor.

An hour later, the water was cold, her bubbles were gone, and she was still without a single solution to her life's riddles.

Suddenly, a loud banging at her front door shook her out of her reverie. Terrified, she leaped out of the bathtub. When the banging persisted, she sat back down and turned on the hot water full blast.

"Stubborn idiot!" she whispered. "Go away!"

The knocking stopped, and she sighed in relief until her cell phone began to ring.

She sat up again.

So much for peace and relaxation.

Her cell phone stopped and then her home phone burst to life.

What was going on?

Her family! She was filled with panic at the thought of a car crash or a heart attack. Then she imagined Joe, backing out of the driveway in his van and running over Gina, who was never where she was supposed to be. Regina shot out of the tub and toweled herself dry.

She put on her thick, terry-cloth robe and ran into the kitchen to find her phone.

"Answer your damned door," Nico yelled.

Nico? Here?

Oh, my God!

She'd left her garage door open, so, of course, he'd seen her car. He'd probably heard her run into the kitchen, too.

Heart racing, she tiptoed to the front door and cracked her shade, gasping when she saw a white stretch limousine gleaming in her driveway.

Although Nico wore a charcoal suit and tie that probably cost a small fortune, he looked as fierce and frightening as a warrior prince from another age on a rampage.

Nico? Nico!

Frantic, she let go of her shade. When it crashed noisily against the window, she screamed.

When big brown knuckles rapped on the windowpane so vigorously she was afraid the glass would shatter, she jumped away. Then, gathering her courage, she clutched her robe tighter and yanked her shade back up again.

Nico crossed his muscular arms, leaned against the door frame and glared at her through the glass. His huge body in that perfectly cut suit was so tense she knew he was barely restraining himself. His blue eyes burned like lasers. A wild thread of fear knotted itself around her heart and pulled tight.

She was naked underneath her robe, but if she took the time to dress, she knew it would try his patience to the extreme, so she unlocked the door.

He blew past her into the foyer, slamming the door so hard the whole house shook.

She'd hung the painting of the little boy playing in the sand in her foyer. When he saw it, he stopped cold and stared at it for long seconds, his frown deepening.

Then, as if it offended him, he turned his back on the painting.

"Why did you call me and then not call me back?" With each word, a blue vein pulsed savagely in his temple.

She let out a strangled cry and sagged against the wall. "I was—"

"Trying to drive me crazy? Because if that was your intent, you damn sure succeeded!"

With her face scrubbed clean of makeup and her hair in wet tangles, she imagined he compared her to the beautiful Viola and found her pathetic.

He strode past her into the kitchen, where he opened and closed drawers, sifting through their contents.

"What are you doing?" she cried. "What are you looking for?"

"Who the hell are you?"

Next he began gazing at all the photographs on her refrigerator. She wanted to scream that he had no right to go through her things, but she watched him, mute, afraid.

Mostly the photographs were of Gina and David and Dino; of Susana and the rest of her family. She'd pinned up a few she'd taken of various sights in Italy.

He lifted them one by one, reading the back of the pictures, as well. It was her habit to methodically jot the names of the people, the location and the time.

"I see there are no pictures of me," he said. "Did you delete them?"

No. No. No. They were on her computer, and she looked at them every night.

When his hand touched E-321's profile, she ran over to the refrigerator to distract him.

He turned, his intense blue eyes cool and calculating now. "Why did you call me and then not call me back? What are you up to? What do you want?"

She couldn't tear her gaze from his dark hand, which rested on E-321's profile.

When he wouldn't stop staring at her, either, her skin grew hot and clammy. Suddenly bile crawled up her throat and her mouth went dry.

Oh, no! No. No!

Cupping her lips, she rushed to the sink and was sick.

When she could lift her head and breathe again, she felt his hard, critical gaze boring into the small of her back. She straightened to her full height and turned slowly to face him.

"You're as white as a sheet," he said without a trace of sympathy. "No makeup."

He opened a cabinet and got out a glass. Then he went to the refrigerator and poured her a glass of icy water.

He gave her the glass, and she sipped the cool liquid gratefully.

She should tell him about the baby now. But she couldn't. Not like this. Not when he was so angry.

"Why are you here? Why are you so upset?" she whispered.

He turned back to the refrigerator and yanked off E-321's profile with a vengeance. *"Why am I here?"*

He wadded up the profile and threw it at her.

When it bounced at her feet, she jumped.

"You're pregnant. That's why."

She sucked in a breath. "You knew even before I was sick. *You knew!*"

"You're hardly in a position to accuse me."

Cornered, her legal mind went on full attack. "That's privileged, private information. I haven't even told my mother yet. You have no right—"

"No right?" Like a predator closing in for the kill, he stalked her.

She skittered backward until her butt hit the cabinets and his tall, muscular body in designer charcoal loomed over her, blocking her escape.

"Who the hell's the father, damn it?"

She looked up at him, and her tongue froze against the roof of her mouth.

He gripped her shoulders so tightly she felt each finger bruising her flesh.

"Is it mine? Or is it the damn sperm donor's? Or some other man's? Did you call me to blackmail me?" The fingers mashed harder, cutting her.

"Blackmail? No! No! No. How can you think…"

She felt as if she were dying inside. She didn't want him here. Not like this.

"Then who's the father?"

She knew she should lie. If he thought she was as low as he was accusing her of being, she should definitely lie. She was a lawyer. Surely she should be able to make up a plausible story that would rid her of him forever.

"Why don't you just tell me the truth for once?" he said.

"You aren't going to like this."

His hands dug even deeper. *"Is it mine?"*

Aware of those rough fingers and of the muscle ticking along his hard jawline, she fought for every breath.

"Nobody has to know," she whispered.

"What? *Nobody has to know?* That's your answer?"

If she'd struck him, he couldn't have looked more stunned. *"I know,"* he said. "I know."

"I wasn't planning to blackmail you. I just wanted to tell you. That's all. I swear."

"Why?"

"I—I…" She broke off. "Because it's yours."

There was no trace of tenderness or even humanity in Nico's face. She'd seen such cold implacability in the courtroom many times. It always spelled doom. No matter what she said, he wasn't going to believe her.

"I'm telling you the truth. That's the only reason I called."

His eyes narrowed until all she could see was glittering blue slits of fire behind his black lashes. "Well, you're not blackmailing anybody because you're going to marry me, you little fool."

"Impossible. You told me we could never be together."

"That was before you became pregnant with my child."

My child, too! she wanted to scream.

"What about Viola? Your family? Your mother?"

"They will have to accept it, as I have to accept it. A higher duty calls."

"You're a prince. I want you to marry Viola. You have to marry her."

"And have my child grow up a bastard in America, raised solely by a woman like you, never knowing him and all the while knowing he'll always feel abandoned by me, his father, knowing, as well, you could use him and threaten to sell your story for your own gain. No! What would that do to him, to have his father abandon him to a mother like you?"

Stung, she almost wept. "I would never do that!"

He stared at her for a long moment. "Did you know who I was that first day? Did you do this deliberately?"

"I don't need you or your title or your money. I'm an attorney. I have my career—"

He laughed. "Some career. You were fired from Merrit, Riley & Whitt. Two days ago."

"How do you know that?"

"Money buys a lot of answers. Being a lawyer, *you* should know that."

"I'll have you know there are privacy laws in this country."

"There should be laws against what you did to me. All your miserable life, you've been out to prove you were somebody."

"How do you know—"

"Is that why you ditched the sperm-donor plan, why you wanted to catch a prince?"

"I—I want you to leave! Now! I—I called you because I thought you were a reasonable person and I wanted to tell you, just to let you know. But now I know who you really are—a total, arrogant bastard."

"As I know who you really are."

"But I'm not what you think and you are what I—"

"All your life, you've felt like an outsider. Your sister was the one everybody loved. You've fought and scraped to climb out of some imaginary gutter. You didn't care who you hurt."

Who had talked to him?

"I don't need you. I can raise my baby without you or anybody else."

"But you're not going to because I won't allow it. You're going to marry me. *For a year.* So I can stake my legal claim to my son."

"I hate you."

His eyes flashed with equal passion. "Surely we can stand each other for a year."

"Are you out of your mind?"

"Yes, and it's your fault." His tone was low and was so maddeningly calm she wanted to slap him, wanted to yank tufts of his thick black hair from his scalp. "After the year is over, you can do what you want."

"My life is here."

"Not for the next year. No child of *mine* is going to be a bastard."

"*My* child, too!"

"If you don't agree to marriage on my terms, I'll fight you for custody. My family is very powerful. Don't force me to lean on you. Believe me, it will not be a pleasant experience."

She tried to swallow. She'd been the legal lackey representing wealthy people and corporations too long not to know the power of big money. He was right. He could crush her.

"So, you will marry me, and fast," he said. "You can seek a divorce when our child is three months old. After our divorce, I will want to see *him* as often as possible."

"*Him?* How can you keep saying *our* baby is a boy?"

Our baby. The phrase echoed in her heart.

"Or her," he corrected.

"If you think I'm going to let you take over my life and my unborn child's life...even for a year..."

"This isn't my fault, you know. You're the one who hired me to be your stud."

"I most certainly did not!"

"You bought that dress, wore that flower, acted like a sad, lonely American woman in need of a gigolo."

The awful G-word gonged like a rusty bell. "I did not!"

"I felt sorry for you," he finished brutally.

"Sorry for me?" She drew a sharp, horrified breath.

"And all the time, you had this plan because you're so damned insecure."

"I did not! I am not!"

"I don't believe you, Miss Tomei. As I said before, your entire life has been about climbing some imaginary ladder." He picked up her phone and began to read aloud from a little black notebook. "Five-five-five, six-four-five…"

He punched in the familiar-sounding string of numbers and waited.

Suddenly, she realized he'd dialed her parents' number and listened in horror when he smiled and said, "Mr. Tomei?"

"Don't you dare!" she screamed. "He doesn't know about any of this!"

"Excuse me, sir." Nico put his hand over the phone. "Then it's time he found out. From what I hear, he's crazy about his other grandchildren."

"You can't just barge in here—"

"Mr. Tomei…"

She took a deep breath to steady herself. Somehow, Nico knew that she'd always wanted her father to think she was special, and that she'd failed, and tonight Nico was determined to destroy her and make her father hate her forever.

"It is a pleasure to meet you, even over the telephone. I am Prince Nico Romano." He said all of his numerous names, which Regina knew she would never be able to remember, even if she stayed married to him for a whole damned year. "Yes, a *real* prince. Yes, we do own a castle. More than one, actually."

Her father, an avid golf fan, who didn't keep up with the lives of celebrities, didn't have a clue who Nico was, no matter how much had been written about him in the tabloids. Nico's voice was low and respectful as he explained who he was, but with every word Regina felt an immense pressure building inside her head until she was nearly sure invisible flames had to be spewing out of her mouth and ears. Otherwise, she would have exploded.

He was going to tell her father! He was determined to ruin her life forever!

"I have only recently learned that your daughter is pregnant with my child."

Oh, my God! He'd said the P-word! Daddy!

I will be the bad daughter forever now! Thanks to you, Prince... no...Principe Don Nico Carlo Giovanni Romano! Even if I do become Principessa Donna Regina Carina Romano di Tomei!

How had she remembered all those names?

Rage must have sharpened her memory.

Time spun backward. Regina was suddenly three years old again. She'd just dropped a jar of peanut butter her father had forbidden her to touch onto the floor. The shattering glass had awakened Susana in her crib, and she'd started crying. Her father had gone to get the baby before returning to the kitchen. Then, as he'd cradled Susana lovingly in his arms, he'd called Regina all sorts of horrid names. Or, in her shame, she'd imagined that he had.

Regina shut her eyes against the awful memory and sagged against the wall. Prince Nico paused and shot her a significant look. Not wanting him to see her vulnerability, she stood up taller and straighter and drew in a calming breath. And then another.

"No, I'm not a sperm donor. I met your daughter in Italy. Love at first sight."

Love. For a second, all she registered was Nico's chiseled male beauty and the intense blue of his eyes. Her entire being blazed. Some incredibly stupid part of her almost believed he was telling the truth, that he'd truly found something rare and beautiful in their brief affair, as she had.

No, she hadn't! And it was impossible that he had, either! He was furious with her. As she was with him—due to his absolutely despicable, totally unforgivable, arrogant behavior of the past five minutes. He was manipulating her and her father. She couldn't possibly ever love such a man!

"You know how it is when something like that catches you by surprise." Nico's white smile flashed.

Why had the devil given him the sexiest smile in the universe?

She squeezed her eyes shut and fought against the memory of their passion. Surely that had been the devil's work, as well.

"Yes, sir. It was like being hit with a thunderbolt."

It had been exactly like that. Was he mocking her?

"Yes, I would like to meet Susana and the children."

Regina's throat tightened with grief and rage and some wild, unnamed emotion that made her feel faint and lost, almost sick again. Nico's sweet lies had exposed that awful, barren place that would be her heart if he really hated her forever.

How humiliating to still want him! To still love him!

With a choked cry, Regina ran to her bedroom, locked her door, tore off her robe and began yanking clothing out of her closet in an attempt to find something to wear.

Through the thin walls, she heard the rest of the conversation.

"I would like to meet all of you as I hope to ask you formally for her hand in marriage."

"Bastard," she breathed. Then she threw a hanger at the wall.

Then Nico hung up, strode to the door and yelled through it. "You'd better hurry. Your father has most graciously invited us to dinner."

"Damn you," she muttered in a low, inaudible voice.

"Tonight. Seven o'clock. I told him I'd buy wine. You have fifteen minutes. Do you need any help?"

Like a child having a tantrum, she tossed the outfits she didn't want to wear into a heap on the floor. Then she stomped up and down on them.

"Fifteen minutes," he repeated. "If you're not dressed, you'll go naked. Your choice."

One glance in the mirror at her nude body and her pale un-made-up face had her gulping in air at a frantic pace. For one second, she entertained the notion of marching into the living room stark naked.

What if she kissed him? Or grabbed his big member? Would his arrogant fury explode into something entirely different? If she threw her arms around him, would he pick her up and carry her to the bedroom? Would sex burn away the hate and open the door to love?

But what if he turned away in disgust?

Shaking, she sank down on the little velvet stool in front of her vanity to apply her makeup.

Why couldn't she have been dressed and gorgeous when he'd arrived instead of being pale and wet headed and wearing her oldest robe? With an effort, she began to concentrate on making the most of her limited time. She even curled her lashes and was pleased with her reflection when she twirled in front of her mirror after he knocked on her door ten minutes later.

Not that wanting to be especially beautiful tonight meant anything. It didn't. But when she opened her door and waltzed into the hall in her low-cut swirly green dress and heels, with her shining hair curling about her face, it pleased her no end when his eyes stalled on her red mouth and then again her breasts. She heard the sharp intake of his breath and fought the urge to smile.

For a long time, she couldn't breathe, either.

Slowly he raised his eyes, but the power of speech had left him, too.

"Ready?" she managed, feeling almost as beautiful as the exquisite Principessa Donna Viola.

Fourteen

Regina's triumph was short-lived. Her beauty, indeed everything about her, seemed to annoy the hell out of him. His face was colder than ever as he stomped out of her house and led her to the car.

She was pregnant, and, therefore, he felt trapped. Her thoughts began to circle around and around, buzzing in a negative loop. By the time she latched her seat belt in the limo, her mood was blacker than his. Nor did being whisked, against her will, through the darkening streets in his luxurious car toward her parents' house improve her mood.

Her family! Why did he have to compound this disaster by dragging them into it?

Nico stopped to buy wine, and, at first, she felt relief at being able to wander through the aisles while he was occupied at the cash register with the clerk. Then she passed a row of brightly colored labels of Italian wines. Instantly, the familiar names and pictures of the wineries took her back to Tuscany where she'd visited her grandmother and then to the Amalfi Coast, which, because of him, had been a dream.

Images of mountains and sea, the cypress-lined roads, the cerulean skies, the flavor of lush dark olives and the sweetness of winter pears in *vino noble* seared her. Most of all, she remembered *him* in that sunlit bar, him on *Simonetta*. Last of all, she remembered her desolation at the airport after she'd made love to him for hours.

Massimo had led her away and, with every step, she'd thought, *Why am I leaving this perfect place and this perfect man?*

For an instant longer, she remained in that lost dream. Again, she felt the cold, stone wall of the deserted farmhouse against her body and Nico's hard warmth surging against hers; his mouth and tongue all over her, and then her own wild abandon as he'd brought her to climax. Sex with other men had never come close. It was as if she were able to be with him on levels that were not possible with anyone else.

And he hated her for trapping him. She didn't want to beg for anyone's love ever again as she'd begged for her father's.

On a strangled sob she ran out of the wine shop and flung herself back into the car. She sank down onto the soft leather, hugging herself in the dark. Much to her surprise, Nico came at once and found her huddled there, feeling as desperate and needy as the lost child she'd once been.

"Are you all right?"

No! I'm not all right! How can you even ask?

"I'm fine."

"Fine? You look unhappy."

"Are you happy? Are you?"

When she looked away, he leaned close enough for her to smell his tangy aftershave. *Lemons.* She remembered the lemon grove outside the farmhouse.

Then his knuckles brushed her cheekbone, causing her heart to race, causing her to hope.

"Are you going to be sick again?" His voice was gentle.

Startled by his concern and even more by his nearness and touch, she jumped away to a far corner of the limo.

"No! I'm not sick! I told you I'm fine. I'm perfectly happy.

Perfectly, perfectly happy, you big, domineering idiot! What could possibly be wrong? I love being forced into a marriage of convenience by a man who feels superior to me, a man who hates me and will hate me forever. Whose entire family will hate me forever." She put her hands over her face and began to sob wildly.

Even to her own ears, her words and tears sounded a bit over the top. But drama-queenery ran in her blood on both sides of her family. The trait had come in handy more times than not in the courtroom although she had been chastised by more than one judge. Not that she was faking this. She felt frightened, wild.

The bleakness that flared in his eyes tore at her heart and instantly stopped her weeping.

"I don't hate you," he said, his tone so low and broken she squeezed her lashes tightly against her cheeks for fear she might burst into tears and humiliate herself all over again.

Was he unhappy, too? Did he grieve for what they had lost, as she did?

Absurd thought.

A wistful moan escaped her lips. For one crazy moment, she wanted to throw herself into his arms and beg his forgiveness. She wanted to trace her fingers through his inky hair and comfort him, to press herself against his wide chest and to find solace herself. She wanted to kiss his brow, his eyelids, his lips. Almost, she could taste him, she wanted him so much.

The last thing she'd ever wanted to do was make him unhappy.

But doubt made her certain he would reject her. So, instead of embracing him or even touching his face as he'd touched hers, or lifting her lips, she turned away, sitting as stiff and rigid as a flagpole, her body language conveying unforgivness.

"I'll be right back," he muttered, his low tone weary now.

The door closed gently. She was aware of him standing there for a moment, as if he were puzzled or worried, but when she finally looked at him, she was disappointed to see his tall, broad-shouldered body striding purposefully through the shop's doors to complete his purchase.

When he returned, he placed the wine bottles on their sides

on the opposite seat. She felt his eyes on her face, but her emotions were still so raw she refused to look at him. She was glad at first that he did not attempt conversation. Then, perversely, she wanted him to say something, anything. Maybe then she could find a way to apologize for the scene she had just made. If he didn't begin, she couldn't. She was so overwrought, she lacked the wisdom to know where or how to start. Once again, an increasingly awkward silence built between them while she sat wrapped in her own misery, and acutely aware of his. If only she could think of something to alter their unhappy state, but she couldn't.

When the limousine braked, and they walked up to the front door, her heart drummed double-time with dread at the prospect of the evening ahead of them.

When Nico rang the bell, he turned. With an effort, he forced himself to speak. "This will be easier if you smile and act happy."

"Easier for you, you mean! Aristocrats spend their lives putting on a show for the world. That's what you do! Well, maybe it's not what I do!"

No sooner had she finished speaking than she wanted to bite her tongue off.

"You're a bride, remember. Your family will only be hurt and worried if they know the whole truth. Is that really what you want? I thought you wanted to please your father."

Her father! Oh, God! What did Nico care about her family or her relationship with her father? Still, she caught something in his controlled tone that made her heart beat even faster.

What if he did care a little?

Suddenly she longed to be back in Italy, skimming across the water in his tender as he pointed out the palazzos and villas and told her stories about his friends and fabled ancestors who lived or had lived in them. She wanted to cling to him again as they entered that secret, hidden, pirate grotto.

She'd asked him to play like a pirate and ravage her.

"I want to make love to you. Will that count? I don't want to hurt you or ravage you."

But he'd held her down as she'd secretly wished. Only he'd made love to her as if he'd cherished her.

"If only happiness was like a switch that one could turn on and off at will," she said, remembering the dark sea cave where he'd dropped the anchor and how silent it had been when he'd cut the engine. She remembered lying with him in the darkness, wrapped in his arms while the boat rocked them like a cradle.

"*If only.*" His tight voice was even gloomier than hers.

"I feel like I'm being kidnapped by a man I don't even know."

"I feel trapped, too."

"I never wanted to make you so—"

She swallowed the word *unhappy,* because at that exact moment, her father threw open the door, extended his arms and hugged Nico fiercely. Then he embraced her and kissed her on each cheek, which was his usual greeting for Susana.

Behind her father, the house was brilliantly lit and redolent with the sweetness of cut flowers and chopped basil from her mother's flower beds. Gina's piping voice could be heard in the backyard.

Her father shook Nico's hand and pulled him inside. Constantin Tomei didn't really understand who Nico was or who his family was or the vastness in social rank and position that separated them. He did not act the least bit awed by the expensive bottles of wine or by the fact that Nico was a prince. Being Italian, he took the wine, appreciated the gift for what it was, a sharing of the vine rooted in an ancient communion between guest and host.

Not that Nico wasn't perceived as a guest of honor.

All the usual clutter, her father's newspapers, her mother's photograph albums and cookbooks had vanished into hiding places, into laundry baskets in the garage probably. The kitchen floor even looked freshly waxed. Regina could smell olive oil and tomatoes and cheeses bubbling on the stove. A screen door banged. She heard her mother and Susana and the children laughing in the kitchen.

Wreathed in smiles, her mother took off her apron and came to the door. Since she never read celebrity magazines and mostly watched cooking shows on those rare occasions when she found the time to watch television, she treated Nico as if he were her equal, too. With many more gracious thank-yous, she accepted the wines Nico had selected when Constantin handed them to her, one for each course, before scurrying back to her domain to stir her pots.

Her mother wasn't a measurer. She simply bought the best available ingredients or grew them and then let them guide her. Much of what she cooked was too simple to be a recipe, but infinitely superior because of her talents.

"Well, he's a catch. No doubt about that," her father said, plucking a halved fig off a platter and nibbling on it when he caught her alone. He and Nico had drunk wine together alone in the den behind closed doors for half an hour by that time and were already great friends, or at least, amiable companions.

"He has a fine mind. We discussed golf and the war."

"The war?"

"World War II. Told me all about what Hitler did to his family. He lost a lot of castles. Then we discussed the wedding."

"The wedding?"

"Yours. He insists his family must pay for it. He says it has to be a very private affair, managed by his staff. He's going to send a jet for us so that we can attend your wedding. He wants me to console your mother because she won't be allowed to plan it. That won't be easy. You know how she is."

All this, *her* wedding, he'd discussed with *her* father. Instead of her.

"Well, you're a sly one. Sperm donor! Gave me a few more gray hairs! Blamed your mother for spoiling you! Ha! Then you went to Italy and snagged yourself a real prince. Well, you had us all worried there for a while." His tone was affectionate, indulgent even.

"I did not snag him."

"You did well, daughter. He's a good man, and I think he's strong enough to deal with you."

Strong enough? As if she were a problem?

"I can't believe…"

Her father swallowed the last of his fig and beamed jovially as he patted her on the waist, the way he often patted Susana, who found them like that when she came in to tell them dinner was on the table.

"I'm going to marry a prince, too," Gina announced when everybody had gathered around the table and were serving themselves.

You could have heard a pin drop as the little girl picked up a piece of ricotta cheese with her fingers, placed it squarely in the middle of her spoon and then, smiling brightly, lifted the utensil with the poorly balanced food to her mouth.

Regina was holding her breath when the cheese toppled onto the floor.

Gina was about to dive for it when her grandmother grabbed her tiara and said, "Leave it there, darling."

Gina looked at her grandmother and then wisely grabbed her tiara and placed it back on her head. She picked up her fork and stabbed a piece of cheese.

"When she heard a prince was coming, she had to wear her blue princess costume," Susana said, smiling at Nico as if she recognized him.

Susana read the tabloids occasionally. If she was in the grocery store and a lurid headline caught her attention, she would thumb through the magazine. If she failed to find the story and read it before the checker finished, she would often buy it.

"Aunt Reggie gave me my princess costume!" Gina piped as the ricotta fell off the fork onto her plate.

"Since you're so much like your aunt, I'm sure you'll marry a prince, too," Nico said, "if you decide you want to."

Regina stiffened.

"I've never cooked for a prince before," Sabrina said. "You probably have a chef."

"More than one. When you come to the palazzo for our wedding, you must give them all lessons." Nico took Regina's hand and squeezed it, but when her furious gaze rose to his, he looked down at the table, his inky lashes sweeping his dark cheeks.

Smooth. He was too smooth, too sure of his charm. And he should be. He had the carved profile of an ancient emperor. He was probably related to emperors. He'd won her when he'd stared at her on that bench, and he'd won her family in less than an hour.

He was probably kin to emperors. This shouldn't be happening! Their worlds were too different. She remembered his palazzo with its gilded antique furnishings.

He'd invaded her family's simple home and had conquered them. Regina was suddenly so mad at the power he had over her that she tried to kick him under the table. When her toe struck the table leg between them, she gasped and bit back a cry of anguish.

He glanced her way, his blue gaze tender.

Pretend tenderness, she thought.

Noting Nico's concern and his daughter's flushed cheeks, Constantin smiled indulgently at them both. "Ah, young love." He met his wife's eyes. "The baked peppers with ricotta and basil are delicious."

"So are the fried zucchini flowers and lemon chicken," Nico said. "You're not eating, darling? More morning sickness?" Again his eyes were ablaze with a disturbing tenderness that could unravel her.

Why did he have to be so good at faking it?

"No! I'm fine!" Her voice was so harsh Susana and Sabrina frowned and shot warning glances her way.

"Try to eat then, dear," her mother said. "For the baby. Try the cheese."

Regina stabbed a chunk of ricotta and lifted it to her lips. Satisfied, her mother got up to see about dessert.

When everybody had finished their meal, Regina jumped up and was about to clear the table when her mother raised her hand. "Before we do that, why don't you tell us how you two met."

"We—I…" Regina sat back down, unable to find the words.

"On the beach in Amalfi," Nico said, his eyes softening every time he looked at Regina. "My grandmother owns a shop in Ravello and she met Cara first…and was charmed by her. She'd sold her a dress, a most fetching dress. So, later, when she saw Cara under a lemon tree, she waved at her. I looked over and when Cara looked at me, I couldn't look away. It was as if—"

He stopped. Somehow his silence was riveting. "Nothing like that had ever happened to me before."

"How romantic," Susana gushed.

"It was, actually," he said, looking tenderly at Regina, whose hand lay on the table near him.

When his own larger hand covered hers, she felt a rush of unwanted excitement.

Lacing his fingers through her tense fingers, he brought her hand to his lips. While everyone watched, he kissed her fingertips as he had the first time in the bar. He was very still, his eyes on her face, his earnest gaze a pledge in front of her family.

Regina swallowed, but the sudden lump in her throat refused to go down.

"She swept me off my feet," he continued, turning her hand and blowing a scorching kiss against her slender blue-veined wrist, a kiss so hot it made the icicles around her heart melt.

The rat! He was only pretending!

Flushing, Regina yanked her hand free. "Everyone finished? Can I take your plates?" Wild with panic, she pushed back from the table and started stacking the plates much too noisily. Nico stood, too, and began to gather the silverware. Susana and Sabrina were about to protest when Dino and David started to howl.

"Bottle time," Susana said, as mother and grandmother galloped toward the cribs.

Thus, Nico and Regina were left to do the honors of clearing the table and preparing the final course. He made a pot of coffee while she ladled mascarpone custard over sliced pears on crystal plates.

"You probably never did anything like this in your life," she said.

"I'll ignore that and carry the desserts to the table."

"Okay, I'll be blunt," she said when he returned for the last two plates. "I want you out of this kitchen and out of my life."

"You're going to have to get used to me, you know."

She was so angry she wanted to scream. When she picked up a spatula, he grabbed it and set it down on the counter.

"You can't just take over somebody's life," she said.

"Then why did you deliberately become pregnant with my child?"

"I didn't."

He stared into her eyes longer than she could bear it.

"I swear I didn't! And you don't have to marry me!"

Without saying anything, he picked up the last two plates. With a sinking heart, she watched him walk into the dining room, sit down and begin joking with her family as if their exchange had never occurred, as if this were a normal evening.

Normal? His being here, his ordinariness with her family, their acceptance of him was driving her crazy.

Did he intend to win them and break their hearts? Was he that cruel? Or was he just being a man and insensitive and blind as a result?

Except for Regina's nervous tension, the dessert and coffee went as smoothly as dinner. If she grew increasingly silent, everybody was too thrilled by him and the thought of a wedding in a castle to care.

Conversation flowed on all sides of her without the least difficulty. Her mother graciously accepted the fact that she would not be allowed to plan her daughter's wedding. It was almost as if Regina's family had been expecting her pregnancy and this marriage and were overjoyed by them.

Who were these people? She'd never mentioned Nico to any of them. How could he just pop into their lives without any warning, take over, and be so totally accepted?

Why couldn't they have ever accepted her this easily? Who she was? Why had she had to work so hard for the slightest praise? When she felt her thoughts heading into one of those negative loops, she put on the brakes. Her family and Nico either loved one another or they deserved Oscars, and that was just the way it was.

Later, when they were all laughing together in the living room while she stood in a dark corner, feeling left out, Nico got up, put his arms around her and led her to the couch, where he pulled her down beside him, so that she was in the heart of the family circle. He took her hand in his again and held on tight, ignoring her every attempt to pull free. And the truth was, under different circumstances, she might have enjoyed herself.

Regina leaned over and whispered in his ear. "Can't we go now?"

Before he could answer, Gina brought a storybook and laid it on his lap.

He laughed. "How can I resist your niece?"

"Read!" Gina commanded.

"Oh, dear, she's got your bossiness," he whispered into Regina's ear. Aloud, he said, "Why don't I read to her while you help your mother clean up in the kitchen?"

"I can do that later," Sabrina said.

But Nico insisted on playing with the children while Regina helped Sabrina in the kitchen, and, thereby, he won her sister and her mother even more completely. Although he did not go so far as to change a diaper, he did feed each twin part of a bottle, and he burped them, too.

"Can you believe it?" Susana said in the kitchen as Sabrina hand-washed and Regina and Susana dried. "He can tell the twins apart. He even called them by their names. Nobody else has ever been able to do that. I can't believe he's a famous prince. I even saw him on television."

"Then you should know he was about to announce his engagement to a princess," Regina whispered. "Only I got pregnant and ruined his life."

"Don't do that! Why do you always do that?"

"Always do what?"

"Doubt yourself. Overthink stuff."

"I don't always doubt myself," Regina snapped.

"Okay. You're right, as always. You're a lawyer. Everything's got to be logical and go along with some plan or list you've made. I learned a long time ago not to argue with you when you're in lawyer mode. But this man loves you."

Susana spoke with all-knowing, completely exasperating confidence.

"You couldn't possibly know that."

"Maybe you made straight A's, but I was the one who was good with men...and feelings."

Ouch. Regina remembered how deftly Susana had stolen Joe right out from under her. Suddenly she was glad Susana had.

"Trust me," Susana said. "Trust him. Trust yourself. And your feelings. For once. He loves you. Sometimes feelings can be smarter than you are."

Susana should know. That's the way she'd always operated. *And everybody loves her,* said a little voice.

By the time the dishes were finished, Nico had read Gina several fairy tales about princesses while she'd stared up at him with big, awed eyes.

"Read *Cinderella* again," Gina begged when the women came out of the kitchen.

"He's already read it three times," her father said.

"Then that's enough," Susana said. "He has to take Regina home. She's going to have a baby, and she needs her rest."

Three whole times? He'd read *Cinderella* three whole times.

"We do have to go," Regina agreed, trying to act like she wasn't the least bit impressed with his talent with children or jealous if he happened to smile at Susana.

"I was having so much fun I didn't realize how late it was," Nico said. "I hope we didn't overstay our welcome."

"Oh, no! No! We loved having you!" her parents and sister gushed.

"I'm going to marry a prince—just like you!" Gina cried. "And live in a castle!"

"Big hug," Nico whispered, kneeling, and the little girl ran into his arms. "When you're all grown-up, I'll introduce you to lots of princes."

When Gina finally released him, he stood up and put his arm around Regina, and for a moment it seemed almost possible that he would be at her side always, that they would have a real marriage.

When he headed toward the door, her family followed them down the sidewalk. Their goodbyes were so warm, her fantasy that they could be a real couple and have a real future persisted a little longer.

At the limousine, her daddy embraced her and wouldn't let her go for several long moments. "I'm so happy for you," he said. "So proud of you."

They smiled at each other in the silvery dark. For the first time since Susana's birth, Regina felt a closeness to him that was almost a completeness.

And she had Nico to thank! Nico, of all people—the enemy!

The two men shook hands. Her mother kissed Nico's cheek.

It was so wrong.

They're all so happy and I'm so happy! But this marriage isn't real! I should tell them now! Tonight! That it won't last a year. I really should tell them!

But, of course, she didn't because she didn't want to, and all too soon she was alone with Nico in the dark, silent limousine again.

Fifteen

"I thought that went well," Nico said a few minutes later as the long car slipped through the silent dark.

"Doesn't it bother you at all that you'll break their hearts?"

"I don't intend to break anybody's heart. That's your specialty."

"I don't want to break anybody's heart," she whispered.

To that he said nothing.

"You didn't have to be *so* nice to them, you know. Especially *so* nice to the children."

"Was that so bad? Do you really think everything I do is to hurt you?"

"After tonight, they'll never understand how awful you are. They'll always be on your side."

"Stop being a lawyer. What if there aren't any sides?"

"There are always sides."

"No. Not always. Two people can become one."

"Not us," she whispered.

As though he were very tired, he leaned back and shut his eyes, seemingly weary of fighting her.

Was he right? Did there always have to be sides? Could two people as different as they were, two families as different as theirs were, live in harmony for the rest of their lives?

She remembered the golden, hazy perfection of Ravello. The pink sunsets, the sea breezes.

What if *they* could? What if...

When she glanced at him and saw the blue-black highlights gleaming in the lock of hair that fell over his brow, she felt a dangerous softening in her heart.

Chiseled profile, olive skin, black hair, sensual lips. Did he have to be *so* incredibly handsome? To act *so* nice, at least, when he wasn't furious? She marveled at his patience, reading *Cinderella* to Gina three times.

Suddenly, Regina wondered where he was staying tonight. The intoxicating memory of him standing naked and as glorious as a well-endowed god or Michelangelo's *David* in her hotel room came back to her.

When the limousine stopped, he let her out and walked her to her front porch. Without a word, he took her key and deftly unlocked her door. She crossed her threshold and then stopped without inviting him in. She was surprised and disappointed when he didn't assume he had the right to follow her inside. Hesitating, she flipped on the light in her foyer and noted the deep shadows under his eyes.

"You look tired," she said, her voice gentle.

"I am. A little."

"Do you want to—" she nodded shyly "—come in?"

He stepped inside and shut the door, and then they both stood there, aware of each other and yet unsure of each other, as well.

Suddenly, she realized how much she wanted to be alone with him, had wanted it all night during the long, drawn-out dinner. Only she hadn't wanted to admit it. And now that she had him all to herself, she didn't know what to do or say. Or even what to think.

What if she simply slipped out of her dress and ran naked into his arms?

Her hand went to the zipper at the back of her dress. Watching her and perhaps reading her intent, he turned on his heel and strode into the kitchen. Cabinet doors banged open and closed until he found her liquor supply. Quickly, he poured himself a double shot of Scotch.

With an acute ache in her heart, she watched him go to her living room and sink into the soft cushions of her deep couch, his dark head falling backward across the navy cushions. His shoulders slumped as he stretched out his long legs and tore his tie loose. She turned a light off. But not before she saw the lines and the gray shadows beneath his eyes again.

He'd flown all the way from Rome. He was probably jet-lagged and utterly exhausted from dealing with her.

"You could sleep here if you wanted," she offered. "I have a spare bedroom. Two, in fact."

His brows lifted in wary surprise. For a long, unnerving moment it seemed to Regina that the word *bedroom* hung heavily in the air.

She didn't know what else she could say or do, so she stood motionless and silent.

"Thank you." He drained his Scotch. "For the offer."

Feeling awkward and yet rejected when he didn't move or state his intentions, she fled down the hall to her own bedroom. Deliberately leaving her door unlocked, she undressed. As she slipped into her sheerest nightgown and washed her face, even as she brushed her teeth, she tried not to think about Nico sprawled on her couch in the living room.

Despite attempts to busy herself in her bathroom by straightening her towel on its towel rack and scrubbing out an immaculate soap dish, all she could think about was him.

Did he still want her? Or was theirs to be only a marriage of convenience? Every time a board creaked in the house, she would glance toward her door, hoping he'd be there.

All of a sudden, nothing mattered except that she was having his baby and he was going to marry her. If they lived together as man and wife, maybe there was still a chance.

She'd forgotten her own anger and all his harsh words and

accusations and even the domineering way he'd proposed. He'd
been sweet to the children and considerate of her family, considerate of her, too, at least, around them.

There was no logic to explain the reason her desire for him
began to feel like a pulsing, all-consuming need. The simple truth
was she could not be around him for long without loving him and
wanting him, even when knowing he could be as bad tempered
as an angry skunk.

She thought about going in to check on him, hoping he'd
notice her in her sheer nightgown. Instead, she pulled back the
sheets and climbed into bed, her heart beating faster and faster.

She turned out the light and waited breathlessly. The little
clock on her bedside table ticked and ticked and ticked, and in the
dark she began to count those maddening passing seconds. Finally,
crazed, she grabbed the clock and stuffed it under a pillow.

Should she go to him? Should she try to explain again? Her
mind whirled, caught in one of those tangled loops.

Hours later, when she was only half awake, she started at what
she thought were heavy footsteps in the hall. Her heart thudding,
her mind blurred with exhaustion, she looked up and saw a
shadowy, wide-shouldered figure looming in her doorway.

Nico.

Her eyes snapped open. Her heart thundered.

"Sorry. I didn't mean to scare you." He leaned against the
doorjamb and combed his thick hair with his fingers. "The Scotch
must have hit me pretty hard. I fell asleep. I'll be going to my
hotel now." His husky voice sounded infinitely weary.

"I know you must have had a long day. You don't have—"

"I'll call you. First thing tomorrow."

His manner was cool, businesslike. *Final.* Abruptly, he turned
on his heel.

She heard her front door close softly and the limousine
drive away.

"It already is…tomorrow."

Filled with conflict and doubts, she lay tossing and turning.
Would he come back? Or was he finished with her?

She was still awake when the sky turned rosy and the phone rang.

"I've chartered a jet," Nico said. "We leave after lunch. I spoke to my mother an hour ago."

Again his voice was cool and deliberately businesslike.

When he hung up, Regina lay against her pillows, feeling more mixed up than ever, but pleased that he'd called and so early. As if he were impatient.

How quickly time brings, if not happiness exactly, acceptance and hope.

All of a sudden, her sleepless night hit her. Pulling her little clock out from under the pillow, she set the alarm to go off in two hours. When she lay down again, she fell instantly and blissfully asleep.

She dreamed of Italy. Again she was lying with Nico in the bottom of his tender in that cool, dark cave that smelled of dank sea things. The water was lapping against the sides of the boat as rhythmically as his warm body drove into hers. And all she knew was that she wanted to be with him forever.

Sixteen

Even though the rain had slowed to a drizzle, the wipers were still slashing the windshield at their highest setting. Nico drove through the tall gates. As he braked the Alpha Romeo in front of the palazzo, Regina sat up straighter.

As if on cue, a horde of whispering servants rushed out of the beautiful pink house.

"Who are they?"

"I told Mother no fuss," Nico said.

A single glance from Abruzzi, the same gaunt, balding gentleman who'd stood guard over Regina not so long ago, soon had everybody lined up in the rain. Each stood as stiffly as a martinet on either side of the granite stairs.

"Oh, no! Why is he making them do that? They'll be soaked!"

Sudden queasiness climbed her throat. Gasping for air, she rolled down her window. There'd been too many long miles, too many narrow, winding roads. And now this.

After she'd gulped in a few breaths and managed a smile, Nico cupped her chin, lifting it.

"Are you all right?" His face was creased with worry.

"I think so."

Harried-looking men and women in black business attire, obviously secretaries, accountants and administrators, rushed out and stood above the maids and cooks, housemen and chauffeurs.

"I'm sorry, but maybe it's for the best," he said. "You had to meet them sometime. The rain will be our excuse for cutting the introductions short."

"My mother doesn't even have a maid. My father mows the lawn."

Nico got out quickly and ran around the front of the car to help her out.

Bone weary from the overnight flight and the long drive from Rome, Regina clung to him throughout the introductions.

Their plane had touched down at Fumichino at ten in the morning in black skies and heavy rain. Due to bad traffic and more storms, not to mention several accidents on the autostrada, they hadn't reached the Amalfi Coast until five.

No sooner had they greeted the staff, and everyone was inside drying themselves off, than Massimo appeared, his plump, tanned face wreathed in smiles. He greeted them warmly, embracing Regina even, before leading them down an elaborately appointed gallery to Gloriana's high-ceilinged, ornate study.

Looking formidable in royal-blue silk and huge diamonds, the princess neither smiled nor rose from her Louis XIV desk when they entered. Her calm blue eyes passed over Regina as if she were a ghost and totally invisible.

With a little pucker between her painted brows the princess focused entirely on Nico. "I need to talk to you. Alone. It's most pressing."

"Mother—"

"Tiberio and Massimo will show Miss Tomei to her suite, the red rooms, so that she can rest. The poor dear looks exhausted."

So, she had seen the ghost, her future daughter-in-law, after all.

Tiberio Abruzzi materialized as if by magic. The princess

nodded at Massimo, who rushed toward the man. Abruzzi turned to Regina, his stern glance ordering her to follow—at once.

Regina seized Nico's hand and clung.

He squeezed her fingers and then released them. "You'll be all right. I won't be long. I promise. I will come for you shortly before dinner, which is at seven."

Feeling abandoned somehow and overwhelmed by the palazzo again, she lifted her cheek, hoping for some scrap of affection. When his lips brushed her cheek, a wild, tumultuous heat flooded her.

Slowly she lifted her chin. Then she followed Massimo, who walked with her a short way and then turned her over to Abruzzi. After that, she had to race to keep up with the tall servant as he sped silently through the many halls and galleries to the red rooms.

An hour later, she was still alone trying to feel at home in the gorgeous, gilded bedroom that had been assigned to her. She forced herself to study the furniture, the crystal, the brocade curtains, and each of the old masters hanging on the red-satin wallpaper. If she were to live here, she must grow used to the beauty of these delightful rooms and objects; she must learn to take them as her due.

She tried to tilt her chin higher so that she could study the ornate ceiling where splashes of turquoise had been combined with crimson and gold. But suddenly her neck hurt, and she realized she'd been awake for many hours and that all she wanted to do was lie down and wait for Nico.

First, she went to the window and opened it, so that she could smell the cool sweetness of the lightly falling rain. Then loosening the buttons of her dress, she went to the bed and pushed the heavy satin spread back and sank tiredly onto the mattress.

Two months ago, it would not have been dark at this hour. Oh, but how nice it was to stretch out horizontally between cool, clean sheets while the rain tap-danced on the balcony and balustrade outside. Her head ached with exhaustion as she strained to hear Nico's footsteps.

Soon he would come. She tried to stay awake, but slowly, the rain was music that lulled her. And a black curtain came down. And she was gone.

When Nico knocked at the door of the red rooms and called her name, she didn't answer, so he slipped inside.

The silent room was shrouded in darkness.

"Cara?"

Above the patter of the rain, he heard her sweet sigh from the bed. He turned just as the moon peeped through the clouds, bathing the bed and her with its silvery light.

She looked like an enchanted princess. *His* princess.

Her lovely face was as pale as alabaster; her hair gleamed like dark satin against her pillows. Her chest, sculpted by the white sheets, moved up and down. Her lips were cherry red and he was eager to wake her and kiss her. But she looked so peaceful asleep; so adorable, almost happy.

His heart swelled with desire and with something even more powerful that he refused to consider. She had not looked like this since he'd dropped her at Fumichino two months ago after they'd made love the whole way to Rome. How her eyes had glimmered with tears at their parting. How she'd clung to him, kissing his cheeks and lips and then burying her face deep into his chest. And only after she'd walked away with Massimo and he'd watched the exact spot where she'd vanished for more than half an hour, the longest thirty minutes in his life, had he even begun to realize how deeply he might need her.

Who was she really? A cynical opportunist who'd used him? Or the gentle, passionate woman he'd fallen in love with?

He didn't care. Whoever she was, he wanted her. Something had begun that he was powerless to stop. From the first, when she'd waved at *Grand-mère* from the bench under the lemon tree, he'd wanted her more than he'd ever wanted any woman. And the wanting had only grown more fierce.

Why? Why her?

Did why ever matter? Some things just were. From the

beginning, he'd been in over his head, his passion having assumed a life of its own.

Love. War. Birth. Death. Human beings thought they could control such matters, but they were an arrogant, doomed species whose passions ruled them.

He stood over her for an hour, his shadow falling across her pale face. The dinner hour came and went, and yet he felt compelled to stay and watch over her. At least, when she was asleep, he could protect her from the forces in this house, in his world, even from the forces within himself that resented and threatened her.

Finally, he leaned down and kissed her lips gently. She stirred and smiled. When she whispered his name, he wanted to kiss her again and again. But he knew that if he did so, he would not stop.

The first thing Regina noticed when she awakened at dawn was the pink sun streaming through the long windows, filling the beautiful room with soft feathers of early light. She felt the pillow beside her and realized she was alone.

Nico had not come.

Seventeen

At eight o'clock sharp, a young maid with creamy skin and a white apron announced to Regina in a beautiful Polish accent that breakfast was to be served on the north terrace at nine and that she would be back to fetch her.

"Where's Nico? I mean, Prince Nico?"

The pretty maid looked confused. "Sorry, *signorina.* Princess Gloriana told me to come. That's all I know."

She curtsied and was about to go when Regina called her back.

"I've been up and dressed for hours. I would like to walk in the garden. Could you show me the way and then come find me there?"

"As you wish, madame."

Nico had not come. With a sickening feeling of abandonment, she followed the girl outside to the pool where the swans made ripples across its dark, glassy surface. Birds were singing in the cypress trees. Exotic blossoms bloomed in the flower beds even though it was autumn.

Some variety of flower must bloom all year here in this centuries-old paradise. But where was Nico? She glanced up at the palazzo and thought she saw a tall, dark man and a blond woman at a long window watching her. Then they vanished, and she wondered if they'd seen her or if she'd merely imagined them.

She began to walk along the intricate gravel paths that wound through the beautiful garden overhanging the sea, this garden that seemed more fantasy than reality. At first, she tried to concentrate on the crunching sound her feet made so that she wouldn't dwell on Nico or the multitude of questions that tortured her heart.

Then she began to enjoy the glories of the garden with its mountains that climbed to the sky on one side and the blue sea that stretched forever on the other.

Her verdant surroundings were so beautiful that soon her walk took over. Her mood became meditative, and she opened her heart to infinite possibilities.

She was here. She was to marry Nico. All her life she'd thought she could plan and that her ambitions and work would take her where she wanted. But she'd lost touch with herself. She'd done things she wasn't proud of. She'd wanted more than her career, more than marriage to a respected professional. Only, she hadn't known what *more* was until now. No man had ever felt so right as Nico, who was from this extravagant world that she had never even imagined.

Life was so much more mysterious than she'd bargained for. One never knew what the next moment would be or bring. As she stared at the palazzo, she couldn't begin to imagine what her life would be like as his wife.

The maid came as she'd promised, startling Regina out of her reverie and then leading her back inside. Regina followed through what seemed like miles of galleries and sitting rooms, all filled with rococo, neoclassical and Louis XVI furnishings. Through the centuries, Romanos must have collected these beautiful things and designed rooms to display them advantageously. As always, the beauty of the palazzo dazzled and overwhelmed her as the garden and its simple pleasures had not.

Suddenly, a door opened, and a slim blond woman, a younger version of Nico's mother, emerged into the hall. Then, as if to catch her breath or regain her composure after some unfortunate encounter, the woman stopped and stood outside the door for a long moment. Then lifting her chin, she turned and headed straight for Regina.

She had fine, delicate features; soft, light-colored hair and luminous violet eyes. Her complexion glowed. She was exquisite and so perfectly made that, except for her stricken expression, she seemed more like a doll than a human.

Principessa Donna Viola Eugenia di Frezano.

Regina gasped in awe and then compassion swept her.

Viola had frozen, too. Then without a word, the princess turned and fled, but not before Regina had seen that her cheeks were streaked with tears.

No servant needed to lead Viola through the maze of gilded rooms. Clearly, even blinded by tears, she knew this maze of ornate rooms by heart.

When Regina looked inside the door from which Viola had come, she saw a grim-faced Nico staring out a tall window. Was it the same window where she'd seen the couple watching her?

"Nico?"

He turned, his expression dazed. For a long moment, it was as if she weren't there.

Was he brokenhearted over having lost Viola?

"Cara?" His dark face registered surprise. He stood up straighter. "Did you sleep well?" His tone was polite, formal.

Regina found his perfect manners, so like his mother's, unendurable. Were they to be man and wife and yet strangers, never to talk about what mattered?

"You said you'd come for me."

"You were asleep."

"I just saw Viola," she whispered.

"For the first and last time."

"You broke your engagement with her?"

"I explained the situation to her. She was very understanding."

"But upset?"

"Yes."

"She looked hurt, devastated."

"I never told her about us, you see. Her staff will speak to the press later today."

"And what will she say?"

"Whatever she wants to say. She will have to move on. As we all will."

"I'm sorry for all the trouble. If you love her, if you prefer her…"

"It is done." He crossed the space that separated them, and yet he felt as far away as ever. "Shall we go down to breakfast together?"

He took her hand. His palm felt cold, and she noticed that he did not bring her fingers to his lips.

"My mother is expecting us."

Would they eat with her every morning? Would they never be alone like a normal couple? Share their own private confidences? Have their own lives? Were they always to live here, with his family?

If only they could have eaten alone this morning.

The Principessa Gloriana was already at a table shaded by a melon-colored umbrella. As they walked up to her, hand in hand, she sipped coffee, patted her lipstick with her napkin, and then gave Nico a chilly smile. Again, she treated Regina as if she didn't exist.

Maybe that was for the best.

"Isn't it a lovely morning," Gloriana said to Nico. "All the dark clouds gone and our glorious Amalfi sun shining so brightly."

"Yes." Regina nodded even though she knew she had not been addressed. "The terrace has such breathtaking views of the water and cliffs."

"It does indeed," Gloriana said. "How lovely to see you again, my dear." Her words were polite, but her blue eyes, so like her son's, were colder than polar ice chips. "I do hope the flight wasn't too tiring and that you rested well. For the baby's sake."

Regina's throat went dry.

Nerves, she hoped. Not morning sickness.

Hot bile climbed her throat. Near panic, she fought to swallow.

Feeling more miserable by the second, she forced a smile. When her mouth twisted, Nico's hand closed over hers.

Then a manservant brought a cart brimming with fruit and cheeses and all kinds of breads including buttery, rich croissants, Regina's favorite. Tiberio Abruzzi, who was standing behind the man and his cart, stared down his nose at her and asked in a lofty tone what the *signorina* would like.

Regina's gaze flicked across luscious thick white lumps of buffalo mozzarella, to raw eggs, omelet makings and then to thick slabs of ham.

"I—I'm not hungry." Clammy with sweat, she sank back in her chair as the awful stuff in her throat bubbled higher.

Terrified of embarrassing herself before Nico, she tried to swallow. But it was hopeless.

Her chair scraped the table as she stood up. Not knowing where a restroom was, she bolted. Behind her, china shattered and the principessa gasped. Regina barely made it to the nearest hedge before she was on the ground losing the contents of whatever she'd managed to eat on the plane.

"Cara—"

She flung herself toward the palazzo, desperate to escape them all, even Nico. A violent cramp shot through her stomach, and she realized she was going to be sick again. There would be no escape. Weakly she stumbled back to the hedge and fell to her knees a second time.

Even before she finished, she felt strong arms around her, supporting her and then Nico was lifting her, holding her tightly because her knees were so rubbery she couldn't stand.

"I'm sorry," she whispered.

"Don't apologize. Don't ever apologize," Nico said.

She caught the citrusy tang of his aftershave, usually a pleasant scent. She swallowed again because she so longed to stay in his arms, but that faint fruity odor ruined it.

"Your aftershave...lemons...awful. I'm sorry." Feeling fuzzy, she fell to her knees again. Only this time, her stomach was empty, so she only had the dry heaves.

Nico's face was lined and grim as he led her back to her room.

"I don't want to make you unhappy," she whispered when she

was sitting down on a little chair in the shade of her balcony as Nico applied a cold towel to her face. Abruzzi stood just inside the door, awaiting further instructions.

"You don't want to marry me," she whispered. "You must let me go. For both our sakes. For your mother's sake. For the baby's sake."

"Hush. Hush. When you feel better, we'll talk. Abruzzi suggested crackers and bananas and some cottage cheese. He said that's all his wife could eat when she was pregnant. Do you think you could eat that?"

She nodded, not wanting to displease him or the terrifying Abruzzi. Then she shook her head miserably.

"No. No crackers."

Abruzzi's stern face fell.

"Ice cream," she said, craving it suddenly. "Chocolate ice cream. Lots of chocolate ice cream…please."

Abruzzi beamed with delight. "Gelato, chocolate, *signorina*, for the baby!" His black eyes came alive as he raced away to do her bidding.

When he brought two heaping bowls, she began eat small spoonfuls. Nico asked if he could leave her briefly to shower.

"So you won't keep wrinkling your nose and rushing to the nearest bush because I smell like lemons."

"Don't even say the word."

He laughed and was gone. When he returned, the bowls of ice cream were gone, and she was feeling much better.

"It's not too late, to change your mind about marrying me," she whispered when he sat down beside her on her balcony.

"I want to marry you."

"But ours won't be a real marriage, if we're already planning to divorce."

His brows shot together. "Cara, nobody must know this isn't a real marriage. Nobody. We who live here say the palazzo has ears in every wall. Rumors start so easily, and, if the media hears even a hint of such things, they can cause great unhappiness. Even my family, Massimo especially, has difficulty keeping secrets. We Italians are extroverts. All we do is talk. I don't want our child's birth surrounded by unnecessary scandal. Do you understand?"

"Yes. You're telling me we'll live a lie, that we'll pretend we love each other. I guess I can at least try, since you're only asking me to do that for a year."

"Damn it." His face dark, his voice held a steely note she hated.

"What do you want me to say then?" she asked.

"Kiss me and pretend you mean it."

She froze. "All right."

She stood up. So did he. She lifted her lips, standing stiffly, regally.

His eyes narrowed as if something about this whole situation displeased him. Then he leaned forward and caressed her shoulders. Her eyes drifted shut as she waited. Then his mouth found hers and even though his lips barely touched hers, her passion flared to life.

She rose onto her tiptoes and threw her arms around his neck. Then she pressed herself closer, closer, until she could feel his heat and hear the drumbeat of his heart.

He deepened the kiss, and she leaned farther into him, offering herself, offering everything.

He drew back, smiling at her, really smiling at her, for the first time in days. Playfully he kissed the tip of her nose.

"You're very good at pretending," he said.

"So are you."

Eager for more, she pulled his head down to hers again and lost herself in more kisses. He began to say soft, caressing things to her in Italian.

"I love it when you do that."

"What?"

"Speak Italian."

He smiled. "I love the language…which melts like kisses and sounds as if it has been writ on satin…syllables which breathe… er…" He struggled for the rest of the line. "Passion."

"Why, that's beautiful."

"Lord Byron, or rather a jumble of Lord Byron. I'm afraid I don't remember the entire poem."

"I like it that you can quote poetry. Dante."

"Memorization is not the loftiest of mental gifts, you know."

"Don't belittle yourself," she said.

"Kissing you is fun. Maybe we should pretend we love each other again," he said, bringing his mouth closer to hers again.

As he gazed down at her, her heart began to flutter nervously. She wet her lips in anticipation.

Then his mouth found hers again, and his tongue came inside her lips. He groaned. She moved her body against his, rubbing her breasts against his massive chest, wanting to be nearer, nearer, aching to be consumed utterly by him.

"Nico, my darling, darling."

When more Italian burst from him, her whole body burned with desire.

Was he saying he loved her, or was he only pretending? He took her hand and was leading her into the bedroom, when there was a sound at the door.

Who knows what might have happened next, if his mother hadn't chosen that moment to appear. As always, she was perfectly groomed and as dazzling as a rare jewel in an absolutely exquisite pink silk suit. Parisian runway, no doubt.

Apologizing politely and lifting her arched brows, she said there was a crisis that needed Nico's attention immediately.

"Can't it wait?" he said in a low, irritable tone.

She shook her head and swept from the room, her footsteps growing fainter in the hall.

"Sorry, darling." There was only a faint echo of passion in his voice. He squeezed Regina's hand and kissed her lightly on the cheek.

Then he was gone, too, and she was left alone on her stone parapet with only her beautiful view for companionship.

Juliet without her Romeo.

Hugging herself, she leaned against the balustrade, shuddering in frustration. She needed a job, something to do, *anything.*

But what? What could she do today? She began to pace the balcony. What did a future princess do to amuse herself all day *in paradise?*

The garden beckoned beneath her. The sunlight was brilliant in the trees. There was an ineffable sweetness of flowers mingling with the scent of the sea.

She dashed out of the red rooms. She would take a walk among the flowers again, a long meditative walk in the garden. She would watch the swans.

When she grew bored with the big white birds, who were content with each other and their placid pond and paid no attention to her, she meandered along the gravel paths until she grew tired of the garden, too. She felt confined, lost.

As she was about to turn back toward the palazzo, she discovered a little gate shrouded with ancient grape vines. A gardener was weeding nearby, so she asked him where the path led.

Yanking an earphone out of his ear, the man stood up. He was dark and thick around the middle. His white shirt was caked with black dirt; his silver curls wet with sweat. His English was as terrible as her Italian, but somehow he managed to make her understand with many smiles and much wild gesticulating that the vine and the path were pre-Roman, that the trail had been used for centuries by the shepherds and their flocks.

How wonderful. She opened the gate and wandered like a child in a land of enchantment for an hour or more, forgetting her restlessness and feeling that she was useless, as she explored the terraced gardens and ochre-colored villas that dotted the cliffs above the sea.

Only when she became thoroughly lost did she notice the time. She sat down on a low rock and pulled out her cell phone, which she must have switched off. When she turned it on, she saw that Nico had called her at least five or six times.

When she rang him, his voice was terse and cold. "Where are you?"

"I don't know. I was walking in the garden. I found a little gate and a shepherd's trail that led down the cliffs. I didn't think. I'm afraid I'm lost."

For a long moment he didn't speak. "I've been worried sick." He asked her to describe her whereabouts.

Five minutes later, he was loping down the steep path toward her. When he saw her, he stopped and sucked in air.

She took three faltering steps up the mountain toward him.

"I thought you'd left me," he said.

"I'm sorry if I worried you."

A long silence followed her statement. He stood very still. How lonely he looked, she suddenly thought, her heart going to him. Did he need her then, just a little?

Or was she only imagining that he did?

Who was he really, this prince she was marrying?

This handsome stranger?

Eighteen

A dazed Princess Donna Regina Carina Tomei di Romano sat in the red rooms alone staring at the glittering band of diamonds on her left hand. She still wore the simple white suit she'd been married in, as well as the little hat with its short veil.

She had married a man she hardly knew.

The private ceremony in the magnificent Salon d'Or with her family and Nico's royal mother watching had been awful, simply awful, at least for her. Because of her morning sickness, Regina's voice had been inaudible to all but Nico, who'd leaned close to hear.

Well, now he was trapped, and so was she. And the whole world was watching, waiting for the first sign of a crack in one of her glass slippers.

The palazzo had notified the press immediately after the ceremony. A trusted journalist, who'd agreed to allow Gloriana final approval of his article, wanted to write Regina's "Cinderella story." Gloriana had personally granted him a private interview with Regina on the terrace.

Unfortunately, his first two questions had made Regina too sick to complete the interview.

Question number one: "Was Prince Nico's 'good friend' Princess Viola on the guest list?"

"The ceremony was small and private. We simply couldn't invite everybody," she'd whispered, wondering why she had to do this on her wedding day.

"And quite sudden, I understand." He'd leaned closer, scribbling furiously.

"I—I… Yes. I suppose it seemed sudden."

"Why the hurry?" When his eyes bored into her, Regina's stomach had rolled.

"I—I don't feel—" She'd arisen and run. Now, she was terrified that she'd given away her secret pregnancy.

Her wedding ring and the red wallpaper blurred. Feeling dreadful about her first failure with a journalist, she walked to her balcony and watched the swans on their placid pool.

Well, at least the ceremony was over.

For Regina, the hasty preparations, the wedding, her family's joyous arrival, which had infected the palazzo with gaiety, had all passed as if in a dream.

Only yesterday, Princess Viola's staff had announced that there was nothing to the rumors of marriage regarding herself and Prince Nico Romano, that they had always been and would continue to be just "good friends." When Nico had been asked to comment, he'd been unavailable.

Nico's "good friend" had not attended the marriage of Prince Nico Romano to *Signorina* Regina Carina Tomei, which had taken place in the magnificent Salon d'Or in the midst of a sea of lilies, roses and orchids.

To Regina, the civil ceremony had felt cold and rushed. Nico's mother hadn't smiled during the ceremony nor during the celebratory reception afterward for one hundred people.

Nico's mood had been equally severe during both events. He'd said all the right words, slipped the ring on her finger, but his lips had felt stiff and cool after doing so.

Only little Gina, and Regina's father and Nico's grandmother, who'd enjoyed causing a stir by upsetting her daughter, had acted happy. Seconds before the wedding, the old lady had arrived unannounced in green veils and wearing so much gold she'd looked like a Gypsy.

Regina's father had been flushed with pride as he'd led her down the grand staircase. He hadn't been the least bit intimidated by the palazzo or by Nico's mother or even by his older sister, Principessa Carolina, who'd flown in from Madrid, demanding to know why she hadn't been told about the wedding sooner.

Maybe it was the morning sickness blurring her senses, but the whole, horrible affair didn't seem real to Regina now.

I'll wake up, she thought, *back in Texas…where I belong.*

She heard a sound and turned. Gloriana, in the same smartly tailored white suit she'd worn to the wedding, stood there.

Wasn't there some rule that a mother-in-law's outfit should not compete with the bride's?

Her blue eyes were huge and luminous and filled with profound grief. She couldn't have looked sadder if she'd buried Nico.

"People are asking where you are. You're upsetting Nico." As always, her voice was pleasant and well modulated.

"How long will it take me to learn that appearances are everything?"

"I should think you would want to be at the reception in your moment of triumph."

"You would think that."

"You caught him when he was weak, grief stricken."

So that was what she thought.

"He is not in love with you. When he comes to his senses, he'll hate you. This marriage is a huge step down for him. You're not even from a princely family, much less a royal one, as he is. You are not even rich. Who are you? An attorney, who was fired for incompetency? How many languages do you speak?"

"I love him."

"I hope, for his sake, that you do."

"We both love him. At least we have that in common."

"No, I *love* him. Someday, soon, you'll know how deep a mother's love is. I want what's best for him." She drew a deep breath. "All I ask is that you at least pretend you love him. Don't hurt him any more than you already have."

"You must teach me how to pretend."

Where this conversation would have gone would always be a mystery because Nico appeared. His mother whirled, her lovely face instantly serene.

"I will leave you to enjoy your bride," she said in a sweet, false tone.

"No time for that—yet. I was looking for both of you. More pictures need to be taken."

"So many pictures? I feel a little like a movie star," Regina said, wishing only to be alone with him.

"These are for the newspapers and television. They won't take long."

After more photographs, Regina stood beside Nico on a balcony and watched a fireworks display in their honor while flashbulbs flickered constantly beneath them.

"The media circus has begun." Nico turned. "Smile at me, *tesorina,* they want the fairy tale."

So do I.

She smiled up at him and he brought her hand to his lips.

"Why so fast?" the reporters demanded of anyone who would answer questions.

"Who is this *Signorina* Regina Carina Tomei?"

"Where did she come from?"

"How did they meet?"

"Why did he marry her?"

Lucy left frantic messages for Regina. Reporters were camped outside her door, demanding to know every intimate detail of her friend's recent vacation in Italy.

"Tell me what to tell them!" Lucy cried in her final message. "I get contractions every time the phone rings!"

So, this is my life. I'm a princess now. Regina felt wonder as she watched streamers of orange fire blossom against a black sky and drizzle bits of gold to earth in her honor.

Nico leaned closer and grasped her hand tightly in his. "You were a planner. Of all the men in the world, why did you pick me? Why me?" His voice was dark and urgent.

"I didn't pick you. I just…" *I just couldn't resist you.*

Ribbons of white curled against the sky.

"You knew who I was, didn't you?" he persisted.

She shook her head.

"I've always been wanted because I'm a Romano and the heir to all this."

"I didn't know who you were."

"But you're a plotter and a planner."

"What if you could believe that I didn't plan any of this?" she said. "That it simply happened, like you once told me?"

"What if?" he whispered, his eyes devouring her.

"I didn't know who you were. I swear."

Regina was wearing a filmy nightgown and a transparent robe that she'd bought in Portofino for her wedding night. Every time she glanced at the great bed and its red satin spread, she trembled.

"I will leave you to wait for him alone if you want me to," Susana said. "Maybe he knows I'm with you. Maybe that's why he hasn't come."

Susana headed toward the door.

"No! Stay! There's something I must tell you—a secret."

Susana ran to her. "This is like a fairy tale."

"No. I can't bear for you to think that." Regina hesitated. "He didn't want to marry me. He wanted to marry Viola. He plans to divorce me in a year."

"Don't do this. Don't always do this. He loves you," Susana whispered. "I know he does. I told you, I can tell."

"You are so naive. Look at this room. Do we…do I belong here?"

"You could. I could if Joe had grown up here. Why are you

always so cynical, so ready to believe nobody can love you? Why? When you are so gifted and talented?"

"Why is loving so easy for you?"

"Maybe because I always had you to protect me and to look up to. I felt safe and happy, protected. Trust me on this. It will work out, even here, in this place, if you love him, too. Do you love him?"

"Yes. But I have always been unlucky in love."

"The past doesn't matter. Not if this is true love. If you really love him and commit, you will do whatever it takes to make him happy, and he will do the same for you. You'll see."

"I wish I could believe you. Daddy was so proud today."

"Yes. He was great until he drank all that champagne and had to go to bed with a headache. Mama is very upset to have missed the dancing."

"And it's all based on a lie."

"Don't say that. Don't even think it."

"I can't help myself. I'm so afraid. Where is Nico? It's late."

Susana glanced at her watch. "Oh! You're right! I need to go check on the twins and Gina and see how Daddy's doing. But I hate to leave you like this. I know how your mind works when you get in a mood like this."

"I'll be fine."

"You're sure?"

Trembling all over, Regina nodded bravely.

They hugged. Susana let her go and then looked up at her, giggling. "My big sister, the princess!"

Alone in the red rooms again, anxiety swept Regina. She began to pace. One minute she felt on fire. In the next, the blood drained from her face and hands, and she was freezing. Then she caught fire all over again.

Terrified, she ran out onto the balcony. When her eyes grew accustomed to the gloom, she saw a tall, dark figure in the moonlight, staring up at her.

She leaned over the railing. "Nico?"

Was he as frightened as she was?

He turned away, and she cried his name again. "Nico! Come to me!"

When he turned back, she slid the transparent robe off her shoulders and let it fall in a swish of silk to the stone floor.

"No!" he yelled. "Don't!"

"You'd better come up here then before I strip for the whole world to see! Even the paparazzi!"

He was running toward the palazzo even before she tore off her nightgown and flung it at him.

Nineteen

Nico raced toward the red rooms like a wild man.

What had she thought? Tearing off that filmy thing with the light behind her? Anyone could have seen her. Photographed her. Why didn't she care that the paparazzi were everywhere?

The mere memory of her slim body, so clearly revealed, made his heart pound faster. He felt like a beast, driven by a savage hunger.

When he banged on the doors to the red suite, and she didn't answer, he kicked the door open and strode inside. Alone in the silent, dark room, all he heard was the harsh rasping of his own breathing.

Then she glided out of the shadows into the moonlight. Except for the gardenia in her hair, she was naked. Slim and curvaceous, she was more beautiful than a goddess from some ancient myth.

He closed his eyes, clenched his fists, fighting the all-consuming fire burning inside him.

"Nico?" she said softly. "I wanted you to come. I waited and waited."

"Were you going to show yourself to the whole world? You're mine. Only mine."

He moved toward her with the swiftness of a jungle beast. Seizing her, he picked her up and carried her to the bed.

"Mine," he said fiercely.

"Always and forever, Nico, *my* darling."

Her eyes were blazing as he stripped, flinging his formal clothes to the floor without a care.

"You win."

She was staring at his erection. "I know."

She smiled up at him. Then she tried to speak again, but his mouth covered hers in a hard, punishing kiss. His hands and lips roamed her silky limbs. Then her body began to twist and writhe beneath his, and nothing mattered, not even his anger. Nothing mattered except being inside her, claiming her for all time.

He made love to her in different positions, in the bed, on the floor, against the wall. And every time, she gave herself to him utterly, and her sweetness and eagerness obliterated every dark emotion and left only love.

Who was she really? The upstart his mother believed her to be, the American who'd ensnared him with her sexual powers because she preferred a prince to a sperm donor? Did he care?

When he had rested, she crawled on top of him and began to eat him with her tongue. He hadn't thought things could get any wilder or any sweeter than the first time, but they did.

Sex was like death, he would think later, when he could think. He couldn't sleep with her and remain whole. Every time he exploded inside her, she stole another piece of his soul. Soon there would be nothing left of him that wasn't hers.

A year. He'd told the upstart he'd believed her to be she had to stay a year. He'd been furious at her in Austin; out of his mind with rage, totally unreasonable and unable to listen to what she'd said in her own defense.

No matter who she was, or what she was, he wanted her forever.

But he loved her too much to force her to stay.

He rolled off the bed and stood up, feeling weary, despising himself for having forced her to marry him.

He dressed hurriedly and walked out onto her balcony.

* * *

Regina didn't know what to do when she woke up and Nico was gone. She couldn't believe she'd done the things she'd done, and yet she could. She'd wanted him so much.

Still, she felt hot with embarrassment every time she thought about it. Was he disgusted with the commoner he'd married? It was terrible of her, but thinking about how her tongue and lips had made love to him, especially that huge part, only made her begin to tremble with fresh need.

Where was he? Why had he left her? Had she totally displeased him?

Oh, why had she flung off her robe outside? He probably found that cheap and low-class. Was he angry about it or ashamed of her?

She arose from the bed and, when she couldn't find her nightgown in the dark, she dragged the heavy satin spread around herself. Trailing red, she was on her way to the bathroom when she saw him slumped on the chair outside, his face white as he stared at the moonlit garden.

"Nico?"

He jumped at the sound of her voice but didn't turn.

Did he hate her that much?

"I'm sorry," he said, his low tone filled with loathing.

Suddenly she was truly afraid. "I don't understand."

"I was out of control. Not myself. I never meant for all that to happen."

"You didn't want to make love to me?"

"I didn't say that."

"Things have a way of getting out of hand with you and me," she whispered, her own heart pounding in fright. "I'm sorry, too."

"I don't want you to be sorry any longer. I was crazy in Austin to say you had to stay a year. I arrogantly thought you wanted me because of who I was. Because I'm a prince, you see. That hurt. I was angry, furious, and concerned about the baby. I wasn't thinking."

"What are you saying?"

"You're not that person. I can't force you. I won't force you. It's not fair to you or the baby."

"Do you mean you want me to go?"

She continued to stare at him, unable to think because of the emotions tearing at her.

He wanted out. As fast as possible. That's all she heard.

"All right then," she said, when he didn't answer. "I understand. Thank you. I'll leave tomorrow with my family. I don't know what I'll say to them. They thought we loved each other."

"You were right. I should never have involved them. I never wanted to hurt them. Or you. I'm sorry. I'm sorry for what will be written in the papers."

"I don't care about the damn papers," she whispered, but so softly he didn't hear her. "I love you, just you, you big idiot."

"I never meant to hurt you," he repeated, his voice low and dull.

She strangled on a wild sob.

But you did. Because you made me believe, for one stupid, glorious moment that you loved me, that I was lovable and special and that you were satisfied with just me.

What a silly fool she was. Nobody had ever loved her like that.

She wasn't Susana.

The limousine raced around a curve and Regina saw the beach and the lemon trees and the dazzling blue water where *Simonetta* was moored.

"Stop!" Regina cried. "Stop the car!"

Dino and David were yelling in the limo while Gina sang the seven dwarves' song from *Snow White,* about whistling while you work, so the driver didn't hear Regina.

Frantic, she pounded on his window. "Stop!"

When he did, she said, "This will just take a minute."

His expression glazed, her father nodded. He had a bit of a hangover. He and her mother had been in shock ever since she'd told them she was leaving Nico and going home with them. Susana, who'd ordered her to quit being her usual bullheaded self and make up with Nico, wasn't speaking to her because Regina had said that wasn't possible.

Slowly, as if in a dream, Regina walked toward the lemon trees and the bench where she'd been sitting when she'd first seen Nico. She sat down and stared at the blue water that was so beautiful it hurt. Why did it have to be the exact shade of Nico's eyes?

Simonetta blurred. Tears, tears that she didn't feel any shame for or try to brush away, leaked out of her eyes and streaked her face.

Everything was the same, but nothing was. She fingered the ornate cross at her throat. She'd felt so much love here. She wondered if such emotions lingered in a place and made it magical for others. Had ancient lovers been here before them? Would someone else find true love in this exact spot?

She buried her face in her hands and sobbed, praying such lovers would be luckier than she was.

"Cara?"

She was sobbing so violently she didn't hear him at first.

"Cara, darling. *Tesorina.*" Then in a deep, dark voice he began to caress her in Italian. "Your sister came to me earlier."

"Nico?" She stood. She couldn't believe he was really here. Then his arms came around her from behind, and she felt his heat against her hips and spine as he molded her against her body.

"Why are you crying, my love?" He stroked her back and her hair.

"Oh, Nico. I know I don't deserve you. I'm not nearly good enough."

"You are perfect in every way."

"Your mother wouldn't want me underfoot all the time."

"My mother has her own household, her own homes, you know."

"I thought you lived with her."

"No. My main residence is outside Florence."

"Why are we talking about houses?" she whispered.

"Maybe because we're afraid of what we feel, of how much we care."

She whirled, half-blind with tears. "Then why did you send me away?"

His dark face was a blur.

"Is that what you thought? You broke my heart when you left."

"Are we both crazy?"

"Crazy in love. All lovers are a little crazy."

When her sobs subsided, she wanted to kiss him. She wanted to kiss him so badly.

"Not here," he said, his eyes scanning their surroundings for cameras.

He took her hand. Then they were running toward his tender and speeding across the blue water to *Simonetta*.

Once they were safely inside his stateroom, she threw her arms around him, and he kissed her.

"I love you," he said, many torrid kisses later.

"I love you, too. Always."

"That, too," he murmured tenderly. *"Always."*

He lifted her hand and began sucking her fingertips. He was tugging her down onto the floor when she remembered.

"Oh, my God!" She ran to a window and stared at Amalfi.

"What?"

"I forgot all about my family. They're in that limousine—still waiting for me."

He pulled out his cell phone and snapped it open. When he hung up, he smiled and said, "Susana said she wanted you to call her as soon as you can. She takes full credit for this happy ending."

Regina grinned. "That may be a while."

"Yes, she's on her way to the States."

"I have a feeling we'll be pretty busy, too," she murmured.

"It's more than a feeling. It's a certainty."

Then they were on the priceless Persian carpet, and she was staring up at him in fascination as he tore off his jeans and then his shirt. He was lean and brown and gorgeous, not to mention, swollen with desire.

Yes—to mention. And he was huge. And all hers.

He loved her. She was loved for herself, just like Susana. She didn't have to be *more* or perfect or even an attorney. She could just be herself. And that was enough.

Then he was disrobing her, kissing each part of her as he removed an item of clothing. Soon, with his lips pressed against intimate, secret flesh, she had no time for thoughts. Only for love.

When he kissed her on the mouth again and began to murmur in Italian, her whole being caught fire.

"Will you marry me for more than a year?"

"Forever," she whispered. "Forever. I love you."

"Then show me."

"With pleasure."

And being a commoner, she did.

* * * * *

Give a 12 month subscription to a friend today!

Call Customer Services
0844 844 1358*

or visit
millsandboon.co.uk/subscription

MILLS & BOON®

Why shop at millsandboon.co.uk?

Each year, thousands of romance readers find their perfect read at millsandboon.co.uk. That's because we're passionate about bringing you the very best romantic fiction. Here are some of the advantages of shopping at www.millsandboon.co.uk:

* **Get new books first**—you'll be able to buy your favourite books one month before they hit the shops

* **Get exclusive discounts**—you'll also be able to buy our specially created monthly collections, with up to 50% off the RRP

* **Find your favourite authors**—latest news, interviews and new releases for all your favourite authors and series on our website, plus ideas for what to try next

* **Join in**—once you've bought your favourite books, don't forget to register with us to rate, review and join in the discussions

Visit **www.millsandboon.co.uk**
for all this and more today!

The World of
MILLS & BOON®

HISTORICAL

*Awaken the romance
of the past*
6 new stories every month

*The ultimate in romantic
medical drama*
6 new stories every month

MODERN™

*Power, passion and
irresistible temptation*
8 new stories every month

By Request

*Relive the romance with the
best of the best*
12 stories every month

WORLD_ M&B2b